THE
CHRONICLES OF
THE UPHEAVALS

SHARIFF M. ABDULLAH

THE CHRONICLES OF THE UPHEAVALS

Commonway Publishing
P. O box 12541
Portland, OR 97212

permissions@commonway.org
publisher@commonway.org

Ordering Information:
This book may be ordered directly from www.amazon.com.

Quantity sales. Special discounts are available on quantity purchases by organizations, associations, and others. For details, contact the publisher at the address above.

Printed in the United States of America

First Printing   (Ver. 1.0) June, 2016

Print ISBN: 1533561389 ISBN-13: 978-1533561381
Digital ISBN: 9781310735240

DEDICATION

For my grandsons:

Solomon
Amir
Talib

And for all grandchildren... of all species...
everywhere.

TABLE OF CONTENTS

So on the eve of our self-destruction, we find ourselves with socio-economic systems designed for a model of human that has never existed—led by people whose *"mental system is failing to comprehend the modern world."* Where will it end?

"In the end," says the Grand Inquisitor in Dostoevsky's parable, *"in the end they will lay their freedom at our feet and say to us, 'Make us your slaves, but feed us.'"* . . .

Jay Hanson, Die-Off (2013)

Introduction by the North American Culture Council

2125 AD

In this writing, we take on a task that many believe to be impossible: to accurately chronicle the times before, during and after the Great Upheavals that engulfed humanity in the 21st Century.

The Upheavals: As many as 4 billion humans died – almost 60% of the human population of this planet at that time. Having so many die, in such a short period of time, from so many different causes seemed like "the end of the world" to many.

And, in some ways, it was.

Although things have begun to stabilize, the suffering was, and still is, unfathomable.

Many view the Upheavals as a fixed event – something that began in the early 2020's and ended in the 2040s. That would be a mistake. Viewing the Upheavals as synonymous with the overt failures of systems and structures limits our view of the magnitude of what happened. The Upheavals did involve massive suffering... But it also involved a massive transformation in what we think of as "human". Without the Upheavals, the Metamorphosis of Humanity would have been impossible.

Many people say that this period should more correctly be identified as the "Transformation". The problem with taking this view is that it makes what happened seem like a singular event. That humanity was in one place, and then transformed to another. In reality, there were a number of "transformations". We can count three distinct "branches" of humanity now... and perhaps more to come. Perhaps we are becoming different "species". (This leads some to suggest that we are witnessing the "fragmentation" of humanity, that we should refer to this writing at "The Great Fragmentation".)

There is no common agreement on when the Upheavals started... and many believe that they are far from over. Some go all the way back to 10–12,000 years ago, with the basic split in our human family – between Holons (those who think and act as One) and Solons (those who think and act as individuals). Others point to the industrial-scale wars of the 20th century, the most barbaric and deadly conflicts the world has ever seen. Still others point to the financial meltdown in the early 21st century, from which the world never fully recovered. Many blame the worldwide terrorist movement, especially that infamous moment when terrorism went nuclear and destroyed one of the world's most beloved cities.

Some advocate using more arcane methods of calculation: the date that the United States went off the gold standard; the date that LSD was invented; the start of the Civil Rights and Black Power movements in America; the date that carbon dioxide went over 350 ppm; the moment of Peak Oil; or the date of the disappearance of Dr. James Harold Moore and the Imaginal Group, the people credited – or blamed – with catalyzing our thinking about our runaway society and what we could do to transform our hopelessness into action.

After much discussion, the Culture Council has decided on the start date of the Upheavals being August of 1945. The twin nuclear atrocities of Hiroshima and Nagasaki marked a singular event in human history: and marked the escalation of... everything.

Fire is what made us "human", one million years ago. The twin fires of Hiroshima and Nagasaki helped transform us into... this.

Regardless of when historians place the start date or end date for the Upheavals, everyone includes the time between 2020 and 2040. This is the time when half of humanity died. Estimates range from 3-4 billion humans died in those decades. (It may be another 15–20 years before we develop the capability of doing an accurate census of those times.)

Some have counseled not to produce a report on the Upheavals. They see no sense in "stirring the pot". Let each endure their own suffering, as best they can. Let more time go by.

We disagree.

For the purpose of this Chronicle, we have chosen to focus our attention on the events directly before and during the disappearance of Dr. Moore and the Imaginal Group. Events prior to their disappearance have been fairly well chronicled and are reasonably accurate. However, so much misunderstanding has been generated by their disappearance (some of it generated by us), and so much misinformation exists in our global history, we believe it is necessary to set the record straight. We attempt to do so here.

This is more than simply an historical narrative about an unfortunate period in human history. This is the beginning of an historical overview of the ongoing transmutation of the human race – something that has not yet fully resolved.

From our point of view of history, the transmutation of humanity seems inevitable... because we have lived it. However, from the point of view of the early 21st Century, there were many, many possible avenues humanity could have taken in the Upheavals. Almost all of them would have led to a complete collapse of human civilization. Not 3 billion lost, but 7 billion. Not a regenerating Earth, but a toxic wasteland. The fact that we of the Culture Council have consciously chosen THIS path needs to be explained to future generations. In fact, it needs to be explained to many of us right now.

Our Methodology:

Once we set upon the task, the question arose: How to go about it? The easiest way (and the way still espoused by some) would be to simply collect the acres of records kept by each Center, combine them with our own records, and make that collection public.

We firmly believe such an inundation of information would serve the opposite effect – it would be so massive, no one human being could ever read it, and no collection of people could derive meaning from it. Such a massive glut of information would put people to sleep, much the way the old Internet did in the Age of Waste.

After much discussion, the Council has opted for a middle-ground approach: to chronicle the lives and times of just a few people, from their novice-hood to their mastery and beyond. A handful of relatively ordinary people. In this way, the kaleidoscope of events, from monumental to mundane, can be witnessed from a human level. Those singular characters can be seen as a living backdrop to historical and transformative actions that took place on a global scale.

By focusing on these characters, we do not hold them up as paragons of virtue, nor do we single them out for ridicule or blame. We see them as fairly ordinary people, doing their best to keep themselves and each other safe and sane during humanity's most challenging and transformative period.

A few historians have asked whether the events set in motion by the Global Culture Councils were worth the deaths of 3 to 4 billion humans. We remain adamant that that is the WRONG question. The real question is: how many more would have died, how many more atrocities suffered, had we <u>not</u> taken these actions? Would the human race have survived, had we not taken these actions?

This is the burden we live with, every day.

So, here is our Chronicle of these times, based on mechanical recordings, public records, mainstream media and our own trusted Observers.

First Councilor Master Lakala,
for the North American Culture Council
Date: 15 September 2125 AD, 15 September xxx AU (After Upheavals)

Foreword from the Archive Committee

Archive Committee: Very few digital records survived the cyber-wars of the 2020's. After converting the world's audio and visual assets into digital form, the world discovered just how vulnerable to attack those digital assets had become.

The age of cyber-warfare was born in the American attack on Iran's nuclear assets in 2010. The largely successful Stuxnet Attack opened the door to other countries and organizations to develop cyber warfare capabilities. Unlike nuclear weapons, there were virtually no moral objections to the development and use of these weapons.

The Cyber-Wars of the 2020's were invisible yet devastating. Whether it was major nations carrying the consciousness of the Cold War into cyberspace, or major corporations finding new ways to attack their competitors and secure market share, or just bored teenagers finding a new outlet for their mean streaks, the Industrial Age disappeared in just a few years. The loss of the world's electrical generation grids, chemical plants, industrial factories, communications facilities... anything with a computer chip was attacked, or so hardened against attack beyond usefulness. The Industrial Age ended, not with a nuclear bang but a digital whimper.

It must be remembered that the Upheavals were NOT "caused" by the cyber-wars, but were a symptom.

Those systems that survived were subject to destruction when electric power failed, or seas rose, or food supplies disappeared or fires burned down entire cities.

Some digital records survive. But passwords, even entire locations, have been forgotten, their guardians dead or compromised. Perhaps, like ancient Egyptian treasures, they will be uncovered hundreds of years from now by the crypto-archeologists in our future.

The only reliable digital records that now exist reside in the Archives of the Culture Council and the various Centers around the world. Early on, the Global Culture Councils made two momentous decisions:

1. Record everything. Only history will determine what is relevant.
2. Keep all records separate from Breaker Society and immune to cyber-attack.

These Chronicles are the results of those decisions. These two decisions have yielded a very ordinary record of humanity's most extraordinary times. Some successes and some painful failures.

One purpose to these Chronicles is to provide the reader with a feel for the size, shape and complexity of the Awakening Centers. While we still refer to them as "Centers", In reality most have grown into cities, with all of the complexities and all of the interlocking systems and structures of urban life.

It's all about perspective. From the perspective of the Age of Waste, the perspective of individuality and exclusivity, a society without poverty, without violence, without want or despair... such a society would have been a fantastic impossibility. From our perspective, it's just the way we do things.

The Banned Books: A Different Lens

If you put the right piece of glass in front of my eyes, I can see the scales on the exoskeleton of an ant, or a super-cluster galaxy at the edge of the Universe.

With the right equipment, I can do a thermal scan on the people sitting in the Sun, drinking beer in this second-floor outdoor café in downtown Leh, with the Himalaya Range as a backdrop – I can see who's getting drunk, and who's got a fever, and who's just getting too much Sun.

It all depends on the lens...

For the past 10,000 years, the predominant lens has been that of the individual human being, what I call the **SOLON**. *What we call "humanity" has been seen as a collection of solons.*

My lens is different. What I see as "humanity" is a collection of inter-dependent, inter-related, inter-active sub-sets... I see **HOLONS**. *I invite you to share this lens.*

Even when Breaker researchers are looking at Holons, they are looking through the lens where they "see" a collection of solons. Even when they "see" holon behavior... they don't see it.

Don't get me wrong: the Breaker researchers have a valid lens. Perhaps even a valuable one. But, it is by no means the only one. It is clearly NOT the lens that will get us out of today's challenges. (The "solon" lens is the one that created the challenges in the first place.)

To solve our problems, we need a re-boot of what we think of as "humanity". It can't happen too soon.

(Banned by Act of Congress)

Part One: The Novice

Section 01: The Novices Adjust (0-6 months)

Few recognize how close we are to human extinction... We will not be colonizing Mars. In the centuries to come, we can speak of success if there are still human colonies on Earth.

Albert Bates (2007)

Processing and Entrance Interview with Unnamed Novice 23 of 30

File No:		File Name:	Processing and Entrance Interview with Unnamed Novice 23 of 30
Location:		Parties:	
Monk/ Master Supervising:	Monk Pico-Laton		

Name:			Pgs:		Date:		Vol:	
Type of Transcript:	**Mechanical** **XXX**							
	Organic							

Preface by North American Archive Committee:

How to achieve a level of diversity in each Center? For the early pioneers, the meta-vision of "A World for All" had to mean more than "A World for All Who Show Up". For every person invited into a Center, there were 10,000 who were turned away.

Some argued that the Centers should select people who were already "awakened". Others argued that no one was "awakened" to the Holonic Mind. Some argued in favor of admission by ability to pay (restricting the Centers to a certain class of people). Still others argued that diversity was important to the Holonic Mind -- that the Selection Committees should be looking for "wild cards". The methodologies used for Collection were... unique and challenging.

This text is being provided in a rough draft format. Communication Access Realtime Translation (CART) facilitates communication accessibility and may not be a totally verbatim record of the proceedings. Let your coordinator know if you would prefer a more verbatim option.

[start of transcript]

Novice 23: What's wrong with the name I got?

Monk Pico-Laton: There's nothing "wrong" with it. The reason that all novices are required to change their names is that your old name will remind you of where you come from, while your new name will remind you of where you're going.

Novice 23: I don't like this! I heard you people do brainwashing in here. What's that? Does it hurt?

Monk Pico-Laton: At any point in time, you can get up, turn around, and walk out that door. We'll even drive you back to where we picked you up. We'll give you back the clothes you came in. There's no one here to stop you, or try to keep you here. So far, all we've done is feed you good food, and give you a clean bed to sleep in. If you don't like that, leave now!

Novice 23: Hey, sorry! Don't get me wrong –the food is cool, and sleeping in a real bed... wow!

I mean... Bam! Everybody's runnin'. Then Bam! Some dude jumps me. Then Bam! I'm out like a light. Then, Bam!... I'm eatin' great food and sleeping in a real bed!

Monk Pico-Laton: So, can I ask you some questions?

Novice 23: Yeah, okay... But my stomach kinda hurts...

Monk Pico-Laton: Your stomach might hurt for a day or so. We put some medicine in your food that will cleanse you of some parasites.

Novice 23: What's a parasite?

Monk Pico-Laton: Something that was growing in you that you don't want growing in your gut. Like a bug.

Novice 23: I got bugs growing in me!?!

Monk Pico-Laton: [sighs]: Not anymore. Now, I've got another seven potential novices to interview today... Do you mind if I ask you some questions?

Novice 23: No, go ahead, ask your questions. Just don't try to wash my brain.

Monk Pico-Laton: I'll try not to. Now, how old are you?

Novice 23: Don't know. Maybe 11.

Monk Pico-Laton: From your size, I'd guess closer to nine or 10... Now, where were you born?

Novice 23: Don't know. Think someplace called Ontario?

Monk Pico-Laton: Do you know where your parents are? What happened to your parents?

Novice 23: Don't know. They just disappeared, when everything went fucked, when the lights went out.

Monk Pico-Laton: When did this happen?

Novice 23: Hey, is this gonna take a long time? You askin' a bunch of questions and me sayin' "don't know"?

Monk Pico-Laton: No, not too long. I know things were crazy for you... I don't expect you to have answers, but this sheet says I have to ask all the questions. Now, do you remember the last time you saw your parents?

Novice 23: Don't know. Maybe when I was five or six.

Monk Pico-Laton: Who took care of you?

Novice 23: My sister did for a while, and then she disappeared, too.

Monk Pico-Laton: Do you know what happened to her?

Novice 23: I think some guys got her. She was about 15. Got with the wrong guys while swapping.

Monk Pico-Laton: What do you mean by "swapping"?

Novice 23: You know, swapping. Trading for food...

Monk Pico-Laton: Trading what?

Novice 23: What the fuck's your problem, lady? You brain-dead? You know... SWAPPING!

Monk Pico-Laton: [pauses]: I know these questions may bring up bad memories for you. It's hard for me to ask them. And I DO know how it is out there. But you've got to answer the questions out loud, so that the recorder can hear you.

Novice 23: [pauses]: You know... Trading sex for food, okay? She was real pretty, so we ate okay. One night she didn't come back.

Monk Pico-Laton: How long ago was that?

[silence]

Monk Pico-Laton: A year? Two years?

Novice 23: Yeah, somethin' like that...

Monk Pico-Laton: Have you ever killed anyone?

Novice 23 [silent, then]: What happens if I say yes? You kick me out?

Monk Pico-Laton: No, we don't kick you out. We know how hard it is to survive out there. We will however, keep a close eye on you, to make sure you don't do anything like that in here.

Novice 23: Well, I tried to. I hurt some guys, real bad. They tried to jump me, but they didn't know I had a knife. A couple of them probably died. At least, I hope so. They kept saying they was gonna eat me.

Monk Pico-Laton: Have you ever eaten human flesh?

Novice 23: Nah... I saw some people eating a lot of meat. Way more than a dog. I knew where it came from. I know it's wrong, but I was so hungry, I tried to get some, but they ran me off... I ate plenty dogs and rats... LOTS of rats...

Monk Pico-Laton: Let's change the subject... What do you know about this place?

Novice 23: The only thing I heard is that they feed you good here, and you have to work real hard, and then you get brainwashed.

Monk Pico-Laton: Well, two out of those three statements are correct!

The Denver Awakening Center is not a "charity". You ate well and you slept well, and we expect you to pay for it. And, if you intend to eat and sleep today, you have to pay for that, too.

Novice 23: Pay how? You know I don't have no money. You even gave me the clothes I'm wearing now... I have to pay for those too? I ain't no good for sex... Is this the part where you wash my brain?

Monk Pico-Laton: [laughing]: Believe me, nobody wants you for sex, and nobody wants your stinky little brain, either!

Novice 23: So, how I pay?

Monk Pico-Laton: You pay through your work. You're required to work every day. In exchange, you get meals, a bed, and our protection.

Novice 23: What's the catch? Once I come in, I can't leave?

Monk Pico-Laton: As I said before, you can leave whenever you want to. The door's right there. However, once you leave, you can't come back. This isn't a revolving door.

Novice 23: What's a revolving door?

Monk Pico-Laton: Never mind. The work will be very hard, very demanding. We don't want you to just move your muscles, we want to exercise your brain, and exercise your spirit, too.

Novice 23: Exercise my brain... What's that mean? Is that the brainwashing?

Monk Pico-Laton: You are really stuck on this brainwashing thing, aren't you? There is no brainwashing here! Exercising your brain means that all of the novices have to go to school.

Novice 23: SCHOOL! I heard of that! My sister said that she went to school and learned things, for a couple years before they closed them down. She really liked it! That's how she taught me to read! I get to go to SCHOOL?

Monk Pico-Laton: [smiling]: Yes, you get to go to school.

Novice 23: Wow... How much I got to pay for THAT?

Monk Pico-Laton: [laughing]: We pay you to go to school!

Novice 23: Are you shitting me?

Monk Pico-Laton: Do you see any shit around here?

Novice 23: Hey, you're alright!

Monk Pico-Laton: Going to school isn't all that you'll do. You have to spend time working in the fields, working to keep the buildings clean, and generating our electricity. The better you work, the harder you work, the more you earn. And, when you earn enough, you can trade for "perks".

Novice 23: What's that?

Monk Pico-Laton: Well, if you have enough credits in your account, you can trade for a better bed, better and different food, and other things. Like your own room. Maybe your own house.

Novice 23: Why you people doing all this?

Monk Pico-Laton: The people who started all this knew that our society was "going to shit", as you would say. Rather than trying to stop it, their goal was to siphon off the best and the brightest, people who could actually use their minds and their hearts, instead of just watching television. Our job is to help guide humanity past these troubles, past the Upheavals, into a new society.

YOU will be one of the Agents creating a new society.

Novice 23: I sure wish I knew what the fuck you talkin' about! But, as long as I get to eat and go to school, it can't be bad!

Monk Pico-Laton: Great attitude! You may go far.

Now, about that name... Let's see: you think you're from the Ontario region, you're "K" class...

Novice 23: What that mean? K class?

Monk Pico-Laton: [pausing]: It means that you didn't come here voluntarily. You were picked up in one of our sweeps.

Novice 23: You mean, those guys that jumped me? If I had known they were taking me here, I would have JUMPED into their net!

You know, the word on the streets is that you people EAT kids in here. That's why nobody volunteers to come here. They say you eat them, because nobody is ever seen again. That's why we run when we see the jump-trucks.

Monk Pico-Laton: Well, do YOU want to leave here and tell them the truth, knowing that you can't come back?

Novice 23: Fuck no! I don't give a fuck what they believe! If everything turns out as you say, those guys jumping me is the best thing ever!

Monk Pico-Laton: You will find that we really don't like cursing around here. You are expected to be mindful of what you say and how you say it.

Okay... From Ontario, K class, and zero criteria...

Novice 23: What's that mean, "zero criteria"?

Monk Pico-Laton: [sighs]: It simply means that you have zero presenting issues. You're not sick, you don't have communicable diseases, you're not significantly mentally disturbed, you're not physically impaired, you don't have a negative attitude, or a history of acute violence, you don't appear traumatized... In a world where "normal" doesn't mean anything anymore, you're pretty close to normal!

Novice 23: Okay, I guess...

Monk Pico-Laton: So, let me finish! Ontario, K, zero, ... I think we will call you "Onko". Now, you'll be in a dormitory with the other boys...

Novice 23: Hey, hold on lady! I ain't no "boy"! I seen more shit than you can ever dream of! I'm a MAN! And, if those fuckers in that dormitory try to punk me, they'll find out the hard way!

Monk Pico-Laton: I think you'll find here that it takes more than "seeing shit" to make you a man. Everyone has "seen shit". We have special dormitories for young people who have been so traumatized from "seeing shit" that they may never be able to re-join human society. We're not sure we can ever let them out again.

But, if being a man is so important to you, that's what we will call you. You'll be called Novice Man-Onko.

Now, if you don't mind, Novice 24 is waiting for her interview.

Novice Man-Onko: No problem... Sorry I went off on you...

Monk Pico-Laton: One last thing: we know that you're carrying a knife...

Novice Man-Onko: Hey, wait a minute...

Monk Pico-Laton: PLEASE! Don't bother trying to deny it. We know it's made of metal, about 5 inches long, and taped to your inner left thigh...

Novice Man-Onko: How the fuck...

Monk Pico-Laton: STOP! Try to listen, without making your mouth move! Around here, just assume that we know everything!

Now, we will let you hold on to your knife for 3 days. That will give you enough time to see that there's no reason to have a knife around here. Within 3 days, I expect you to bring that knife to me. If you don't... both you and your knife will be sent Outside.

Novice Man-Onko: Okay...

Monk Pico-Laton: I'm not asking for your okay. This will HAPPEN, whether you agree or not. Now you may leave.

Novice Man-Onko: One thing... if I decide to split, I get my knife back?

Monk Pico-Laton: If you return Outside, it will be with all your belongings, including your clothes.

Novice Man-Onko: [pauses]: Okay, you just holdin' it, see?

[Novice Man-Onko releases knife]

Monk Pico-Laton: You are surprising – I think you might go far. Just wait while I write you a receipt...

Novice Man-Onko: What's that?

Monk Pico-Laton: [sighs]: Never mind. Just more paperwork...

You really have potential. Now, please report to your dormitory.

Novice Man-Onko: That's the place with all the beds? Cool!

[end of transcript]

The Orientation

File No:		File Name:	The Orientation
Location:	Denver AC	Parties:	All Masters All Monks All Novices
Monk/ Master Supervising:	Master Still Light, Abbot		

Name:		Pgs:		Date:		Vol:	
Type of Transcript:	**Mechanical**						
	XXX						
	Organic						

Preface by North American Archive Committee:

In the early days of the Awakening Movement, the parties were creating a CULTURE. The accumulation of small items of behavior turned into cultural and ideological norms. Our style of clothing. The double-stomp. Practicing reverence toward our masters and elders.

And, most importantly, growing up believing in our role as transformers of society...

This text is being provided in a rough draft format. Communication Access Realtime Translation (CART) facilitates communication accessibility and may not be a totally verbatim record of the proceedings. Let your coordinator know if you would prefer a more verbatim option.

[start of transcript]

[6 pods, of 5-6 novices each]

Pods:
1. Maple Leaf
2. Sparrow
3. Gopher
4. Cricket
5. Frog
6. Rose

Abbot Still Light, of Denver Awakening Center, accompanied by all monks and masters

Abbot Still Light: Greetings, young ones! And, we get to do this opening again! I'm walking back out, and this time, when I walk in, I want you to all stand up, put your hands together like this, and bow to me. Okay, let's try it.

[pause for re-entry]

Abbot Still Light: Better! We do that to honor the Masters – people like me, the ones with the hats with corners and wearing purple. And to honor the Monks – people like these, the ones with the round hats and wearing red.

We do this for respect... something that most of you don't know a lot about. Yet.

Like everything else, this thing with standing and bowing will seem weird or strange to you at first. It will take a few weeks, perhaps a few months, before you get the hang of it.

My name is Still Light, and I am a Master here at the Center. I am also the Abbot, which means I've been elected by the other monks and masters to oversee and facilitate Center operations.

You've all been here about a week, and other than everybody telling you what to do, things aren't too bad, are they?

All of the changes that you are experiencing are necessary – you can't bring your old culture, behavior and attitudes in here. If you did, this place would start to look like Outside in no time flat. You are welcome; your old behavior is not.

The US Army had a system for their recruits, called "Boot Camp". That was to force the soldiers to accept their role as killers and to make sure they never questioned authority.

Our goals are exactly the opposite. We want you to be healers, not killers. We want you to always question, even those in authority.

[Aside to other monks and masters:] Perhaps we should call this "Kid Glove Camp".

[laughter among monks and masters]

We have the opposite of Boot Camp. Instead of punishments and harsh conditions, we're giving you good food, clean sheets, pleasant surroundings and lots of encouragement.

We do have discipline here. A few of you have already found that out. But, even our discipline is different – we don't punish you, we counsel you.

Of course, there is one ultimate punishment... you can go back to where you came from. We won't stop you if you want to leave. A few of you we will encourage.

Another difference here: you will be working together in units that we call "pods". This is to encourage you to think and act as a group, not as isolated individuals.

Each of you will be assigned to a pod. All of your work is done through a pod, and all of your payments are assigned to your pod, not to you as individuals.

[General rumbling. Hands raised for attention.]

Abbot Still Light: I see that several of you have raised your hands for attention. Here at the Center, novices just stand up until you are recognized. What's your name, Novice?

Dorado: Stevie... I mean, Dorado!

[Laughter]

Abbot Still Light: Yes, please try to use your Center names at all times. It will help in your transition.

DORADO: Well, since you know what my name was, how 'bout you tell me what yours was?

Abbot Still Light: Novice Dorado, it is considered VERY rude to ask for, or to reveal, your former name.

DORADO: Oops...

Abbot Still Light: Not a problem... this time.

So, Novice Dorado, what brings you to your feet today?

DORADO: Well, umm...

Abbot Still Light: You may refer to me as "Abbot" or "Master".

DORADO: Well, uh, Master... Being paid as a pod doesn't seem fair. What if one person works harder than another? What if somebody is just lazy? What if someone is a bully, and wants to keep all the money?

Abbot Still Light: All of these things can and do occur. And you develop ways to deal with them. And we will be keeping an eye on all of your arrangements.

DORADO: Can we change pods, get rid of dead weight?

Abbot Still Light: Almost never. You are together for a reason... your task is to discover the reasons and work things out.

In 3 to 6 months, there will be some reassignments, as some novices leave and a few new ones are admitted. But, other than slight numerical changes, your pod will be intact throughout your time as novices. Perhaps beyond – some pods stay together all the way into their training as monks.

Are there any other questions?

[Five novices stand]

Abbot Still Light: How about you...

Novice Man-Onko: Hey, you guys have trouble counting?

Abbot Still Light: I don't think any of us have lost the ability to count.

And, by the way, I am to be addressed as "Abbot" or "Master". Even "sir" is better than "you guys".

Novice Man-Onko: Yeah. Check. So, uhh... Abbot, why come some of us have to sleep outside, in tents? Or sleep in the greenhouse? It's COLD in there!

Abbot Still Light: Well, it's cold until you put a dozen young novices in there. Then it heats up pretty fast!

Novice Man-Onko: What? Y'all too cheap to turn up the heat? You guys... you MONKS... forget to pay your gas bill or somethin'?

[laughter]

Abbot Still Light: Novice, what is your name?

Novice Man-Onko: They name y'all give me is Man-Onko.

Abbot Still Light: Well Novice Man-Onko, tell me: which do you think is cheaper? Coal, natural gas, or novice sweat?

Novice Man-Onko: You mean you do that on purpose? I mean, shouldn't you like, PAY us?

Abbot Still Light: We do. You remember that we charge you for your beds. On the days when you bunk in the greenhouses, we charge you a lot less.

Even with that, it's still more efficient to heat with novices that with coal or oil. Each of you generates close to 100 degrees of body heat, constantly. Put 12 novices in the greenhouse and we have to prop open the windows to let some of the heat out!

Novice Man-Onko: But not in the first hour! We freeze our... our buns off.

Abbot Still Light: Thank you for being mindful just then. Cursing is about as pleasant as someone passing gas. Try to do less... of both.

[laughing]

Novice Man-Onko: Check. But what about the tents? You got a reason for us sleeping in tents? ...Master?

Abbot Still Light: Yes. Quite simple. We do know how to count. We predict that a certain number of you will leave within the first 3 to 6 months. As you leave, we collapse the extra tents.

Novice Man-Onko: What if they don't leave? You kick them out?

Abbot Still Light: [pauses] No one gets kicked out just to make room. [pauses] We're pretty sure who is going to leave, when and why.

Novice Man-Onko: Why come you know? You spyin' on us? Secret cameras?

Abbot Still Light: [pauses] Eventually, you will learn that we know everything that's going on around here, and without cameras or recording devices. We'll tell you, once you get more experience with our operations... and more mature in your own behavior.

And with that, let us wrap up this Orientation. The young novices will stay and receive their pod assignments... the rest of you may go.

Young novices: You will stand with your hands folded until your monks and masters have filed out. Then, Monk Pico-Laton will give you your assignments.

Now together:

May I be well,
May I be secure,
May I be happy.

May you be well,
May you be secure,
May you be happy.

May all beings be well,
May all beings be secure,
May all beings be happy.

[end of transcript]

The Banned Books: A Story Waiting to Pierce You

Cultures are created, and destroyed in ecstasy – and for every moment in between there is nothing that keeps a world alive aside from the breath of ecstatics.

People in general sincerely believe they know what life and the past and present are, although they know nothing. The news, the huge archives, the carefully written books are all about nothing. They're not even about the shadows of reality, or about moving chairs on the deck of a ship that soon could go down. They are absolutely nothing.

There is no such thing as true movement in this world. We can seem to run, push, dance, fly; make our way into space. But the only movement that really exists is the restlessness of our busy minds.

The whole existence is an elaborate illusion to make everyone believe that something can be done here, even though nothing is ever done. In spite of the personal dreams, the collective degrees, and the associations, nothing whatsoever is altered because the real something all happened somewhere else.

...

We have the strange idea in the West that civilizations just happen, that they come into existence in a hit or miss affair and then we bumble along creating and inventing and making it better.

But this is not how things are done at all.

Civilizations never just happen. They are brought into existence quite consciously, with unbelievable will, passion and determination, from another world. Then the job of people experienced in ecstasy is to prepare the soil for them; carefully sow and plant them; watch them grow.

...

In our unconsciousness we take credit where no credit is due, oblivious to the real source of everything we pretend is ours – the sacred origin not just of religion but also of everything else, of science and technology and education and law, of medicine, logic, architecture, ordinary daily life, the cry of longing, the excruciating ache of the awakening love for wisdom.

And then there are those who quietly go about doing whatever is needed: the ones who wait in a state of ecstasy to help bring new civilizations into being, the ones without whom nothing is possible.

But not only are these people needed to bring new worlds into existence. They even are needed to bring them to end so as to help make way for the new.

A Story Waiting to Pierce You

Peter Kingsley

(Banned by Act of Congress)

News Article: **Candidates Debate Ends in Bloodshed**

Both Democratic and Republican candidates for the upcoming Congressional seat ended in bloodshed last night, as a fight that started in the Convention Center spilled out into the streets.

"Neither side has a clue what's going on out here! They're talking about taxes and immigration, when people are STARVING on the streets!"

Candidates were admitted and released from X Hospital, treated for cuts and bruises from the altercation.

Others were not so fortunate. Police reported 7 deaths, and 25 admitted to hospital with life threatening conditions.

Police arrested 43 people on a variety of charges, and used tear gas and water cannons to disperse crowds that ranged as high as several thousand people. Fiercest fighting took place in area near the campaign headquarters of both parties.

Both parties have asked for additional security to cover the upcoming debates. "We can't let a few hotheads disrupt our democratic processes. In the future, we may rely more on 'virtual' debates, and less on just throwing the doors open for just anybody to show up."

Disciplinary Proceedings Regarding Novice Man-Onko

File No:		File Name:	Disciplinary Proceedings Regarding Novice Man-Onko
Location:	Denver AW	Parties:	
Monk/ Master Supervising:	Monk Pico-Laton		

Name:		Pgs:		Date:		Vol:	
Type of Transcript:	**Mechanical** XXX						
	Organic						

Notes:
Preface by North American Archive Committee:

Discipline has always been an issue at the Awakening Centers.

On the one hand: the intention was to foster an atmosphere of openness, inclusivity and respect for the opinion of others. We also recognized that bringing in many different cultures, including our "wild cards", would create major security concerns, from both inside and outside the Center.

What is "discipline"? How did the notion of "discipline" fit with the ideal of "Inclusivity"? How could an opportunity for discipline become an opportunity for learning?

This text is being provided in a rough draft format. Communication Access Realtime Translation (CART) facilitates communication accessibility and may not be a totally verbatim record of the proceedings. Let your coordinator know if you would prefer a more verbatim option.

[start of transcript]

Monk Pico-Laton: For the record, you know that I am not a Disciplinarian. You asked for me in this matter specifically.

Novice Man-Onko: Yeah. You get me, better than these other pukes.

Monk Pico-Laton: I'm going to act like I didn't hear that. Or, you'd be looking at three counts, instead of just two.

Novice Man-Onko: Shit. Looks like I can't do nothin' right around here...

Monk Pico-Laton: Or maybe FOUR. You know how we feel about cursing.

But, it's not so bad. Everybody has discipline problems at first. You're actually lucky that you only have two.

Novice Man-Onko: Funny, I don't feel lucky.

Monk Pico-Laton: Let's take a look at what's in your folder... Looks like you have one count of refusing to work, and another count of fighting in the dormitory.

Novice Man-Onko: I get to explain my side?

Monk Pico-Laton: Yes, of course. But don't spend a lot of time on this... The likelihood that you're in the wrong is really high.

Novice Man-Onko: I mean, can I get a lawyer or something, before you kick me out? Don't I get a judge?

Monk Pico-Laton: No one's going to kick you out! These are considered minor offenses. We just want to get you adjusted, before they turn into major ones.

Novice Man-Onko: Oh! Okay! But, what do you do? I mean, I don't want no beating...

Monk Pico-Laton: So, it's gone from brainwashing to beating! It's okay... you're not gonna get kicked out, and no one here is beating anybody else.

Now, for the first count, it seems as though you refused your job assignment of cleaning toilets.

Novice Man-Onko: Fuck yeah! I don't know what they think I am! I ain't cleaning nobody's shit!

Monk Pico-Laton: Novice Man-Onko, you will learn to stop using foul language in the presence of a Monk or a Master. And, you will learn to modulate the tone of your voice in our presence!

Novice Man-Onko: Sorry, sorry..., What's "modulate" mean?

Monk Pico-Laton: [smiling]: It means lower your voice. And, try thinking before you make your mouth move.

Novice Man-Onko: Okay... But, I ain't cleaning no toilets!

Monk Pico-Laton: [smiling]: Well, you don't have to! And, you're about to get a lesson in inclusive economics!

Novice Man-Onko: How come I get the feeling I'm not going to like this?

Monk Pico-Laton: Now, if you do all of your work, and attend all of your classes, at the end of a week you will earn 200 credits. That's what you earned last week. And, to pay for your food, your bed, your clothes, the laundry, the electricity, the water, ... That will cost you about 150 credits. So, at the end of the week, you will have in your account 50 credits. Are you following me?

Novice Man-Onko: Yeah, I get it. It's like the swapping that we would do out on the streets, but we didn't call it "credits". Sometimes, the swap wasn't even, so you built up a "count".

Monk Pico-Laton: Same thing here. You have 50 credits in your "account".

Now, when you refuse to do a job, you don't get the credits from that work. In this case, the 50 credits assigned to doing latrine duty.

So, to get that work done, the work that you refuse to do, we have to "hire" someone else, one of the other novices or monks, to do your job. And, because the toilet duty is so unpopular, we have to pay someone 100 credits to cover your work.

Now, guess where that 100 credits comes from?

Novice Man-Onko: Shit... From my account?

Monk Pico-Laton: Exactly. You're pretty quick. Your toilet duty is six hours a week. But, to make up for that 100 credit deficit in your account, it will take you over 20 hours. Is it worth that much to you?

Novice Man-Onko: But... I don't have that much in my account. What happens then?

Monk Pico-Laton: Small deficits iron themselves out, but you are not allowed to run a big deficit. If you don't have a positive credit account, or a way to make it positive, you leave. You can't afford to live here.

But, I want you to be clear about this: we are not kicking you out – it's your attitude that is kicking you out.

Novice Man-Onko: But, I see some folks down in the toilets, they're always cleaning up! Isn't cleaning toilets their job? Aren't they hired to do that? Why do I have to do it, if it's their job?

Monk Pico-Laton: No, they're just like you... They have their assigned time to clean toilets, and then they volunteer for extra time, because they're trying to build their credit account.

Novice Man-Onko: Why? Ain't shit to buy here! Oops! Excuse the language...

Monk Pico-Laton: Most of those doing the extra duty are trying to mount "search and rescue" operations.

Novice Man-Onko: What's that?

Monk Pico-Laton: Let's say that you could locate your sister. Would you want her to be in here, or out in the streets?

Novice Man-Onko: [rising]: You can find my sister?

Monk Pico-Laton: Sit down! Thank you! Yes, we can try to find her... But it would be very expensive. Over 1,000 credits just to find her. If she wanted to go, but was being held against her will, another 5 to10,000 credits or more. And, if you wanted her taken involuntarily... That could go up to 100,000 credits. That's a LOT of toilet scrubbing.

But, would your sister be worth it?

Novice Man- Onko: If you folks can find my sister, I'll scrub every toilet in this place, every day! (Rising) How do I sign up?

Monk Pico-Laton: It starts with patience. Sit down! First we've got to deal with this second count. Assuming of course that you are now willing to scrub toilets?

Novice Man-Onko: Abso-fucking-lutely! Sorry!

Monk Pico-Laton: Now, what was this fight about?

Novice Man-Onko: Some of them pukes... I mean some of the other novices, they think that they're better than the rest of us. They call us names. They call the ones got jumped here "kidnaps" and "criminals" and "cannibals". And, when you monks are around, they refer to us as "kids"... for "kidnaps". So, it looks like we're fighting over nothing. They call themselves "volunteers" or "vols".

Monk Pico-Laton: [pausing]: Yes, we're aware of this problem. We are trying to find ways of solving it.

Novice Man-Onko: Hey, just turn your backs for a few minutes... I'll solve it for you!

Monk Pico-Laton: Violence solves nothing... aren't you learning that in your classes?

There are three ways a young person becomes a novice. Some, like you, are, as you put it, "jumped". We call it "Collected". Brought in involuntarily. One of our Agents close to the streets sees your potential and alerts us. We are looking for... a certain kind of temperament. Someone who will benefit from our brand of discipline, direction and devotion.

Some are volunteers. Thousands show up at the gates, trying to get in. Thousands of parents try to give us (or even sell us) their children. They want what they can no longer supply – a decent life for their children.

Some of them we let in – about 1 out of 1,000. We admit as many as we can sustainably take – and catch hell because we don't take more. Some of the parents of the voluntaries don't want us to take ANY Collecteds. That's why we spread the rumor that we eat children, or brainwash them – to try to cut down on the folks who come to our door.

Incidentally – once you give us her name and description, if your sister showed up at our door, or the door of any Center, she would be immediately admitted... as long as you want her here, and as long as your account is positive. You would be guaranteeing her.

And, some gain admission by paying a very hefty tuition. These are the children of rich families, who send their offspring to us, for protection, for education, and for discipline. The families of the tuition children pay three times what they cost us. In effect, they pay for both the volunteers, and you Collecteds.

Because these are old families, that still have "money", they feel that they are better than the rest of you, and more privileged. These "elites" have formed a temporary alliance with the "voluntaries" – but that will end once they think they've got the "involuntaries" out of the way.

Novice Man-Onko: Why don't you just kick out these elite pukes?

Monk Pico-Laton: Please... language! We don't kick them out, because, frankly, we need the money. These Centers are constantly expanding, constantly taking in more novices, trying to rescue people from the shattered remnants of the old society. The resources have to come from somewhere...

You will notice that none of the elites ever get "latrine duty". They pay an exorbitant fee – a lot of money – to not have to do such things. And we let them pay their way out, because we need the money. We really hope it won't be like that for long.

Novice Man-Onko: Okay, so the elite pukes... NOVICES, sorry! These elite guys get to walk all over us, because you need money, right?

Monk Pico-Laton: [pauses]: We are really trying to do something about that. We really are. This place isn't perfect, and we don't have all the answers.

Man-Onko, I would really encourage you to NOT react when they taunt you. And, if you could encourage the other novices who were Collected, I would really appreciate it. Give us some time to work this out – maybe a few months. This place works well enough, but we're constantly trying to improve. Things take time...

Novice Man-Onko: Well, okay... But, if I'm doing this for you, what you gonna do for ME?

Monk Pico-Laton: Novice, we don't do deals. You don't understand now, but what I'm asking is for YOU, not for me.

And... based on this conversation, I will recommend that the refusal of work charge be dropped, and the fighting count go on your record but be suspended, pending no other incidents of fighting.

Novice Man-Onko: Okay... So... we cool?

Monk Pico-Laton: Try saying it this way: "Are my charges dismissed, Sister?"

Novice Man-Onko: How come you my sister, but you treat me like my mother?

Monk Pico-Laton: Are you just trying to get on my nerves?

Novice Man-Onko: No! I just don't understand most of this shit... this STUFF. It's like I landed on a different planet.

Monk Pico-Laton: I apologize. I sometimes forget how different our environment is, and that you've only been here for a week.

Novice Man-Onko: Hey! YOU apologizing to ME? Cool! That mean I bring charges against you? We get to swap seats?

Monk Pico-Laton: [laughing]: Not in any of your pathetic dreams! It's only when you become a Monk that you'll learn how many rights you novices DON'T have. This place runs as a democracy... but not for novices!

Novice Man-Onko: Hey, Lady... Hey SISTER... I don't know what "democracy" means, but as long as you keep the food and the beds coming, I don't care!

Monk Pico-Laton: Fair enough. Now, you are dismissed. Time for your next class.

Novice Man-Onko: Food, bed and SCHOOL. And toilets to clean! Life don't get no better!

Monk Pico-Laton: And, Novice Man-Onko... you have to pay for my TIME in this disciplinary hearing. 50 credits. It will certainly be in your best interests not to violate the rules again.

Novice Man-Onko: I got to PAY?? SHIT!! SORRY!!

[end of transcript]

The Banned Books: The Tao Te Ching

It is close at hand, stands indeed at our very side; yet is intangible, a thing that by reaching for cannot be got.

Remote it seems as the furthest limit of the Infinite. Yet it is not far off; every day we use its power. For the Way of the Vital Spirit fills our whole frames, yet one cannot keep track of it. It goes, yet has not departed.

It comes, yet is not here. It is muted, makes no note that can be heard, yet all of a sudden we find that it is there in the mind.

It is dim and dark, showing no outward form, yet in a great stream it flowed into us at our birth.

The Tao Te Ching
Lao Tzu (translated by Huston Smith)

(Banned by Act of Congress)

The Television Interview

File No:		File Name:	Television Interview: 60 Minutes
Location:	Denver AW	Parties:	**Lester Grant, Interviewer Margaret "Maggie" Schmidt**
Monk/ Master Supervising:	General archives		

Name:		Pgs:		Date:		Vol:	
Type of Transcript:	**Mechanical XXX**						
	Organic						

Preface by North American Archive Committee:

Very few video records survived the cyber-wars of the 2020's. What follows is the written transcript of a video record from the "60 Minutes" news program, an interview between award-winning correspondent Lester Grant and former model and actress Margaret Schmidt, an early Investor in the Awakening Movement.

This text is being provided in a rough draft format. Communication Access Realtime Translation (CART) facilitates communication accessibility and may not be a totally verbatim record of the proceedings. Let your coordinator know if you would prefer a more verbatim option.

[start of transcript]

Grant: Tonight we are looking into the affairs of the Imaginal Group, and their so-called "Awakening Centers".   Some have said they are an essentially harmless group of do-gooders. Others have labelled them a dangerous cult. The US Congress has lumped them with groups like Al-Qaeda and Islamic State, as an organization with goals and intentions that are detrimental to the American way of life.

Tonight, we will delve below the surface. We'll take a look inside one of their "Awakening Centers", talk with Congressman Frank Hammond about the official view of the government toward these Centers and the movement as a whole, then talk to actress turned activist Margaret Schmidt.

[Video segment on the history of "utopian" and cultist movements in America omitted.]

[Video segment on Congressman Francis Hammond and Congressman Charles Baker interviews omitted.]

Grant: Now, as part of our ongoing investigations into the Imaginal Group and the activities of James Harold Moore, we come to our interview with Margaret Schmidt, former model, former actress, former wife of billionaire businessman Gregory Scott, and now supporter and financer of the Imaginal Group and the Awakening Centers.

Starting out early as a supermodel, Ms. Schmidt broke into Hollywood as the "icy blond" in the popular and critically acclaimed remakes of the Alfred Hitchcock movies, starting with "Rear Window" and continuing through to "Psycho". Along the way, she picked up a reputation for lavish parties and lavish living.

Grant: Thank you so much for appearing on our program. Many of the other members of IG have been reluctant to appear.

MS: Well, thank you Lester, but I'm not really sure that you can call me a member of IG.

LG: Why not?

MS: Well, I'm not really sure IG actually exists! I think it is more of a convenient place holder, a fiction created by the media to explain an event to people who need simple explanations.

LG: Are you trying to minimize your involvement? Did you not attend the seminal meeting with Dr. Moore and the other members of IG?

MS: Oh yes, I attended a conference on "Imaginal Cells and Society" that Dr. Moore held five years ago. Like everyone else invited, I was deeply moved by what he said: the peril of the status quo, and the promise of changing tracks.

As a consequence of that meeting, I made a donation to Dr. Moore's foundation, and I bought shares in the "Awakening Movement".

However, I don't think...

LG: Hang on there. Are you denying that you are an integral member of IG? You just said that you've made both donations and investments to the group. I don't think you can have it both ways.

MS: This is what I'm talking about! Does making an investment, a smart investment, make me some kind of a conspirator? Does a donation mean you are a "member" of something?

Some of the people who attended Dr. Moore's conference have continued to meet regularly. I meet with them once in a while, but mostly not. Some have made this work with creating "Awakening Centers" their life's work. Me? I'm just along for the ride!

LG: well, Ms. Schmidt, can you tell us...

MS: Call me Maggie!

LG: [smiling]: Well, Maggie, can you tell us what "along for the ride" means to you? You've put substantial funds into IG...

MS: I keep telling you, there is no IG! James asked us to invest in his nonprofit foundation, which some of us did. In addition, he asked us to invest in his idea of "Awakening Centers". Some of us did. Neither making donations nor making investments in legal entities is illegal. There is no organization called "Imaginal Group". If there is, I've never heard of it, and I haven't invested in it. There is no vast and dark "conspiracy"!

LG: So, why is Congress so intent to investigate? Why does Congress see your actions as so dangerous to our way of life?

MS: I know you're going to have Congressmen Hammond and Baker on your program. You're going to have to ask them!

LG: Fair enough. Changing our subjects: can you tell us something – what do you get for your massive investment in this movement?

MS: First of all, I'd hardly call it massive! I had a good career as both a model and an actress, and...

LG: Yes, all of us remember fondly your roles in the remakes of those Hitchcock movies!

MS: Yes, Lester, I've had some really fortunate rolls in my brief Hollywood career. And, I've had some really good financial advisors over the years, who helped me not squander all my money in my wilder days!

LG: Yes, and you married one of those financial advisors, didn't you?

MS: (pauses): Lester, I'd rather not talk about my relationship with Gregory. As you know, we're divorced now, but we're still best friends. However, let me say one thing: the reason I married him was NOT for his money or his financial advice!

LG: Fair enough!

MS: So, investing $10 million in the "Awakening Centers" was a significant, but not a vast sum of money for me.

LG: Maggie, let's cut to the chase: what do you get for $10 million?

MS: The Awakening Centers operate sort of like the old timeshares did, before they collapsed. For an amount of money, you get to buy "time" at one of the many centers around the world.

LG: So, I have to come up with $10 million in order to get a seat on their ride?

MS: Not at all! right now, a "basic" day at an awakening center costs about $100...

LG: $100! Why, at a $10 million investment, that would buy you...

MS: It would buy a few centuries! I have a lot more than the "basic" model! While my units at the "Awakening Centers" are tiny in comparison with my houses in Beverly Hills or Miami Beach, they are mansions in comparison with the standard cabins at the "Awakening Centers".

LG: Why is that?

MS: Well, Lester... I like long baths! My bathroom at the Awakening Center is larger than some people's cabins!

LG: Wow... Mentioning "baths" is bringing up for me your shower scene in "Psycho"!

Changing the subject a bit... would you call yourself an "activist"?

MS: You know that I used to demonstrate for various "causes". I was arrested a few times for this demonstration or that demonstration. Back then, I would have called myself an "activist" ...

Now? I don't think so. I think of myself as a person just living her life, but doing it in such a way that is healthy for herself, and healthy for her community and healthy for her planet. The only one she's got!

LG: You compared your investment to "timeshares". Would you refer to these Awakening Centers as being "all inclusive"?

MS: Well, yes and no. At my rate, I don't have to lift a finger to do anything. However, there are many people in the Awakening Centers who can't afford even $100 a day. They get to work their way along...

LG: You say you don't have to lift a finger, but it looks like you've been lifting more than just a finger!

[Cut to photos and videos of MS, in T-shirts and overalls, building structures and working in the Gardens.]

LG: That doesn't look like "not lifting a finger". to me!

MS: That's not WORK! That's what I call having FUN! It feels SO GOOD to work hard like that all day!

LG: You are sometimes working besides really poor people, homeless people. How does it feel to have people like that in your community?

MS: There are the same number of poor people in your community, Lester. You just manage to ignore them.

Working with formerly homeless people has really opened my eyes to what's wrong with this society. You know, we're paid for our work, but I never take my credits – I leave them for my work buddies. The fresh air, sunshine, doing high-quality work with others... It's just great! That's payment enough for me!

LG: Well, how's this for fresh air and sunshine?

[Cut to video of MS and others, covered in mud, laughing, during a torrential rain storm. Apparently standing in a mud pit.]

MS: [laughing]: That day was great! I've never been so dirty in my life!

LG: What were you doing?

MS: We were building rammed earth houses, and got caught in this amazing rain storm, that washed all our work away! We were trying to sandbag it, then gave up and just had a mud fight! From the picture, you can see that I lost! God, that was so great!

LG: Would you say that your working there has been... Therapeutic?

MS: (pauses): Well, Lester... You know I had some difficulties when I was working in Hollywood. The hectic schedules, the pressure, the drugs... A while back, I just snapped. Signed myself into a sanitarium.

While that got me back on my feet, I didn't know which direction my feet were pointing! On the one hand, I had enough money to live on to last me the rest of my life. On the other hand... I didn't know who I was! I didn't know what I wanted to do!

If I went back into movies, I'd just be creating a revolving door back to the sanitarium. There had to be another way for me. A friend suggested that I attend that lecture on the Imaginal Society. The rest is history!

LG: Thank you for sharing that with us, Maggie. I know that part of your life is painful for you to recall.

But, I have another question: there are those who say that Dr. Moore and his cronies caught you at a very delicate point in time in your life, and have used you and your money for their own purposes. They say that these "Awakening Centers" are more like cults than businesses. That once you get in, it's very hard for you to get out again.

What do you say to all this?

MS: (pause): Lester, it would be really easy for me just to say "Of course not!" and move on. However, I think both you and your audience deserve a better, deeper answer than that.

Yes, I became aware of the Awakening Centers at a pivotal point in my life. ALL OF US are at that same pivotal point. Yours may not be as dramatic as mine. The person watching this program may not have the money and resources to sign themselves into a high-class sanitarium, like I did. They may be trying to fix their craziness with illegal drugs or by taking it out on their wives and children. They may be struggling to find enough food, or living in a car. They may be medicating themselves, just so they can go back to a boring, dead-end job.

The sanitarium fixed me up, so that I could go back and participate in the kinds of activities that sent me to the sanitarium in the first place. That's called CRAZY! I needed something else, and Dr. Moore and his Awakening Centers provided it.

Is that a cult? Can I leave whenever I want to? Of course I can! I'm here, aren't I? I still travel around the world, I still buy nice shoes and go to parties once in a while. But that's just not my life anymore... That fun isn't fun anymore. Compared with growing tomatoes...

LG: ...and getting real dirty!

MS: Yes! Getting really muddy with some great new friends! Compared with that, getting drunk and wrecking a $200,000 car just doesn't seem like that much fun anymore!

LG: Well, Maggie, it has been a pleasure to talk with you!

MS: And Lester, please feel free to come visit me, and have some tomatoes!

LG: And get dirty?

MS: It's not dirt... It's mud!

[end of transcript]

News Article: Congress Subpoenas Moore and Imaginal Group to Hearings

Statement by Congressman Francis Hammond, R-OK, Chair of the Congressional Oversight Committee for Homeland Security, on why Congress issued a subpoena for Dr. James Harold Moore and the other members of the Imaginal Group:

"We invited him to come, and he refused. We were even willing to work around their schedules... Whatever THAT is! His refusal to testify under oath, or even to send a representative, is a slap in the face of every American.

"We want to hear from these characters that call themselves the "Imaginal Group". We want to hear why their predictions have been so damn close to the reality of what's actually happening out on our streets. I mean, how could they PREDICT what is happening, so closely, unless they were actually CAUSING it?

We know that Moore was a leading cadre in the Black Power movement, which nearly tore this country apart. Some of us still remember our cities in flames in the Sixties. It was people like Moore and the others holding the matches.

"We know he made a point of visiting all of the hot spots around the world. Some of them show up on his travel record. Russia... Cuba... Sri Lanka... His passport reads like a checklist for the "Terrorism Tour".

"And who knows where else he's been? Who knows who else he's talked to? That's why we want him HERE, under oath, before God and the United States Congress, to answer our questions about his role in instigating this Mess! We cannot develop an effective strategy to repair the damage that's been done without an accounting from Mr. Moore on how much damage he's actually caused, and the TRUE purpose for those "Centers" he has created!"

Responding to the Congressional subpoena, Penelope Starnes, attorney for the Imaginal Group, issued the following statement:

"While my firm has been hired to represent the legal interests of Dr. Moore and the Imaginal Group, we have no idea of their whereabouts. I've never met any of them. Our office has been hired specifically to respond to the Congressional subpoena. The response is in the form of this statement by Dr. Moore. This statement was prepared by him -- we neither advised nor condoned this course of action on his part.

Statement by Dr. James Harold Moore:

"I have no intention of participating in the Congressional witch-hunt. The flames of the Upheavals have been smoldering for over half a century, and all Congress has done in that time frame is pour gasoline and fan the flames. Now, they still do nothing, while looking for a culprit. They need only look in the mirror.

"50 years of supporting energy waste, militarism, pollution, Big Oil, Big Pharma, Big EVERYTHING...

<u>*All*</u> *of the predictions of <u>everyone</u> paying attention have come true. Climate change, Peak Oil, Peak Water, everything has been analyzed and predicted, much more thoroughly than I have. Yet, the Imaginal Group has been singled out as the "cause". Why?*

The answer to that is as sad as it is simple: Of all the predictors of bad times, we are the only ones who have proposed a solution that DOES NOT NEED THE US GOVERNMENT TO ACT. As long as people are petitioning Congress or the President or the Supreme

Court to act (through pleas, promises, demonstrations or threats), they reinforce the mythology that these institutions have POWER. Through the Awakening Centers, we stuck a pin in that bubble.

We choose not to participate in this distracting spectacle. We choose not to be the scapegoat for 50 years of Democratic and Republican ineptitude. We've delivered the message -- pardon us if we choose not to stick around to get shot."

The Banned Books: **The Need for Bonding & Community**

Over time, religions have learned techniques to bypass cognitive functions and tie groups of people to each other and to open the doors to the Transcendent.

On the one hand, we have a need for the new, the innovative and exciting. On the other hand, we need to know that we are part of an existing or established ORDER, to note that what we're doing is in accord with our ancestors and will be honored by our descendants.

Without this, people experience a dis-ease, an unexplained anxiety.

Some believe that continuity is experienced through doctrine and dogma. The exact opposite is true... the doctrines and dogmas, rules and regulations are the very things that separate us from each other.

Catholics, Buddhists and Muslims, along with many others, all use prayer beads. Even the number of beads on a string are common: 20, 22, 33, 99 or 108. However, the exclusivist doctrines that are attached to each of these groups prevents them from seeing that they have a common practice.

In the Spiritual Commons, we can create places where we practice all of the things we inadvertently rejected... Places where we practice with those who hold different beliefs, but have a similar practice.

"The Ecstatic Society"

Shariff M. Abdullah

(Banned by Act of Congress)

The Parade

File No:		File Name:	The Parade – Counseling Between Monk Ariel and Novice Man-Onko
Location:	**Denver AC**	**Parties:**	
Monk/ Master Supervising:	*Monk Ariel, Head of Leadership Development*		*Initial leadership assessment and evaluation session for Novice Man-Onko.*

Name:		Pgs:		Date:		Vol:	
Type of Transcript:	**Mechanical**						
	Organic – Observer 294						

Preface by North American Archive Committee:

Novices were encouraged/ required to leave their past dysfunctional culture behind. Everything. That requirement led to some interesting challenges...

The US Army relied on "Boot Camp", a prescribed set of harsh and demeaning behaviors, to erase the ties to past cultures. The Awakening Centers relied on... something else.

This text is being provided in a rough draft format. Communication Access Realtime Translation (CART) facilitates communication accessibility and may not be a totally verbatim record of the proceedings. Let your coordinator know if you would prefer a more verbatim option.

[start of transcript]

Monk Ariel: Come in and sit down. And stop looking like you're the guest of honor at an execution! Will you have some tea?

Novice Man-Onko: No, I don't want any...

Monk Ariel: Here's a hint: if a monk or master offers you tea around here, take it. Just trust me on this.

Novice Man-Onko: I don't get it – why you being nice, just so to punish me?

Monk Ariel: Why do you think this is punishment?

Novice Man-Onko: Well, I'm here because I was mouthing off in the lecture today, right? Bout the dumb shit... STUFF! We have to do at the Parade...

Monk Ariel: Well, yes, you're right. You're here because you were "mouthing off". But what makes you think talking to me is "punishment"?

Novice Man-Onko: Well, I don't see nobody gettin' awards for mouthing off!

Monk Ariel: But, I just did! I just offered you tea!

Novice Man-Onko: This place gets weirder by the minute... Yeah, okay, I'll take some tea.

[Pause for making tea]

Monk Ariel: So, what seems to be your problem with the Parade?

Novice Man-Onko: Look, I said already that I would do it, right? I've been out three times, and I'll keep going out, long as you tell me to. I'll do your goofy little dances. I don't see why we got to talk about it....

Monk Ariel: We call these "chat sessions". We don't have to do this... If you'd feel better, we'll put this off to some other time. We just want you to be able to ask questions freely, not necessarily in the environment in the Lecture hall.

Novice Man-Onko: I just don't get it. Why you do this Parade every week? It seems like... a waste.

Monk Ariel: Why does it seem like a waste to you?

Novice Man-Onko: Why you folks always turn my questions back into questions for me? We do a lot of talking, but I don't see the straight shit... the straight stuff, sorry.

Monk Ariel: Don't worry about your language while we're having our "chat". That's mainly for when you are in social situations.

And, we ask questions to make your brain work! It's something that most people from Outside aren't used to doing, which is why it seems strange or weird to you.

So, my question: why does the Parade seem like a waste to you?

Novice Man-Onko: It's not just givin' away food and clothes. I get that part – that's the "compassion" stuff y'all always talking about. I'm okay with that...

But why drag all of US Outside to do that? The novices? Why the little puppet show, with us dancing around and singing? Why not just drop off a wagon full of food and be done with it?

Monk Ariel: You don't like dancing and singing?

Novice Man-Onko: [pauses] Well, you said this was just a "chat", so I'll tell you... Fuck no! It seems... like kid-shit. Especially since we all HAVE to do it! We put a lot of time into learning those stupid dances! And a different dance every week! It just don't make no sense!

Grow food? I'm down with it. Make energy? I'm cool. I'm even okay with cleaning the toilets. But why we entertainin' the Outsiders?

Monk Ariel: Is it because you are wearing your robes on the Outside?

Novice Man-Onko: Yeah, that too! I MUCH rather have my street clothes on! But that's not really the problem... It's the whole thing!! It don't make no SENSE!

Monk Ariel: Well, you're doing a lot of things that are different now, that don't "make sense" to how you used to do things. But the only thing you're having problems with is the Parade. You seem to like the chants and the meditations and the song circles okay...

Novice Man-Onko: Yeah! They're cool! I mean, they're strange, but I kinda "get" what they're all about. 'Specially that dude with that deep voice!

Monk Ariel: ... that "monk".

Novice Man-Onko: Yeah, sorry, that monk doing that strange singing. Sounds like he's gargling!

Monk Ariel: That's called tuvan throat chanting, and you can learn that if you want to.

Novice Man-Onko: ME? Cool!

Monk Ariel: But let's go back a minute. You said that you "get" the chanting, but you don't "get" the Parade. What's the difference?

Novice Man-Onko: [pauses] Well...

Monk Ariel: Let me ask the question a different way. You think both the chanting and the Parade are weird, right?

Novice Man-Onko: Check.

Monk Ariel: Is it that one is done here at the Center and the other is done Outside?

Novice Man-Onko: [pauses] I don't think so. I'd do our chanting on the Outside. Especially the throat dude! Monk!

Monk Ariel: So, what's the difference? Why are we having this talk?

Novice Man-Onko: [pauses] You have to TEACH us those dumb dances. If it was like the chanting, you wouldn't have to teach us. It would just... you know...

Monk Ariel: Flow?

Novice Man-Onko: Yeah! Like water! That's what it feels like when we're in the circles – like we're floating in warm water.

Monk Ariel: [pauses] That was an excellent metaphor.

Novice Man-Onko: What's a metaphor?

Monk Ariel: [sighs] See your Languages teacher.

Answer this: If you could change one thing about the Parade, what would you change?

Novice Man-Onko: [pauses]: Well... I just wouldn't do it! Once a week, I'd drag a wagon full of food Outside and just leave it! Whoever gets it gets it. Leave off the show. Leave off the handouts and the smiles.

Monk Ariel: Therefore... You're saying that "the show" must be really important, because we spend so much time and energy on it and get nothing out of it. You're also saying that it goes beyond "compassion". And you don't understand the importance.

Novice Man-Onko: Thank you! That's EXACTLY what I'm saying! We spend so much time on it, and get nothin' from it.

Monk Ariel: My pleasure. So, let's look at why we do the Parade. As you can see, a great deal of our resources go into this "show" every week, so it must be important. What is the most important aspect of the Parade?

Novice Man-Onko: Well, it's NOT giving away food. You can do that a lot easier and a lot... you know, smarter.

Monk Ariel: We would say "efficiently".

Novice Man-Onko: Yeah, that. So, I think the Parade part is like saying, like "we're having fun and you're not".

Monk Ariel: Exactly! You nailed it with one try! That's exactly what we're saying to the people out there! Now: why do we want to say that?

Novice Man-Onko: Well... This is hard! [pauses]: The easiest thing is if you want to recruit them. But, you don't, at least I don't think you do. You're turning people away at the gates every day... Why go out and recruit more?

Monk Ariel: Yes, why would we?

Novice Man-Onko: Okay, so now you're back to the trick questions! Well [pauses] You don't really want them in here, right? You just want them to WANT to be in here. You want them to WANT the Center.

Monk Ariel: [pauses] I can see why Monk Pico-Laton thinks you will go far. You nailed it again! So, why do we want that?

Novice Man-Onko: I'm working on it... [Longer pause] You don't want them to want THEIR current life, you want them to want OUR current life. You changed my actions by dragging me Inside. And, you are trying to change their actions, while they are still Outside.

Monk Ariel: Very perceptive. Now, why...

Novice Man-Onko: Hang on a minute: if they are acting more like US, they are less of a security threat to us!

Monk Ariel: Again, very perceptive. But it's not just about stopping security threats. We want them to really <u>want</u> this kind of life.

It's easy for them to fall into the routine of the life they have right now. It would be easy, especially for the children, to grow up thinking that bad food, bad water, bad clothes, bad health and no government are the norm. It would be easy for them to start believing that the "Age of Waste" was some kind of "Golden Age". That the Age of Waste was GOOD. It would be VERY easy for them to keep wanting THAT. It would be easy for them to accept the current "Dark Ages" or work to return to the "Age of Waste".

It would be easy for them to want the present, or want the past... we want them to want the FUTURE. OUR future.

Novice Man-Onko: Yeah... So that the Parade is to help keep them out of fantasy land, and into reality. OUR reality.

Okay... But why the stupid dances? Why have us dressed up in robes and dancing around, singing stupid songs? Why not just have us walk out on the street and give away the food? We ain't showin' them our reality, we showin' them... a FANTASY of our reality!

Monk Ariel: Again, very perceptive. [pause] What did you know about the Center before you came here?

Novice Man-Onko: Well, that you had lots of food and that all of you were brainwashed. Now, how does that... Wait a minute! Okay! So, during the Parade, the novices are running around, acting like we're brainwashed! That makes the idea stronger in the Outsiders!

Monk Ariel: We call it "positive reinforcement". We're sending them a subtle message: that we really do brainwash little children.

Now, why is that important?

Novice Man-Onko: [pauses]: This is tricky... [Pauses] I know why we tell people about the brainwashing – to keep them away. But why make that stronger? Why reinforce that?

Monk Ariel: You've done very well in our "chat", so I'll give you this one.

Some people are going to say bad things about the Centers, because it's in their nature to say bad things. We can't go in and change their nature... At least, not yet!

So instead we FEED them the "bad" stuff to talk about! If they are talking about the dumb stuff we feed them, like how we eat children or brainwash them, they won't spend any time trying to fight the parts we really ARE changing, like practicing inclusivity and having alternative economic, energy and governance systems, for example. We don't want them protesting the Latent Powers...

Novice Man-Onko: What's the 'Latent Powers'?

Monk Ariel: Something... you'll learn about another day.

The opposition, if and when it organizes, will be organized to stop us from brainwashing little children, or stop us from eating babies... and not stop us from practicing sustainability or... anything else we want to do.

Novice Man-Onko: Okay... So the Parade is a fake...

Monk Ariel: We call it a "feint" ... move one way to hide another.

Novice Man-Onko: Yeah, that's what I mean. But, why not just TELL us novices about it? About the fenk...

Monk Ariel: "Feint."

Novice Man-Onko: Yeah, that. Feint. Why not just tell us?

Monk Ariel: You know what I'm about to do, so why don't you just answer your question!

Novice Man-Onko: Man... Okay... So, you don't tell us, because we might give something away.

Monk Ariel: Yes. And?

Novice Man-Onko: And... [pause] There's something about US you're checking out...

Monk Ariel: Yes. We're looking at leadership potential in the novices.

Novice Man-Onko: Leadership? Bullshit! Leadership in who can do the best square dance? What kind of leadership is that?

Monk Ariel: We're not looking at your dance moves. We're looking at your CONSCIOUSNESS while you're out there square dancing.

Stress. Embarrassment. Memorization. Unfamiliar movement. Being on display. Working with others. Being back Outside. ALL of these things put each of you in a position to reveal what is really inside you. Not just the surface "you", but the inner "you".

We know you, Novice Man-Onko. Right now, we know you better than you know yourself. For example: you have a knack at getting along with others. People like you, are relaxed around you. But YOU are not relaxed around THEM. While you're telling jokes and cutting up, you are constantly looking for advantage, for a way to come out on top.

Novice Man-Onko: Hey, man, what the fuck? What you sayin'? What I do wrong?

Monk Ariel: Relax! Have some more tea! That wasn't a criticism... that's what we call "leadership potential". And the way we see it is by having you learn and perform those stupid little dances.

You and I are having this talk, because you have that potential. You aren't doing anything wrong. You're drinking my tea because you have the potential to do things right.

And, there's something we want you to do. A test of leadership.

Novice Man-Onko: Okay. Cool. What do you want?

Monk Ariel: Your English isn't bad at all, when you are calm and relaxed. Try to stay that way.

Your task: Try to get the other novices to go along with the "Parade", to be more participative, less holding back. Try to get them to get into the act.

Novice Man-Onko: Sure, no problem. I get it now...

Monk Ariel: Wait. Big problem. You cannot tell them what we talked about here.

Novice Man-Onko: [pause] Nothing?

Monk Ariel: Not one word. That would be too easy. I could do that myself. Instead, we want to see your "leadership", when its not something that benefits you directly.

Novice Man-Onko: [pause] What the fuck... Okay. I'll be star student in the "Weird Academy". Why not...

[end of transcript]

[Afternote: Novice Man-Onko excelled in his leadership classes with Monk Ariel.

However, after one year, "The Parade" was suspended at this Center, due to the growth of a permanent "Commons" in the city, which made the Parade unnecessary.]

The Dream

File No:		File Name:	The Dream
Location:	Denver Awareness Center	Parties:	Novice Man-Onko
Monk/ Master Supervising:	Monk Ariel		Voluntary counseling session

Name:		Pgs:	Date:	Vol:
Type of Transcript:	Mechanical xxx			
	Organic			

Preface by the North American Centers Archive Committee:

From the very beginning of their residency, Novices participate in a number of practices and activities designed to awaken the experience of the Latent Powers. Daily meditation sessions, tai chi, counseling... all designed to help the Novices access the Holonic Mind.

When it began, it usually started in their dreams...

[start of transcript]

Ariel: Sit down. I believe this is the first time you've come to see me voluntarily. Will you have some tea?

Man-Onko: That's the strongest you've got?

Ariel: Like that, huh? Well, let's make it a black tea this time.

[Pause for tea]

Ariel: Well, let's talk about the dreams that are troubling you...

Man-Onko: WHAT? How the – how did you know what I wanted to talk about?

Ariel: This falls into the "We Know Everything" category...

And, also, all of you Novices are having the same dream right around now...

Man-Onko: Okay, you're makin' my head hurt! How can ALL of us have the SAME DREAM?

Ariel: What is a dream?

Man-Onko: Hey, isn't this MY session? Don't I ever get to ask questions?

Ariel: Of course you can ask questions! Just don't expect any of us monks to ever give you any answers!

Now, answer mine: what is a dream?

Man-Onko: I don't know. Just the stuff that's runnin' around in your head, from whatever you were doing the day before.

Ariel: Actually, not bad! That "stuff" has a name. It's called CONSCIOUSNESS.

Man-Onko: Okay, I remember that from one of my classes.

So, my consciousness picks up a lot of sh--, of stuff from the day, and plays it back at night?

Ariel: Yes and no. It's not just playing back random scenes. It's trying to reach RESOLUTION. It's trying to FIX things.

Man-Onko: Well, my fixer must be stuck. I keep having the same dream, over and over, and it ain't fixed. I don't think it can be fixed.

Ariel: This dream is about your mother and your sister on the Outside, and you in the Center, right?

Man-Onko: [pauses]: You're gonna tell me how you crawl up my nose at night and see into my brain. This shit ain't funny.

Ariel: Man-Onko, all I can tell you is that 6 months from now, you will know the answer to that question, without me telling you. Right now, all I can ask is that you trust me.

[pauses]: May I go on?

Man-Onko: Yes...

Ariel: So, your dreams are about your mother and your sister?

Man-Onko: Yes...

Ariel: In the dream, you're having fun here in the Center.

Man-Onko: Yes...

Ariel: And you can see them on the Outside.

Man-Onko: Yes...

Ariel: And they've got it pretty bad.

Man-Onko: [pauses]: Yes...

Ariel: In some of the dreams, you see them with you, happy in the Center. But then you wake up and they aren't here. It depresses you.

Man-Onko: Damn! I forgot about those! Yes! Those are the worse!

Ariel: So... while these dreams are depressing, they are not particularly scary or frightening, are they?

Man-Onko: No...

Ariel: And, unfortunately, these dreams are pretty accurate, aren't they? You are Inside, you are enjoying yourself and they are Outside, and probably not enjoying themselves.

Man-Onko: Yes...

Ariel: The subject of the dreams is the same for all of the Novices. Different loved ones: parents, siblings, friends...

So,... how about we work on changing the dreams?

Man-Onko: [pauses]: So... now you're gonna crawl up my nose tonight and CHANGE how I'm dreaming?

Ariel: [laughing]: Taking your colorful language out of it... yes!

What did you come to me for? Did you come to just talk about your problem, or do something about it?

On the Outside, they had these people called "psychiatrists". They would spend hours and hours, sometimes years and years, just listening to people talking about their problems. Sometimes they got better, sometimes they didn't.

We are doing things differently.

I won't bother asking you if you know what "lucid dreaming" is. It's like being awake in your dream.

Man-Onko: Hey, I kinda know what you're talking about! Some dreams are like, CLEARER than others.

Ariel: Excellent!

Well, we've taken lucid dreaming a step further. I can be awake in YOUR dream. Not just yours, but all of you Novices.

In a few days, we're going to start steering your dreams. You will start to understand the lesson-value of these dreams.

Man-Onko: Why wait? I'm ready NOW.

Ariel: Indeed you are. But some of the others haven't gotten to your point in the dreams yet. Just be patient – help is on the way.

Man-Onko: And then what happens?

Ariel: What do you think happens?

Man-Onko: You quit crawling up my nose, and I quit having bad dreams.

Ariel: No and no. We'll be doing the "nose-crawling" so often, we've developed a name for it: "Night School". While your body is resting, your mind and spirit will be joining with others and going places... including other dimensions.

Man-Onko: Okay, more "Weirdo Academy" stuff. And I'm sure you're gonna say that we'll be doing this the rest of our lives...

Ariel: Actually... it seems like it's going to be much longer than that!

[end of transcript]

[Afternote: Four days after the counseling session, all Novices underwent their first "Night School" session. 35% experienced lucidity on the first attempt (including Man-Onko). All of them experienced a resolution of the "guilt" dream.

Within one year, 92% of Novices experienced lucidity in at least one Night School session, and 60% were experiencing lucidity in the majority of the sessions.]

News Article: CITIES ON FIRE!!

File No:		File Name:	News Article: CITIES ON FIRE!!
Location:		Parties:	
Monk/ Master Supervising:			

Name:		Pgs:		Date:		Vol:	
Type of Transcript:	Mechanical xxx						
	Organic						

Preface by the North American Archives Committee:

When the Upheavals happened, they didn't happen all at once. They didn't happen to everyone evenly. They were not uniform in their results.

Some effects were remote and isolated. Some systems failures triggered others. Most were recurring.

From the beginning, the goal of the Awakening Movement was not to ameliorate the effects of the Mess. In the caterpillar, the systems and structures break down – a necessary step in the formation of the flying beauty of a butterfly.

The goal was not to prevent what was happening. The goal was to create NEW systems and structures, ones that respond to the needs of the butterfly.

In the face of major conflagrations, the Awakening Centers guarded their water supplies. This was not a lack of compassion. This was triage.

NEWS ARTICLE:
Several US cities have major fires raging out-of-control, spread by a combination of unprecedented heat, social unrest and failing municipal services.

"We don't know where to start. We don't know what's feeding it. It should have burned out by now- there's nothing left to burn. I don't know what to do..." Chief Ken Simmons of the fire-weary Kansas City Fire Department. "We've got firefighters passing out from exhaustion. I haven't slept in 3 days. Our water is running low, and the fire still spreads. At some point ... we're gonna have to pull back, cut our losses."

Kansas City is not the only urban area to experience runaway conflagrations. In Rapid City, the local fire department has issued the first city-wide evacuation order since Hurricane Katrina three decades ago. Said Chief William Smythe, "When those gas lines exploded, it was all over. There's nothing we can do, besides get people out of the way of the fire."

"The asphalt streets are BURNING! I didn't know anything could get that hot! The streets melted one of our fire trucks! The only thing we can do is get people out of the way. We don't know how far we have to run..."

Things are not so grim in Richmond, VA. "We're blessed by the river," said Chief Chuck Barker. "We've got 3 fire boats going full blast, aimed at the downtown business district. Not a single ember is getting by us!"

However, some residents of the city are not so positive. "Yeah, they're protecting downtown, but they're letting whole neighborhoods burn! Look! The fire's only 10 blocks away! And we haven't seen a fire truck all day!"

Chief Barker was sober in his response: "That's not an accident. We've had to make some hard choices. We simply don't have the resources to stop every fire in every neighborhood. If we tried, we'd lose everything-including the places we tried to save. Some areas just have to be sacrificed for the greater good."

Said one resident, "Why come all the neighborhoods being sacrificed are black? Why come rich white folks ain't sacrificed?"

The Banned Books: The Laws of LIFE

What is a "field"? It's something you cannot detect with your senses, but which has a powerful effect on almost everything that you <u>can</u> detect with your senses.

LIFE is a field. And, there's only one field, one LIFE. Most of us do not accept that there is one LIFE field. This is because, ever since you were a child, people had different explanations for what they saw as the phenomena of LIFE.

LIFE, the Life Energy Field, is the least studied of the fields. You can't major in it in college. No one hands out Nobel Prizes in "Life Energy Field Studies". This is mainly because just about every scientist denies that there is one. And most of us act like the Field doesn't exist.

I am attempting to correct this oversight. Newton did not "discover" gravity. He simply explained what everyone could see - in a way that MADE SENSE.

"The Ecstatic Society"

Shariff M. Abdullah

(Banned by Act of Congress)

The Table

File No:		File Name:	Novice Exercise: "The Table"	Class "The Table"
Location:	Denver AC; Canteen	Parties:		
Monk/ Master Supervising:	Monk Green-Man		15 Novices, Novice Teams: Pod Gopher, Pod Maple Leaf, Pod Sparrow	

Name:		Pgs:		Date:		Vol:	
Type of Transcript:	Mechanical						
	Organic						

Preface by North American Archive Committee:

How do you teach morality, humanity, VALUES, to young people who had experienced the trauma of a dysfunctional society and the horrors of the Upheavals? Early on, the Centers discovered that the best lessons were those that came outside of regular "classes".

This text is being provided in a rough draft format. Communication Access Realtime Translation (CART) facilitates communication accessibility and may not be a totally verbatim record of the proceedings. Let your coordinator know if you would prefer a more verbatim option.

[start of transcript]

Gopher Pod members [Table B position]:
· Novice Man-Onko
· Novice Victory
· Novice Dorado
· Novice Breener
· Novice Krista-lin

Novice Man-Onko: Hey, where's everybody? And where's the food?

Monk Green-Man: Okay, everybody pipe down! This is an exercise...

Novice Victory: Exercise? How bout we eat, then exercise!

Monk Green-Man: I said SILENCE!

[silence]

Monk Green-Man: Good. You're all getting better at that. Now, find a seat with your name on it, sit down and stay shut up.

[shuffling sounds]

Monk Green-Man: Okay. There are three tables. There are 5 of you at each table. You will be served your food soon. It won't be enough for everyone at your table. You will have to decide what to do.

There will NOT be any more food available until dinner time. I know you were worked pretty hard this morning, so you're all hungry right now.

You will stay at your table. You can LOOK at the other tables, but you cannot discuss the problem with them. You have to solve your problems on your own.

Last point: If you don't decide what to do within 30 minutes... we take the food back.

Novice Man-Onko: Hey, what about...

Monk Green-Man: NO QUESTIONS! Figure it out the best you can. Please bring out the food now.

[shuffling sounds as servers bring out food]

[What follows is the conversation at Table B]

Novice Victory: Man, this is bogus! That's only a bowl of soup and one piece of bread! I eat more than that myself!

Novice Breener: Bogus is right! What do they expect us to do, starve?

Novice Man-Onko: No, they expect us to start fighting over that little bit of food.

Novice Dorado: Well, if we was Outside, we would, right?

Novice Victory: Yeah, but this ain't Outside. If we start fighting, we should be fighting THEM.

Novice Krista-lin: I don't want to fight nobody...

Novice Victory: That mean I can have your share, sweetie?

Novice Man-Onko: Wait a minute! We're goin' right where they want us to go! Let's figure this out!

Novice Dorado: Man, talkin' won't make that bread grow into a loaf...

Novice Krista-lin: I don't want to be here...

Novice Victory: Yeah, well you are, you little chicken, so best you get with the program...

Novice Man-Onko: Man, we don't even know what the program is! Why don't you leave her alone, and help us figure out what to do?

Novice Dorado: I want to figure out what that table is doin' [indicates Table C]. Looks like they're prayin' or sleepin'.

Novice Breener: Maybe they're all faint with hunger!

[General laughing]

Novice Man-Onko: Come on, let's figure out what to do, before we all faint!

Novice Breener: Or we have to give the food back!

Novice Victory: How bout we all draw straws?

Novice Dorado: Man, you see any straws?

Novice Krista-lin: I... I... I don't want to fight...

Novice Man-Onko: We could divide it up five ways...

Novice Dorado: Man, get real! We'd each get about a mouthful. What would that do?

[Altercation in the room, at Table A]

Novice Dorado: Well, looks like that table just "decided" what to do! That big asshole just grabbed the bread!

Novice Man-Onko: Yeah, but the other ones took him down! And spilled the soup!

Novice Dorado: Hey, those turkeys over at the other table are still asleep... maybe we should creep over and help ourselves to theirs!

Novice Krista-lin: I don't... I don't want to be here...

Novice Victory: Okay, bitch, NOTED! Now just shut the fuck up, if you can't be helpful!

Novice Man-Onko: Leave her alone...

Novice Victory: But she's creepin' me out!

Novice Man-Onko: Look, right now, we are running THEIR PROGRAM. We're fighting with each other, over a mouthful of food. That guy got punched out for a mouthful of bread, and those other pukes'll probly get kicked out for fighting!

Now, the only question is: did we learn anything in the past 5 weeks, or are we still Outside?

[silence]

Novice Dorado: Seems to me the only things to do are either divide it up, or everyone agree to give it to one of us.

And... Whatever happens, we should AGREE.

[mutual assent]

Novice Man-Onko: Okay, which way we go?

Novice Krista-lin: I don't...

Novice Victory: Yeah, Honey, we know. You don't want to fight and you don't want to be here. Anything else?

Novice Man-Onko: Leave her alone.

Novice Dorado: Maybe she should leave us alone.

Novice Man-Onko: Okay, how bout we vote? All in favor of dividing...

Novice Victory: Wait a minute. That other table just woke up...

[sounds of movement]

Novice Victory: Hey, they're heading over here!

Hey, you guys can't be over here... if you're talking to us, you'll get in trouble!

Table C Spokesman: We're not here to talk to you. We're here to make you a gift.

[Places bread and soup on Table B]

Table C Spokesman: We realized that this is a game, and we decided not to play. We've all been way hungrier than we are right now. Hunger is in our minds, and we decided to move the hunger out of our minds.

Novice Man-Onko: Damn...

Table C Spokesman: Let us finish, so no one can say that we were "discussing".

We know it's still not enough food, but it might make your decision-making easier if you have it.

And, don't thank us. The extra food might make your decision-making harder...

[Table C exits the canteen]

Novice Man-Onko: Damn...

Novice Breener: Yeah... But, it does make things a little easier. I vote now for dividing it up...

Novice Man-Onko: No! Wait...

Novice Dorado: What? More for one person...?

Novice Man-Onko: No... I... I.... I think we should do what they did. I think we shouldn't eat any of it.

Novice Victory: What? Give it to the fighting assholes?

Novice Man-Onko: No. [pause] I think we should give it back.

[silence]

Novice Breener: Damn. And fuck.

Novice Man-Onko: Is that yes or no?

Novice Breener: Shit. Wow.... Yes. Although my hunger sounds like its still in my belly, not in my head!

Novice Victory: Agreed. Fuck their game. We'll choose not to play, like those other guys.

Novice Breener: Hey... Yeah, but its more than that. We are choosing not to be hungry. We've all seen worse times than this – let's be strong!

Novice Dorado: I'm cool. What about you, Princess?

Novice Krista-lin: I don't... I mean...[pause] Yes, I agree.

Novice Man-Onko: Okay... we're solid. Let's go! Everybody grab a plate or bowl... and no drinking on the way!

[end of transcript]

[AFTERNOTE: Tables B & C received commendations for solving the game, and in record time: 17 minutes.

Table A received demerits for fighting. Novice Ran-ka, the protagonist, has been noted for additional psychological screening and possible adjustment.

All novices at Table C are being observed for possible early apprenticeship. Also Novice Man-Onko from Table B. Novice Krista-lin from Table B has been noted for additional psychological screening and possible adjustment.]

News Article: **Nationwide Manhunt Underway for Imaginal Group**

"He's going to answer to us for his actions. He will find that we have more resolve on this matter than he gives us credit for. This committee will not rest until James Harold Moore and his band of domestic terrorists are locked up and testifying about their role in the Upheavals."

Mary Huntlee, Acting Director of the FBI, issued a statement from her office: "Congress has made the search for the Imaginal Group (IG) a top priority, allocating additional resources from other agencies, including Border Patrol and Homeland Security. Their bank accounts have been frozen and Cloud accounts have been seized. Interpol has been alerted to our search and has pledged cooperation. We believe it is only a matter of time before IG is apprehended and brought to justice."

Senior officials in the FBI, speaking on condition of anonymity, paint a very different picture. "Everyone knows this is just a show," said an official close to the investigation. "Europe loves this guy. He could go over there and die of old age before Interpol moves against him. And, there are large sections of our own cities that are 'no-go' zones for law enforcement officials. We would need an Army battalion to get into some of them. And IG is very popular in places like that."

"And then there are those Centers. Any one of them would gladly harbor all of the IG members. We don't even know how many there are! Some of them are vast -- hundreds of acres or more. We don't have the resources to comb every square inch. Especially if they don't want us to find them.

"We don't even know how they communicate with each other! We can tap any phone, anywhere in the world...

but these folks must be sending smoke signals! Using invisible smoke!

"And... some of our agents are in sympathy with Moore and IG. He makes too much sense to be ignored."

Memorandum – Water Triage

TRANSCRIPT OF TOP SECRET SECUITY BRIEFING

REMARKS OF HARVARD PROFESSOR GRANT EDWARDS, HYDROLOGY AND SECURITY

"Reshaping the American Landscape: Hydrology, Security and the Limits of State Power"

Audience:
- Heads of selected major private universities
- Representatives of selected State National Guards
- Representatives of Federal and State disaster management agencies

DR. LESLIE TOWERS: Greetings, friends. Let's settle down, because we've got a long day ahead of us and some hard choices to make.

My first speaker is Professor Grant Edwards, head of the Department of Hydrology and Security at Harvard University's School of Water Studies. He's been working on the issue of water security for quite awhile... I think everyone in the room knows about him and his reputation as a straight-shooter.

Because of the security level of this briefing, you've all had to relinquish your electronic devices at the door, as well as sign non-disclosure agreements. Professor Edwards' recommendations are going to be pretty hard-hitting and are definitely NOT for attribution or public consumption.

Without further ado, my friend and colleague Grant Edwards.

GRANT EDWARDS: Thanks for that introduction, Leslie. It's been a pleasure visiting with you, Alan and your kids for the past few days.

As she said, we don't have a lot of time, and we have a lot of ground to cover. Let's get started.

My first point: You've all read in my books about the concept of "societal triage". You've all read my books, right? [Laughter] For the couple of you who haven't [Laughter], "societal triage" means just that – we as a society have to make some hard choices about where we apply our limited resources.

Just as a battlefield medic has to scan the entire battlefield and make some hard choices, we are faced with a similar situation. Basically, he or she has to decide who is NOT going to get any resources. They can't just run up to the first person they see bleeding and start applying bandages. They have to think about the whole, first. This is the basic concept of "triage"... determining who gets your help... and who doesn't.

The first choice of those to let suffer are those who are hurting, but will be able to make it on their own. A soldier with a broken leg, with the bone sticking through his flesh, may be hurting like hell, but he's not going to die from that broken leg. No resources. That's Level One.

The second choice is harder, but just as clear: Level Five marks someone who's not going to make it, no matter how many resources you administer. The soldier who's been cut in half by machine gun fire, or is missing half their chest cavity isn't going to make it. Even administering pain reduction medication is wasting a resource on that person... medication that would better go to a soldier whose life may be saved with that medication.

Those are the two extremes. As hard as those choices are, they are relatively easy compared to the next two.

If Level One is what we would call the "walking wounded", Level Two are the people who COULD die unless they receive your resources. A person with a simple bone break, but is bleeding from an artery and needs a compress or a tourniquet. The other side of the equation is Level Four, the people who absolutely WILL die, unless you use heroic measures to save them.

I said Levels One and Five were easy. Now I think you can see what I mean. Telling someone who <u>might</u> die unless they get your aid, or someone who <u>WILL</u> die unless they get your aid, that you will not give them any resources will be the hardest things you will ever have to do.

And you will have to do it. Starting today.

You know from my books that I've applied this "triage" model to our present and future water crises in this country. In those books, I've hinted at the US government having to make some hard choices. In the past, I've never been specific. Today I get specific.

Look around this room. There is no one in this room from institutions or agencies that are West of the Rocky Mountains. We've already done the first level of triage, right here in this room.

There's no one here from the water-rich Pacific Northwest. Yes, we are aware that there are water wars between the thirsty cities of Seattle and Portland and the desperate farmers and ranchers of Eastern Oregon, Eastern Washington and most of Idaho. We know that they are begging for us to intervene, to help them divide up the water more equitably. We will do nothing. They are Level One. They're on their own.

Likewise, there's no one here from the water-poor Southwest. They are at Level Five. They will die, and there's nothing we can or will do to save them. For those of you who have friends or family in Phoenix or Tucson or Las Vegas, I fully expect you to be on your cellphones the moment they're given back to you. And, your calls should be very short. In fact, they should consist of one word: "MOVE!"

Move to where? Move to a city that's on a river that you've actually heard of. The Mississippi. The Columbia. The Missouri. The Delaware. The Savannah. The Potomac. The Hudson. The Ohio.

And I stress that you tell people to move to a city that is ON a river. Cities like New York, New Haven, Philadelphia and Washington, DC will make it. Atlanta, Georgia will NOT. We have placed Atlanta at Level Four. It will not receive our heroic efforts to survive.

That leaves the Level Three cities: those that will survive, but only if we intervene.

Levels Zero to One: (no-few problems): Seattle, Portland, Boston, New York, Philadelphia, Washington, DC... San Francisco? Sacramento?

Level Two: Worcester... Birmingham??

Level Three: Fresno, Lexington, Greensboro/Raleigh/Durham... Denver??

Level Four: Atlanta, Charlotte, Orlando, Dallas/ Ft. Worth... Houston??

Level Five: Phoenix, Tucson, Las Vegas, Los Angeles, San Diego

San Francisco? Sacramento? Even though they are in highly volatile California, they'll probably be alright, unless they allow others to steal their water. Not only do we predict state to state violence over water, but states like California may fragment over water issues. Northern, Central and Southern California may have three very different destinies, based solely on the presence of water.

Also, we have had disagreements as to where to place Houston and Birmingham. Some think that they are Level Four, while others place them at Level Five. The distinction is obviously important to where we place our resources.

All of this leads to the next question: What is going to happen when the word gets out that certain cities are not going to receive federal aid? We predict water wars, massive migration and massive deaths in the Southwest, and a mad scramble for available freshwater resources in the Southeast.

The one thing that SHOULD happen is the one thing we absolutely predict will NOT happen – we predict that people will NOT abandon the Level Four and Five cities. We believe those areas will call in all of their political favors, political clout, military force, public opinion... Anything and everything other than deal with the reality that they've run out of water.

And finally that gets us to the real purpose of this meeting. The real reason that we restricted this meeting as "Top Secret – Eyes Only". The real reason that every one of you needs to act like the life of our nation depends on our next actions.

Once word of this meeting gets out, Congress will start to make short-term political decisions – all the wrong ones. They will try to allocate water resources based on which cities have the most clout, or have the most to lose. They will allocate all of our resources on the Level Five cities... and ALL of them will go under, even Levels One and Two. All will go under, and take all of our resources with them. Unless you act.

You must stop them. There are two things that you must do:

1. Do not reveal the contents of this briefing to anyone. Not even your friends and family that you are trying to get out of the Level Four and Five cities. Say nothing to anyone – especially Congress or the press. The longer we can hold this, the better Part 2 will work. If we can hold the line for just 6 months, we all stand a chance.

2. Allocate ALL of your resources, right now, to the Level 3 cities. Right now. ALL IN. Hold nothing back. Don't wait for Congress to act. By the time Congress gets around to snatching your resources, you should be so committed to your Level 3 cities you don't have anything for Congressional pie-in-the-sky rescue operations of Level 5 cities.

3. Throw "water rights" right out the window. Make some decisions that should have been made decades ago. People watching their children die from lack of water won't care one bit about "legally senior water rights". Growing water-wasting crops like cotton and rice in the middle of a desert, just so a millionaire farmer can maintain his water rights, is wasteful and nonsensical. Your focus must be on "highest use", not "most senior use".

Now, a few of the big water agencies in the room might try resource allocation for a few Level 4 cities. Choose carefully. Choose wisely. Let your compassion be tempered not by need but by possibility.

Are there any questions?

[end of transcript]

[AFTERNOTE: The "Edwards Plan" did not survive the conference. As soon as they were given their cellphones, fifteen participants called their Congressmen or the press. (One called both.)

Congressman Ted Dawkins, whose Congressional district included Phoenix, moved immediately to freeze the budgets of all of the participating agencies, and called Professor Edwards into hearings to explain his theories.

Branding Edwards a "domestic terrorist", Dawkins had him investigated for possible links to Al Qaeda and ISIS. Because of Congressional pressure on scholastic budgets, Edwards was forced to resign his position at Harvard University.

Dawkins proposed the "American Water Freedom Act" (also known as the Dawkins Plan). Passed unanimously by Congress, the AWFA directed the nation's water agencies to place all of their resources on Level Five cities and farms... including transferring it from Level One cities.

Congressman Dawkins had the Bellagio Fountain in Las Vegas declared a "National Icon of the strength and power of the American people". He said that continuing to operate the fountain was the equivalent of "flying the American flag at Fort Sumter".

The Dawkins Plan was a disaster. As bad as "doing nothing" would have been, the Dawkins Plan was worse. As Professor Edwards predicted, the attempt to keep the Level Five cities functioning exhausted the water management agencies. The willingness to de-stabilize the Levels One and Two cities to support the survival of the Level Five cities placed them all at risk.

The Chipmunk

File No:		File Name:	The Chipmunk: Counseling Session
Location:	Denver AC: Masters' Counseling Rooms	Parties:	Novice Man-Onko
Monk/ Master Supervising:	Master Auroron		

Name:		Pgs:	Date:	Vol:	
Type of Transcript:	Mechanical				
	Organic				

Preface by North American Archive Committee:

Some negative behaviors were relatively easy to spot- violence, lying, theft...

Others were harder to detect and adjust. How could you see hoarding, or fear of lack, when the novices have so little to hoard?

This text is being provided in a rough draft format. Communication Access Realtime Translation (CART) facilitates communication accessibility and may not be a totally verbatim record of the proceedings. Let your coordinator know if you would prefer a more verbatim option.

[start of transcript]

Novice Man-Onko: Hey man, you don't have one of those Observers!

Master Auroron: Before you speak to me, you will BOW to me!

Novice Man-Onko: Oh yeah, I forget...

[pause]

Novice Man-Onko: So, why not get one of those creepy Observers? You don't rate?

Master Auroron: Before you speak to me, you will sit in silence and wait for me to speak first.

Novice Man-Onko: [under breath]: Damn...

[long pause, then bell rings]

Master Auroron: You should know, Novice Man-Onko, that I do not usually waste my time sitting with novices. However, several of your monks have asked me to take a look at you, which is why you are here.

So, Novice Man-Onko, I believe you had a question...

Novice Man-Onko: Hey, I forgot it by now!

Master Auroron: Which means that your question was not important to you. However, your question was important to ME, so I will remind you and then answer it. You were inquiring about why I still use a digital recorder, and not use the services of one of our Observers.

Novice Man-Onko: Yeah, right, that was it!

Master Auroron: I don't use the Observers because I don't think that is a respectful use for human consciousness. I also do not approve of the techniques they use to enhance the memory capacities of the Observers.

Novice Man-Onko: Oh yeah? What do they do? Jack 'em up with drugs?

Master Auroron: Do you really care about the answer? Or, are you just talking because you haven't learned the discipline of keeping one's mouth shut?

Novice Man-Onko: Hey, you guys... MONKS... are always tellin' us to be 'curious' and 'creative'! I'm just tryin' to learn!

Master Auroron: Are you trying to learn right now? Do you really want to know how Observers are enhanced?

Novice Man-Onko: Uh... yeah! Of course!

Master Auroron: Well, transfer 10 credits into my account, and I will tell you.

Novice Man-Onko: Ten credits! Why should I pay? Ain't... ISN'T... learning supposed to be free? How come you're profiting from my learning?

Master Auroron: Fair enough. I should not profit from your learning. Instead of transferring the 10 credits to me, I want you to transfer ten credits to that chipmunk outside my window.

Novice Man-Onko: WHAT? Are you brain-dead? That chipmunk don't have no account!!

Master Auroron: The more excited you get, the worse your language gets. Do not forget that I am a Master. Please repeat what you said.

Novice Man-Onko: [pause]: Sorry for saying you're brain-dead. But, that chipmunk doesn't have an account, so I can't transfer any credits to him.

Master Auroron: To her, actually. Her name is Roberta, and she has an account balance larger than yours is right now.

Novice Man-Onko: What? Why's a chipmunk need an account balance? What does it do with the credits?

Master Auroron: And that question will be our lesson for today.

Novice Man-Onko: [pauses]: You know, of all the weirdoes here at "Weirdo Academy", you really take the cake. I really want to find the stuff that you're smokin'.

Master Auroron: My smoking habits will be the subject of another day. Right now, we're talking about Roberta's account balance. Why does she need one?

Novice Man-Onko: She DOESN'T. She's a fuckin'... excuse me. She's an ANIMAL. She eats nuts, climbs trees and gets humped regularly. Probably in that order. She don't need my 10 credits to do any of that!

Master Auroron: True... so why does she have one?

Novice Man-Onko: Because... [pause] you guys are WEIRDOES!

Master Auroron: Do you really think that's an answer I will accept?

Novice Man-Onko: [long pause]: I give up. I don't know.

Master Auroron: Why do you check your account balance 3 or 4 times a day?

Novice Man-Onko: What? How do you know that?

Master Auroron: One day, you will figure out HOW we know everything. Right now, just answer the question.

Novice Man-Onko: [pause]: I just want to know that no one is cheating me out of credits.

Master Auroron: Have you found any cheating?

Novice Man-Onko: No...

Master Auroron: Speak up! Sit up straight!

Novice Man-Onko: No, sir!

Master Auroron: You've been here six weeks. Why do you still check every day, several times a day?

Novice Man-Onko: [pause]: Is there something wrong with checking?

Master Auroron: [pause]: There is nothing wrong with checking your balance. I'm not here to talk about your account balance. I'm here to help you find out WHO YOU ARE.

[long pause]

Master Auroron: I think you're discovering something about yourself.

Novice Man-Onko: I feel... funny inside. Can we talk later?

Master Auroron: We will talk now. Let's try to bring that funny feeling from inside to outside.

Since you check your balance so often, what do you know about your totals?

Novice Man-Onko: They keep going up.

Master Auroron: Have they EVER gone down?

Novice Man-Onko: [pauses]: No.

Master Auroron: If you work and go to school, your totals go up. Not by a lot, but at the end of the week, you have more credits than you started with. After we deduct for your food, your clothes, your bed, all the extra ice cream you eat at meals... you still have more at the end of the week than you did before.

Didn't we promise you that on the first day you arrived here?

Novice Man-Onko: Yes...

Master Auroron: You will SPEAK UP! Have we kept our promise?

Novice Man-Onko: Yes, sir.

Master Auroron: Now... how often do you think Roberta checks her account balance?

Novice Man-Onko: I get it...

Master Auroron: Please answer me.

Novice Man-Onko: She doesn't check it, because she doesn't HAVE to check it. She gets fed, whether she has a high or a low balance.

Master Auroron: Are you planning on leaving the Center?

Novice Man-Onko: What? No! Or... I mean, I don't have any plans on leaving.

Master Auroron: Good. We would miss you. I would miss you. But frequent balance checks is a sign of someone about to jump the fence.

So, if you're not a fence-jumper, why do you do it?

Novice Man-Onko: Okay, I'll try to check less...

Master Auroron: That doesn't answer my question! I want to know WHO YOU ARE. I want to know the kind of person you are. I don't want you walking around here like a zombie, reacting blindly, unconsciously, like the people on the Outside do.

Why do you keep checking your balance?

Novice Man-Onko: [long pause]: I don't know...

Master Auroron: That... is actually a good answer. Good enough for right now, anyway.

You have a new assignment. You are still free to check your balance as many times a day as you like. But, you MUST check it, at least twice a day – every morning and evening. When you check it, you will do these things:

1. Before you check, you will meditate for 5 minutes on my question: Why are you checking? Write down any answers that come to you.

2. You will check Roberta's balance FIRST. Then yours.

3. You will write down both of the balances, yours and Roberta's.

4. You will find Roberta and tell her what her balance is, every time you check yours.

Understand?

Novice Man-Onko: Wow. Man, this is really heavy...

Master Auroron: And... once I give you Roberta's account number, there will be nothing to stop you from transferring her balance to you. You will have the power to steal from her.

Novice Man-Onko: Steal from... that. It gets weirder by the minute. Wow...

Master Auroron: You are doing something very important. You are revealing yourself... to yourself.

Novice Man-Onko: Yeah... and to a fucking squirrel.

Master Auroron: She's a chipmunk.

[end of transcript]

[AFTERNOTE: One week after receiving his assignment, Novice Man-Onko wrote the following note to Master Auroron:

"Roberta doesn't care about her account balance. Neither do I. We're both getting enough nuts. I still don't know who I am, but I know I'm not Outside anymore, and I'm not hungry.

And yes, I can steal from Roberta, but that would make me stupider than a ~~squirrel~~ CHIPMUNK."

Based on this note, Master Auroron canceled further counseling sessions.]

News Article: FEMA Cities Springing Up

In the face of the multiple crises stretching America's urban infrastructure to the breaking point, many cities have seen the growth of emergency encampments within their borders. These so-called "FEMA Cities" are places where people can get food, shelter and basic services.

Some of the temporary facilities have been in large municipal buildings, like stadiums. And some have been tent cities...But FEMA is running short on tents – and everything else.

"We are prepared for hurricanes, or earthquakes. We are NOT prepared for THIS!" said Sergio Hernandez, regional director for FEMA in the Southwest. "Everything's gone wrong, and it's all gone wrong at the same time! We can't feed and house hundreds of thousands of people, indefinitely!"

In a strange turn of events, the recent bankruptcy of the National Basketball Association (NBA) has turned into a blessing of sorts for FEMA. "There were these large stadiums in most big cities, huge buildings with no tenants. We are using these as temporary shelters and storage facilities for food and equipment. Just until both America and the NBA are back on their feet."

Congressional Hearings for Awakening Center Donors

Date:

Congressional hearing called to question donors of the Awakening Centers

Transcript of official Recording with Mr. Frazier, Mr. Younger and Ms. Kingsley. Rep Charles Baker D- MS.

Baker: These proceedings will come to order. We are here to investigate the vast sums of money that some people gave to James Harold Moore to start these so-called "Awakening Centers". We're here to find out what they intended to gain from these so-called "donations", and to get some insight into why the "Imaginal Group" fugitives are still at large. Are these donors aiding and abetting the IG evasion of justice? Or, is Moore just a pawn, and these so-called "donors" the real powers behind the so-called "Awakening Centers"?

As I understand it, only one of the three witnesses summoned by this committee chooses to make an opening statement.

Frazier: That is correct. My colleagues agree with my statement, but do not want to co-sign it.

Baker: Why is that?

Frazier: That will be obvious from the statement itself.

Baker: Proceed.

Frazier: Dear ladies and gentlemen of Congress. Actually, I speak not so much to you as to the people you claim to represent.

Calling these hearings, first on the Imaginal Group and then on us as donors, people who made legal and legitimate nonprofit donations to a valid 501(c)(3) organization, is a waste of taxpayers' time and money. You're looking in the wrong direction for a reason for the Upheavals on the streets.

Basically, Congress is fully to blame for all of the conditions that they claim to be investigating. And, they are looking for a scapegoat rather than explain their own behavior. Scapegoating is the best they can do. Once the American people...

Baker: Hold on! Wait a minute! You can't say that to us! I'll have you all thrown in jail for contempt of Congress!

Frazier: Now you can see why my colleagues, while agreeing with me have declined to sign this. Only I am subject to jail. And that bank of lawyers sitting behind me have advised me that I won't go to jail for exercising my First Amendment rights.

Baker: I won't have you soiling the name and reputation of Congress...

Frazier: You can come down off your high horse. I don't have a need to say any of this. My remarks are in writing and I've given them to the media already. It's already on the Internet and about to go viral. And, a copy will be included in the Federal Register.

Baker: No it won't. You think that we'll put that kind of scandalous language in our record, you better...scandalous...

[Aide whispers to Baker]

Baker: Well... Let's get on with this hearing...

Mr. Frazier, our records indicate that you've provided aid and support to James Harold Moore and the Imaginal Group in the amount of $8 million over the course of the past three years. Is that correct?

Frazier: No, it is not correct.

Baker: What do you mean by that? Our records indicate...

Frazier: Your records indicate that I provided money to Commonway Institute, a valid 501(c)(3) organization. I have never given any money to Dr. Moore. The so-called "Imaginal Group" isn't even an organization - its just a group of people who attended a conference. And, by the way, I gave Commonway $10 million, not $8 million.

Baker: Isn't giving money to his organization the same as giving money to him?

Frazier: Of course not. Dr. Moore is a living, breathing human being. Commonway is a legal fiction, a piece of paper. You folks never figured out that difference. That's why you work so hard for corporations and so little for your voters.

Baker: I'm not here to bandy words with you!

Frazier: Oh yes you are! That's all you people do!

[General laughter in the room.]

Baker: Mrs. Kingsley, let me ask you: what did you think you were buying with your donation?

Kingsley: Nothing. You don't buy things with nonprofit donations. What law school did you graduate from?

Baker: Just answer my questions! Why did you make your donation of $6 million?

Kingsley: That money, and the funds I will give in the future, are my investment in a world that works for all beings.

Baker: Oh yes, now we're back to Moore's pet phrase!

Kingsley: I know that's how you see it. But, it's not a phrase... It's a perspective. A point of view, one that obviously you don't understand or share.

Baker: I don't know anything about "all beings". I DO know the American people! And I know that they will not tolerate the disruption of their society!

Kingsley: You know the American people? Last night, from my hotel room, I could hear gunfire in the streets below! Automatic gunfire! Which of your "American citizens" was doing the firing? And who were they firing on?

Couldn't you hear them? Automatic weapons fired right here in the nation's capital, and not a word of it in the morning newspapers! Do you think Dr. Moore was down there, with an automatic rifle, firing in the streets to disrupt things?

Guns and bullets are where YOUR money goes. Ours goes for a different purpose. A better world.

Baker: If he is so interested in a better world, why doesn't he come forward, come to these hearings and clear his name?

Youngen: His name is doing pretty well out there with the public. His books are selling like hotcakes. The only people who seem to have a problem with Dr. Moore's purpose and intent are you people in Congress. And, I have it on good authority that he just doesn't give a shit about your opinions.

Baker: Stop saying that! This is outrageous! I'm going to have you all behind bars!

Youngen: I know you really want to lock someone up. I know you want to show that you're tough. I know you want to show the handful of people you call your constituents that you're "doing something".

But, I'm willing to bet the hourly fees of that bus load of lawyers sitting behind us that you don't get tough with us. I'll bet you that none of us spend even 5 minutes in jail.

[end of transcript]

[Afternote: Hearings were suspended at this point. Other donors refused to participate and appear.

In a legal proceeding, the Federal District Court held that donors did not have to answer to Congress for valid donations to registered non-profit groups.]

The Banned Books: Emergence – A Conversation with LIFE

Think of Emergence as a conversation between beings... one that takes place without words, or even concepts. Or, think of Emergence as a political governance system... one where all parties share the same vision, mission and values, where none are in conflict, because all can see the Big Picture, the Emergent Vision.

The Conversation through Emergence is a Conversation with LIFE.

It is the activation of the LIFE Energy Field. (More on THAT later.) This conversation is something that happens at a level that an individual simply cannot comprehend.

This is a conversation that does not take place in the realm of words and thoughts. Because the conversation starts and ends beyond the "individual", it lies beyond the individualized human mind, but can be perceived by the human heart.

But, before you think I am lapsing into sappy sentimentality, I believe the Emergent conversation is (and can be) both powerful and objectively measured. (And, more on THAT later.)

Humans who can think and act through Emergence, who act from the Inclusive Consciousness are (and will be) simply SMARTER than those who cannot. Not smarter in terms of grades or degrees, but smarter in terms of LIFE. Because they will be seeing from a different perspective, they will be perceiving in the longer term, and acting more comprehensively than others.

Smarter... not better. Consider three people, watching a news event on television. One of them is blindfolded, so they can only hear what's going on. The second has earplugs – they can see, but not hear.

And one can do both. They are simply better informed than the other two.

Inclusive consciousness will be the doorway into true sustainability.

Inclusive consciousness is not the sole domain of human beings, but is cross-, inter-, and trans-species. Inclusive consciousness transcends species, just as it transcends individuals within species.

At one time, Breakers did not believe that all "human" beings were capable of consciousness. (In their world-view, me and my black ancestors were not capable of consciousness... and they locked the doors to their educational institutions and put my ancestors in chains to insure the survival of that "belief".) The descendants of those Breakers will scoff at my notion that animals, plants and I share the same consciousness.

The implications of creating community, across species, open the doors to vast possibilities.

"The Ecstatic Society"

Shariff M. Abdullah

(Banned by Act of Congress)

The Fish

File No:		File Name:	The Fish
Location:	Denver	Parties:	Gopher Pod Frog Pod
Monk/ Master Supervising:	Tanu, Master		Transcript of novice lesson

Name:		Pgs:	Date:	Vol:	
Type of Transcript:	Mechanical xxx				
	Organic				

Preface by the North American Centers Archive Committee:

All who come to the Awakening Centers understand "We are One" as a concept, a principle. It takes a while to get inclusivity as a REALITY.

This text is being provided in a rough draft format. Communication Access Realtime Translation (CART) facilitates communication accessibility and may not be a totally verbatim record of the proceedings. Let your coordinator know if you would prefer a more verbatim option.

[start of transcript]

Master Tanu: No, no one is going swimming today. Or for a few weeks in the future, at this time of day.

Man-Onko: Come on! Did you happen to notice that it's HOT out here? What gives?

Master Tanu: Our nature seers have determined that your swimming is disturbing the fish. This is their sensitive mating season, and we want to...

Man-Onko: WHAT? We gotta be hot, just so some fish can FUCK? Sorry... have sex?

Novice Victory: Yeah! Tell 'em to get a room! Hell, they can have ours – it's hot as hell for them!

Master Tanu: Hold it! This isn't a negotiation! The fish have asked for privacy, and they're going to get it!

Now, you can go around griping like a bunch of little kids, or you can LISTEN TO ME and figure out what's going on!

[Silence]

Master Tanu: Better!

The fish have asked for privacy. We humans will honor that. This river belongs to us, and it also belongs to all of the other beings that use it. Especially those beings that were here before us.

Novice Krista-lin: I think I understand...

Novice Victory: Yeah, you would...

Novice Man-Onko: Hey, leave her...

Novice Victory: Yeah, I know. 'Leave her alone.' You got another song on that CD?

Novice Man-Onko: How about we listen to the man?

Master Tanu: Thank you. But that's "Master" to you.

Novice Man-Onko: Sorry...

Master Tanu: How about we listen to Novice Krista-lin first?

Novice Krista-lin: I... I don't know. Well... But... Well, if we leave them alone now, and they can make more babies...

Novice Victory: EGGS! Fish don't have babies!

Novice Man-Onko: Stuff it! You know what she means!

Novice Krista-lin: Well, if there are more fish, we... we... all benefit next year, right?

Master Tanu: You're right, but you're only partially right.

Yes, if we don't disturb the fish, we ought to get more fish later. That would be good. But that's not why we're doing this. We're doing this because they ASKED. We're doing this because they NEED IT. If the frogs had asked, we would do the same thing... and we don't eat frogs.

There once was a world that revolved around human wants. There was a world that didn't pay attention to the needs of others. WE RESCUED YOU FROM THAT. Do you remember? Do you remember living in that world? Did you forget so easily? That world is what you call

"Outside". Do you want to go back there? Do you want to bring that kind of thinking and acting in here?

[Silence]

I didn't think so. NOBODY wants to live in that world anymore. Even the people that created it.

This is something important for you to learn: the world does not revolve around humans. The world does NOT revolve around humans. Just because you want something doesn't mean you should have it. It doesn't mean your wants are good for you, or good for other species, or good for the planet.

All of us here are learning how to live WITH LIFE, not controlling or harnessing it as if it were a wild enemy that needs to be tamed and controlled.

Now, in time, you will be able to hear these voices yourselves. You will speak to the fish directly. You will hear the other Beings asking for our help, or giving us direction. But, until you do, you are going to listen to US, when we tell you that the swimming hole is off limits.

[Silence.]

Master Tanu: Good. Now, for the next two weeks, while the swimming hole is off limits, we are opening the monks' swimming pool to novices in the afternoons...

Novice Man-Onko: LET'S GO!!!

[end of transcript]

The Banned Books: What Exactly Is 'Ordinary Ecstasy'?

We generally associate the term "ecstasy" with peak experiences – usually religious or sexual. That would be a mistake.

Many of us experience "ordinary ecstasy" in our daily lives, examples of ecstasy in the everyday, the commonplace. It happens in ongoing situations and circumstances.

I think back to the lines of women I saw selling vegetables on the main streets, in the Ladakhi towns of Leh and Diskit. The tourists take their pictures, because they encompass the "quality without a name". They take pictures, because the vegetable women hold a timeless, non-self-referent quality. In some way, the tourists know these women are BEAUTIFUL.

Ordinary ecstasy happens when we become One with a purpose greater than our own. That purpose may be exalted or very, very everyday. Selling vegetables in the market. Steering a herd of yaks over a mountain pass. Seeing a rainbow in an oily rain puddle on a sidewalk.

And, perhaps... writing these words that you are now reading.

When ordinary ecstasy happens, SOMETHING gets triggered. Something that we don't have a lot of words for, something that, once we have it, we know we want it AGAIN.

This is the very thing that has kept religions going for ages. All religions have correctly said that religion is merely a window into a larger Reality. This is true. The trouble starts when they claim to be the ONLY window, or when they make negative inferences about OTHERS windows.

It is the promise of ecstasy, the promise of an experience of transcendence that keeps religions going, even when the adherents no longer adhere to the tenets of their faith.

What happens when we DON'T have the experience of Transcendence? We numb out in front of our televisions. We try to sublimate the need for Transcendence via other experiences, like "extreme" sports and risky social activities. And... we commit suicide – in greater and greater numbers.

People NEED to be in touch with the Transcendent. It is as important as food, or dreaming, or bonding...

"The Ecstatic Society"
Shariff M. Abdullah

(Banned by Act of Congress)

News Article: **Congress Passes Emergency Legislation, Issues Arrest Orders for Imaginal Group, Bans "Subversive" Writings**

"There's 'Freedom of Speech', then there's freedom to throw bombs in buses or spread disease in a crowded city. We banned these books, especially "The Ecstatic Society", in an effort to curb the infectious disease that has invaded our cities!

"In this time of crisis, the Imaginal Group is encouraging people to turn away from their government, as though some vague notion of "community", not our democratic institutions, will save us.

"Make no mistake: Our present troubles are a direct result of this group dabbling in "powers" that rightfully belong to God alone. These so-called "Latent Powers" that they talk about are opening the door to moral corruption. The Bible talks about what happened when people tried to usurp the powers of God by building the Tower of Babel. The so-called Imaginal Group is the modern equivalent of that.

"But they won't succeed. Not this time. We won't let them!"

In an increasingly effective counter-movement, websites in Europe, Asia and South America have been posting Imaginal Group writings on the Internet. A senior official with the European Union, speaking on condition of anonymity, said: "We think it is irresponsible to deny access to this material. Officially, our governments will not publish this material, but likewise we will not prevent our citizens from doing so."

The response from the President was characteristically blunt. "These writings are dangerous. WE have to protect our people, especially in these times of trouble." And, in a veiled reference to the European Union and others, the President stated, "Anyone sponsoring this material will be deemed acting against our national and strategic interests, and we will act accordingly."

The Four Principles

File No:		File Name:	The Four Principles
Location:	Denver	Parties:	Gopher Pod Sparrow Pod
Monk/ Master Supervising:	Bright Flower, Master		Transcript of novice lesson

Name:		Pgs:		Date:		Vol:	
Type of Transcript:	Mechanical xxx						
	Organic						

Preface by the North American Centers Archive Committee:

The novices learned how to grow food, wash dishes and plant trees. While this was important, it was also important to impart to them WHY they were doing so...

[start of transcript]

Sparrow Pod: Tanur, Nacom-Li, Harma, Wenna
Gopher Pod: Victory, Dorado, Man-Onko and Krista-Lin

Master: today, we'll return to the Four Principles. Who can tell me what we learned yesterday?

(20 novices rise). Novice Harma?

Harma: We learned about the 12 Global Challenges. And we learned there were four challenges that were more... important and difficult. We call them the "Four Principles": food and water, energy and spirit.

Master: Excellent. Why are they more important?

Harma: If we are not successful with those four, we don't get a chance to deal with the rest!

Master: Why do we lump them together like that? Novice Victory?

Victory: All four are important, but they also have resonance with each other. Without food, water becomes less relevant. Without water, food becomes impossible. Energy and spirit are...

Nacom-Li: Energy and spirit are like each other, I guess. Maybe energy is a form of spirit? Or maybe spirit is a form of energy?

Master: Are you asking or are you telling?

Nacom-Li: I am... Telling?

Master: Sounds an awful lot like a question to me!

Man-Onko: Well, this is tricky. I know we are told that energy is spirit and spirit is energy. But, it's hard for me to look at the generator powering these lights as "spirit".

Dorado: Yes, especially when I'm the one who has to pedal it!

(Laughter)

Nacom-Li: Yes, I agree. Isn't energy a THING? I mean, you have batteries, generators, light bulbs...

Dorado: Well, that's the tricky part! The batteries and generators are things. But the energy isn't the battery or the generator. The energy is in someway IN the battery...

Nacom-Li: Maybe it's like the energy is in YOU, and by pedaling the generator, the energy leaves you and goes into the generator...

Harma: And maybe that energy is also spirit?

Master: I see you are back to questions again! I keep thinking that's MY job!

Harma: Sorry...

Master: All of you are essentially correct. So, what's this have to do with "spirit"?

Harma: Well, on the Outside, they used to sell food without any energy in it. Is that the same as saying that the food doesn't have any Spirit?

Master: Do you have any idea about the difference between a question and a statement?

Harma: Sorry again! (Hesitates) The food on the Outside does not have any energy. Therefore, the food on the Outside does not have any spirit.

Master: Better. The people on the Outside will tell you, though, that they added chemical vitamins and nutrients to their food. Doesn't that give it energy?

Dorado: That's the attitude that got everything in the Mess that it's in now. They tried to FORCE things to have energy.

Harma: They only saw the PHYSICAL effects of energy, not any of the Mental, emotional and... Spiritual? Spiritual! The spiritual energy that the food had.

Master: Are we just talking about food here?

Harma: No! This is about EVERYTHING! Wow! They did this with everything! They can see that their society ran out of physical energy, in the form of fossil fuels. They can't drive their cars anymore. But, it's deeper than that, isn't it? Isn't it that ALL of their activities ran out of energy, at the same time?

Master: I really...

Harma: Wait! Sorry! All of their activities ran out of energy at the same time, with a period.

Master: Much better. Now, what about...

Krista-Lin: Why aren't there FIVE principles? My... my... father... my father... used to say that people needed food, Water and SHELTER. Why isn't shelter one of the principles?

Dorado: Yeah, and clothing! What about clothing?

Master: Since it looks like all of you are playing the role of master today, I guess I can go take a break! However, that is a valid question... Why not? Why doesn't the list include shelter and clothing?

Man-Onko: In the Urban Geography class, Master Neled said that shelter won't be a principal need in our society, because those Wasters overbuilt the physical environment. It will be centuries before we can occupy all of their abandoned and under-used buildings, before we have a real need for shelter.

Krista-Lin: And, so many people died... they all died...

Dorado: I remember that class. He said that once corporations started losing their shelter, human beings and other beings will have plenty of room.

Victory: Yeah! I saw eagles nesting in the upper floors of a skyscraper, when we went out on a field trip...

Master: We digress. Why isn't education one of the principles?

Wenna: That's easy. Master Tanu said that we novices were all sponges – we absorb everything. We are programmed that way – humans are. All beings are. The purpose of the Center is simply to DIRECT our education, not give it to us.

Master: She said that, but do you believe her?

Wenna: Well... Yes. I mean, what we're doing is really hard – but we keep coming back here for it! I don't know if this is called learning or not, but it seems like the right thing to do. It seems like I WANT to do it.

Master: On that high note, I think we'll end for the day!

(Novices rise and bow to the master, as she exits.)

[end of transcript]

The Food Wagon

File No:		File Name:	The Food Wagon
Location:		Parties:	Gopher Pod Frog Pod
Monk/ Master Supervising:	Monk Ariel		

Name:		Pgs:		Date:		Vol:	
Type of Transcript:	Mechanical XXX						
	Organic						

Notes:
Preface by North American Archive Committee:

The decades before the onslaught of the Upheavals have been referred to as "The Age of Waste". Given that so much of our resources were squandered on wasteful ventures (from ever-bigger cars and houses, to ever-bigger wars), it was easy to see how the name fit.

The Upheavals focused the human population on essentials. Enough food. Adequate, clean water. Enough heat in the cold climates, enough transportation to get away from danger...

While it was relatively easy to see that "food" is an essential, it's a little harder to see that "SYSTEM" was just as essential. Perhaps even more so...

[start of transcript]

Ariel: Okay, Gophers on this side of the wagon, Frogs on the other!

[sounds of scrambling]

Man-Onko: Hey Ariel, where's all this food going?

Ariel: To hungry people... so get a move on!

[more scrambling]

Man-Onko: Okay, we're up and away... check! Horses delivering horse-power, check! Novices delivering novice-power, check! So back to my question: Where's this food going?

Victory: And, where's it come from? I thought we didn't have enough food to give away.

Ariel: Well! Seems like when it comes to food, you two are really paying attention!

[Laughter]

Ariel: So, a straight answer: the food is coming from people who aren't ours. And, the food is going to people who aren't ours. And, I'm sure that's the end of your questions!

Man-Onko: Yep! No more from me! Except... maybe one. Why are we out here, freezing our asses off, for food that ain't ours and people that ain't ours!?!?

[chorus of applause and shouts of "Amen!" from both pods]

Ariel: A good question! So, Man-Onko, why don't you answer it?

Victory: The end of straight answers, and the beginning of crooked ones...

Man-Onko: Hey, stow it! I'm about to be brilliant!

Ariel: Everybody settle down! Let's hear this brilliance heading our way...

Man-Onko: Well, if we're being delivery boys...

Tanura: ... and GIRLS!

Man-Onko: SORRY! If we're being delivery PERSONS...

Dorado: ... delivery BEINGS! Don't forget the horses!

Man-Onko: If we're doing the delivery, I'll bet we're being paid well to do so.

Ariel: Actually, that answer is... not too bad! Yes, we get paid, and paid in the kind of "cash" we like – the kind we can EAT! But, that's not the main reason we're doing this. Anyone else?

Tanura: I'm just guessing here... but I'll bet it has something to do with compassion...

Ariel: Interesting... Say more...

Tanura: It's probably hard on the farmers to try to get their crops into the city. Probably dangerous. And, it's probably dangerous for the people in the city to come out to the farms, with the bad roads and the gangs and all...

Ariel: Right on both counts... but understated. It's not hard on Appearance Farm and the other farmers... it's near fatal. They would be picked to shreds by the looters before they got anywhere near the city limits. And for the city people, it's just impossible. With no fuel, dangerous roads and looters, the likelihood they'd make it out and back... let's just say it's really bad odds on making it back alive, food or no food.

With this wagon, there are 100 families that will get a week's worth of food, and Appearance Farm gets to stay in business.

So yes, compassion drives us... but that's not the main reason we are out here today. Anyone else?

[pause]

Man-Onko: I know this is kind of insane, but couldn't you, like, TELL US? I mean, it would save some time...

Ariel: Those horses up there are pulling this wagon at about 5 miles per hour. At that rate, we'll reach the city right before evening. So, we've got all the time in the world. Any other ideas about why we're out here?

Krista-Lin: Well, um, excuse me, um, I don't know...

Victory: Looks like the mental midget is trying to get warmed up...

Man-Onko: Man, some day somebody's gonna shut that mouth of yours...

Victory: I'm gonna look forward to seeing what's left of you if you ever try...

Breen: You guys are so tiring...

Dorado: Cool it! Both of you! Let's see what our Princess has to say...

Krista-Lin: Well... this might be wrong, but... um... when we were getting on, I had the feeling that we were BAIT.

[silence]

Krista-Lin: I'm sorry! I didn't mean to...

Ariel: No! You're right! I'm just kind of... shocked that you figured that out, so quickly.

And, I can't really talk about that, except to say... [pause] for every one of you on this wagon, there's 3 or 4 of us, out in the field, looking for the bad guys. It may be invisible, but you are really protected up here. While you're riding shotgun...

Victory: Shotgun? We're riding SHOTGUN? Can I get a SHOTGUN? Bam! Bam!

[laughter]

Ariel: You don't seem to understand! "Riding shotgun" means that you get to ride up here, while people point shotguns at you!

[laughter]

Krista-Lin: That's why the food is on the inside of the wagon and the novices are on the outside, right?

[silence]

Victory: Princess Buzzkill...

Man-Onko: Damn. For once, I agree with you...

Ariel: Let's just say that it's important to us to secure this stretch of road. And that this wagon is really important in drawing out any... gaps in security.

Victory: Yeah... bait.

Man-Onko: Low-value bait. It'll be awhile before they run out of novices to get shot at.

Dorado: I'm surprised they use the horses. They're a higher-value target than us novices...

Ariel: How about if we change the subject? Besides compassion, and besides getting paid, why...

Victory: ... And besides being target practice for homicidal maniacs!

Ariel: [pauses]: Besides being "bait". Why are we doing this?

[pause]

Dorado: Okay, my turn for ridicule. If it's not about the FOOD, it has to be about the SYSTEM, right?

Ariel: Straight from your classes. But, what system? We're not growing this food, and we're not eating it...

Victory: Damn, this is hard!

Ariel: Language...

Victory: Sorry... It's like... it's like THIS WAGON is important. That this wagon is the "system". But, I don't know WHY it's the system.

Dorado: Hold it! I think you got it! That farm full of food is NOTHING without people to eat it. If that food is sitting there, away from the city... that farm would die inside of one season.

Tanura: And the other side! Without this wagon, 100 families in the city would die... and shorter than a whole season!

Ariel: Yes, now you're getting...

Man-Onko: Wait! This wagon like... it... c'mon, what's the word?

Breen: Catalyzes!

Man-Onko: Right! This wagon catalyzes both the farm and the people in the city. The wagon makes them... like... okay, what's the other word I'm thinking about?

Breen: Inter-dependency!

Man-Onko: Bingo! The farm and the city become inter-dependency... I mean, inter-dependent, right? They need each other. They both live, with this wagon. And they both die, without this wagon.

Ariel: Y'all are really hot right now! You're almost there... What else happens because of the wagon?

Victory: Well... We're taking this ride during the day, when others can see us. We could do this at night, and on back roads. We could put an engine on this wagon, and be in the city inside of an hour. We want them to see this system...

Krista-Lin: If we're bait, it makes it easier for the bad guys to shoot us.

Victory: Damn, girl! Why don't you ride up front and wave your arms around?

Ariel: Easy, there. Show some respect. Keep going with your theory...

Victory: [pauses]: We're riding this wagon past farms that are going belly-up. Nice and slow. Look over there! We could probably buy that guy out for pocket change. This wagon is saying to them, "You can live... but you've got to do things OUR way."

Ariel: And what's "our way"?

Tanura: No violence, inclusive, compassionate...

Breen: Organic, not wasting anything, recycling...

Ariel: Yes... but that's the easy stuff. If that farmer over there promised to do all that stuff, we still may not work with him. Why would we deal with Appearance Farm and not that guy?

[pauses]

Dorado: When in doubt, go back to the classes. "It's all about systems..."

Tanura: Yeah... What do the Appearance folks have that Farmer Hardluck over there doesn't have?

Man-Onko: Wow... I got it...

Breen: You gonna share it?

Man-Onko: It's about SYSTEMS!

Breen: Gee... didn't I just say that?

Man-Onko: No! Yes! But, you're thinking about the wrong systems! It's about CONSCIOUSNESS! Farmer

Hardluck is having hard luck because he invested in the wrong system! His CONSCIOUSNESS is in the wrong system! Changing the details... like going organic, or recycling... doesn't change his basic consciousness. It isn't changing his mental system! If things shifted back, Farmer Hardluck would start selling to McDonald's again so fast, it would make your celery wilt!

[laughter]

Victory: Yeah... like you GOT celery!

[laughter]

Ariel: Okay, cool it! We're not here to talk about anyone's vegetative capacity!

[laughter]

Ariel: Man-Onko, you're right on point. Keep going...

Man-Onko: Well, if he changed his consciousness, we would expand...

Nasur: Hey, wait a minute! How do we KNOW he hasn't changed his consciousness? I mean, let's say he's doing all our stuff – organics, recycling, nonviolence... that stuff. Who are we to judge that he "doesn't get it"?

Tanura: Yeah! I think...

Ariel: Hold it, everyone! Stop the horses! We've got spotters coming in!

[Wagon pauses. Silently, a glider flies overhead, and fires an arrow 10 feet ahead of them in the road.]

Ariel: Okay, let's get started. And Man-Onko, you had the most right answers, so you get to jump down and get that arrow.

Man-Onko: Wow, what a reward!

[pause while Ariel reads the message attached to the arrow.]

Ariel: It says the next 15 miles is okay... they're still working on the rest. Now, where were we?

Victory: Wait a minute... You started the horses, before you read the message! What if it said, "Turn around and run!"?

Ariel: Then, the message would have been fired BEHIND us, not in front. And, if we were under imminent attack, it would have been fired ON the wagon... on that flat space up top.

Victory: What if the arrow went through Man-Onko? What would that mean?

Ariel: Just that there's a monk up in the glider he really pissed off!

[laughter]

Man-Onko: Very funny...

Dorado: Before we go on... can we go back to the part where we're target practice for hungry, homicidal maniacs? I mean, what do you do with them? How do you stop them... nonviolently?

Ariel: As you well know, I'm not supposed to say, and you're not supposed to ASK.

Man-Onko: C'mon! We're out on this wagon, in the middle of nowhere! Who's gonna know?

Ariel: Well, every single novice in the Center, as soon as we got back!

Victory: Hey, you don't have to say anything... we already know. You mind-wipe their asses!

Ariel: I think you need to pay more attention in your anatomy classes!

[laughter]

Victory: Hey, I don't know! That might be where they do their thinking!

[laughter]

Ariel: On that light note, we'll change the subject...

Dorado: Yeah, for them, mind-wiping is a fate worse than death. Zap, and you can't even remember your name – all you know is that you love us!

Ariel: Hold on...

Man-Onko: Yeah, I bet we only wipe the leaders... the rest of them will get the message pretty quick! Mess with the Awakening Centers and somebody's gonna have to change your diapers! For life!

Victory: And they spread the word!

Tanura: Yeah, but do we have to take them someplace to do that? Or, can we do mind-wipes in the field?

Man-Onko: I heard...

Ariel: I said "SILENCE"!

[Silence]

Ariel: Okay... everyone who wants to volunteer to be the subject of a mind-wipe, please keep talking about it!

[Silence]

Ariel: No takers? Okay... how about if we go back to talking about agricultural systems and structures? Any objections?

Nasur: No objections... but I'd just like to point out that your threat of a mind-wipe implies that mind-wiping exists.

Ariel: Okay, enough! We were talking about systems and consciousness...

Man-Onko: Yeah, that's right! In some way, this wagon isn't just "bait". It isn't just moving food from here to there. It's... changing consciousness. But... I haven't worked out how... yet.

Ariel: Good. Anyone worked it out, yet?

Nasur: No... but how about a hypo? Let's say Mr. X, somebody on the Outside, has a working car and a working bicycle. Let's say he's healthy, and it's a nice day. Let's say he has to go on a 5-mile trip. Whether he chooses the car or the bike reflects his consciousness.

Dorado: Sure... what's new?

Nasur: Wait, I'm not finished! Change the hypo: Let's say there's no fuel around. So everybody's riding around on their bikes. How could you tell whether Mr. X is on his bike because he believes in it, or just because there isn't any fuel?

Victory: Well... offer him some gas and see what he does. See if he trashes his bike.

Tanura: Or... wait for a rainy day and see if he still is riding.

Dorado: Or... ask to buy his car! If he refuses to sell, it might be because he's attached to it.

Breen: Or... offer to swap his bike for a tank of gas!

Man-Onko: How about...

Ariel: Enough! Lots of good ideas! You are really tying together the external cues, like you've been taught. Adding one and one gets you a lot more than two. And... once you develop and trust your intuition, you won't have to rely on looking at external clues.

Dorado: Yeah, good hypo, Nasur! So, what we want are the farmers that actually WANT to do things differently, not the ones riding their bikes out of desperation.

Man-Onko: Okay, here's a guess: I bet you guys can do your mind mumbo-jumbo stuff, and sniff out the real ones from the fakes, right?

Ariel: [pauses]: Changing your language to something that approximates what we actually do, the answer is yes, we can tell the real ones from the desperate ones. Without external clues.

Man-Onko: So you leave the fakers swingin' in the breeze, right?

Ariel: [pauses]: I'm really looking forward to the time you start practicing standard English, Man-Onko.

Breen: Don't worry about him. He knows how to talk. He just does that to get a rise out of you...

Ariel: Actually, that's not why he does it, not at all. We know why he does it... and he doesn't.

Breen: [to Man-Onko]: Hey, Man, you better be cool! These folks have scoped you! Your fly's open!

[laughter]

Man-Onko: Yeah... as though these cute pants had flys!

[laughter]

Man-Onko: Okay, Mr. All-Seeing Monk, sir, I have the same question. What do you do with the farmers you've scanned with your magic x-ray vision and see that they're faking?

Ariel: That's supposed to be better? Oh well... What we do is buy their tomatoes. But, we pay a lot less than we pay the authentic farmers. We won't do long-term contracts with them. We won't make loans to them. They have to sell to US, not to folks in the city. And, the second we see them sliding backwards, we cut them off, completely.

Dorado: Which you can do, because nobody in the city is dependent on them.

Ariel: You're getting it. Same goes for folks in the city. If they're behaving themselves, we'll sell them food... but OUR food, not from the farmers down the road.

We're building new SYSTEMS. And sometimes, while you're building the system, you've got to make some hard choices.

Man-Onko: Like, if Farmer Butthead has a nice wife and 4 children...

Victory: Yeah, four little Buttheads!

Man-Onko: ... yeah, our compassion says that we help them, but the systems approach says let 'em twist in the wind, right?

Ariel: [pauses]: Not quite that cut and dried, Man-Onko. Let's say the farmer has an adult child, over 18. We might deal with the kid, cut the father out, strengthen his hand in the family dynamic... there are a number of ways we can play that.

Man-Onko: Yeah, like using your super-duper mental-ray powers to mind-wipe Mr. Butthead into a turnip!

[laughter]

Ariel: How do you know we haven't used our X-ray powers already on YOU?

Breen: You mean, he used to be worse than THIS?

[end of transcript]

Part One: The Novice
Section 02: How Things Work

INTERLUDE -- WHERE WERE YOU IN THIS STORY?

You, the reader of these Chronicles, are the children of those who survived the Upheavals. You may remember your parents telling you about those times. What role did they play in the Upheavals?

Were they one of the MONKS and MASTERS of an Awakening Center, imparting valuable information to others on how to live a new life?

Were they NOVICES or students, learning new ways to live?

Were they PUBLIC OFFICIALS or SOCIAL WORKERS, trying to hold together what could no longer be held together?

Were they SURVIVORS, trying to find the "FEWS" (enough food, energy, water and shelter) to last another day, waiting for things to go back to "normal"?

Were they DENIERS, using money or power to maintain the semblance of normalcy?

Were they SCAVENGERS, living off the refuse of others?

Were they VICTIMS, thrown about by the forces that engulfed them?

Regardless of which one: WHY DID YOUR PARENTS CHOOSE THAT STORY?

The Six Month Mark

File No:		File Name:	The Six Month Mark
Location:		Parties:	[All 6-month pods]
Monk/ Master Supervising:	Monk Pico-Laton		

Name:		Pgs:		Date:		Vol:	
Type of Transcript:	Mechanical						
	Organic						

Preface by North American Archive Committee:

The process of blending into an Awakening Center was gradual. As they gained in experience and maturity, they gained some rights and privileges.

[start of transcript]

Monk Pico-Laton: Alright, settle down!

You've all been here at the Center for about six months. That's the time when you "graduate", sort of... You've got some new privileges, and you've also got some new responsibilities.

In terms of the new privileges – you won't have to go out on "The Parade" anymore!

[Wild cheering]

Monk Pico-Laton: Alright, I already said settle down! And, in the future remember this: instead of cheering like that, mature apprentices and monks will stomp twice as their way of saying they agree. Let's try it now.

[General rumbling noises]

Monk Pico-Laton: That will NEVER do! By now, you should be starting to "read" each other! You can SENSE when the right time to do the double stomp. You're not acting as individuals you're acting as a TEAM! Now, let's try it again!

[Clear double stop]

Monk Pico-Laton: There you go! That's better!

Now, along with not doing the "Parade", you can start to select your own teammates for work. And, instead of being assigned your work, your Pod can start to bid on some of the tasks around here.

As you know, the easier or "fun" work is highly bid, and generally goes months in advance. Masters have work preference over monks, and monks over senior novices.

If you want to fill up your account here, I would suggest bidding on some of the less popular tasks...

Novice Man-Onko: Back to the toilets!

[General laughter]

Monk Pico-Laton: If you want to change the composition of your pod, you'll have two weeks to select new teammates. You don't have to change if you don't want to, but if you do, you get to select three members, and the other two will be assigned to you.

Novice Victory: Does that mean we could wind up with "dead weight" again?

Monk Pico-Laton: I don't know what you mean by dead weight. It could be that other novices here think that YOU are dead weight!

What that means is that you will be assigned teammates that will balance out your team. Learning to work together, practicing inclusivity through the adversity of our times, is how we build this Center.

Now...

Novice Dorado: But, what sense does it mean make to change our present team, if we can still wind up with people we don't want to work with?

Monk Pico-Laton: That's a good question. Many six month novices don't bother to change their teams.

Moving on... You'll get to see more of the Center in this next phase. You'll be doing many different kinds of jobs. This is to give you a better idea of whether or not you want to stay here or go back Outside.

Novice Man-Onko: No more toilets!

[General laughter]

Monk Pico-Laton: The next six months will be very important to you. You spent the last few months working off your addictions and bad habits. You now know how to live in a <u>society</u>, not a dystopia.

Now, you get the next six months to think about your future. You've got three different directions that you can go: In, Out and Up.

You may choose to stay here, as a student or an Apprentice. Students are like "super novices", while Apprentices have made a long-term commitment to the Center – they are monk-candidates. Student commitments are for one-year terms, and can be renewed indefinitely, so long as your account balance is positive.

Some of you may choose to go back "Outside". You can do this either by cashing out and taking your chances Outside. Or, we would recommend that you become an AGENT of the Center.

Novice Victory: An agent? Wow, we get spy stuff? 007? Guns and cars?

Monk Pico-Laton: That's really pathetic!

In reality, an Agent lives and works on the Outside, while holding the values and training of the Center. They get to hold onto their account here, and get to "come home" when things get really rough out there.

Agents are set up in work environments, where they are supplying needed goods and services.

Many of them work and live in "The Commons". And, we try to establish a few secure neighborhoods out there, so that living there isn't as bad as living on the streets. However, there are no guarantees. Things are bad out there, much worse than just a few weeks ago. And its going downhill, fast. We predict that things will get worse. Much worse. People who choose to live as Agents know that they are taking a risk.

Novice Man-Onko: So, why do it? Why not stay here, all comfy and warm?

Monk Pico-Laton: Ignoring your sarcasm... for now. Most Agents are committed to what we call the "Hospice Path" – they are actively trying to make the Upheavals less bad for those on the Outside. They are following the path of selfless compassion.

And, some Agents still feel attached to elements of the old society. You can't imagine the number of Agents who are Outside just so they can watch the remnants of television!

Some can't deal with the very different culture here inside the Center. They are trying different experiments, in different kinds of culture. Some of the Agents just don't like being out here in the country. They form what looks and functions just like a Center, but inside a city, instead of being out here in the rural areas.

And some we ask to go Outside. We need certain kinds of information and we need to be able to affect the outside culture as it develops. For example, now that you are senior novices, you can know that the Mayor and a majority of City Council are our agents.

[General rumbling]

Novice Victory: Cool! Now that's what I'm talking about! So, I can leave here and become Mayor?

Monk Pico-Laton: That is a dangerous, thankless job. I'd rather stay in here and scrub toilets every day!

Novice Victory: Why? You get prestige and power as mayor! People look up to you. You get to tell people what to do!

Monk Pico-Laton: You really should pay more attention to your classes! Yes, the mayor does have power... Over a city that is largely out of anyone's control, with no resources, and everyone looking to her for a solution and blaming her when they don't see the results! If there's another riot in the city, she could get assassinated! And, if she does her job really, really well, if she minimizes the death and suffering... people will still blame her for everything that goes wrong.

If that's your idea of "power and prestige", you can have it!

Novice Victory: Okay, but why she's out there?

Monk Pico-Laton: She's performing a crucial role. She's trying to make things LESS BAD. We all know that no one can stop the Upheavals... but we CAN make them of shorter duration and not as deadly. While we are Inside, trying to follow the Vision, she and the others are Outside, working tirelessly to help a terrible situation not get worse. By doing that, they relieve a lot of the pressure on the Center.

Right now, she's got 100,000 people living in FEMA tents or on the streets and eating government rations... when they can find them. Without her, those 100,000 people would be trying to climb OUR fences. She's got so much violence happening in the city, the police don't bother answering 911 calls anymore. As bad as that is, it's better than half a million people starving to death, or freezing to death.

So, do you think ANY of the 100,000 people are going to turn to her and say, "Gee, thanks a lot! I really enjoyed my time eating bad food and living in tents!"

I fully expect Mayor Smith and her City Council will be forced out of office in the next few years, forced to retire here, inside the Center. The city will soon be too dangerous for them.

Novice Man-Onko: I thought you said "Once out, always out"? You would let them back in?

Monk Pico-Laton: We make exceptions. For our purposes, they are not really out...

Novice Man-Onko: But...

Monk Pico-Laton: No more questions! I need to get through with this session sometime today!

I said that there was "In, Out and Up". What do I mean by "up"?

Novice Dorado: You mean, become a master?

Monk Pico-Laton: Are you making a statement, or are you asking me a question?

Novice Dorado: You become a master!

Monk Pico-Laton: Thank you.

The Masters here are monks who have taken additional training to become very good at a task that is beneficial to the Center. It's hard work, and generally involves three years or more of working and learning.

I noticed that some of you have already started to gravitate towards certain kinds of jobs and tasks. Once we've taken "Money" out of the system, you can start to pay attention to what is really calling you, as opposed to doing things for the most money.

And then, there are other levels. You can become an Administrator here, or even the Abbot. And, you can become a Councilor on the Culture Council – regional, continental, even global.

Novice Man-Onko: What's that?

Monk Pico-Laton: Those are the folks that run the show here. Those are the folks who will be responsible for catalyzing our new world order, the metamorphosis of humanity.

And... right now, that's all you need to know about them for now. Most likely, you will never run into a member of the Culture Council in your entire life. You won't have to. A lot of their work takes place behind the scenes – and that's where it should stay.

[end of transcript]

Snow Umbrellas

File No:		File Name:	Snow Umbrellas
Location:		Parties:	Gopher Pod
Monk/ Master Supervising:	Tala, Master		

Name:		Pgs:		Date:		Vol:	
Type of Transcript:	Mechanical xxx						
	Organic						

Preface by North American Archive Committee:

Even during the Age of Waste, many of the Wasters professed an intention to "recycle". Some diverted part of their waste stream into recycling bins. Others cut down on the amounts of electricity they consumed, by purchasing energy-efficient light bulbs and appliances. Still others cut down on a fraction of the fossil fuels they wasted by purchasing an "energy efficient" vehicle.

In the end, none of these actions mattered. It was the Awakening Centers' core values that made the difference:

"If you don't produce it, don't consume it. And if you do produce it, you HAVE TO consume it..."

[start of transcript]

Recorded lesson between Gopher Pod and Master Tala...

Master Tala: You're kicking them wrong! Don't kick them like you're angry at them. Kick them like a friend you're playing with. You want to knock off that snow, not damage them!

Man-Onko: Got it. And why are we planting these things? And why do you call them "umbrellas"? They can't keep the rain off...

Master Tala: They're not rain umbrellas, dear. They're SNOW umbrellas. They don't keep the snow off... they just keep it from piling up too high.

We're trying to entice the Snow Beings back into this valley, but they won't come if it means burying and killing the young evergreens we planted.

Man-Onko: And.. how do you know this? You talked to the snow?

Master Tala: Of course, dear. Can't you?

Man-Onko: Yeah! Sure! Hey, somebody come check her meds...

Master Tala: Oh, you must be the little sassy one they're talking about. Man-Onko, right?

Man-Onko: Hey, I ain't little!

Master Tala: Pretty tiny, from where I stand.

Man-Onko: Lady, I swear... [pause] Is this where I'm supposed to practice that nonviolence you're all talking about?

Master Tala: I'd say you were microscopic. Perhaps we should call you "Nano-Onko".

Man-Onko: Shit, I'm outta here!

Master Tala: STOP! Before you leave, just one thing: How you feel right now is how others feel when you tease them. When you make fun of them. Even if you don't "mean" it, it still hurts, doesn't it?

If you don't like it for you, perhaps you don't like it for them?

Man-Onko: [pauses]: You got funny ways of teaching a lesson.

Master Tala: No... You've just got funny ways of learning them.

And I meant what I said about listening to the Snow Beings. You can hear them, if you choose to.

Man-Onko: Do I have to?

Master Tala: Absolutely not! You DO have to treat all beings with respect, but that doesn't mean learning to listen to them.

Man-Onko: Okay, I'll pass then.

Master Tala: Fine. But, I do expect you to listen to ME, when I tell you that tree says you're planting your umbrella wrong. It won't shelter the tree, and it'll snap off in the first strong wind.

Man-Onko: Okay, got it. More like this?

Master Tala: Yes, that's it, dear. How about a little deeper?

Man-Onko: Okay, okay, got it...

Master Tala: See? Now, when the wind blows, it'll twist instead of bend. And when it twists, it'll knock the snow off.

Man-Onko: Cool...

Krista-Lin: I... I think... I think I'd like to hear the Snow Beings...

Victory: Yeah, that would be the creepy thing to do. Better than listening to humans, right?

Krista-Lin: No. I like listening to humans. I'd really like to listen to you, Victory... if you ever have anything to say.

Dorado: Hey! Score another one for the Mighty Mite! Better watch your back, Victory! She's discovering she's got vocal chords!

Victory: Very funny...

Dorado: Hey, how come these things...

Master Tala: Snow umbrellas, dear.

Dorado: Yeah, how come the snow umbrellas' so heavy? Isn't bamboo supposed to be light?

Master Tala: They're heavy because they're filled with goodness!

Man-Onko: I got a bad feeling about this...

Dorado: What's "goodness"?

Master Tala: Tell me: What's the best meal that you get in the canteen?

Dorado: Me? I love the fake spaghetti and fake meatballs!

Man-Onko: Yeah, me too! I never had the real thing, so the fake stuff ain't fake to me!

Master Tala: Well, that's what's in here!

[pause]

Man-Onko: Okay... I'm not supposed to make fun and talk about your meds... but, are you CRAZY?

Master Tala: Spaghetti, and ice cream and cake and pie...

Man-Onko: And off she goes! How did you get to be a monk?

Master Tala: Actually, I'm a Master.

[pause]

Man-Onko: Watch out, everybody. She's about to get really deep.

Master Tala: Everything's in the bamboo pipes that I said. It's just been processed.

Dorado: Processed? By what?

Man-Onko: I got a bad feeling about this...

Master Tala: Not what, dear. Who.

Dorado: Who? What do you mean?

Man-Onko: She means the pipes are filled with our SHIT.

[general uproar]

Master Tala: Try not to say "shit" dears. "Excrement" or "compost" is better.

Victory: Lady... Master... That pipe is filled with our... compost?

Master Tala: Where did you think it went?

Man-Onko: Actually, I didn't give a... excrement.

Master Tala: That was quite clever!

Dorado: This is disgusting!

Master Tala: Why? That pipe you just dropped is filled with your spaghetti and meatballs and all your other favorites.

Dorado: Yeah, but now it's SHIT!

Master Tala: And what's the difference?

Man-Onko: Told you. I knew she was gonna get heavy on us.

Dorado: It's.... It's....

Master Tala: Everything is food for everything else. You breathe out a poisonous gas. This tree, your brother, breathes it in. That tree takes your processed food and turns it into... more food.

Actually, you Novices are an important part of the operation of the Center.

Dorado: We are?

Master Tala: Well, actually, not you. Your excrement.

After the toilet, the first stop for your poo is the methane gas digesters. You know how your Pod has to raise and lower your flags every morning and evening? The raising and lowering stirs up the poo in the tanks underneath, to extract the maximum methane value.

Man-Onko: I hate to ask, but... what do you do with the gas?

Master Tala: That's how we cook your meals and light the paths at night.

Man-Onko: EEYewww!!! Gross!!

Dorado: We're being punished. Victory's farts cooking our dinner...

Victory: Leave me alone! She said everybody contributed!

Man-Onko: Yeah... Some a lot more than others.

Master Tala: Excuse me, dears, may I finish?

After the methane tanks, the "spent fuel" is delivered to Composting, then...

Krista-Lin: Then to the gardens?

Master Tala: No dearest, I'm sorry, but novice poo is considered too toxic for vegetables. That's why your goodness is going to the trees.

Man-Onko: Yeah, Victory's so potent, he'd cause the tomatoes to mutate!

Dorado: Yeah! If this hillside is dead next year, we'll know the reason.

Victory: Master, is aiming a fart at a fellow novice considered an act of violence?

Man-Onko: From you, it would be an act of homicide!

[end of transcript]

News Article: FEMA Pulls the Plug on Some Cities; Sets up Regional Centers

"FEMA was never meant to provide a long-term solution to societal ills. These are not 'emergencies' as much as social breakdowns," said Ruth Auburne, recently taking the reins as the fourth Director of FEMA this year. "Having people in perpetual crisis is taking away from our ability to respond to REAL emergencies."

Director Auburne announced a series of measures designed to reduce the strain on an already compromised organization. The new measures include:

- A "lifetime" cap of six months for receiving FEMA resources. "We have to draw the line somewhere. People can't live in our tents forever."
- Restrictions on the types of "emergencies" that FEMA will respond to. "We can't respond to environmental disasters like fires and floods anymore. The other agencies will just have to do a better job in water management and fire suppression. If a city burns, its not on us."
- Establishing regional food and shelter centers. "There are so many cities needing so much assistance, it's just efficient on our part to place those resources in reasonable reach of the maximum number of people. Most people on the East Coast will be within 75 miles of a FEMA distribution center."

"Yes, that's 100 miles by driving... where's the gasoline? Where are there roads safe enough to drive? Has she ever tried walking 100 miles, with two children? Has she ever left her armed convoy behind?", said Marjorie Nolan, living with her two children in the FEMA center in Rapid City, Iowa, set up after the devastating fire that laid waste to over 30% of that city. "We've been in these tents for 8 months – they're just gonna cut us off? Is that fair? What are we gonna do?"

Many have complained about the new rules, from embattled state officials to current FEMA recipients. One Indiana state official, speaking on condition of anonymity, said, "Auburne told us that an emergency is something that lasts 48 hours or less. She said they wouldn't respond to anything that lasts longer than 48 hours! We've had FIRES burn longer than that! The East Coast has had HURRICANES lasting longer than that! What about Hurricane Claudette, the one that hit Miami, bounced back and hit it again! According to Auburne, that's not an "emergency"! FEMA won't respond! She's got to be kidding!"

In the face of criticism, Director Auburne remains adamant. "As long as resources are finite, tough choices have to be made. There's no other way. These are challenging times, and FEMA must maintain its ability to respond to emergencies. REAL emergencies. Churches and other organizations will have to take up the slack."

Rev. Nancy Sloane, the Director of National Ecumenical Ministries, disagreed. "There is no way that the faith-based organizations can respond to even a fraction of the need that's out there. We're the "social safety net". We can't catch an entire population in need.

"This problem belongs to the government. And they aren't responding. The federal government is going ahead with the damned space launch! How is putting men back on the Moon going to help us down here? Why don't they take NASA's budget and give it to FEMA?"

Eric Shapiro, the President's Press Secretary, defended the NASA budget. "Putting men back on the Moon will demonstrate to the world that America is as strong as ever. We're in a race with China to establish the first permanent human colony on the Moon, and we're not about to come out second-best!"

Softening his tone, Mr. Shapiro had conciliatory words for those in FEMA camps. "Our hearts go out to those who are facing temporary challenges. We've had a run of bad luck, but America has always bounced back from every crisis we've ever faced, and we'll bounce back from this one!"

A Confidential Request

File No:		File Name:	A Confidential Request
Location:		Parties:	Novice Man-Onko
Monk/ Master Supervising:	Auroron, Master		

Name:		Pgs:	Date:	Vol:	
Type of Transcript:	Mechanical XXX				
	Organic				

Preface by the North American Archive Committee:

The Archive Committee asked for and received special authority to access and reveal this transcript, given the extremely sensitive nature of the material it contains. It was felt that this material helps the reader understand some of the complexities of the decisions the Awakening Movement faced...

This text is being provided in a rough draft format. Communication Access Realtime Translation (CART) facilitates communication accessibility and may not be a totally verbatim record of the proceedings. Let your coordinator know if you would prefer a more verbatim option.

[start of transcript]

[Counseling session called by Master Auroron, with Novice Man-Onko.]

Master Auroron: Come in. Please have a seat.

[pause]

Master Auroron: I see you're learning to control your random talking impulses, your "monkey mind".

Novice Man-Onko: I've learned that if I keep my mouth shut around you Masters, it increases the likelihood that I'll be offered tea.

Master Auroron: [laughter]: And so it does! Would you like some tea?

Novice Man-Onko: Yes, please.

[pause for tea]:

Master Auroron: You have matured a great deal since our last meeting. You are paying attention to your words, not just blurting them out. And, you are losing some of your fear of introspection. You are not so afraid to ask the question of who you are.

Novice Man-Onko: Thanks. I still remember your lesson – I still speak to Roberta the chipmunk, every day!

But, I'm gonna bet you didn't call me in here to tell me how wonderful I am. I'm gonna bet that I've screwed up something in the past week or so.

Master Auroron: You lose your bet.

[pause]

Novice Man-Onko: Okay... Thanks for the tea. I'll be seeing you...

Master Auroron: You are not here because you "screwed up". You're here because I have a request. A favor. It's important and its difficult for us to ask this of you. You will be well within your rights to say "no", but I ask that you hear me out before making up your mind.

Novice Man-Onko: Okay, shoot.

Master Auroron: "Hearing me out" means that I'm going to tell you some very confidential information. I'm going to ask that this conversation stay in this room.

Novice Man-Onko: This just gets more and more interesting. Okay, lips are sealed. Pledge in blood. Cross my heart.

Master Auroron: Fine. We know there has been animosity between you and Novice Victory, from the very beginning. And we know that you've been planning to have Gopher Pod consist of you, Krista-lin, Breener and Dorado.

We are asking that you not do this. It is important for Gopher Pod to remain intact.

Novice Man-Onko: Wow... I didn't see that coming.

[pauses]

Okay, I can put up with Victory's bullshit for another 6 months. But, at least get Krista-lin out of that situation. He's riding her all the time. For some reason, he gets angry every time she opens her mouth. And she's really defenseless – she can't take care of herself. Get her out, and I'll stick with Gopher for another six.

Master Auroron: It is very, very important that Gopher remain intact. It is important that Gopher Pod maintain its present configuration.

Novice Man-Onko: Do I have any choice in this? Are you ordering me to stop trying to dump Victory?

Master Auroron: If we could, we would. It's that important. But we can't. So please listen.

Novice Man-Onko: [pauses]: Okay. I'm listening.

Master Auroron: When you first came in, we told you that some of our novices were so damaged, they could not function in our society. We told you that others were borderline and we had to constantly monitor them. You have one of the borderline cases in your pod.

Novice Man-Onko: Well, that explains a lot about Victory...

Master Auroron: I'm not talking about Victory. I'm talking about Krista-Lin.

Novice Man-Onko: WHAT? Stop! Krista-Lin couldn't hurt a fly! I'm constantly trying to get her to stand up for herself!

Master Auroron: We know. We keep a very careful watch on her. She's killed more people than she can count. Before the age of 12. Her father ran a very sick meat processing and protection racket. He thought having his baby daughter running the guillotine would "toughen her up".

She can't talk about it. She can barely talk at all. The conflict of beheading screaming humans and the conflict of not confronting her deranged father has driven her to the brink of insanity.

The National Guard broke up the operation, killing her mother and father in front of her eyes. When they found her, she was still covered in the arterial blood of her last beheading. They brought her here, because they had no idea what else to do with her.

She cannot handle conflict. In every conflict situation, she tries to withdraw. In every conflict she has only one of two responses: withdraw or kill.

We don't want her to withdraw. We definitely DON'T want her to kill. We want her to learn HOW to deal with a healthy degree of conflict, not just withdraw... or attack and kill.

Novice Man-Onko: So... you put her with Victory on purpose?

Master Auroron: Yes.

Novice Man-Onko: So... why don't you let the two of them make out, and leave me out of it?

Master Auroron: You don't understand – Gopher Pod was carefully selected. You are a TEAM. Each of you brings something valuable to the table.

Novice Man-Onko: Okay, so, we've got one homicidal maniac, pretending to be a cute little girl, one bully, pretending to be a bully, one spineless guy who goes along with everything, and then me. Did I miss someone?

Master Auroron: What are positive reasons for Gopher Pod?

Novice Man-Onko: Got me. That's the reason I'm trying to exit right now.

Master Auroron: You aren't trying to get out. You're trying to get Victory out. But, let's start with Dorado. You say he goes along with everything.

Novice Man-Onko: Yes...

Master Auroron: Does he? Or, is he the one that helps Gopher Pod come to consensus? Can you think of a single decision that Dorado was against? Has Gopher Pod ever done anything, before Dorado signals his direction and agreement?

Novice Man-Onko: Wow. I never thought about it like that...

Master Auroron: You say Victory is a bully. Is he that, or does he force each of you to articulate your reasons for acting? Victory makes sure your reasoning is RIGHT. It only LOOKS like he's harder on Krista-Lin, because it's harder for her to articulate her reasoning.

Novice Man-Onko: Wow again.

Master Auroron: Dorado is your pod's "Consensus Maker". And Victory is your "Contrarian". He helps all of you understand your consensus.

Novice Man-Onko: But, does he have to go against EVERYONE?

Master Auroron: He doesn't go against everyone. He only goes against YOU. For being so articulate. And, Krista-Lin, for not being clear about her positions.

Try to name one thing that Victory was against that Dorado was in favor of. Once Dorado indicates Gopher's consensus, Victory lines right up. Everyone lines up, including you. And Dorado does it in such a way that you never see that he was the key decision-maker. HE doesn't even see it.

Novice Man-Onko: Wow. Heavy again. There really is balance...

Master Auroron: Gopher Pod is incredibly balanced. So much so, we can't afford to add anyone to it, or change its dynamic in any way. That's why there will be only four of you.

Novice Man-Onko: Four? What about Breener?

Master Auroron: We believe he'll be leaving this Center soon.

Novice Man-Onko: No! Outside?? Not Breener!

Master Auroron: Not Outside. To another Center... we think.

And now, we are beginning to see where the challenge is in these relationships. We are beginning to see the true challenge for Gopher Pod.

Novice Man-Onko: Yes, I agree. I'll stick with Gopher Pod. I'll go easy on Victory...

Master Auroron: Not so fast. What we've been talking about is only part of the dynamic. We need to look at your role in the pod.

Novice Man-Onko: Listen, I said I'd go along! I won't cause any trouble...

Master Auroron: What is your sister's name?

Novice Man-Onko: [pauses]: Look. Stop. I don't want to talk about this. I'm not going to do this.

Master Auroron: I asked you a question. What is your sister's name?

Novice Man-Onko: [pauses]: Her name is Paulette.

Master Auroron: You will repeat what I say. It doesn't matter whether or not you believe it, it only matters that you repeat it. You only have to say these few sentences out loud and then you can leave. Do you understand?

Novice Man-Onko: I don't want to do this...

Master Auroron: The sooner we get this part done, the sooner you can leave. Now, are you ready to repeat these sentences?

Novice Man-Onko: [pauses]: Yes.

Master Auroron: Repeat after me. "Krista-Lin is not Paulette."

Novice Man-Onko: "Krista-Lin..." [Sobbing uncontrollably]

[Long pause]

Master Auroron: That's right, deep breathing. Yes. You and I will get through this together. Sit up straight and look at me. Look at me through your tears. There is nothing to be ashamed of in crying.

Novice Man-Onko: Oh yeah?... Why don't YOU do the crying, and I'll sit back and sip my tea, hand out tissues, and say it's all okay?

Master Auroron: Novice, at the rate you are progressing, that may actually happen in a few years. Now, are you ready?

Novice Man-Onko: (pauses) Yes.

Master Auroron: Repeat after me. "Krista-Lin is not Paulette".

Novice Man-Onko: "Krista-Lin is not Paulette".

Master Auroron: "Victory did not take Paulette from me."

Novice Man-Onko: "Victory did not take Paulette from me."

Master Auroron: "Defending Krista-Lin will not bring Paulette back to me."

[Pause]

Novice Man-Onko: I know what you're trying to do. I can see it now. Paulette may not have been jumped at all. Maybe she was just tired of having to take care of me, tired of having to work twice as hard so she could feed me. Maybe she just walked away. Maybe my parents just walked away.

Master Auroron: That wasn't repeating what I said, but I think you get it now. Removing your block can let you see Victory as Victory and Krista-Lin as Krista-Lin.

Novice Man-Onko: And Paulette as Paulette. Man, I feel... strange... light... kinda dizzy.

Master Auroron: You stopped carrying a burden that wasn't yours to carry. You may actually feel dizzy for a couple of days. And, pay attention to what's happening in your heart for the next day or two.

Novice Man-Onko: Okay, will do. And thanks for the tea and the tissues.

Master Auroron: So, what are your decisions?

Novice Man-Onko: I won't try to get Gopher Pod dissolved. If they want to stick together, I'll stick with them.

Master Auroron: Excellent. I know that Victory was particularly concerned about being abandoned by his pod.

Novice Man-Onko: Victory? He has a strange way of showing it.

Master Auroron: Don't you all.

Novice Man-Onko: I guess.

Master Auroron: And what is your decision regarding Krista-Lin?

Novice Man-Onko: I guess I back off, let them go after each other.

Master Auroron: Actually, we want you to stay involved, just in another role. Instead of being Krista-Lin's "Protector", we want you to be a "Referee" for both of them. You are their "score-keeper". Help them to "fight fair".

Novice Man-Onko: Okay. Though, it's gonna be hard, watching Victory go after her.

Master Auroron: Remember the dynamic. What's hard about watching a loud-mouth but essentially nonviolent Novice, going up against a young woman who has killed more people than she can count?

Novice Man-Onko: Wow and wow and wow. Okay. I'm the referee, until little Krista-Lin gets in a murderin' mood. Then, I'm running!

[end of transcript]

(Afterword: To the surprise of many, Gopher Pod elected to stay intact.)

How Things Work – The Swarm

File No:		File Name:	How Things Work – The Swarm
Location:	Denver Awakening Center	Parties:	Gopher Pod Otter Pod Brightwater Pod
Monk/ Master Supervising:	Monk Ariel		

Name:		Pgs:		Date:		Vol:	
Type of Transcript:	Mechanical xxx						
	Organic						

Preface by the North American Centers Archive Committee:

While similar to the "intentional communities" that sprang up during the Age of Waste, Awakening Centers were not "communities", in the sense of places for people to live. The purpose of the Awakening Centers was to activate the mission and goals of the Awakening Movement... avoiding the worst of the dysfunctional period known as the Upheavals, while ushering in a profound human evolution.

As such, the Awakening Centers were never "stable", but were constantly growing, adapting and changing, based on the constantly changing circumstances of the Upheavals.

How did Centers grow? How did they insure a stable food supply? Where did their energy come from?

And, most importantly... given the great need, where did new Centers come from?

[start of transcript]

Ariel: Heave ho, me hearties! Each Pod has to get 5 tents up before nightfall! That means, before DINNER!

Man-Onko: Hey, where'd all these tents come from?

Ariel: Think you can talk and work at the same time, Novice?

Man-Onko: Hey, can't screw in the pipes until my podmates finish unrolling the... walls?

Dorado: Yeah, I think they're walls. Whatever they are, they're labelled "Step 4", so they're next.

Man-Onko: Yeah, I'm Step 5...

Ariel: Okay. The short answer: the tents came out of our storage. But I don't think that's what you're asking...

Man-Onko: Yeah... Like, how come you've got so many tents in storage? And why are they so BIG? And so many?

Ariel: I'll answer... but I think it's time for you to do your thing with the pipes.

[Long pause. Sounds of scuffling.]

Ariel: I'm back. Sorry for the delay. The Brightwater folks seem to have forgotten how to count! "Step 11" doesn't come before "Step 6"!

Sorry, Novice... what was your question?

Man-Onko: I wanted to know why we got all these tents? And why we're setting them up? And why they're so... BIG?

Ariel: Great questions! And, they've all got one answer: we are hosting a "SWARM".

Any other questions?

Man-Onko: Hey! I get to play monk! Watch this: "Well, Novice Ariel, you already know my question, so why don't you answer it?"

Victory: Hey, why don't you play "worker", and slip that loop through that pulley, like the instructions say?

[Pause, sounds of work]

Ariel: Okay. Now, our newest "monk", Man-Onko, demands that I answer his question about the Swarm.

And, of course, I'll answer with a question: how do you think Centers are started?

Man-Onko: Well, my monkhood didn't last long...

Dorado: Somebody has to start them, right? Like, some rich people get together and buy some land?

Ariel: That's where the land comes from. Where do all the people come from? There are close to 3,000 people in this Center alone... where did they come from?

Krista-Lin: I, well, I don't... Umm...

Victory: Damn! Why can't you talk?

Man-Onko: Why do you talk so much?

Ariel: Give her time...

Krista-Lin: Well... you know... didn't you, like... umm... kidnap them?

Ariel: Yes, though we prefer to say "Collected". A lot were Collected. But, what about all the monks and Masters? You can't have a Center with just novices, can you?

[pause]

Man-Onko: It's amazing how we never thought about any of that.

Ariel: Well, as long as you don't slow down with your tent assembly, I'll tell you!

[sounds of scuffling]

Ariel: You are about to participate in something that happens only once every 3 or 4 years. We call it a "Swarm".

The Awakening Movement grows by cell division, just like you studied in your Biology classes. This Center is about to divide in two.

First thing that happens is that we're about to get a LOT bigger. We'll come close to doubling in size... we'll go up to about 5,000 folks, maybe more. So, we need a place for 2,000 more people to sleep and eat. So... you're putting up tents.

Then we'll divide. Some will stay here. Others will travel to the new Center. They will take some of this Center's resources with them. They won't have to start from scratch. They'll take two of our generators, a couple of our kitchens, plenty of tents, clothes, bedding...

We've had four years to double up on everything we need to run a Center. Now, we divide, give them half of our essentials... and then start building up again, for the next Swarm 3 or 4 years from now.

Krista-Lin: Where, um... how... Where do they come from? The Swarm people?

Ariel: All over the Awakening Movement. They've been traveling in from all of our Centers, all around the world. Every Center participates.

Dorado: How are people chosen to come?

Ariel: Some want to get out of their Centers. Broken relationships, bad blood, disagreements on policy... They apply to be part of the Swarm. Some have trouble fitting in where they are. Their Abbots "suggest" that they go to a Swarm. Some have valuable skills that will be needed in a new Center. They are requested to participate in a Swarm.

Krista-Lin: Do you... do you, like... have to?

Victory: Can I suggest someone go to the Swarm?

[pause]

Dorado: Wow... Mo missed an opportunity to tell you to shut up.

Ariel: Settle down! Novice Krista-Lin, the short answer is "yes", people have to participate.

Krista-Lin: But... this is their... their... home!

Ariel: No, the Awakening Movement is our home. The Movement, not a particular Center. This means that you are always subject to the call.

But, you can announce that you'd like not to participate. So, unless you've got a special skill that's in great demand, you probably can be exempt from participating. And, even if you get sent against your wishes, you can apply to come back after a few years.

Krista-Lin: What about... novices?

Ariel: Novices also participate in the Swarm.

Krista-Lin: I don't want to go! I don't, I don't...

Victory: Hey, you gotta go! You have that special talent: being annoying and freaky...

[pause]

Dorado: Mo? Are you feeling okay?

Ariel: All of you – Pipe down! I shouldn't have said anything!

The fact is, the selection process is occurring... on another level. Once you are calm and open, you'll just "know" if you are supposed to stay or go. You may feel called to another area. Or feel called to participate. Or...

Breener: Hey... Is the new Center gonna be in a hot, wet area? I keep having dreams about being really hot, and being on water...

Ariel: Interesting... We'll talk later, okay?

Dorado: You said, "Or". "Or" what?

Ariel: By intuition, folks in the Swarm will know to Stay, to Go... or to Go On. Of the 5,000 people in the Swarm, 2,000 will form a new Center, 2,000 will stay here to rebuild this Center, get us back up to 3,000. And 1,000 will go on to the next Swarm.

Man-Onko: You said that the Swarm only happens every 3 or 4 years. That won't make a lot of new Centers.

Ariel: The Swarm happens here only every 3 or 4 years. But, there are dozens of Centers, hosting dozens of Swarms per year. We're growing like weeds. Sometimes it's hard to keep track of who's who!

Dorado: Are there any people in the Swarm who like, never settle down?

Ariel: Frankly, yes. We never anticipated it, but there are some permanent "Swarmers". We're calling them "Nomads". The Culture Council doesn't exactly know what to do with them. Some want to force them to join a Center. Others want to let them roll, see how the experiment plays out.

Victory: What's the "Culture Council"?

Ariel: Damn... The folks who are running this show. And that's all you need to know right now. You'll know more in the next few months... assuming you last that long! And that assumes you get these tents done before midnight!

Man-Onko: Hey, chill! We've only got two more tents to go! We'll get dinner near our regular time!

[end of transcript]

[AFTERNOTE: The Denver Swarm was successful. Their new sister Center is located in Baton Rouge.

Novice Breener from Gopher Pod was selected to move to the new Center. The Denver Abbot took the necessary but highly unusual step of leaving Gopher Pod with only four Novices: Man-Onko, Dorado, Victory and Krista-Lin.]

The Banned Books: The Collapse of Economics

We exist, beyond any shadow of any doubt, in an environment of absolute fakery where nothing is real...

...the market continues to rise. ... Nothing is real. I can't stress this enough... we're going to continue to see more fakery... and manipulation and twisting of this entire system... We now exist in an environment where the financial system as a whole has been flipped upside down just to make it function... and that's very scary. ... We've never seen anything like this in the history of the world... The Federal Reserve has never been in a situation like this... we are completely in uncharted territory where the world's central banks have ...negative interest rates... it's all an illusion to keep the stock market booming.

... Every single asset now... I don't care what asset... you want to look at currency, debt, housing, metals, the stock market... pick an asset... there's no price discovery mechanism behind it whatsoever... it's all fake... it's all being distorted. ... The system is built upon on one premise and that is confidence that it will work... if that confidence is rattled the whole thing will implode... our policy makers are well aware of this... there is collusion between central banks and their respective governments... and it will not stop until it implodes...

Millions upon millions of people are going to die on a world-wide scale when the debt bubble bursts. And I'm saying when, not if...

Greg Mannarino

"Traders Choice" (2016)

(Banned by Act of Congress)

How Things Work: Tight-Line Communications

File No:		File Name:	How Things Work: Tight-Line Communications
Location:		Parties:	Gopher Pod
Monk/ Master Supervising:	Lazarus, Security Monk		

Name:		Pgs:	Date:	Vol:	
Type of Transcript:	Mechanical				
	Organic				

Preface by North American Archive Committee:

In every system, communications is a vital element. Most of the time, participants don't think about the technology of communication – whether open air, telegraph signals, the Internet... or something else.

The US government invested billions of dollars in spying on its own citizens. The solution was to change the technology. When the game is rigged, play a different game...

This text is being provided in a rough draft format. Communication Access Realtime Translation (CART) facilitates communication accessibility and may not be a totally verbatim record of the proceedings. Let your coordinator know if you would prefer a more verbatim option.

[start of transcript]

Lazarus: Okay, listen up. This is the first time that Gopher Pod has pulled tight-line duty, so make sure you pay close attention!

This is a VERY DANGEROUS ASSIGNMENT! The biggest danger is that you are about to be BORED TO DEATH!

[Laughter]

Seriously, the hardest thing you will be involved in is the drive out here today. That done, the rest of this evening is straight downhill.

Okay, see that red handle sticking out from the side of the van? There's one on each side of the van. I want one of you on each handle...

Man-Onko: What do I do?

Lazarus: Stand there and look cute, sweetheart.

Man-Onko: Hey, funny guy....

Lazarus: Okay, when you've got your handle, I want you to twist it like this to unlock it, then pull the cable straight out from the roof rack of the van, as far as it will go. [Demonstrates.] Once the cable extends out 100 feet or so, you tether it down with this stake and hammer. Make sure its in there good. [Demonstrates].

Man-Onko: What? You're trying to make sure the van doesn't blow away?

Lazarus: Novice, do us a favor and don't use your mouth for the next five minutes, okay? We already know you're not using your brain...

[Laughter]

Lazarus: Seriously, you'll get an education inside of five minutes. You are the key to this operation. Now everyone with a line pull it straight out like this and tie it down.

[Long pause]

Lazarus: Okay, back to me!

In ten seconds, you'll find out what this is all about, and see the reason I'M SO BORED!

[Top of van opens. A large helium balloon fills and lifts.]

Lazarus: And there goes the boring balloon!

Man-Onko: Did you do something to turn that on?

Lazarus: No! Boring! And I'm about to not do something else!

[A cylinder the size of a small trash can, covered with lenses, rises from the van, and is lifted by the balloon.]

Lazarus: And there goes the boring tightline!

[The four staked cables are lifted by the tightline.]

Lazarus: And there go the boring stabilization cables!

And our heroic work is done! The work a trained MONKEY could do! But, why waste the talents of one monkey, when I've got FOUR NOVICES to remind me how unnecessary I am?

Novice Dorado: Anybody bring violins?

Man-Onko: Earplugs would be nice about now...

Lazarus: Earplugs??? You'd miss the best part! When I spend 3 hours, out here in the middle of nowhere, explaining to you what I could explain in 20 minutes back at the Center. No open fire, no marshmallows – no lights!

Man-Onko: Hey, how about explaining it in 20 minutes, then all of us can get some SLEEP?

Lazarus: Unfortunately, not all of us. Somebody has to stay awake, standing guard and responding to a system alarm – which NEVER comes, by the way!

Okay, enough whining. Here's the straight poop.

This is a tightline communications node. It's how all the Centers, all around the world, stay in contact with each other.

Dorado: Well, what about the Internet? It's gotten spotty, but I hear it still works...

Lazarus: Sure, it works. And it is heavily monitored by... well, everyone. Governments, major corporations, private militias, probably my kid sister, if she's still out there. Oh, almost forgot – US, too. The Centers monitor what's left of the Internet, to stay on top of what's happening on the Outside.

Same for phone, video links, telegraph... If the Breakers created it, they've also infiltrated it.

So, we invented our own system.

Victory: That trash can up there?

Lazarus: Yup, our intensely boring trash can.

Man-Onko: How come everyone can infiltrate the Internet?

Dorado: Cause, well, the signal goes everywhere... right?

Lazarus: Head of the class. Everybody gets the signal, and everybody can do whatever they want with it. It's like the old Indians, sending smoke signals. Anybody with eyeballs could see the smoke.

Krista-lin: But... I mean... don't you have to know the... you know... the LANGUAGE?

Lazarus: Your turn at the head of the class. You can encode the language, so all you're looking at is smoke, not meaning.

Victory: Yep... waiting for someone to hack your code.

Lazarus: Exactly! So how...

Man-Onko: Hey, is this the 20-minute version? I'm getting sleepy...

Lazarus: Actually, it is! And, thanks for volunteering to stay up with me on guard duty!

Man-Onko: But...

Lazarus: And, interrupt me again, and you'll be doing it by YOURSELF!

[Silence]

Lazarus: Okay, where was I? Okay... how do you make your smoke signals hack-proof? Anyone?

Dorado: [pause]: Okay... this is just a guess, but I'd say our trash can is a way for only our people to see the smoke...

Lazarus: Do you see why I'm so bored? There's just nothing exciting about any of this.

So, cut to the chase: 20 or 30 lasers up there, part of a system narrow-casting to hundreds of Centers on this continent. Same setup on other continents. Then, an inter-continental setup for messages across the oceans. A bunch of receivers for the lasers at other Centers that are pointed to our friend up there. Relays to other Centers that are over the "line of sight" horizon.

The only way the government could "see our smoke" is to stand directly between our trash can and the one at, say, Cedar Rapids Awakening Center. And I mean directly! If they miss it by five feet, they'll see nothing. If they miss it by 5 inches, they see nothing.

Dorado: Well... what if they put up a balloon 100 feet across? Or 200 feet across? If they had a general idea of where to look, wouldn't they catch the smoke then?

Lazarus: Y'all are doing way too much thinking! Yes, let's say they intercept the signal – but all that would do is tell both Denver and Cedar Rapids that something is blocking their signal. And that crashes the whole system, until we identify who's sniffing our smoke.

Victory: But... how does the system know where all the trash cans are?

Lazarus: A complex algorithm is generated at the end of each tightline session, sent to all continental sites, telling us where to set up the next night. Always somewhere different. And, before you ask, based on GPS.

Victory: I thought GPS was dead.

Lazarus: Nope. The domestic companies that read it and interpreted it for you are dead as doornails, but the satellites are still up there and still broadcasting.

Victory: What happens when the satellites come down?

Lazarus: By that time, the Centers should be strong enough to put up our own satellites...

Dorado: Wow... We've got a SPACE program?

Lazarus: ...Or, we'll all be dead! Either way, it'll work!

Actually... while we are interested in putting up satellites, there are other folks looking into other ways of moving and delivering packets of information. Remember: information is just energy. And, we've got some folks working on some real trippy, "next-level" stuff about moving information.

Dorado: Like what?

Lazarus: Like... way beyond your pay grade, youngster.

Man-Onko: How come you guys always talk about "pay grade", when none of us gets paid?

Krista-Lin: But... Umm... don't we, like... still use something like the Internet?

Lazarus: Yes. We load it with all the info that we don't care if anyone sees – crop reports, weather reports... LOTS of reports!

Plus, lots of misinformation! If there's something we don't care that they know, we send it through regular. If there's misinformation we want to make sure they pay attention to, we encrypt it! Gives them something to do! Otherwise, they'd be as bored as me!

Dorado: Do they believe our mis-information?

Lazarus: Absolutely! The government believes that because we don't lie to each other, we won't lie to them! We can feed them nearly anything!

Victory: Hey, this stuff is probably important! Why are you so bored?

Lazarus: Because the system works so damn well! One person could set this up, so we send out three! Or, in the case of tonight, FIVE!

Victory: Why so many?

Lazarus: We think most of the old government has no idea that this communication system exists. For those that think they know, they think it is located on the INSIDE of the gate, not the OUTSIDE. For those who know its mobile... well, this van would be Acquisition Target Number One.

Our job is to make sure it doesn't get acquired. And even THAT is automated! If the van follows a route that is different from the one established by the system, or if any one of us is more than 250 feet from the van, the van disables itself and the entire contents of the van are melted.

Dorado: How about hurricanes, thunderstorms, tsunamis...

Lazarus: Taken care of, automatically. See the trash can? It constantly reads wind speed and direction, and makes micro-adjustments to its position by pulling on the 4 cables. We never have to make an adjustment.

Dorado: What if one of the cables snaps?
Victory: More likely, doofus, what happens when you set yours wrong?

Man-Onko: Man, why are you...

Lazarus: Everybody can it! Even your bickering is boring!

You want to find out what happens when the system goes out of sync? Go jump as high as you can, grab that cable and hang on.

Dorado: Are you serious?

Lazarus: Sure... our excitement for the night!

[Dorado runs and grabs a stabilizing cable, and brings it to the ground. Immediately, a high-pitched alarm goes off for five seconds, then stops.]

Lazarus: See? For those 5 seconds, the system was out of sync. Right now, its re-sending and re-verifying all of the information – in, out and transfer – for those 5 seconds.

Okay, now let go of the cable.

[Dorado lets go. There is no alarm.]

Dorado: Nothing happened that time.

Lazarus: No... the system was expecting it. We can deploy this thing in a tropical storm and barely get an alarm.

Dorado: Cool!

Lazarus: Yes, cool... and boring. My most exciting part of tonight is having to log why there was an alarm just now.

Man-Onko: Actually, the most exciting part of your evening... and your LIFE... is spending guard duty with me.

Lazarus: Does anybody have a sharp knife? I'm feeling the urge to slit my throat...

[end of transcript]

File No:		File Name:	Moving Water
Location:		Parties:	Gopher Pod
			Cricket Pod
Monk/ Master Supervising:	Waterman, Master		

How Things Work: Moving Water

Name:		Pgs:		Date:		Vol:	
Type of Transcript:	Mechanical						
	XXX						
	Organic						

Preface by North American Archive Committee:

The Age of Waste created a devastated, toxic landscape – the dry fuel for the Upheavals.

Nowhere was the waste more evident than in our relationship to water. Water was LIFE... and we poisoned it, wasted it, used it for purposes from frivolous to insane... Wasters acted like it would always be there, then turned on each other when it wasn't.

This text is being provided in a rough draft format. Communication Access Realtime

[start of transcript]

Master Waterman: Okay, time for the youngsters to learn about the birds and the bees....

Man-Onko: I thought we were supposed to learn about water.

Master Waterman: Picky, picky! Birds, bees and water, okay?

Man-Onko: What's to learn? Water falls from the sky as rain. Then we pick it up and use it to wash dishes in the canteen. Did I leave anything out?

Master Waterman: Thank you, Novice Genius! We can all leave early!

Man-Onko: Oh, you're welcome. Glad to be ...

Master Waterman: You won't mind if I expand on your brilliance, do you?

Man-Onko: If possible... Go ahead.

Master Waterman: Well, the very first thing you said was wrong...

Victory: Why isn't that surprising?

Master Waterman: Rain DOESN'T fall from the sky. Not anymore.

Or, more correctly: too little rain falls where we need it. Too much falls where we don't want it.

Man-Onko: Well... Don't mean to be smart-mouth, but so what? I mean, we're doing fine. Look how green everything is, all up and down the valley!
Master Waterman: And why is that?

Dorado: Because everything is irrigated. Hundreds of novices, running in their gerbil wheels, spreading joy and water throughout the valley.. .

Master Waterman: And where is the irrigation water coming from?

(Silence)

Master Waterman: Mr. Novice Genius? Any words of wisdom?

Man-Onko: Ahhh... Wells?

Master Waterman: Not a bad guess! WRONG, but not bad.

Man-Onko: Whew! I'd hate to be "bad"...

Master Waterman: Can't use well water, 'cause the Breakers DRANK it all! Didn't drink it as much as wasted it. Golf courses and gold mines. Huge fountains in Las Vegas, in the middle of the desert! Flushing away 5 ounces of pee with 5 gallons of drinkable water!

Dorado: Hey, the water in the ground was called something...

Victory: Yeah... Dinosaur water, I think.

Man-Onko: You think wrong. It was "fossil" water.

Victory: I was close! Fossils, dinosaurs, same thing!

Master Waterman: Close enough! Whatever you call it, its ancient history.

What you young'uns are doing up on this fine hill on this fine day at this fine sunset isn't just admiring the view. You're about to take a delivery of water.

Okay everyone! ABOUT FACE! God... that means turn around! What do they teach you guys down there?

Man-Onko: Well, they teach us to say "turn around" when they.. Hey, what's that?

Master Waterman: What's it look like?

Dorado: Looks like a flying pillow.

Victory: Looks like a cloud... Going in the wrong direction!

Dorado: It's coming here! Its heading this way!

Man-Onko: That sucker is HUGE!

Krista-Lin: I don't like this. I don't want to be here!

Victory: Wow, been waiting for that.

Master Waterman: What you're gawking at is a swimming pool worth of water, flying through the air. Don't see that every day!

Victory: That looks bigger than a swimming pool!

Master Waterman: How observant! You are looking at the water through the envelope of hydrogen gas- which is how the water can fly.

Dorado: Where's the water come from?

Master Waterman: This load is from the Great Lakes, but it can come from anywhere there's more fresh water than average.

Krista-Lin: Um, I'm sorry, um, I have a question? I mean, like, is this SUSTAINABLE? Shouldn't we be learning how to live with the water we've got?

Master Waterman: Hmmm. Good question. I wonder what our resident genius has to say about that?

Victory: Yeah... Especially since he has yet to be RIGHT.

Man-Onko: Ummm. She's right?

Master Waterman: Yes. This is an example of "conscious instability". No, this water operation is not sustainable, not in the short run. But, our challenge was to import water or abandon this Center completely. Actually, abandon the western part of this country.

Without these shipments, this valley would be a desert, and all of us would be fighting for food.

Man-Onko: Okay, Master, great! Nice talking to you! But that thing's getting BIGGER! Shouldn't we be doing something? Like RUNNING?

Master Waterman: Why? You got a problem with having several hundred tons of water landing on you?

As usual, your lesson involves working! See those four ropes hanging down from the pillow? Each of you grab one of them. Do NOT hang on to it! If the pillow pulls away, let it go! We don't need any flying novices today!

Now, take your line and attach it to one of those steel rings. That's right, all the way through. That stabilizes the pillow.

[Sounds of activity]

Man-Onko: What's that thing called?

Master Waterman: Actually, we call it "The Pillow"! And, Mr. Genius Boy, you get to tie all this off!

See that guy up there in the Pillow? Actually, she's not a guy! She's waiting for your tie-off signal.

Man-Onko: What's that?

Master Waterman: She's waiting for you to tell her that the lines are tied. She can't see the corners of the Pillow.

Man-Onko: How do I do that? Yell? She's pretty far up there.

Master Waterman: You use sign language. Point to your podmates. No, face them and use both arms. Right, now turn and point to the next one. And the next one. And the final one.

Now, she knows you looked at all 4 lines. Take this green flag and wave it 4 times.

Okay, now the fun begins! She's dropping the snorkel! Now, grab the end and attach it to that coupling on the ground. Great! Now run!

Man-Onko: Seriously?

Master Waterman: You wanna find out the hard way? This whole bowl is gonna fill up FAST!

(Sounds of running)

Master Waterman: Here it comes! It's in the interest of the Pillow pilots to dump their loads ASAP.

And, they also have to burn or dump hydrogen- see the lift? See how all the lines are stretched? She can't take off unless she dumps both water and hydrogen.

So, she fills up this bowl. Dumps the H, slacks the lines, then takes off for the next run.

Dorado: How many runs does she make a day?

Master Waterman: Two or three... per NIGHT. We have very few daylight runs - attracts too much of the wrong kind of attention.

If she's running out of the Gulf, she may only do 1-2 per night.

Depending on our needs, the water is diverted from up here to the fields, or the living quarters, or the research wing... And... Back into the ground. We are trying to recharge the aquifer. Half the water for the present, half for the future.

Man-Onko: Wow. How many Pillows will that take?

Master Waterman: We're guessing over half a million Pillows. Probably 20 years or so.

Dorado: What do we get out of sticking water in the ground?

Master Waterman: Basically nothing. Nothing direct. Some of us think that if the aquifers are recharged, the weather patterns will change and the rains will return. And we won't have to do this anymore.

Dorado: Hey... don't the folks we're taking water from mind us scarfing their water?

Master Waterman: Try asking an Iowa farmer whose field is under 6 feet of water if they mind us snorkeling up the water! They PAY us to do it! If they're organic, we'll take part of their crop.

Dorado: If they're not organic?

Master Waterman: We sail on by. They have nothing we need.

Man-Onko: Wow. Ain't that kind of... cold?

Master Waterman: [pauses]: Each of you knows how it is Outside. You each CAME from it. You know there's more need than our ability to meet that need.

Our pillow pilots fly swimming pools of water over farms that are parched, dying of thirst. They see people begging us for water. Or begging us to take their water away. Or begging us to drop food. Or begging us to take their children...

Think about it: the pillow pilots are flying over desperate people, flying water to us, so we can stick it in the ground. Are they cold and uncaring? Or, are they thinking about the Big Picture? We call this compassion... for the future. Something the Breakers never understood.

Once in awhile, a farm will convert to organics. If they do, we might do a swap with them.

Or, they'll LIE and tell us they're organic when they're not. Or, they'll get rifles and try to bring a Pillow down, along with the water it's carrying.

Dorado: Hey, isn't shooting at big bags of hydrogen... dangerous?

Master Waterman: Not much. We designed it so that most of the water is on the bottom of the pillow, most of the hydrogen is on the top. Most bullet holes are self-sealing. We get drips, but no explosions.

There was an anarchist group in Illinois that used flaming arrows! Very non-dramatic... they got wet!

Man-Onko: How about if they...

Master Waterman: No more questions! Got to get busy! She's done dumping water!

Okay, Mr. Ground Control, get ready with your flags! Wave the green ones up and down 3 times. That tells her that you know she's finished. You others, get on your lines! Don't touch them yet! NEVER try to release a line while it's tight! Not if you still enjoy wearing your head!

Look! See that she's lowered a little, that there's slack on the lines? Okay, Ground Control, point both of your green flags to one of your podmates. Keep pointing until they release the line. Okay, the next one. And the next one. Now the last one. Now, 3 more up and down waves, let her know you cleared all 4 lines.

Man-Onko: Hey, what about the snorkel? It's under 10 feet of water!

Master Waterman: 15 feet, actually. Just watch – she can control it from above. There it goes! And there she goes!

When she lifts off, it's customary to salute her, like this. [pause.] Some folks think it's carryover military crap and don't do it, but I think it's a nice way to say "thank you".

208

[end of transcript]

File No:		File Name:	The Fire
Location:	Denver	Parties:	All Novice Pods
Monk/ Master Supervising:	All Monks All Masters		

The Fire

Name:		Pgs:	Date:	Vol:	
Type of Transcript:	Mechanical xxx				
	Organic				

Preface by the North American Centers Archive Committee:

Emergencies are stressful times. When an unscheduled event happens, systems and structures are pulled to their breaking point... and sometimes beyond.

Fires are not disasters. They are naturally occurring events. The "disaster" is in not being prepared for them.

Preparation is not just external. The fire is not just an external event...

This text is being provided in a rough draft format. Communication Access Realtime Translation (CART) facilitates communication accessibility and may not be a totally

[Transcript of All-Center emergency procedures drill. Transcript of Gopher Pod...]

Dorado: I wonder how long we're gonna be down here.

Victory: Until this blows over, I guess.

Man-Onko: Or, until we're all baked potatoes down here. Is it my imagination, or is it getting HOT?

Dorado: It's your sick imagination! I was last one in, and the fire looked like it was over 10 miles away.

Man-Onko: KILOMETERS, Novice Dorado! Here at the Center, we speak in metrics!

Dorado: Oh, pardon me, Master Man-Onko! The fire looked like it was 20 *kilometers* away.

Man-Onko: Well said, my Novice! With any luck, you will join me in the exalted ranks of monkhood one day!

Victory: With any luck, you two pukes won't make me vomit!

Dorado: If you toss it down here, the sound's gonna carry!

Man-Onko: Yeah, and you'll have 200 novices following your exalted example!

Victory: Well, just don't talk about revolting subjects... like Mo being a monk!

Man-Onko: That was Master...

Dorado: Hey! Can it! Here comes the real thing!

[pause. Gopher Pod is joined by Ariel.]

Ariel: Everything okay? Just going around checking on the pods.

Dorado: We're cool...

Ariel: I think this is the first burn for all of you, right?

[General assent]

Ariel: Well, don't worry. It's my third. We'll be okay.

Man-Onko: Is this why we build with so much rammed earth?

Ariel: Great guess, novice! Everything made out of wood is down here in the caves, or at the bottom of the water tanks.

Dorado: What about the wooden beams in the Assembly Hall?

Ariel: We're wrapping them in water-soaked blankets right now.

Dorado: Isn't that cutting it kind of close?

Ariel: The fire's slowing down as it approaches. We've got time. It might miss us completely. Enjoy your time doing nothing!

[Pause as Ariel moves on to another pod.]

Dorado: He's pretty relaxed. But, I guess that's 'cause he's down here with us, breathing filtered air...

Krista-Lin: The air.... The air.... It's not... not filtered.

Victory: So, we hear from Creepy Corner at last!

[pause]

Dorado: Why'd you say it's not filtered? They said we'd be breathing filtered air down here.

Krista-Lin: We... we don't.... don't need to, not yet. That... that monk, over there. He's got the switch that brings in the air from down in the caves. This air still smells smoky. The air from down below is cold, and will smell like... bat guano.

Victory: Are you LISTENING to her shit? Miss Bat-Shit for Brains knows a lot about bat guano, I'm sure!

[pause]

Dorado: Well, in the surprising silence of Man-Onko, I guess it's my turn to tell you to shut up, Victory. [To Krista-Lin:] Or, why don't you tell him to shut up, yourself? You don't have to take his shit...

Krista-Lin: I... I... don't want Victory to shut up. I want... I want him to continue to reveal himself.

[pause]

Man-Onko: I have the feeling that things are about to get heavy.

Victory: What the fuck are you...

Dorado: Hey! Let her finish talking! [To Krista-Lin:] What do you mean "reveal himself"?

Krista-Lin: Master... Master Neled said that... that we always reveal ourselves, in everything we do. How we do our chores, or eat our food, or even go to sleep. How... how we talk to each other. The more we reveal, the more we can see our "true selves".

[to Victory]: Victory. You... you... you always give me a hard time.   But, not just me. You give ALL the girls a hard time.

Dorado: Hey, he gives EVERYBODY a hard time!

Krista-Lin: Yes, he talks bad to the guys, if you give him a reason, like when you tease him. But, he talks bad to the girls ALL THE TIME. And, with us, he... he MEANS IT!

Victory: I don't have to listen to this shit! She's talkin' out of her gourd! She's a...

Dorado: HEY! DON'T INTERRUPT HER! You can stay here and listen, or you can get up and walk away! But, don't interrupt! This is the most she's ever said in almost a year! And, so far, she's SPOT ON! Stay or go – but I think you ought to shut up and listen.

[Pause as Monk Pico-Laton joins Gopher Pod]

Pico-Laton: I'm just making the rounds... everything okay here?

Dorado: We're okay... Just dealing with some... pod business.

Pico-Laton: Pod business is okay – just keep it down, so it doesn't become everyone else's business, okay?

Dorado: Got it.

Man-Onko: How's the fire?   Are we gonna turn into baked potatoes down here?

Pico-Laton: I haven't been outside, but the last report was that the fire was moving around the fields and the buildings.

Man-Onko: Yay! I'd hate to lose those fields. We worked real hard on those crops...

Pico-Laton: Well, Farmer Man-Onko, you'll be pleased to know that you'll continue to be eating well.

Man-Onko: Actually, it's more like I'll be pleased to be eating AT ALL. I remember a year ago when I wasn't.

Dorado: So true.

Pico-Laton: Well. Fire or not, you won't have to worry about not eating.   We've got enough dried beans and vegetables stored down here to last a few years.

Man-Onko: BEANS???   You'd give Victory BEANS?? Inside of a CAVE?? Don't you fear EXPLOSIONS?

Dorado: [LAUGHING]:   I'll take my chances with the FIRE!

Victory: You guys are SOOOO funny.

Pico-Laton: I will leave you to your "pod business". Just keep a lid on it, okay?

Dorado: Aye, aye, Captain!

[Pause as Pico-Laton departs]

Victory: I got something to say...

Dorado: Yeah, but Krista-Lin had the floor.

Victory: Okay, but after she finishes scraping me along the floor, I got something to say.

Dorado: Fair enough. [To Krista-Lin:] What were you saying, before we got monked?

Krista-Lin: Just... just that... Well... Master Neled said that we were never angry for the reasons that we think. So, I think Victory isn't angry at ME, or at the other girls. I think he's angry at WOMEN. Even the female monks and masters. He always obeys them, but he never SAYS anything to them.

Victory: [Seething]: Shit. Fuck...

Dorado: You cool?

Victory: [Pauses]: I'm cool...

Man-Onko: Well, you're gonna be really cool! The vents just kicked in – cold cave air and guano!

Dorado: Okay, back to business... Anything else?

Krista-Lin: Can... Can I say just one more thing? Master Neled... He said that the basis of anger was fear. That means that Victory is really afraid of women and girls, and covers it up by acting angry.

Dorado: Do you think that you can say that directly to Victory?

Krista-Lin: [Pauses]: Yes. [pauses]: Victory...

Victory: That's okay.

Dorado: I think it's best if she...

Victory: SHUT UP!! I DON'T WANT TO HEAR IT AGAIN!! ALRIGHT?? [Begins sobbing uncontrollably]

[Long pause, as Victory regains his composure.]

Man-Onko: Well, so much for "Keeping pod business to ourselves"... Everybody's staring at us...

Victory: Before they Collected me, I was in this truly fucked-up "camp". Six or seven families. We didn't even pretend it was a "community". The men would go out stealing from other camps all day, come back with food and liquor, get drunk and beat and fuck the women... Just beat the kids.

Then, during the day, while the men were gone, the women would take it out on the boys in the camp. We'd get beat for just... being there. Being male.

Man-Onko: Even your mother?

Victory: Especially my mother. All the mothers beat their own sons extra-hard. I think it was because we reminded them of our fathers. My Mom would refer to me and the other boys as "The Next Generation of Nigger-Men".

And if that wasn't bad enough, the girls in the camp would crap on us, also. My own sister! If we said anything to the girls, they'd tell the mothers and we'd get beat! And, if the mothers left marks, the men would come back and beat us again!

Man-Onko: Damn...

Victory: Damn, yeah. So, when I got here, and saw that the girls weren't protected, I just thought... [Pause] Well, maybe I didn't think.

Krista-Lin: You thought...you thought... it was time for pay-back?

Victory: [pauses]: Yeah. I thought it was, like, okay – I wasn't, like beating on them...

Dorado: You think you can say that directly to her?

[Long pause]

Victory: Okay... Okay... Maybe sometimes I don't think you're all that creepy, okay?

Krista-Lin: Okay.

Dorado: Not so fast. Isn't there some more?

Victory: What? I said I'm sorry!

Dorado: Well, you didn't, but we'll let that pass. Isn't there another reason you've been dumping on her?

Victory: Hey, come on, give me a break!

Krista-Lin: Something else?

Man-Onko: Yeah. Like he thinks you're HOT.

Krista-Lin: WHAT?? NO!! DON'T SAY THAT!

Victory: HEY! WHAT?

Dorado: Looks like more "pod business" coming up...

Man-Onko: Okay, let's try to work this out, okay? Quietly?

Krista-Lin: I DON'T WANT TO BE HERE!!!

Man-Onko: Is this the first time someone said you were pretty?

Krista-Lin: STOP IT! DON'T SAY THAT! DON'T SAY THAT! (Sobbing)

Dorado: Damn... okay, maybe we'll save that piece of pod business for later.

Krista-Lin: I DON'T WANT TO BE HERE!! I DON'T WANT TO BE HERE!! (Sobbing...)

Dorado: It's okay! We won't talk about it! You can uncover your ears!

Victory: Shit! All this time, I thought she was stuck up! All this time, and she's really...

Man-Onko: Clueless? Oblivious? On another planet?

Victory: Yeah, something like that...

Krista-Lin: EMILY IS A GOOD GIRL! EMILY IS A GOOD GIRL!

Man-Onko: Uh-oh..

Victory: Who the hell is 'Emily'?

Dorado: It's okay! Keep it down! We'll talk about this later...

Man-Onko: Looks like every monk in this joint is on their way over here...

Victory: Hey! Would it make you feel better if I called you a "Creepazoid"?

Krista-Lin: [Pauses, takes a long breath]: It might. [Pause.] But, I don't want to be "Miss Bat-Shit".

Victory: Okay, she stays "Miss Creepy". But, NO "Bat-Shit"! [Stands up, addresses the cave]: Hear that, everybody? I'll call you... "Miss GUANO"!

[Everyone laughs, including Krista-Lin]

Dorado: Looks like the monks are gonna be cool...

Ariel: OKAY EVERYONE, LISTEN UP! Looks like the fire's passing us! There's been minimal damage to the fields, and NO damage to our buildings!

[Laughter and cheering]

Ariel: Okay, listen! We're going to stay down here another half hour or so, until the smoke clears. But, it looks like we'll have dinner on time!

[More cheering]

Ariel: Those novices responsible for fixing dinner should report to the canteen, pronto! That would be Pods Frog, Gopher, Rose...

Man-Onko: What a world... after enlightenment, the dishes.

[end of transcript]

The Birds

File No:		File Name:	The Birds: Novice Lecture on Inter-Species, Trans-Species and Cross-Species Communication
Location:		Parties:	Angel, Gopher, Rose & Frog
Monk/ Master Supervising:	Open Sky, Master (Bird Man)		

Name:		Pgs:		Date:		Vol:	
Type of Transcript:	Mechanical xxx						
	Organic						

Preface by North American Archive Committee:

Wasters had two attitudes toward the living world: "pets" or "pests". Beings to be brought under your control, or beings to be killed. "Crops" or "weeds".

In the Awakening Movement, there were no pets. Or pests. There were LOTS of "partners"...

This text is being provided in a rough draft format. Communication Access Realtime Translation (CART) facilitates communication accessibility and may not be a totally verbatim record of the proceedings. Let your coordinator know if you would prefer a more verbatim option.

[start of transcript]

Bird-Man: Welcome to the Great Outdoors! Or, the Great Inside! My "monk" name is Open Sky, but you can call me "Bird Man"! Everybody does! At least, my friends do... And we're all friends, right?

I am SO happy to see you all! I love working with new novices!

I'm a "master", but don't call me that. I just like doing my work. And, my work is with... Birds!

So, what am I doing with birds, especially, what am I doing with CROWS?

[Five novices stand]

Bird-Man: How about you?

Novice Man-Onko: Nothing! You can't eat them! I'm told they don't taste very good!

Bird-Man: I'm not trying to eat them! I'm trying to TALK to them!

I see some of you rolling your eyes right now. So, let's do a demonstration.

[Suddenly, the air is filled with hundreds of crows, swirling all around Master Bird-Man. After two minutes of swirling, they all settle down and perch in the nearby trees.]

Bird-Man: So, what do you think of THAT?

[3 novices stand]

Bird-Man: Back to you... How'd you like that?

Novice Man-Onko: I think it's a fake. I think you did a good job of training those birds. Birds are as dumb as... excrement.

Bird-Man: [turning to birds]: Well, what do you think of what he said?

[Birds swarm and peck at Novice Man-Onko, who ducks and covers. After one minute, birds subside]

Novice Man-Onko: Okay... That still doesn't prove anything. So you've got the birds trained to act on certain keywords. I still say... So what?

Bird-Man: [Laughing] A hard-head! We've got a real critic in the audience! Let's try a more complicated experiment.

Put your tablet on the table. Now, pick any bird that you want, just point to one...

[Man-Onko points. Bird flies down and lands on table, near tablet.]

Now, what are the chances that this random bird can get your password in one try?

[Crow taps in 4-digit password]

Novice Man-Onko: Holy crap...

Bird-Man: We're not finished yet. Pick up your tablet, and change the password. [pauses]: Now, put it back down and select a different bird.

Novice Man-Onko: No... I want the same one! I know that one wasn't looking over my shoulder!

Bird-Man: Fair enough! Put your tablet back down... (Bird taps out new password.)

Novice Man-Onko: Damn...

Bird-Man: I can tell that you still don't believe me. How about you THINK of a different four-digit password for your tablet?

[Bird taps out new password]

Novice Man-Onko: Wow... How do you do that?

Bird-Man: I am not doing anything. The birds can pick up your resonant frequency, and translate that into action. You can call it "Mind Reading", but it's just a matter of broadcasting and receiving frequencies.

Novice Man-Onko: Can the birds do that with everyone, or just me?

Bird-Man: Well, let's see! When you came here, you were all given an envelope. In your envelope you will see a card. On the card is a picture of either a dead crow or a crow being fed.

I want you to concentrate on the picture.

[The crows land near the novices holding positive images, while staying away from the novices holding negative images.]

Bird-Man: This isn't just fun and games. The crows alert us to the potential for attacks, sometimes tens of miles away. They can tell us how many people are involved, what kinds of weapons they have... The whole thing. Things don't happen around us by surprise!

This is really important. You know how light our human security teams are. We can't watch everywhere, all the time. By opening ourselves to the crows, and the crows opening themselves to us, we can target our resources very effectively... and to Outsiders, we look a lot more powerful than we are!

Man-Onko: Yeah... and I think I'm starting to see how the monks know so much about what's going on with us novices!

Bird-Man: Ha, ha! That's really funny! Really! As though what you novices are doing is important enough to merit the attention of a crow!

[end of transcript]

News Article: "WE CAN'T COUNT THE BODIES." FEMA Loses Control over Food Distribution Centers

All twelve of the FEMA distribution centers are in disarray, as thousands of hungry people have overrun the security and administration of the centers, in the face of ever more stringent FEMA rules.

"They weren't getting enough as it is. Then, when they heard that they were getting even less... I guess something snapped," said Colonel Sharpes, Army head of security for FEMA's Northeast Distribution Center. "People came over the fence. If it were a couple dozen, we could have stopped them. But, they came over the fence by the hundreds, the thousands. There's no way we could have stopped them."

Some of the distribution centers tried. In the FEMA Distribution Center outside of Savannah, GA, the private security firm hired by FEMA to maintain order in the Center opened fire on the advancing crowd. "We were hired to stop them. We stopped them," said a spokesman, identified only as "Mr. Evans". "They were trying to break the law. We stopped them from doing that. We preserved the order."

Preserving the order came at a heavy toll. "We can't count the bodies! They just opened fire on everyone! The only reason I wasn't hit was because I dived behind the bodies of people who had already been killed. It was a nightmare." Kathleen Sullivan, a social worker who was working in the camp at the time, spoke to [this reporter] on a cell phone smuggled into the camp. "I saw thousands of bodies, just were I was. I could hear machine gun fire all over the camp. It was like they're trying to kill everyone!"

Molly Knudson, a camp resident, agreed. "This was a police riot – the people doing the shooting and the looting were the cops! The food in the center disappeared... and we sure don't have it!"

FEMA officials have provided no figures on the numbers of deaths in the camps. Said Director Andrew Smith, who took over the reins from the embattled Director Auburne 8 months ago, "We are currently assessing the situation in the distribution centers. We'll report to you when we've got reliable information."

Kathleen Sullivan said, "We haven't seen a single FEMA official since the shooting started a day ago. No one. The bodies are just lying there on the ground. There's no one distributing any food. No one is picking up the bodies. Everyone's afraid to approach the fence. There is no security. There is no food. There is no water, no electricity, no heat. I don't know what we're going to do."

How Things Work: The Muscle Train

File No:		File Name:	How Things Work: The Muscle Train
Location:	On the rails between Denver and Grand Junction	Parties:	Frog Pod Gopher Pod
Monk/ Master Supervising:	Train Master Bax		On board H-PRCS, the "Human-Powered Rail Conveyance System" (aka "Muscle Train").

Name:		Pgs:		Date:		Vol:	
Type of Transcript:	Mechanical						
	Organic						

Preface by North American Archive Committee:

The first question was not "How do you get from Point A to Point B?" The first question was: "Why do you want to go?"

Once transportation was reduced to its essentials, finding new ways to move people and goods became essential...

This text is being provided in a rough draft format. Communication Access Realtime Translation (CART) facilitates communication accessibility and may not be a totally verbatim record of the proceedings. Let your coordinator know if you would prefer a more verbatim option.

[start of transcript]

Bax: Okay, basics of how we get from here to there. And DON'T STOP PEDALING while I'm talking!

We're using the old national railway system. We're hacked into their computers - what's left of them - so we know when they're not using the line... Which is most of the time. There's nothing to move, no one to move it, no energy to fuel it, and no one to pay for it.

Once in awhile, there's a military shipment... but most of the time, they're so big and slow, we can get out of their way.

Their rail cars are big, heavy and steel. Ours are light and bamboo. When theirs break, they have to wait for parts that may never come. When ours break, we just grow some more!

Okay, see that box down there? Look, right near your pedals! That's the master controller. That's what converts your pedal power into electricity, then feeds that to the electric motors on each wheel.

Man-Onko: Hey, what's this thing for?

Bax: That's your credit chip. That's how we keep score on you little turkeys. Keep it around your neck.

It doesn't matter how many times you turn your crank. It doesn't matter how fast you try to go.

What matters is how many watts you generate.

Man-Onko: What's a "watt"?

Bax: Is that a real question, or are you trying to be cute?

Man-Onko: Uhh... Both?

Bax: Ha! Fair enough!

A watt is a unit of electricity. Never mind... You'll get more about it in your Science class.

So, you adjust the gears so you've got a comfortable pace. Not TOO comfortable, or you won't make any watts. Not too hard, or you'll get too tired too quickly.

So, your fare from here to Grand Junction or New York would be your base fare, minus whatever credits you earned.

Victory: Our fare? Why come we gotta pay? We didn't ask to be out here!

Bax: You didn't?

Victory: No! They just told us to report to you.

Bax: A STOWAWAY!! THROW HIS ASS OVERBOARD! Guards!

(Laughter)

Bax: All novices get a "training" trip, then one other free trip of your choice. No cost and it's all credits.

And... Once in awhile, we may have to "draft" you. If we've got a shipment to get from A to B, and not enough volunteers to move it, we may "volun-tell" some of you. Don't worry... It rarely happens, and when it does, you'll get rewarded for it.

Dorado: Hey, this is a breeze! We can get to New York in no time!

Bax: First of all, Ace, you're pointing in the wrong direction.

Secondly, you've got your gears set too low. You're pedaling furiously, but you're not making much power. (pause) Yeah, that's better.

ThirDorado: let's see how much a "breeze" it is when you're pulling two or three cars of grain or fat-assed passengers behind you, on a 3-mile grade!

Victory: Yeah... and why would you want to go to New York anyway? I heard it's a big fat cesspool.

Man-Onko: Nah... Dorado's gonna move into one of those remodeled skyscrapers, livin' large, with guards and stuff!

Victory: Yeah... those folks'll get eaten LAST.

Dorado: I will invite both of my pod-mates to shut the heck up. Back to the point: I thought passengers had to pedal!

Bax: You thought wrong. The passengers can pedal, but they don't have to. We still get passengers that can pay and don't want to lose their oblate figures.

Victory: That doesn't seem fair. We have to haul their extra weight around, and they don't want to contribute?

Bax: We don't sell tickets by the person. We sell by the KILOGRAM and by the KILOMETER.

Man-Onko: Whoa! So a person twice my weight has to pay twice as much?

Bax: More than that. We've got an algorithm for that.

Krista-Lin: What's a "al-go-rim"?

Bax: She talks! I was wondering if we'd ever hear from the Silent Partner.

It's just a math formula, one that says you pay through the nose if you're overweight and not willing to work.

Hey, and the rest of you, pay attention! Look at how she's got her gears set! She's racking up maximum watts - more than Mr. Speed Demon over there.

Man-Onko: Hey, gimme a break! I never SEEN a bicycle before, let alone the gears!

Victory: Looks like Ms. Creepy finally does something right.

Krista-Lin: If... If... If I'm creepy and I'm doing it RIGHT, what... what does that make you?

(Hoots and laughter...)

Man-Onko: The Mighty Mite SCORES!

Victory: (subdued): Don't make her less creepy...

Dorado: Actually... It DOES!

Bax: Hello? I'm over here? Anybody mind if we get back to talking about the TRAIN?

Train rules are pretty simple and obvious:

-- No fires or anything that might combust. The last place you want to be with fire is inside this bamboo box!

-- no uncoupling the cars. It has to be done at the right time, in the right way.

-- Unless you're a passenger, stay out of the passenger car. Put delicately... When you sweat, you STINK!

-- It's okay if you want to stop pedaling and enjoy the scenery. But, if you do, unplug your card and leave your station. Someone else may want a go.

Okay, any questions?

Krista-Lin: Well, maybe one? What about, well, you know, people who don't have any legs, or can't use their legs or something like that...

Bax: Sweetie, see that red knob right between your pedals? Pull it out, then bring it forward... All the way until it clicks. Now, bring your pedals up, about chest-high... Yeah, that's right! Now push the red knob back in... Now you can use your hands instead of your feet!

Some of the high-power mules will switch up every hour between their hands and their feet, keep their energy flowing all over their body.

Man-Onko: Mules? What's a mule?

Bax: Oops. We're not supposed to call them that. A "mule" is someone who commits to pedaling for the Muscle Train. Some folks do it for a few months, to lose weight or clear their heads or whatever. Some think of it as a meditation. Then, some do it full-time... I'm not sure about their motivations...

Dorado: Are those the "mind-wipes" we've been hearing about?

Bax: You know the drill. The Culture Council discourages people from asking about whether mind-wiping exists. So... you go around asking about mind-wiping, you could get yourself wiped!

Dorado: Yeah... but, what do you think?

Bax: "Those who say don't know. Those who know don't say. And those who know and say get mind-wiped!"

Dorado: Okay, okay... I'm cool!

Bax: Back to the Muscle Train, okay? Follow the rules, pay your fare, don't set anything on fire, pedal once in awhile, don't stink the place up... I think that just about covers it.

Man-Onko: If we were regular passengers, how much would we pay for a ticket?

Bax: Okay, let's assume you were regular size, going a reasonable distance, hauling 3-5 passenger cars and 3-5 cars of grain. If you ate regular meals and pedaled about half the time, your fare would be free. If you pedaled the whole time, at the end of the journey, WE would owe YOU money!

Man-Onko: Cool!

Dorado: I'd hate to be labeled a pessimist, but...

Man-Onko: Here it comes...

Dorado: BUT... what happens if a real train comes?

Bax: THIS IS A REAL TRAIN!!

Dorado: Hey, don't be so touchy! You know what I mean... a METAL train.

Bax: Well, we have to deal with that "real" stuff all the time. While we can see the national grid pretty well, there are plenty of rogues and outlaws riding the rails. Also some military. We're...

Victory: Hey, aren't WE rogues and outlaws?

Bax: You're really itching to get thrown overboard, aren't you?

Ignoring that last comment... We're faster than all of the other hand-powered jobs – we help THEM get off the tracks when we overtake them.

When a STEEL train is using the same tracks, we have to hop off, FAST. That's where being made of plastic and bamboo comes in handy.

All of the cars have hinge joints that slide everything sideways. Uncouple the car, pop the hinge joints, slide the cargo sideways until the center of gravity lifts the wheels off of the track, then keep pushing until the wheels are completely up in the air and everything is away from the track. Then, once the Steel Beast has passed, just reverse the process. Easy-peasy... to get off the tracks takes about 3 minutes per car, only a minute if you're in a hurry. To get back on takes 10-15 minutes, more for a grain car.

Dorado: So, who pays us to be a passenger on our Bamboo Train?

Bax: Rich people have enough money to buy or rent an old-style steel train and ride around. Poor folks take their chances on the roads... highway robbers, slavers, cultists, nut-jobs, religious freaks, cannibals... In my humble opinion, not worth the risk.

So, we're the alternative, for people who want to get from A to B, and keep their scalps while doing it.

Dorado: Nobody tries to rob us?

Bax: Well, it's been tried. Once a group tried to board us with horses! Right out of the Old West! They had no idea how fast electric motors were! We blew past them before they even knew what was going on!

Victory: So how fast can this sucker go?

Bax: Faster than everything else. We can hit 100 mph without working up a sweat.

Victory: Cool!

Bax: I was on a train that got up to 130 mph. One of your Steel Beast "real" trains tried to overtake us once. They managed to get up to about 65 mph before they gave up. We made them look like they were standing still!

Actually, 200 mph or better is possible. But, the faster you go, the more vibrations you set up in the cars. I wouldn't want to be on a train that shook apart. This is our cruising speed... a nice 60 mph.

Dorado: Back to the bad guys who want to rob us?

Bax: Yeah... A couple of times groups have tried blockading the tracks. See that mortar up on top the engine? We stop a mile away, lob over some sleepy-time grenades, put them all to sleep, take all their shit, especially their weapons, remove the barricades and on we go!

One group came BACK at us a few months later! They found some gas masks and thought they could have another go.

Dorado: What did you do?

Bax: Just kept lobbing sleepy-time at them. The gas masks had a charge of 60 minutes. We had 10 hours of grenades.

This time, we weren't so nice. Gave them a free ride to "Somewhere Else".

Dorado: What... you KILLED them?

Bax: Is that what they're teaching you in classes that we do? Or, were you just asleep when they were talking about NONVIOLENCE?

We literally gave them a free ride. We rode them down an abandoned rail line, 100 miles from the nearest human settlement, and left them with enough food and water to last 3 days.

Man-Onko: What happened to them? Did they die?

Bax: Don't know and don't care. We didn't kill 'em, and they learned a very valuable lesson: It doesn't pay to mess with us.

Dorado: Hey! What's THAT up ahead?!?! Is that a blockade?

Man-Onko: Hey, we're slowing down! What do we do??

Bax: CHILL!! Everybody just chill!!

That's not a blockade, it's a rest stop! We'll be pulling in for a 15-minute stop.

Dorado: Hey, cool, I knew that! I wasn't worried!

Victory: Yeah, Mr. "I'm-Not-Worried" looked like he was about to pee himself!

Krista-lin: That's not... not... not Center people.

Bax: [pauses]: Very observant, Little Lady.

Some folks Outside have contacted us for trading. They set up little rest stops, selling meals to passengers, water, trinkets. To us, they sell energy, food, essential crafts...

Dorado: Is it all barter?

Bax: Who gave you permission to be intelligent? No, it's not all barter. They will take Center credits – good for some of the things that we sell them. Like greenhouses... very good in places that get way too much Sun and way too little rain. Or, our energy generators, so they can work less hard to produce power – to sell back to us! Sometimes, we sell them shelters, or kitchens, or water. Or security – ways to deal with bandits and the such roaming around here... nonviolently, of course!

This is how we're building new systems and structures. You see that collection of 10 buildings we're slowing down to? 100 years from now, that's going to be a city of 100,000 people – one of the biggest cities in the region.

People take Center credits because they know they can be traded for something. They don't lose value the way the old money does. A ticket for a Muscle Train ride is gonna cost the same two years from now as it does today.

Dorado: Unless you get fat.

Bax: Indeed! Speaking of weight... see that woman standing over there? The one that's as wide as she is tall, holding those two pies? Best apple pies this side of a Center! And both of them are MINE!

Krista-lin: But... is that part of a healthy diet?

Bax: (laughing): Now, Sweetie Pie just discovered one of the hidden benefits of the Muscle Train! Just wait until you brats learn how to say, "cheeseburger"!

Okay, up and out! Stops are 15 minutes, which means you've got to be back in your saddles in 12! You don't want to find out how much you'd have to pay if you get left in a rest stop like this!

[end of transcript]

The Strike

File No:		File Name:	The Strike
Location:		Parties:	Gopher Pod Cricket Pod
Monk/ Master Supervising:	Bird- Man, Master		

Name:		Pgs:		Date:		Vol:	
Type of Transcript:	Mechanical xxx						
	Organic						

Preface by the North American Centers Archive Committee:

Humans are not superior to other beings. We all live to cooperate and support one another.

All of us know this. However, when the other beings don't speak English and can't attend a meeting, it's easy for us to ACT like we respect and cooperate with them. It's easy to believe that we "hear" their voices... especially when those voices are saying what we want to hear.

All beings have both volition and permission. When they are denied volition or permission, they turn into "pets". Or slaves.

It's always interesting to find out what's really going on...

[start of transcript]

Bird-Man: That's right... now, ask them to wheel counter-clockwise. Great! Now, ask them all to fly to the tops of the trees. Yes! Now, all of them fly to that one tree over there. Great! You're all getting the hang of this. You're going to be better than me at "crow wrangling"!

Now, ask them to settle down, so we can have a chat.

[Pause while birds return to trees.]

Bird-Man: Now you can see how powerful and how important our trans-species communication is. We can fine-tune our communications with them. They can be our eyes and our ears.

Dorado: How accurate are they?

Bird-Man: Depends on what you're asking them to see. The larger, the more accurate. And, they have problems seeing man-made objects that are made to look like natural objects. They would have problems finding a gun if it were made to look like a stick, for example.

Man-Onko: So, they don't handle camouflage clothes, huh?

Bird-Man: No, actually! For some reason, camo clothes stand out for them. They really hate it! The camo would have to actually LOOK like leaves, in three dimensions. Anything else, they can spot miles away.

Dorado: What else can they do?

Bird-Man: Right now, we're teaching them how to smell explosives. Also, certain classes of drugs. This will help us a great deal, when we start to re-take certain sections of the city... it will tell us where the baddies are concentrated, and when they are moving.

Novice Krista-lin: So... What do the crows get out of it?

Bird-Man: We take care of them very well. They get food, nesting space, treats and our protection.

Novice Man-Onko: Yeah... But that's not what they want.

Bird-Man: [pause]: What do you think they want?

Novice Man-Onko: What they want is people out of their space.

Novice Krista-lin: They want their own space – without people.

Novice Man-Onko: Actually... THAT space, over there, with those trees.

Bird-Man: [Pause] How do you know that?

Novice Man-Onko: Well, it's obvious how they're flying around! They're really raising a stink about it... I can smell them!

Bird-Man: Well... It's not obvious to anybody but you! Is anybody else getting that message?

Novice Dorado: I don't know... Maybe me.

Novice Victory: Yeah, you're half bird-brain yourself!

Bird-Man: Okay, settle down! Well, young novice, I've been getting that message for a while now! I've tried to tell the Council about it, but they don't believe me... They think I'm just coddling these birds. They think I'm treating them like pets, but I'm not! The Council doesn't take me seriously.

Novice Man-Onko: Well, why don't you DO something about that?

Bird-Man: Do what? I've tried to present proof, and demonstrations, but the Abbot won't even come to look...

Novice Man-Onko: It's real simple...

[Birds suddenly fly up and away]

Bird-Man: Who did that? Where'd they go? I can't FEEL them anymore!

Novice Man-Onko: I just gave them the idea that they should go on strike! No more information, until they get land of their own! How many humans will it take to replace the crows' information?

Bird-Man: Bring them back! We can't replace them! We're blind! I'M BLIND!!

Novice Man-Onko: So, perhaps the Abbot and the Head of Security will pay attention now! The crows don't want much land... Just a few acres down there...[pointing] You're not using that anyway!

Bird-Man: Okay, just bring them back and we'll talk about it!

Novice Man-Onko: You don't know how a strike works, do you? They go back to work when they have a CONTRACT!

Bird-Man: This is terrible! This is terrible! I can't FEEL them! We're wide open! [Breaks into tears.] [to the crows]: I thought you were loyal to me! I thought you LIKED me!

Novice Man-Onko: They like you, but they like themselves MORE. I just showed them how to be loyal to themselves.

[Other novices join in chat: Strike! Strike! Strike!]

[end of transcript]

[After note: After two days, the Denver Council set aside a 10-acre tract of land as a "no humans allowed" zone for all other-than-human beings. Other Centers have been invited to follow their example.]

[Novice Man-Onko received a reprimand in his file for disrupting the lecture on interspecies communication, and another reprimand for jeopardizing the security of the Center. These reprimands were offset by credits for his cooperation in securing the trans-species contract – and more credits for demonstrating the necessity for it.]

The End of Gopher

File No:		File Name:	The End of Gopher
Location:	Denver	**Parties:**	**Novice Man-Onko**
Monk/ Master Supervising:	Monk Pico-Laton		Evaluation Meeting for Apprenticeship (Monk Candidacy)

Name:			Pgs:		Date:		Vol:	
Type of Transcript:	**Mechanical** **XXX**							
	Organic							

Preface by North American Archive Committee:

When the time is right, it's time for more Awakening...

[start of transcript]

Man-Onko: Why are we meeting in here? I think I've only been in this building 2 or 3 times...

Monk Pico-Laton: This is where we do Assessments. You came through that door 12 months ago, thinking we were going to either eat you or brainwash you!

I'm hoping that, when we're through talking today, you will decide to become Apprentice Man-Onko, and walk out THAT door.

Novice Man-Onko: Well, I'm interested... But, I need to hear the real reasons why I would want to start on the road to become a monk.

Monk Pico-Laton: All of your teachers – ALL of them – talk about how perceptive you are. In your old language, you would say that you can "see through bullshit".

Novice Man-Onko: Yeah... enough to know that you didn't say anything just now.

Monk Pico-Laton: Okay, so let me say something. In your "Current Affairs" class, you have been researching the state of our sorry world. The deaths, the wars, the famines... the INHUMANITY. In the past 5 years, we estimate we've lost almost two billion humans around the world.

Here in America, there's no real government to speak of, there are fantastically rich people, and many others who survive by cannibalism... For a long time now, the leading cause of death has been suicide.

If you were able to, would you change this?

Novice Man-Onko: [pause]: That's a bogus question. Or a trick question. In "Society" class, Master Neled said all that stuff, all "The Upheavals" was... was... destined to happen.

Monk Pico-Laton: Inevitable?

Novice Man-Onko: Yeah. Nothing we can do about it. So, the question either doesn't make sense, or it's a set-up for something else.

Monk Pico-Laton: Now it's your turn for a straight answer. You didn't answer my question. Despite the inevitability of the Upheavals, if you could change this situation, WOULD YOU?

Novice Man-Onko: [Longer pause, then]: Yes...

Monk Pico-Laton: Why?

Novice Man-Onko: I remember the streets. I remember how bad things were. I remember looking up at the hills, thinking how any one of those folks living behind their walls and guards, or floating out in the bays in their party-boats, surrounded by guards who made sure they never SEE us... any one of them could help us – and they don't.

Now that I'm okay, with enough to eat and a secure place to sleep, do I just forget about the folks still on the street? Forget about my sister? Forget about everyone else? I don't think so.

Monk Pico-Laton: And THAT, Novice Man-Onko, is why I believe you will become Apprentice Man-Onko. There is a term for what you just said. It's called COMPASSION. It's the single driving force for all Monks in our Order.

Novice Man-Onko: But, what good is compassion? If Master Neled is right, being compassionate won't matter a hill of beans.

Monk Pico-Laton: My next question: What if the Upheavals are inevitable, but the SEVERITY of them is not? What if, instead of all humans on Earth dying, only HALF of them do so? Or even less than half? Would you work to stop the complete destruction of the human race?

Novice Man-Onko: Yes! Okay! I get it! The Centers aren't about just making the monks rich and comfortable – you could do that pretty easy, with what you've got here. There's a bigger plan going on, some "A" level stuff...

Monk Pico-Laton: Absolutely. And, perhaps you now see why we go to the trouble to collect young people off the streets. Many of the tuition novices come to us "compassion-impaired". They have lost the ability to be concerned for others... even care for themselves.

We have found that living on the streets can awaken compassion. Or completely kill it.

You may have heard the collection teams referring to the collected youth as "M&M's". It's a reference to a candy that was popular in the days candy was manufactured in huge factories. Now, it means "Monks & Monsters". When a collection team goes out, they know they're going to bring back one or the other.

Novice Man-Onko: Probably not so many "Monsters". I know what you mean... I've seen them. People who would kill you just for looking in the wrong direction. I saw a guy cut off a girl's tit, just to see if his knife was sharp.

Monk Pico-Laton: That's one kind of monster – they are easy to spot, and easy to avoid. We stay far away from them – the Collectors never bring them in - although we do take a few that are borderline. I think you know what I mean...

Novice Man-Onko: Yeah... in my own Pod.

But, there's another kind of "monster". The other kind are the ones that smile, or cry, or laugh on cue. They always say the right thing, do the right thing... while plotting how to "win", how to "get over".

Tell me: When Novice Ramskar tried to get you to score some drugs for him, why didn't you go along?

Novice Man-Onko: WHAT? How did you know about that?

Monk Pico-Laton: Remember what I told you in your first interview? Just assume that we know everything... Answer me – why didn't you go along? So many other novices were hooking up with him. Why did you go against the grain?

Novice Man-Onko: I can't really explain it... It just SMELLED BAD.

Monk Pico-Laton: On the other hanDorado: What about that betting ring you set up, betting on the meals served in the cafeteria?

Novice Man-Onko: How did you...

Monk Pico-Laton: [Hand raised]: Please. When are you going to actually believe that we know everything?

Why did you rig it so that some novices knew the right answers in advance?

Novice Man-Onko: So, I'm being questioned about illegal activity WITHIN an illegal activity?

Monk Pico-Laton: Just answer the question.

Novice Man-Onko: [pauses]: Well... It's checking the balance between the garden delivery and the garbage take-away. When the balances...

Monk Pico-Laton: Stop. We know HOW you did it. We want to know WHY you did it – why you told some of the novices the answers in advance?

Novice Man-Onko: Well... They were running behind on their credit balances. They were in danger of losing some privileges, or even getting kicked out. I gave them a little "boost". It didn't cost me nothing...

Monk Pico-Laton: But it did. If you hadn't done that, you would have made MORE credits for yourself. That was a sign of your COMPASSION. A person without compassion would have simply tried to maximize his or her profits.

Novice Man-Onko: You don't care that I broke the rules?

Monk Pico-Laton: We don't care that you break rules – we care WHY you do. Had you kept the credits for yourself, we would have penalized you so many credits, you'd be back to scrubbing toilets. As it is, your "Illegal" scheme accelerated you into being a Monk-Candidate.

Novice Man-Onko: Wow. Just when I think I've got my head around this joint, you throw me another curve!

So... what do I have to do? Sign in blood?

Monk Pico-Laton: Something like that. If you agree, you will leave here, accompanied by two guards. You will speak to no one while you clean out your locker, collect your personal things, and are ushered out the door.

Once out, you will have transport to the Awakening Center in Columbus, Ohio, where you will...

Novice Man-Onko: Wait a minute! I don't want to leave here! Some of these novices are my friends! What about my pod-mates?...

Monk Pico-Laton: One way or another, this is the end of Gopher Pod. This must be done. There simply cannot be "friendships" between novices and monks. The easiest way to break them is to transfer you. ALL Monk-Candidates get transferred out. No exceptions. I don't have enough time to explain the wisdom of this. All of you are travelling on different trajectories, and trying to maintain old friendships will simply slow you down.

Novice Man-Onko: I'll never see Dorado, Krista-lin and Victory again?

Monk Pico-Laton: Not for at least a year. If they decide to take the steps toward monk-hood, they will be sent to different Centers. If they stay at this Center, you'll see them when you return. If they go Outside... you'll probably never see them again.

Novice Man-Onko: But, why the criminal treatment? The guards and... stuff.

Monk Pico-Laton: We will plant the rumor that you were expelled for your gambling scheme. Novices who are expelled aren't looked for anymore. If and when you come back, anyone still a novice won't recognize you, not even by your name.

Novice Man-Onko: "IF" I come back?

Monk Pico-Laton: Yes. You will spend at least ten years on the road. Think of this as your high school and beginning of college education.

After six months in Ohio, you will spend at least six months each in other Centers, in different regions. You will continue that rotation for up to ten years.

Then, you can either settle down in one place, or keep up the six-month rotation until you visit all of the Centers. That would take you about 30 years – probably a lot longer, at the rate we are growing. Or, you can settle on one Center... including, if you want, this one.

Novice Man-Onko: So, I'm out of here for ten years... sounds like forever. What else?

Monk Pico-Laton: One of those tours will be to a Center overseas...

Novice Man-Onko: Overseas!?! You've got to be kidding... How do I get over there? There's no more planes flying...

Monk Pico-Laton: You'll see... like I said, we still have a few surprises up our sleeves.

In that ten-year time frame, you will be given a chance to see the "big picture" game plan – how we are trying to mitigate the Upheavals... what the next big steps for humanity are.

Novice Man-Onko: Wait a minute... let's go back. A month or so ago, Novice Ramskar was escorted out... did HE become an Apprentice?

Monk Pico-Laton: [pauses]: No, that was an old-fashioned expulsion.

Novice Man-Onko: Wow... expulsion for drugs...

Monk Pico-Laton: No, the drug scheme was the least of his crimes against the Center. He was plotting murder...

Novice Man-Onko: Wow! How could he pull that off in here? Who was he going to kill?

Monk Pico-Laton: He wasn't going to kill anyone. He was arranging a series of "accidents". Three people... one of them being YOU.

Novice Man-Onko: ME? You're kidding me! Why me? I thought I got along with him!

Monk Pico-Laton: Now you see what I mean by a "quiet monster". He determined that you were popular and were on a fast track to become a monk. He wanted that for himself... without ever understanding WHY he wanted it.

Novice Man-Onko: Wow... so, you booted him out.

Monk Pico-Laton: No, we had him killed.

Novice Man-Onko: WHAT?? Now you really ARE shitting me!

Monk Pico-Laton: No "shit", to borrow your phrase for a moment. It's a practice we call "Extreme Expulsion". We stripped him of his credits, everything he possessed, and dropped him off in Old Town wearing only a pair of shorts. How long do you think he lasted?

Novice Man-Onko: Damn. Without a gun or at least a knife, he wouldn't last 5 minutes in Old Town.

Monk Pico-Laton: Actually, he lasted 26 hours, which we attribute to his ability to run fast and talk faster. But, at some point, he had to go to sleep...

We had a sub-dermal tracker on him. At the 26-hour mark, the tracker melted. We assume he was killed, roasted and eaten. His only value in that world was the protein in his well-fed body.

Novice Man-Onko: Double damn...

Monk Pico-Laton: I'm not telling you this to shock you or scare you. I'm telling you this to let you know that these are the kinds of decisions that monks have to make, day in and day out. WE don't kill people – but we do set up the circumstances where others can do so for us.

And... there are a lot of us here that don't approve of "Extreme Expulsion", even think it's in violation of our prime values. Many Centers don't do it. And, I think some Centers do it too much...

Novice Man-Onko: But... what about "inclusivity"? Isn't it a bit harsh to have someone EATEN because he was plotting against me? I mean, a fine and upstanding person like me deserves to be protected, but couldn't....

Monk Pico-Laton: Stow it! We didn't do an Extreme Expulsion for what he planned to do – we did that for what he DID. He was responsible for Novice April's death.

Novice Man-Onko: Triple damn. You guys told us that was an accident.

Monk Pico-Laton: It was. We didn't lie to you. Just as we said, the rope broke when she was washing windows. But, the rope was CUT... and not by Ramskar, but by one of his flunkies. His hands were "clean". We knew he was plotting something, but we weren't fast enough to save April.

By the way: He never thought we would go through with it. The entire time we were interrogating him and stripping him, he acted like all this would breeze over. He thought we would turn him over to what's left of the civilian authority. He kept talking about "a nice warm prison cell". He would have had a prison organized and under his control within a year -- guards and all...

Novice Man-Onko: Wait a minute... you guys are always telling us that you "know everything". How come you didn't know Ramskar was going off the rails?

Monk Pico-Laton: [pauses] I'm not quite ready to tell you how we "know everything". We knew Ramskar was a problem, but couldn't see how deep it was, or where it manifested itself. While we are adept at "seeing", he was adept at "hiding". A real natural. We didn't see how adept he was until after April was killed.

Novice Man-Onko: Wow. [pauses] So... how many people do you have eaten every year?

Monk Pico-Laton: Please don't put it like that. Not many face Extreme Expulsion. Most are not novices, but are people trying to breach our perimeter.

Novice Man-Onko: Like the folks that beat you up a while ago? They kick the crap out of you, and wind up as someone's pot roast?

Monk Pico-Laton: Ignoring the way you put that... There are 3 kinds of people who try to climb the wall. The good-hearted but desperate – those receive "Simple Expulsion". We drop them off near a farm that sometimes takes in people – miles away from here. If they have weapons, we confiscate them. Not as good as being in a Center, but better than being Outside.

The aggressive ones, like last night – they receive "Serious Expulsion". We'll confiscate everything, especially their weapons, leave them clothing and enough food and water to last 24 hours, then drop them within 2-5 miles of an Old Town – in another city. They help us put the word out that if you try to steal from us, you will LOSE.

Then, there are the folks like the federal agents who plan to attack us in a week or two. They will come armed to the gills, with orders to shoot to kill. If they don't kill anyone, we will schedule them all for mind-wiping. Or, sometimes we let their agencies buy them back. Sometimes, we sell them back after mind-wiping! The Feds get real burnt up about THAT.

If they kill one of us – they'll get Old Town, Ground Zero. Extreme Expulsion.

Novice Man-Onko: If I were the feds, I'd stake out a troop transport in Old Town to pick them up...

Monk Pico-Laton: "Old Town" is a metaphor. There's any of a dozen different places in a hundred different cities where people walk in but don't walk out. And, we've got a lot of cities to choose from.

But, let's get back on track. In order to be a Monk-Candidate, you need two Sponsors. One sponsor here, at your Home Center, and another sponsor, in the Columbus Center, or wherever you wind up. Once you arrive there, you will have two weeks to find a sponsor... or they toss you back here or further forward. This is true at each of the Centers – find a sponsor or move on.

Novice Man-Onko: What about here? Will you be my Sponsor here?

Monk Pico-Laton: [rising]: Monk-Candidate Man-Onko, I would be honored to be your Sponsor!

Novice Man-Onko: Cool! Last question: When do I get a cute little hat like yours?

Monk Pico-Laton: [sitting]: Monk-Candidate Man-Onko, I think you should leave, before I come to my senses and change my mind!

Novice Man-Onko: Cool... just so long as changing your mind it doesn't involve me getting eaten...

Monk Pico-Laton: [laughing]: Get out!

[end of transcript]

[AFTERNOTE: Monk-Candidate Man-Onko left the Denver Center that same day.]

Part Two: The Apprentice

Year One

Compassion is not something one person has for another, but rather something that arises when one begins to see all others as ones own self. As real compassion develops within, the sense of 'other' begins to lessen.

Amma

News Article: National Guard Cooperates with Awakening Centers

As events continue to spiral out of control in many areas, National Guard units in 4 states have announced that they are actively cooperating with the Awakening Centers in their areas.

Commander Bradley Factor was upbeat about working with the Awakening Centers. "As our resources are stretched thin, it makes sense for us to make cooperative agreements with those organizations that have a good reputation and a good track record of helping people."

"Some of the Awakening Centers have gotten a bad rap. We've studied them pretty carefully. They are not religious organizations, so we don't have a "church and state" separation problem. And, they offer to help everyone – very few strings attached. We sit down with them and make agreements, so that no one is left out of their assistance.

Others in the National Guard operation paint a slightly different picture. Said Lt. Helen Bean, charged with the logistics of getting aid to people: "There are no 'cooperative agreements'. We just find the Centers, then give them everything they ask for- food to flashlights. It's either that, or have this stuff rot in our warehouses. We have no ability to get this material out to people. We're giving them everything they want."

Center Director Bright Horizon: "That's not quite true. They give us everything they've GOT- which isn't much. Not enough food to help many people. Generators, but no fuel to run them. Guns, ammo, Kevlar vests, armored vehicles, even mini guns - all of which we refuse. Not much of a shopping list ..."

When asked if there is any conflict in having the National Guard assist their Center, Director Bright Horizon was dismissive. "Assist US? Are you kidding? We won't eat that food! We actually put warning labels on it before we give it to others! Yes, eating crap is better than starving... but just barely."

"They're not helping our Center. They're helping the people on the Outside. They're USING us... And we're happy to help!

Pinch Me

File No:		File Name:	Pinch Me
Location:	Denver	Parties:	The Franklin Family
Monk/ Master Supervising:	Monk Pico-Laton, assisted by Apprentice Man-Onko		

Name:		Pgs:	Date:	Vol:	
Type of Transcript:	Mechanical xxx				
	Organic				

Preface by North American Archive Committee:

Even before the Upheavals were in full swing, getting into an Awakening Center was every struggling family's dream.

However, it was vitally important to bring in the family... not their behavior...

This text is being provided in a rough draft format. Communication Access Realtime Translation (CART) facilitates communication accessibility and may not be a totally verbatim record of the proceedings. Let your coordinator know if you would prefer a more verbatim option.

[start of transcript]

[Intake interview with mother (Martha), father (Frank) and three children. Intake conducted by Monk Pico-Laton, assisted by Novice Man-Onko.]

Martha: (crying) What did we do to deserve all this?
Pico-Laton: Wish we could help everyone. We have to be selective - we don't want to bring in bad influences.
Frank: Not us! We're gonna be model citizens! And we'll make sure these brats behave...
Pico-Laton: We'll get to that in a moment. Right now, we need to discuss your living arrangements...

Martha: Did you know we were all sleepin' in a car? The car wouldn't even run anymore. We had no gas for it. All of us in a car. But, better there than under a bridge, or one of those FEMA death camps...

Pico-Laton: Yes, that's changing now.

Martha: You know, we got kicked out of the FEMA camp in Kansas City? Said we maxed out our time there. But, we wouldn't go to the FEMA regional center... we heard some really bad...

Pico-Laton: Let me explain how this is going to work...

Martha: And these girls! All cooped up in that car all the time! It's just...
Pico-Laton: PLEASE! Let's put all that behind us! I'm trying to find out what kind of housing you need now.

Martha: Oh, I'm so sorry, going on like this! I'm just so... HAPPY! This is like Christmas and birthday all rolled into one! You know, these girls have never had a proper Christmas. We try to figure out what day...

Pico-Laton: Excuse me! Will you and your husband both be working?

Martha: Sorry! Yes, both of us are hard workers, and both of us will do our fair share, and then some! We'll...

Pico-Laton: And! What about your children? Are they going to work, also?

Martha: Well... yes, if there's something you think they can do, and it's not too hard. The young one's...

Pico-Laton: The five-year-old is too young for formal work. The nine and fifteen year olds can work with you, or can work on their own, or can go to school...

Martha: Oh, we'd love it if they could go to school, but it might be a while before we could afford to send them...

Pico-Laton: We pay them to go to school...

Martha: Oh, pinch me! You've got to be kidding! This place is a dream!

Pico-Laton: There's a pretty complicated formula for how young ones can work and go to school. And school is different from what they had in the past.

(pause)

You see those young ones over there? The ones with those aluminum rods? They are learning how to bend and cut those strips. They're making casings for windows. Last session, they smelted the metal to make the rods. Next session, they'll learn how to fit the windows into that four story building those students over there are building...

Frank: They're working? It just looks like a free for all in a mud pit! They get paid for mud wrestling?

Pico-Laton: Do you know anything about cob construction?

Frank: Cob what?

Pico-Laton: It's a construction method. And they're the experts.

Martha: Experts? They just look like a bunch of kids, having fun!

Pico-Laton: Who said that working and learning can't be fun, also?

Three months from now, there'll be a four story building right there, ready for aluminum - casing windows - and in the winter, they learn the math and physics for all that they're doing now...

Frank: You can't teach physics to a seven-year-old!

Pico-Laton: Of course we can. Mainly because we believe we can. But, let's get back to getting you housing. With both adults working, and all three children doing work-study, I suggest you start out with two bedrooms. One for adults, one for children...

Martha: That's fine...

Pico-Laton: ...Then you can trade up to a larger apartment later, when your account balance is built up...

Martha: Oh, that sounds like heaven...

Pico-Laton: And, once you've built up your account, you can think about building your own home...

Martha: No! Oh God! Pinch me, pinch me...

Frank: It's alright, honey...

Martha: It's just been so hard those years...

Pico-Laton: Well, there are some requirements and rules...

Frank: Like what? Do we have to join your religion or something?

Pico-Laton: (laughing) First, there isn't a religion here! There are a number of "interest groups," and you can join any or all of them. Or none of them.... There are a number of "Christian interest groups" meeting on Sunday mornings, for example...

Martha: What's an "interest group"?

Pico-Laton: The Christian interest groups meet on Sundays, the Muslim interest groups meet on Fridays, the Jews and Buddhists meet on Saturdays... And the Atheist interest groups meet whenever they feel like!

Martha: Do we have to join one?

Pico-Laton: Absolutely not. And, you can join as many as you've got time for.

But, let's get to the rules for staying here. Our rules are simple, yet strict. Violation is cause for dismissal:

The five no's:
1) No violence, no weapons, no coercion. This applies to all beings, not just humans.
2) No stealing.

3) No drunkenness or inebriation to the point you cannot positively function in the community. And that's got a catch to it...

4) No undeclared intimate relationships.

5) Everyone must be an asset to the community. At a minimum, that means keeping a positive account balance.

Frank: Piece of cake! I was worried for a second...

Pico-Laton: Frank, it's the third rule I want to talk with you about...

Frank: Hey, no problem, all of them sound...

Pico-Laton: Frank, there IS a problem. When we were doing your medical exams, we detected your blood alcohol level was significantly elevated...

Martha: Oh Frank! You promised!

Frank: Hey, I was nervous coming here! I just had one little drink...

Pico-Laton: The medical report indicated that you drink heavily, and every day...

Martha: Frank! Not now! Not while we're so close!!

Frank: Hey, what's the problem?! It's not like I can get anything in this place, is there?

Pico-Laton: Frank... We've already found the three containers of moonshine you had hidden in your luggage...

Martha: FRANK!!

Pico-Laton: ... we poured it out.

Frank: NO!!

Pico-Laton: And we are charging you a toxic waste disposal charge.

Martha: You promised, you promised, you promised...

Frank: OK, I'll clean up my act. I'll go straight...

Pico-Laton: Frankly, we doubt it. Some on the committee want to turn you all down flat... You've already violated Rule Three.

Martha: (crying)

Pico-Laton: Instead, we are offering you a provisional entry. You will undergo a daily screening for alcohol...

Frank: That's OK. That's fair...

Pico-Laton: We already know that you know how to defeat a breathalyzer. It will be daily blood tests...

Frank: Wait! That's not fair!

Martha: You have no intention of changing, do you?

Frank: How long for the daily tests?

Pico-Laton: Six months.

Frank: God, six months... Alright...

Pico-Laton: Then periodic tests of breath, blood and/or urine.

Frank: For how long?

Pico-Laton: Forever.

Frank: What?

Pico-Laton: Frank, this is one of those life defining moments. I hope you can see that.

Martha, our conditional offer of admittance is for YOU, not for Frank. You and your girls.

Martha: Frank, I love you, but I love these girls more. I love ME more. I ain't gonna let your demon ruin our chance of happiness. You broke every promise you ever made to me. You love me, but you love that bottle MORE. So, it's either me and the girls or you, the bottle and that goddamn car.

Frank: You're right, baby. I've been wrong, an asshole. But, I swear, I'm straightening up as of right now. No more booze! My hand to God...

Pico-Laton: Oh, spare us! That's just more of the alcohol talking. From here, you're going only one of two places. Either into an isolation tank for four days, where we see what fresh air, good food and sunshine do to you... or out the front gate.

Martha, if Frank survives his time in the isolation tank, he'll be sent to a men's dormitory for an indefinite period – at least six months. Only after he convinces us that he's cured will he be admitted and allowed to live with you.

If you object to this, you'll all be sent back outside the gate.

Martha: We accept. I accept for my girls...

Frank: Don't I get a chance to appeal, to talk to someone else...

Pico-Laton: This is the end of that line. You'll get up and follow me to the isolation room, or you'll follow those two young men to the front gate.

Frank: Wait! I'm sick! I need treatment! You can't just...

Pico-Laton: We can and we will. There are billions of people out there, and we can only help a few. There are lots of good, deserving people who are going to die without our assistance. We have offered to help your family. You? You're going to prove that you'll take our help and not be a constant drain on our resources. It's not up to us, it's up to YOU.

[end of transcript]

[After four days in isolation, Frank elected to join the community on a provisional level, and was placed in a men's dormitory. A hard worker, Frank paid for his isolation and treatment, and earned enough credits to start an intensive alcohol recovery program, including spiritual plant medicines and deep counseling.

Six months after their conditional admission, Martha and Frank were reunited. The family has been a credit to the Center.]

Community Center Opening

File No:		File Name:	Community Center Opening
Location:	Denton, TX	Parties:	Master Xavier Monk-Candidate Man-Onko Mayor and city officials
Monk/ Master Supervising:	Xavier, Master & Abbot		Remarks made at the opening of the Community Center in Denton Texas.

Name:		Pgs:		Date:		Vol:	
Type of Transcript:	Mechanical XXX						
	Organic						

Preface by North American Archive Committee:

Some locations resisted the Awakening Centers at every step (with economic sanctions, civil procedures and even violence).

Others welcomed the new thinking, the changes in resource utilization, and the visionary focus that the Centers provide.

Confrontation was possible. So was cooperation and partnership...

This text is being provided in a rough draft format. Communication Access Realtime Translation (CART) facilitates communication accessibility and may not be a totally verbatim record of the proceedings. Let your coordinator know if you would prefer a more verbatim option.

[start of transcript]

Xavier: Thank you Mr. Mayor. We don't often get invited to this kind of public speaking. In the interest of time, and in the interest of the children being able to get to those hotdogs and ice cream we've provided, I'll keep my remarks short!

You thanked us for our contribution in the creation of this new community. There is no need to do that. We're just doing our job.

Mr. Mayor, you said something in your remarks that I would like to both contradict and clarify. You said in your introduction that we were giving the residents of this community "new hope". In fact, you proposed that as a name for this community. We rejected that, and we reject the idea that we are providing anyone with "hope".

A person with hope is looking at their future, not their present. They're striving for something that they don't have, rather than realizing what they do. A person with "hope" focuses on themselves as an individual, rather than looking at the reality of their total circumstances.

I am anticipating that people living in this new community will be living "hope free". That they and their neighbors can live together on a day-to-day basis, each day is good for them, and leads to a more balanced, more sustainable and a richer spiritual experience in their future.

As we all know, a number of people in the city balked at the idea of the Awareness Center being involved in this community development project. Many people are afraid of us. Many are fearful that we are some kind of religious cult. Many don't know our intentions – and many know them, yet don't believe us.

We intend from this kind of partnership to dispel a lot of rumors and myth. Our intentions are simple and in some ways selfish. The more people who are living a decent and sustainable life on the Outside will spend less time and effort trying to climb over our walls. Helping them is helping us.

I know that occasions like this are supposed to be all happy talk, but that is not our style. This project simply could not have been done without our Awareness Center. I hope you realize that. The city got our labor, resources, and organizational methodology to put together a living and sustainable community for 300 people.

I want to introduce you to our young Monk-Candidate Man-Onko. Just a few years ago, he lived on the streets, eating garbage and worse, living the "American Nightmare". Now he is a vital part of a thriving community.

We received a lot of criticism for the style and configuration of these houses. People objected to their size, saying they were too small. They are not small – they are TINY. But, as you can see in the smiling faces surrounding us, "tiny is beautiful".

People said that small wasn't "American". They deeply objected to our response: "you are correct". It is the idea of "Americanism" as being wasteful, Individualistic, extravagant, inappropriate, nonsustainable and BIG that got us in these Upheavals in the first place. Yes, we consciously reject all of that.

If you want to see the future of that America, just look over on Front Street, at those "luxury" condos that were never finished, but sit there like a sore thumb.

People also objected to how our tiny houses are configured. No streets. No spaces for cars. Set so the houses face a central fire pit. Set off in the woods. None of this looks like a modern urban environment. And it's not! It's an experiment, a living laboratory, a new way of living. We are trying to encourage, even force people to interact with each other, to build a meaningful community – one where people actually NEED each other.

And, it truly is an experiment. We built all of the houses on pads, so that we can pick them up and reconfigure them, as we work to see the best arrangement for the people AND all of the other beings living in that space.

What we got out of this partnership was the only thing that the city has left to offer – land. We built this current Community Center on one of the city's former municipal golf courses. To pay for our time, labor, resources and expertise, we received the OTHER municipal golf course. We will be digging that up and planting vegetables... 300 people need food to eat!

For many, the repurposing of these golf courses represents a failure, a sadness. We see the exact opposite: that these former symbols of wasteful, extravagant luxury for a few can be brought to serve people, to serve all other beings, and the healing of the Earth Herself. And that is something for which all of us can be proud!

[Applause]

[end of transcript]

The Airport Memo

Much of the information flowing into the Centers came from Awakening Agents still embedded in the dying system. This memo is an example...

MEMORANDUM

FROM: The Federal Aviation Administration, in cooperation with:

      The Department of Homeland Security

      The Transportation Safety Administration

      The Federal Bureau of Investigation

      The Department of State

FOR IMMEDIATE RELEASE:

NEW PROCEDURES TO PROTECT THE NATION'S AIRPORTS

Due to shifts in demand and increased security concerns, the FAA, in cooperation with the above-referenced agencies, hereby announces new security and operating measures for the nation's airports. Our goal is to keep America flying and safe.

Due to the recent attacks on airports in Chicago, New York and Los Angeles, along with civil unrest near airports in over 20 additional cities, the FAA takes the following measures to insure the safety of the flying public.

We ask the public to be patient with these changes. These are the minimal restrictions necessary to insure the health and safety of the flying public.

1.   All airports will experience restricted days and hours of operation:

a.   Airports landing flights of international origin will be open only on odd-numbered days. Those landings will take place only after sunset.

b.   Airports without international flights (domestic only) will be open at the discretion of the airport manager.

2.   Please be advised that these changes are NOT due to the recent bankruptcy proceedings of the major airlines. Despite their losses in the recent terrorist attacks, the nation's airlines remain flying. It is anticipated that normal scheduling will resume shortly.

3.   Due to enhanced security procedures, passengers at all airports will be screened in secure, off-airport locations established by the Department of Homeland Security, then transported to the airport in secure vehicles supplied by the DHS.

4.   Unauthorized vehicles will NOT be allowed to approach airport property, under any circumstances! Any vehicle approaching an airport will be stopped and seized, and its occupants placed under arrest. Any vehicle exhibiting a profile similar to the recent terrorist bombings (older vehicles with a single occupant) will be stopped and/or destroyed at a distance.

5.   In an administrative matter, passengers to certain so-called "destination" countries will no longer be able to purchase one-way tickets to those countries. In recent days, flights returning from New Zealand, South Africa, the European Union, Ecuador, Costa Rica, Mexico

(certain areas) and Canada have been returning nearly empty. This negatively affects the financial picture of the US airlines, and fuels unwarranted speculation that Americans are abandoning their country. Nothing could be further from the truth. As a measure of increased financial security, only round-trip flights will be booked to the above-named destination countries.

6. None of the above measures pertains to charter flights. Registered charter flights can take off and land on any day, for any destination.

With these temporary safety measures, we believe that our skies will be safer than ever, and we will return to normal operations as quickly as possible.

With Respect,

William Gunderson, Chairman

Federal Aviation Administration

[AFTERNOTE: These measures did not stem the tide of people attempting to escape America... nor the people attacking them for doing so.

What was eventually billed as "The Great Escape" turned into short-lived class warfare in the cities, as wealthy people who had purchased properties in foreign countries found that they could not get to them. Routes to the airports of America were blocked by tens of thousands of the poor, trying to hold hostage those who had the means and opportunity to escape.

In many cities, the routes to the airports were forced open when security forces opened fire on the blockaders. In some cities, the blockaders fired back.

Disruption spread, as protestors entered the airports and did battle with the TSA screeners, preventing flights from departing.

The remote screening facilities proved even more vulnerable to attack, resulting in thousands of deaths and screening locations closing almost as fast as they were opened.

During "The Great Escape", the most prevalent form of identity theft was the theft and re-sale of "hot" boarding passes.

Eight months after the date of this announcement, commercial passenger aviation in America ceased to exist. Airports were open only to charter flights (usually one way) cargo flights and "pillow" flights to and from Awakening Centers.]

Incident Report – Category 3 Security Breach

File No:		File Name:	Incident Report – Category 3 Security Breach at Columbus Awakening Center
Location:	Columbus (OH) Awakening Center	Parties:	
Monk/ Master Supervising:			

Name:		Pgs:		Date:		Vol:	
Type of Transcript:	Mechanical						
	Organic						

Preface by the North American Centers Archive Committee:

No one is perfect. Here is the most infamous instance where both the Awakening Center and the Culture Council completely mis-read the local situation. In hindsight, the reasons for the mis-reading were understandable. The consequences of this mis-reading were grave.

This text is being provided in a rough draft format. Communication Access Realtime Translation (CART) facilitates communication accessibility and may not be a totally verbatim record of the proceedings. Let your coordinator know if you would prefer a more verbatim option.

FR: **COUNCIL SECURITY**
TO: **ALL SECURITY DIRECTORS, ALL CENTERS**
RE: **Incident report – Category 3 Security Breach at Columbus Ohio Awakening Center**

All Centers should be on alert for military – level incidents. High priority.

Background: As you know, all of the Awakening Centers have experienced security incidents. These have fallen into one of two different types:

Category 1. Security parameters have been breached by people who are hungry and desperate.

Category 2. More sophisticated (and violent) breaches have taken place by semi-organized paramilitary groups, bent on looting and/or destruction. Also included in Category 2 are reconnaissance missions by organized governmental groups, whether armed or unarmed.

Because of the effectiveness of our passive defensive perimeters, and the watchfulness of the monks in forecasting incursions, as well as the monks who are on guard duty, these incidents have been relatively minor and easily repulsed.

[Note: it is acknowledged that there is continued dissent to the Council's policy that all people involved in Category 2 attempts to breach the parameters of the Centers be stripped of all of their belongings (especially weapons) and relocated. It is noted that there are many within the Centers that believe that this policy is not compassionate, and even unusually cruel, especially in the cold latitudes.

[After deep debate, the majority of the Council remains adamant that, given the ongoing conditions of the Upheavals, the only way, the most compassionate way, to help the majority of people is to maintain the integrity of the Centers. That means that the word must spread that attacking or invading the Centers is a losing proposition. The Centers cannot be maintained in the presence of ongoing, military-style attacks. Expulsion remains a viable recourse for dissuading security breaches.

[This policy is also based on our "no free ride" doctrine - that those who create the necessity for security should be the ones who pay for it. That this policy is successful is evidenced by the dramatic fall off of perimeter breaches Categories 1 and 2.]

The Columbus incident introduces a new category of attack: **Category 3.**
Organized, professional attempt at breaching.

The incident:

At 2:32 AM, monks on security duty along the perimeter noticed an incursion. (This incursion was NOT predicted by the forecasting teams.) After setting the alarm, they went to investigate. They were captured by the invaders. After capture, and according to plan, they discharged their pheromonal defense grenades – and put everyone to sleep, including themselves. The follow-up team secured the area.

Upon examination, it was determined that these were no ordinary invaders. Despite their attempt to look like typical internal refugees (dirty and ripped clothing, and dirt smeared on their faces and hands,) these invaders were well fed, well muscled, and exhibited military discipline in the attack. They carried no identification. They all wore surgical gloves - they intended to leave no fingerprints.

Columbus Center Security planned to hold these invaders for screening and possible ransom to the government agency responsible for the attack. It would have been instructive to see who showed up for them.

However, these plans were thwarted when a SECOND attack was mounted, and the captured invaders were rescued by their companions. During this rescue mission, three monks were injured by the rescuers, one seriously.

The sophisticated nature of the attack, along with the fact there was a pre-organized rescue operation, leads the Council to believe that this will be the first in a series of attacks. Therefore, we issue this warning to all North American Awakening Centers.

Of further concern is that the Columbus Future Forecasting Group (FFG) did not see/predict either the sophisticated incursion nor the rescue operation. Because of the nature of the events, the attack should have been easily predictable by FFG.

The Council strongly recommends that Columbus FFG review its procedures for developing forecasts, increase the training of the monks and masters making their forecasts, and make any other changes necessary to improve the accuracy and reliability of their forecasting methods.

The Council contacted all appropriate governmental and paramilitary organizations, to find out who initiated the attack. We were unable to do so. All government agencies that retain the ability and interest to mount such an attack have denied knowledge or involvement. We will continue to probe this matter.

Centers should be extra vigilant in the maintenance of security. Council forecasters predict a 75% probability that the government will attempt another Category 3 incursion. This one is likely to be coordinated, with at least three Centers being targeted, in geographically distant locations. Centers should be prepared and trained to nonviolently subdue and repel waves of attackers, including would-be rescue missions.

Centers are being asked to step up security, with new security procedures that will be coming to you by tight-beams and word-of-mouth couriers.

[AFTERNOTE: There were no subsequent attacks, at least, not of this nature. There were no government agencies responsible. This was the first known example of the Culture Council completely misreading both the nature and the source of the attack.

It would take another confrontation, in a completely different realm, before the Culture Council perceived the true nature and the near-fatal threat posed by its invisible adversary.]

File No:		File Name:	Exit Interview – No Beggars
Location:	Tampa Bay/ Clearwater Awakening Center	Parties:	Jason Wright, temporary guest Monk-Candidate Man-Onko
Monk/ Master Supervising:	Monk Karriem		

Exit Interview -- No Beggars

Name:		Pgs:	Date:	Vol:	
Type of Transcript:	Mechanical xxx				
	Organic				

Preface by the North American Centers Archive Committee:

In a world where "money" had replaced and corrupted all other social values, it was challenging (and sometimes impossible) to get people to understand what it means to contribute to society.

[start of transcript]

Monk Karriem: This room has two exits. One of them leads back to the Center. The other leads out.

Wright: What? You're kicking me OUT?

Monk Karriem: No, you're kicking yourself out. You don't have enough credits to stay, and you won't work.

Wright: I will so work! I've done some work around here! I just won't live by your bullshit rules and regulations!

Monk Karriem: Well, that amounts to about the same thing. You can't do whatever you feel like doing, whenever you feel like doing it. You have to work according to a SCHEDULE...

Wright: Yeah? Well, Fuck the schedule! This is about being FREE, not a bunch of rules and schedules! I see how you treat those poor novices! It's like they're slaves. This is just like back on the Outside!

Monk Karriem: No it isn't. You know that isn't true, you know what those young ones would face Outside. You know what YOU are facing outside that door. Which is why you're trying to stay here for so long on a free ride.

If being "free" is so important, you are welcome to live that way ... on the other side of that door.

We are one of the lucky Centers. We don't have thousands of people camped out on our doorstep, trying to get in. We have the luxury of bringing in people as "Temporary Guests". But, you've abused the privilege...

We have a number of different types of people here in the Center. Monks and masters, who are residents here. Students of various levels, from Novices to Interns. And several different categories of "Guests"... from people visiting from other Centers, to people who pay to become more or less permanent "residents".

The Centers are based on a different economic construct. You either pay or work. No exceptions. If you don't...

Wright: What do you mean no exceptions? There are plenty of people around here who haven't lifted a finger!

Monk Karriem: Yes, that's true. They are not novices or monks. They are GUESTS, who have paid handsomely, in money or resources, to reside here. You yourself entered here as a Guest, paid for a few days, and now want to live here forever, with someone else paying for your room and board. That won't happen.

Wright: I don't see why I can't stay! You folks are RICH! If people knew how much food you've got stored here, they'd be breaking down the doors! You could feed an army for years! One more mouth won't matter!

Monk Karriem: Sit down and stop screaming. Screaming won't get you any closer to being inside.

I know it seems to you that we are sitting on mountains of food. But that's not the case. We have calculated how much food, energy and water it will take to support our Center, for the years when we predict that there will be no food coming through that gate. And, we have an obligation to GROW, to create 2 to 4 new Centers in the near term.

Right now, we don't have enough. We are buying up all of the storable food we can get our hands on. And, we're buying or renting all of the arable land we can get.

But that's besides the case. The new SYSTEM just can't work with dead weight. And that's what you are – dead weight. You say that you worked, but you show up to a work crew, work half heartedly, then wander off, leaving your work to others. The credits that you think that you earned have gone to compensate the crews that had to pick up your slack.

You would work on a crew for one day, then just not show up the next. We don't operate like that...

Wright: I'm a free spirit! I wake up, and I feel like writing, or composing music, or just sitting by the river, waiting for inspiration! I can't be tied to a work schedule! And, I see PLENTY of people doing that – sitting by the river, doing nothing!

Monk Karriem: Every person sitting by the river has paid for that privilege in some way. They paid money, or they have a full account from working and have taken some days off, or they have someone who is sponsoring them - working so that they don't have to.

You think that you can wander into the cafeteria, eat as much as you want, wander into the pub at night and drink as much as you want, and that some way, something just "balances out". It doesn't work that way.

Wright: The folks at the pub like my music! Maybe they will support me!

Monk Karriem: No one is supported by music, or art, at least not yet. The Upheavals have started, and we don't really know how long they're going to last. The only thing that we know is that things Outside are going to get harder than they are right now, and things inside are going to get tighter. Which is why you're leaving.

Monk-Candidate Man-Onko: It's not about what you FEEL like doing, get that through your thick skull! It's not about YOU at all! It's about what the CENTER needs! It's about saving humanity! Not about what you feel like doing, or not doing! I know you can't understand that, which is why you're going to be using that other door there.

Monk Karriem: Now, Monk-Candidate, please try to refrain...

Wright: You can't kick me out! I LIKE it in here!

Monk Karriem: All your life, you've been able to make other people take care of you. We are not your mother and father. We are not your friends on the outside, who let you eat and sleep because they felt sorry, or guilty, or generous to you.

We are building a new society. One in which every single person, every single CELL in this organism has meaning, has function and has value. This is something that has to...

Wright: Yeah? What about that crazy ass guy, the one who pushes that wagon up and down all day? Are you trying to tell me that HE has meaning and value?

Monk Karriem: (pauses): The "crazy ass guy" has a name. His name is Roy. Roy has a purpose- it's delivering goods from one end of our large Center to the other. His entire life is dedicated to pushing his wagon.

His value to this Center is... immense. If he stopped working, it would take 3 or 4 people to replace him. Right now, he could sit by the river for 5 years, and still have credits in his account.

Wright: Okay, okay I get it. How much is this going to cost? I can probably come up with some money... I'll try to make a few phone calls. How much is this going to cost me?

Monk Karriem: (sighs): You just don't get it...

Monk-Candidate Man-Onko: Any phone calls you will be making will be done from the outside, not from inside the Center. And, if you wish to be readmitted, you can show up and fill out an application, like everyone else.

In order to be readmitted, you will have to deposit at least $1,000. $500 of that is to pay off your existing balance in here and $500 will buy you five days of sitting by the river and "doing nothing".

Wright: WHAT?? Are you out of your fucking mind!?! Where am I supposed to find money like that!?

Monk Karriem: And now you see what five hours of real work is really worth. At some point in time somewhere along the line, SOMEBODY has to put in some real work. You don't realize that, simply because it's never been YOU.

You get assigned a task, then don't do it. Somebody has to register that, monitor you. Someone else has to post the job you didn't do on the jobs board...usually at a premium, in order to get the work done quickly. Someone else has to do the accounting for your lack of work. Instead of working FOR our community, you are taking away from it.

Wright: Okay! Okay! I'll try to work harder. I'll try to put in more regular hours...

Monk Karriem: It doesn't work like that. Right now, no one wants you on their work crew. And, without a crew, you can't work. Crews are paid TOGETHER, not as individuals. And, if you're on their crew, they earn less – in fact, they have to carry you. And no one feels like carrying you anymore.

Wright: What about some of the people I hang out with, like Rory, Atom and Ann? They only work a few hours, then they hang out by the river, or in the pub.

Monk-Candidate Man-Onko: They are VOLUNTEERS. They are fully paid up guests, with money or resources – Rory has paid with money, Atom and Ann have paid by transferring their land to the Center. AND they also work a few hours every day. They don't have to lift a finger... but they do. They don't work because they have to, they do it because they recognize the value of WORK.

Wright: Okay! Okay! I'll talk to a few of the guys and see which crew I can slip on to. We get along well at the pub...

Monk Karriem: No you won't. You're going out THAT door. I have the authority to give you "one last chance", but I've seen nothing in this interview to indicate that you have had a change of heart or attitude.

The guys at the pub LOVE you, because they get well compensated when you don't show up for work. They get to do your work, and do it at a premium. And that's why you have a deficit account here.

I wish it were otherwise, you really are a nice guy. I hope you find a role out there, where your skills at being a "nice guy" may have value.

Wright: Okay, let me go get my things and I'll be on my way...

Monk Karriem: Your things have been collected and assembled. You will find them outside that door and down the corridor. Outside the next-door you will find... Outside. I wish you well.

Wright: Hey! Hold on! Where are you going –

[end of transcript]

[AFTER NOTE: Jason Wright showed up at the Center's Intake Office several times, arguing why he should be given free admission to the Center. After 6 months, he stopped coming.]

A Lesson in Center Justice

File No:		File Name:	A Lesson in Center Justice
Location:	Tampa Bay/ Clearwater Awakening Center	Parties:	All Senior Novices (35)
Monk/ Master Supervising:	Allison, Master assisted by Monk-Candidate Man-Onko		

Name:		Pgs:		Date:		Vol:	
Type of Transcript:	**Mechanical** xxx						
	Organic						

Preface by North American Archive Committee:

What is "law"? How do you maintain "order"? What is "justice"? Who gets it... and who doesn't?

In the Age of Waste, most people didn't think about these concepts. As long as things worked for them, their family and friends, they went along. They were most willing to exchange justice for contentment.

The Awakening Centers were different. How do you create new systems and structures for creating and maintaining law and order... based on a radically different way of seeing the world? How do you maintain order without violence? How can you have law and inclusivity?

This text is being provided in a rough draft format. Communication Access Realtime Translation (CART) facilitates communication accessibility and may not be a totally verbatim record of the proceedings. Let your coordinator know if you would prefer a more verbatim option.

[start of transcript]

Master Allison: Recently, you ended your temporary status. Because of that, you now have a few more freedoms, a few more responsibilities, and we will show you a little more of how this Center operates. We feel that you are ready to start taking your place as full members of the society.

(Double stomp, signifying assent.)

Master Allison: So, we'd like to show you more of our justice system, how we keep things in line around here. However, first of all, what do you know about how the so-called Criminal Justice System operated on the outside?

(Three novices rise: Novice Counter, Novice Betterman and Novice Greenleaf)

Master Allison: Okay, Novice Counter, what can you tell us about the old system?

Novice Counter: Well, it was based on a bunch of really old laws, that came from Europe... mainly England. And those laws were based on people being individuals and people being property.

Novice Betterman: I can't understand how anybody thought that anybody else was property!

Novice Counter: Yeah, me too! But, that's what they tell us here...

Master Allison: What happened when you broke one of these laws based on property?

Novice Greenleaf: They locked you up!

Master Allison: Why did they lock you up? What was supposed to be the purpose of that?

Novice Greenleaf: Well, the person locked up was supposed to hate being locked up so much, they would not commit the crime again.

Master Allison: Is that the only reason? Was there any other purpose in locking the person up?

Novice Betterman: Well... That person isn't on the streets anymore. They can't steal anymore, or beat anybody else up...

Master Allison: But, why lock someone up? Why not whip them, or burn them, or chop off their arms and legs?

Novice Betterman: Yuck! Probably because it was messy!

Master Allison: Was that the only reason for not doing that?

Novice Counter: Well, probably some places did that. But, here people said that doing things like that was "cruel and unusual punishment".

Master Allison: You get points for remembering that...

Novice Betterman: Wait a minute. Some people did get beaten and chopped up, didn't they? Didn't some black people get whipped and beaten and chopped up?

Novice Greenleaf: That was just during slavery...

Novice Betterman: No it wasn't! That was happening all the way until the Upheavals started!

Master Allison: Yes, but a little off of our subject for today. Basically, you are saying that society felt that locking a person up worked better than the other alternatives. Did it?

(All three novices) NO!

Master Allison: So, if it didn't work, what happened?

Novice Greenleaf: Basically, what's happening Outside right now. People do pretty much whatever they want to do, to whoever they want to do it, and there's no one to stop them.

Novice Counter: Yeah, I can tell you, it's pretty bad out there. I've seen some things...

Master Allison: Yes, we've all seen some things. Why do people act like that?

Novice Counter: Some people are crazy, some are trying to survive, and some just don't care.

Master Allison: Yes... I think you just covered it all.

So, what's the answer? If that system doesn't work, what will?

Novice Counter: Well... I know what you want us to say. I know you want us to say that the Center system is the answer. But, I don't really see how it is.

Master Allison: Do you care to explain that?

Novice Counter: Well, I see the monks spending an awful lot of time talking to each other, sometimes arguing a lot. I see a lot of things that could get stolen, but not getting stolen. I see the monks who were arguing one minute meditating the next. And...

Master Allison: And?

Novice Counter: Well... We see a lot of people... disappear. One day they're here, next day... Nobody sees them again or knows where they've gone. And you're not supposed to ask.

Master Allison: What do you think happens to them?

Novice Greenleaf: I think you ice their asses.

Master Allison: By that phrase, I assume you mean that you think we kill them?

(novices are silent)

Master Allison: Well, it may interest you to know that we are not nearly as bloodthirsty as you think we are. We don't kill people. We don't lock them up - not our own citizenship. And, we try not to punish them at all.

Novice Counter: Come on! You don't kill anyone? You don't punish anyone? Do you mean that all the people you kick out of the Center are alive and well?

Master Allison: Let me tell you about how things operate here. There are...

Novice Counter: No, I'd like an answer to my question! Are you saying that all the people you've kicked out of here are still alive?

Master Allison: I will give you an answer, but you may not understand it.

Novice Counter: Go ahead... Try me.

Master: Be careful of your tone... You are speaking to a Master.

Novice Counter: Sorry...

Master Allison: To answer your question: We don't kill ANYONE. If a person commits a violent act here in the Center, we evict them. Send them Outside. And, for those we eject from the center for committing violent acts, those people are dead, generally within 12 hours after being evicted.

(Silence from the novices)

Master Allison: When it is decided that a person can't function in our society, under our rules, they are returned to the world outside. And, we return them to the kind of community that they came from. This is called the "Return to Kind" policy.

I should add that this rarely happens. There are some who are seriously addicted to some aspect of the Outside life -- like, for example, someone addicted to violence, or to various types of control paradigms or chemical addictions. We've got a great track record of fixing these things, and we're developing even better techniques. But we simply can't keep a person in here against their will.

There are people who cannot control their behavior, despite their efforts and our own. People who cannot control being violent. For example, people who cannot control being rapists -- despite our best efforts.

So, a violent person would be returned to a violent community. And, all of you know that a person without contacts or resources in that kind of community doesn't last long.

Novice Counter: Master, Isn't that the same thing as killing them? With respect – isn't having someone else pull the trigger for you the same as pulling the trigger yourself?

Master Allison: This is one of the most difficult and the most contentious aspects of our Center system. There are some here that would agree with you. There are many monks who disagree with this policy, and some who choose to leave this Center because of our policy.

There are some Centers that operate under a different policy. And, they have a whole different set of problems because of that.

If you leave here to return Outside, you leave with a great deal of knowledge of how our system operates. You know aspects of our security system. You know where the food is kept. That kind of knowledge on the outside can be very valuable and very dangerous to us. The Centers that operate without the "return to kind" policy have a lot more external violence aimed at them. A few may not survive.

However, don't look so glum! This is RARELY done. Most of the "disappearances" that you see are people transferring from one Center to another, or transferring from one area or level to another. We don't throw everyone to the wolves.

A few Centers are trying a different approach. What if they could have a person FORGET the security layout of a Center? That way, when they are released, they don't have any inside information to exchange for food, or protection.

Then, one step further: what if they could have the person FORGET the behavior that is causing them to be ejected in the first place? What if they could make a person forget that they are violent, or that they are a compulsive thief? That way, the person would not have to leave the Center in the first place.

Novice Greenleaf: Hey, is this the "mind-wiping" that we've been hearing about?

Master Allison: There is no such thing as "mind-wiping", despite everything you've heard. The technique I'm speaking of is called DCI, for "Direct Consciousness Intervention".

This Center is not researching this development – for us, it sounds too much like "brainwashing". However, we'll see how things develop in the future. It could be that DCI replaces "Return to Kind".

If you really object to the "Return to Kind" policy, you can ask to transfer elsewhere, to another Center. This is why we're telling you this. We will do everything in our power to help you, if you decide to leave over this policy issue.

But, perhaps you'll see that our policy, in the long run, really is beneficial to all.

[end of transcript]

Year Two:

...darkness in the human experience is overcome, not by avoidance, but through shining the light of awareness on it and choosing otherwise.

Dianne Eippler Adams

The Housing Project

File No:		File Name:	The Housing Project
Location:	City Hall, Omaha, NB	Parties:	Mayor, City Council, selected service agencies (public, private and faith-based)
Monk/ Master Supervising:	Abbot Still Light, Master, assisted by Monk-Candidate Man-Onko		Meeting: "Joint Task Force to resolve the Current Housing Crisis"

Name:		Pgs:		Date:		Vol:	
Type of Transcript:	Mechanical xxx						
	Organic						

Preface by North American Archives Committee:

The challenges that some cities found overwhelming and insurmountable were never crises of resources or politics or economics. They were challenges of PERSPECTIVE. The city leaders that were able to shift their perspective fared better than those who could not.

Sometimes, that shift in perspective took a little encouragement...

[start of transcript]

Mayor: I've convened this gathering to try to find our way in our current debacle. Our situation was desperate when FEMA was providing food and shelter. Now that they are reallocating their resources, we are going to have an even bigger challenge. How do we address...

Councilor Miller: "Reallocating"? They're pulling out, pure and simple. Pulling out and leaving us high and dry. They wouldn't even send a rep to this meeting.

Mayor: I'm... I'm going to suggest that we not engage in recrimination. It may relieve some of our anger and frustration, but it's not going to get anyone fed or sheltered.

Councilor Miller: Sorry. But, it really is frustrating...

Mayor: We've got a report that we passed out earlier. Karen Anderson from the Housing Authority may want to take us through that report. Karen?

Housing Director Anderson: Thank you, Mr. Mayor. If you all turn to page 5 of the Executive Summary, you will see...

Still Light: Excuse me. I don't want to interrupt you, but I feel that the Housing Authority's document is not a good starting point for this conversation. Your bottom line is that you need an additional 5,000 units of housing. Our estimate is that the city needs at least 25,000 units of housing.

[General commotion...]

Mayor: Okay, everyone, simmer down!

Councilor Smythe: Mr. Mayor! I think Abbot Still Light's done us a favor by cutting to the chase. My own numbers indicated that the Housing Authority's numbers were low. FEMA was feeding and sheltering somewhere around 8,000 to 10,000 people. There are more people sleeping under the bridges, in the parks and in their cars. So, like Still Light said, the number is a lot higher than 5,000. But, I'd like to hear how she got a figure as high as 25,000.

Still Light: Actually, 25,000 is our low figure. It's possible that the number is twice that.

The Housing Authority has based its figures on the number of people calling them asking for housing, and the number of people who have filled out applications. But, you must consider the number of people who don't apply, because they already know that you don't have any housing. Or, who don't apply because they can't get down to the office, or they no longer have phone or internet service, or because they know it's a useless gesture.

In addition to the Housing Authority's 5,000, and in addition to the ones already mentioned by Councilor Smythe, we add those who are shacking up in abandoned houses, those who are living on others couches, the thousands who line up nightly for the opportunity to sleep on the bug infested cots in the city's "emergency" shelters ... we get to 25,000 fairly easily.

Also, we need to add that much of the housing that is currently "on the market" is substandard and unfit for human habitation. Once you add...

Anderson: Well, we don't add the sub-standard housing, because, frankly, that will make an impossible situation... more impossible.

Still Light: We feel that the only way to address your challenges is to know the extent of your challenge. Otherwise, you'll show up to paint a 50 foot wall with a 15-foot ladder.

Anderson: We can't build 25,000 units of housing!

Still Light: You believe that it's impossible to build 5,000 units. Why do you struggle with the notion of a greater impossibility?

Anderson: NO ONE can build 5,000 units of housing!

Still Light: [pauses]: The person who believes something can't be done should not interrupt the person DOING it.

[To the Mayor]: Mr. Mayor, the Omaha Awakening Center will construct 35,000 housing units, at the rate of 7,000 per year, for the next five years.

[General commotion]

Mayor: Okay, hold it down! Hold it down! Abbot Still Light, we really respect what the Awakening Center has done. We really want your help. But we really need a REALISTIC estimate of what you can do... This is...

Still Light: Impossible? So was landing on the Moon, when President Kennedy set the goal. Just because it's never been done does not mean it CAN'T be done.

Anderson: Where's the money coming from? We've got the lowest per-unit rate for constructing housing. It would take hundreds of millions of dollars to construct the housing. And where's the land coming from? You're talking about a billion-dollar project, maybe more!

Still Light: All that's true... the way you build housing. Our way is different.

The land? You are going to transfer two of your city parks to our control. Standing Bear and Hummel. We're going put the housing there.

Mayor: What? But...

Still Light: Please. Let me finish, then you can tell me why it's impossible.

We've already drawn up plans for ten "neighborhoods" of 3,000 to 4,000 people each. Ranging from studios to multi-family. A modular design... and we will build the modules.

Mayor: I'm sorry, but we just CAN'T turn those parks over to you!

Still Light: You already HAVE turned the parks over... to the thieves, the rapists, the drug lords, the morally corrupted. We all know that the police won't enter those parks, day or night. You have lost all control over them. What we're offering is a chance to get them BACK.

[Pauses]

We will cut down the trees for wood to construct the housing, then...

Mayor: Cut down all the trees??? We can't let that happen!!

Still Light: Please. No one said we would cut down all the trees. Our plans call for harvesting 1/3 of the trees. Selective harvest of some of the trees will actually energize the environment, along with providing the land for building.

You're going to lose more than that in the next few years, with all the squatters you have living in the parks now. They're going to burn down all of your trees, then turn on each other, then starve.

Your choice will be to lose 1/3 of your trees and have housing for thousands, or lose ALL of your trees, have housing for none, and a blighted wasteland where the trees were located.

Now... may I continue?

Mayor: [pauses]: Yes, please continue.

Still Light: Lumber work, digging the foundations, shoring, construction of the modules, maintenance... this will provide good work and right livelihood for those who will live in the housing. It will give us a chance to impart some of our Center discipline into a very chaotic situation.

The first few thousand units will...

Anderson: Excuse me, Still Light, I know we're not supposed to ask questions yet, but you still haven't accounted for how all this gets paid for. Where's the money coming from? Even if you use the potential residents for some labor, you've got the skilled crafts to account for. The labor unions, the electrical unions, the plumbing unions... That's going to eat up the lion's share of your costs. You've got to pay for appraisers, attorney fees, HVAC, insulation, windows, doors. You've got to have inspectors, engineers, the people who approve of the engineers... MORE attorneys.

I'm really afraid you don't know how the world works, my friend. I think your plan is naïve. If I could do without all of those people, I could build a lot of housing for a lot less money.

Still Light: Yes, Karen, you've spotted the exact reason why there are thousands of people living on your streets, with thousands more about to join them.

The source of the money is simple. The city will turn its entire housing budget over to the Awakening Center. Everything. You will fire all of your workers, and turn the funds over to us.

[Silence]

Still Light: I guess that got your attention. We are not naïve. We will hire back those workers who are currently maintaining your existing housing stock. We will hire those who will help us build the new houses. We will hire back people who are actually working, but not those who are paid handsomely for maintaining a useless, dysfunctional bureaucracy.

We will take your workers, but NOT your HUD regulations, City codes and zoning ordinances, union contracts, or anything else from the old consciousness. We will take the people who can "think outside the box". It is that old-style consciousness that prevents you from seeing and solving the problems. We will be free of that.

Councilor Joseph Miller: Wow. I'm stunned. Is what she said even possible?

Anderson: Yes, I think "stunned" is the right word. Please forgive me for saying that you were naïve. Perhaps we are the naïve ones, for either thinking that we could solve the problems with all the shackles and old thinking in place, or for thinking that the problem could not be solved, because we could not see beyond our shackles.

[To Councilor Miller:] Joe, your answer is "yes", you can toss out everything. People will grumble, some may sue you, but really all it takes is political will.

Rev. Page: If this is possible, I can assure you that the faith-based communities will be behind it! We came to this table, ready to offer to build an additional 200 units of housing. But, if we can leverage our involvement and help get to 25,000 units of housing... Heck, we're all in!

Still Light: Excellent! But our offer is for 35,000 units. I hope you won't object to an additional 10,000 units.

Rev. Page: [Laughing]

Still Light: I'll take that to be a "yes"!

But, I see Councilor Cornell is frowning...

Councilor Cornell: Don't get me wrong... I'm going to vote in favor of all this. I don't quite believe you can pull all this off, but we'd be crazy not to try. Even if you fail by 50%, we'll still have almost 20,000 more units of housing.

But I want to understand you. From what you propose, we are supplying the land. We are supplying most of the building components. We are supplying all of the money and the skilled workers.

What exactly are YOU supplying?

Still Light: That's simple, Mr. Cornell. We are supplying the SOLUTION.

In the Awakening Center, we have a name for this project. We call it "Operation Stone Soup".

[end of transcript]

[Afternote: In one way, "Operation Stone Soup" did fail to meet its lofty goals. Instead of 35,000 units of new housing, the partners managed to create "only" 28,000. Instead of 7 years, it took 9 years.

In another way, Operation Stone Soup was a smashing success. Once 100-year-old statutes and codes about what constituted "housing" were relaxed, amended or abandoned, many new developers emerged. Preferring to be called "housing facilitators", this repurposed private sector built an additional 12,000 units of housing, bringing the total to 40,000.

One of the unintended positive consequences of building and populating the new communities was a drastic reduction in behaviors that were classified under the heading of "mental illness". The partners soon recognized that "mental illness" was in reality "societal illness" – the behavioral problems stemmed from marginalized living in a hopeless situation.

The Omaha Stone Soup Solution became a model for other cities in dealing with their housing crises.]

News Article: Awakening Centers Disavow Imaginal Group

Joint Statement by the North American Awakening Centers:

"We agree with the principles, values and vision as they have been articulated by Dr. James Harold Moore and the others of the so-called Imaginal Group. We also agree that the Imaginal Group is currently being uniquely and wrongly targeted by the US government, as the "cause" of conditions that have been festering for decades, sometimes for centuries.

"IG is not the issue -- The Upheavals are. IG has taken themselves out of the equation by disappearing. They have made themselves and their whereabouts irrelevant. We wish them well – wherever they may be located.

"We do not know where they are. We cannot locate them, nor do we care to try. They are not located within any of our Centers. We will gladly and voluntarily open our doors to any UNARMED representatives of the US government who wish to verify the absence of Dr. Moore or any other IG representatives from our premises.

However, we will <u>not</u> respond to any Congressional subpoenas, nor will we open our gates for inspection by anyone carrying arms or threatening violence.

While the Centers have been locations where people could purchase the writings and other materials of the Imaginal Group, we voluntarily choose to suspend that practice. We will provide NO excuses for armed intervention into our grounds, by anyone.

For Congress to pursue this meaningless "investigation", in the face of the untold suffering that is happening in our cities and on our streets, is the height of irresponsibility. We will do nothing to feed their irresponsibility.

The Culture Council, for
The North American Awakening Centers

The Collapse of Money

File No:		File Name: The Collapse of Money	
Location:		Parties: Sarah Harrington, Center guest	
Monk/ Master Supervising:	Monk Montana, assisted by Monk- Candidate Man-Onko		

Name:		Pgs:		Date:		Vol:	
Type of Transcript:	Mechanical xxx						
	Organic						

Preface by the North American Centers Archive Committee:

For many, the salient point in the Upheavals was the collapse of the US monetary system. Cities could catch fire, people could starve, open warfare could exist on our streets, but as long as dollars were dollars, many held the belief that everything would eventually "snap back".

Before the breakdown of money, the middle and upper classes believed they could buy themselves out of the Upheavals. Moneyed classes created elaborate exit strategies, involving dual citizenships, second homes in friendly tropical countries, ocean-going yachts, "secured" banking, private security services... In the end, they merely managed to delay, not avoid, the inevitable.

Some even involved the Awakening Centers in their plans...

This text is being provided in a rough draft format. Communication Access Realtime Translation (CART) facilitates communication accessibility and may not be a totally verbatim record of the proceedings. Let your coordinator know if you would prefer a more verbatim option.

[start of transcript]

Harrington: This is outrageous! I want to talk to James Harold Moore, NOW!

Montana: I'm sorry Miss Harrington, but Dr. Moore has disappeared. We do not know where he is. Please, let me help you sort this out.

Harrington: There's nothing to sort out! James himself told me that I would never have to work here, as long as I paid! Now, you're telling me I have to work!

Montana: Yes, what Dr. Moore said is correct. The problem is, you cannot pay.

Harrington: That's ridiculous! I have millions of dollars in the bank! MILLIONS! The problem is, you people won't take my money anymore!

Montana: Ms. Harrington, you know that the country is in hyperinflation right now. Your millions just simply aren't worth anything anymore.

Harrington: Other people are still taking them!

Montana: The Awakening Centers have stopped playing the money game. We took dollars only so long as we were not yet self-sufficient, and the dollar still held some value. Now, most of the Centers are fully sufficient and the US dollar is in free-fall, and will never come back. So, you got these alternatives...

Harrington: The President just said yesterday that the dollar will be back, stronger than ever! The government will GUARANTEE the value of my money!

Montana: And who will guarantee the government? They're printing money like it's going out of style... which it is!

If you want to pin your hopes on what the President believes, you're free to leave here and take your chances. However, if you want to stay, you do have options. Do you want to hear them?

Harrington: [pauses] Go ahead.

Montana: You can work here for 6 to 8 hours a day. If you move out of your suite, into a smaller unit, you might be able to stay inside the walls of the Awakening Center forever.

Harrington: I am NOT going to work beside those filthy people that you drag in from the streets!

Montana: [Pauses]: You never really got the whole "inclusivity" thing, did you?

Harrington: Look, don't get me wrong. I love the idea that you people are helping those unfortunate ones. But, I don't want to work with them. I don't want to work at all! I don't see why I have to.

Montana: You have to work because you don't have any money! If you wanted to, you could convert your US dollars into a currency that we still accept, like euros or even yen.

Harrington: If I converted, I'd lose 90% of the value!

Montana: Yes, probably more than that. That's what I've been saying – you don't have any money! Now, your third option would be to take your remaining credits with us, and arrange a safe conduct travel package to a location of your desire.

Harrington: Where could I go?

Montana: Well, I'm sure some of your family could take you in...

Harrington: I am not a charity case! And, my children don't speak to me, since I wrote them out of my will.

Montana: Why did you do that?

Harrington: They were being greedy! All they wanted was my money! Well, I saw to it that they weren't going to get any of it!

Montana: Now, all that's irrelevant. They don't have your money, and neither do YOU!

If you refuse to work, if you refuse to convert your funds, and if you refuse to go anywhere else, at the end of the month, we will set your belongings outside the gate, along with yourself. You'll get to see exactly how far your millions will take you.

Harrington: If I converted my currency, I still couldn't stay here for longer than six months.

Montana: Yes, that's true. Not in your luxury suite. You couldn't stay here, unless you worked.

Harrington: Manual labor is beneath my station!

Montana: Lady, you really need to get a grip! Who do you think you're talking to? I used to have millions in the bank, too! I was a high-priced New York attorney, making over $1 million a year! I had a wife, a mistress, five houses and three cars!

Now, I've got a small cabin, I work four hours in the vegetable gardens and spend the other four hours between the admin desk and teaching. And, I've never been so happy in my life!

Those "filthy people" that you complain about have taught me more about life and living then I ever learned in my other life. I used to pay thousands of dollars to a psychiatrist... now I realize that I wasn't crazy – the society was!

And, I'll tell you something else: I was smart enough to transfer ALL of my money to the Awakening Center, before the crash! When it actually had value! I don't have to work, ever again! I don't do this work because I have to, I do it because it makes me feel GOOD!

And you'd feel good too, if you just let go of the illusion of your money and learn how to LIVE!

Harrington: You can't talk to me like that!

Montana: That's just it: this is a new reality! I can talk to you like that, and I just did! There's no one here to protect you from the reality of your own creation. You have used money as a buffer, to shield you from what was actually happening in the world. Now, it's caught up with you, and you don't know what to do!

Harrington: [crying]: You're right! I don't know what to do! And you're not being nice to me!

Montana: When money won't work, you fall back onto infantile behavior! I'm being more than nice to you – I'm being COMPASSIONATE. And compassion doesn't mean being shielded from reality.

This is my suggestion for you: convert all of your currency into euros and pay yourself up here. Do it today, while it's still worth a little something. If you move out of that suite and into a basic unit, you can get up to 14 more months here. If you take a roommate, and start making your own bed and eating your meals in the cafeteria with the rest of us, you could make that over two years.

And, in those years, I would strongly suggest that you start WORKING! Start with just two or three hours a day. And, work ALL of the positions here at the Awakening Center, from kitchen to nursery to gardens to security. In that year, you'll get a feel for what you're good at. And, you'll get an idea of what we're all about. And, you'll get rid of some of your hang-ups, and find out what inclusivity really means.

Harrington: You people just want all of my money...

Montana: You aren't listening to a word I'm saying, are you? My second suggestion, if you don't like the first, is that you leave. Take your chances Outside. That suite you're in can hold a dozen people dormitory style. And, we're going to have a lot more people coming in, now that money isn't any good anymore.

Harrington: Who says money isn't any good!?! The President just said...

Montana: Okay... [pauses] Why don't you go back to your suite and think about it? You've got another 20 days before you have to make a decision. But in 20 days, your millions might be worth zero.

Harrington: I don't think you can do this to me! I still want to see Dr. Moore! And, I'm going to contact a lawyer as soon as I walk out of here!

Montana: You do that. Goodbye.

[end of transcript]

[Afternote: After five days, Sarah Harrington chose the first option. After converting all of her currency to yen, and liquidating her other paper assets, and by downsizing to a small unit, she had enough credits to live in the Awakening Center for 2.5 years. She started working a three hour per day shift, rotating through all of the work available. She settled on a four hour per day split shift between Administration and the Nursery.

Sarah Harrington passed on eight years later, leaving an accrued time credit of 11.5 years. In her credit disposition request, she asked that half of her accrued credits be used to rescue street children, and the other half be used to find and rescue her biological children.]

The Tampa Accords

File No:		File Name:	The Tampa Accords
Location:	Tampa Awakening Center	Parties:	Mayor and Police Chief of Tampa, FL
Monk/ Master Supervising:	East Wind, Master, Abbot, assisted by Monk-Candidate Man-Onko		

Name:		Pgs:		Date:		Vol:	
Type of Transcript:	Mechanical xxx						
	Organic						

Preface by the North American Centers Archive Committee:

From the beginning of the Awakening Movement, it was understood that the Awakening Centers could never hold everyone. Not only was it not possible, it was not desirable.

From the beginning, it was understood that America's urban areas would be transformed. And, it was understood that some of the early transformations would involve some... friction.

This text is being provided in a rough draft format. Communication Access Realtime Translation (CART) facilitates communication accessibility and may not be a totally verbatim record of the proceedings. Let your coordinator know if you would prefer a more verbatim option.

[start of transcript]

Abbot: We are not a religious order...

Police Chief: I'll be damned if you aren't! Why else would you jokers run around wearing robes and singing all day!? You call yourselves MONKS! And who the hell is this other guy? He's just a kid! Get him out of here!

Mayor: Now Chief, this kind of talk isn't going to get us any place! I invited the two of you to come here to my office so that we can talk about our present crisis and how we're going to solve it.

Abbot: Well let me talk! By the way, this is Apprentice Man-Onko. He is studying to be a monk and is assigned to be my confidential recorder.

No Chief, we are NOT a religious order: We have no religious acts or vows that we take, no religious dogma, and, frankly find religion to be... Out of date. Some of our people are religious, but that's their choice...

Police Chief: Well, you must be some kind of cult, then...

Mayor: CHIEF! That just isn't helpful! [Quieter] Now, Abbot, I asked you to come here about our food crisis. It looks like it may be up to a week or two before we can get adequate food supplies into Tampa. If we all cooperate together, we can get through this crisis and back on the road...

Abbot: And where is that road going?

Mayor: What do you mean? We have had our ups and downs, but we are still essentially a good place for people to live in.

Abbot: No, Mayor – you have BEEN a good place to live in. Now, you are... something else. And it's time you adjusted to your new reality. Both of you.

Police Chief [to Mayor]: I don't know why we have to listen to this horseshit! We should just go down there to their little cult, and seize their stockpiles of food, so that the rest of us can survive!

[To Abbot]: Tampa has been here for hundreds of years, and will be here for hundreds of years more! The road we are traveling is the road we have ALWAYS traveled! It's time for you to stop smoking whatever it is you're smoking in your little hole in the ground out there, and come up for air!

Abbot: You have no food. You have an inadequate amount of electricity and gas – you've got rolling blackouts and gasoline rationing. You have no money... You can't pay your city workers, or anyone else. You have workers walking off the job... including police officers. And you can't get help from the state or federal levels, because they're worse off than you.

That's the road you're on. That's the road you're going to be on, for your foreseeable future. You can continue business as usual, or you can start doing things differently, and have a chance of surviving. "Business as usual" gives you more of what you see outside your windows right now. Are you looking? Seriously... I'm pointing right now -- are you looking out that window?

Police Chief: You can't talk to me...

Mayor: What do you call... Different?

Abbot: You want our help. Yes, we have adequate supplies of food and energy. We are willing to exchange food for WORK.

Police Chief: Now, what do you call "work"? Building your little fantasy empire out there?

Abbot: We don't refer to it as an "Empire". We refer to it as an "Awakening Center" or an "Imaginal Center". I'd appreciate it if you would use the correct...

Police Chief: I don't give a shit what you call it! The people of Tampa are not going to be turned into slave labor for a bunch of lunatics! We can just go to your little Paradise down there and TAKE the food! And you WILL take our IOU in return! We're not thieves...

Abbot: Oh, yes you are.

Mayor: PLEASE! Let's all talk....

Abbot: Our food stores have been relocated and distributed. They've also been booby-trapped. You won't find very much to take, if you try to take it by force. And, our people will resist you, nonviolently, at every step you take onto our property without our permission.

Police Chief: Then we'll arrest all of you!

Abbot: Yes, but how will you FEED us?

Mayor: Hold on! No one is talking about taking anything!

Abbot: He is.

Mayor: You asked the Chief to be here. I can send him away, and you and I can come to some kind of an arrangement.

Abbot: [pauses]: No, the agreement has to be with the both of you, or it won't work. As unpleasant as I find this, I don't see that there is any other way.

Our work isn't "slavery". We find that working for one's food is the opposite of slavery —it empowers people to help themselves and their community. People work hard but feel good about what they achieve. Everyone is fairly treated, because everyone works and manages the work – there are no "overseers". And, the food we produce tastes really good!"

Mayor: How long would they have to work?

Abbot: As long as they are hungry. We work four hour shifts. One person working two shifts a day will feed a family of 4.

If you are right and this "blows over", they won't be working long. If I'm right, they will be working... forever.

Police Chief: I've heard that you've got BABIES working down there! That's downright sinful!

Abbot: Your intelligence gathering is rather faulty, Mr. Police Chief. Babies don't work, for the simple reason that they can't. However, everyone of the age 12 and over who intends to eat has to work for that food.

Police Chief: Bullshit! We've got intel that you have children as young as seven or eight working down there!

Abbot: Yes, some of the younger children like accompanying their family on work detail. "Watching your parents" is how children have learned since the beginning of Time. And not just human children learn that way.

They are not required to work – they simply want to learn. And, if they happen to do something useful, they're paid for it. Why is that such a problem for you?

Police Chief: Because IT'S AGAINST THE LAW!

Abbot: In case you haven't noticed, most of what's going on in Tampa right now is against the law. Just look outside your window. THAT window! Do you see all those people camped out in your car park? Do you see those young girls, trying to prostitute themselves? Try to find something that ISN'T illegal! Right down there!

Right under your noses, there are hundreds, maybe thousands of people, doing illegal acts that demoralize and destabilize your society. And you do nothing. We are doing illegal acts that build community and high moral values... and you want to shut us down and steal our food.

As I said before, you're traveling down a new road, and you better learn what it looks like.

Mayor: We can't ask our citizens to go out on your work details.

Abbot: There's no need to. They can sit in your emergency shelters, doing nothing, watching TV, until the TV stations shut down and the food runs out. Then they can start rioting, and the police chief here will shoot them down in the streets. Because that's the law.

Mayor: [pauses]: That's... not a very pretty picture that you paint.

Abbot: I'm not painting. I'm telling you about the reports that we're getting from other cities. We know you're getting the same reports. I'm telling you what you can see on the news tonight. IF the electricity is working. IF the stations are still broadcasting. That's what's down your road. It's time for you to take a different way...

Mayor: I can't ask a family to make their 12-year-old work for you.

Abbot: You don't have to. If you tell people that we have food for work, they can make their own decisions. If a family with two children doesn't want their children to work, that's fine with us. After working a shift, they will be given enough food for two adults. They can split that anyway they want to.

Police Chief: You people barely give those folks enough food to eat anyway! There's not enough to split!

Abbot: Our food does take a little getting used to. The "Average American diet" has been a recipe for disaster. Overstuffed guts and zero nutrition.

People get more than adequate nutrition from our food, but it doesn't FEEL as filling as a trip to McDonald's. Or, the empty garbage that you feed them that you call "emergency rations". Our people are simply healthier than yours.

Mayor: What do you have the 12-year-olds doing?

Abbot: Nothing a 12-year-old can't do.

Mayor: Listen... Why don't you just take our IOU? I will pay you handsomely for the food, and when this thing blows over, you'll be sitting pretty.

Abbot: We wouldn't sell you our food, even if you were paying in gold. We don't want your money and we don't want your IOUs. Just saying that means that you still believe that our present situation is "temporary".

NOTHING is blowing over. The fact that you're even talking to me is more than adequate proof that it isn't.

Mayor: Well... Let me think about this some more. Maybe can get together in the next week or two...

Abbot: In the next week or two, the only thing that will change is that your situation will be more desperate. You'll have more people in your shelters. You'll have fewer police to contain their fear and anger. In two weeks, the police chief will have worked himself up into doing something monumentally stupid.

And, in two weeks, I won't be saying a single thing that I'm not saying right now.

Mayor: I just can't get past this notion of asking the citizens of Tampa to work for your... Center.

Abbot: And, you don't have to. People can choose to work in our Center, or can work in any of the tasks that we mutually agree on. We are willing to provide food to caretakers, teachers, and certain civil servants. Even... some police.

Mayor: Huh?

Abbot: Regardless of the faulty intelligence reports of your police chief, we have no need for your citizens to build our Center. If they wish to do so, fine. If not, they can work for YOU.

We're trying to reinstate a concept that has been a part of America for a long time – the concept of working for the betterment of one's society. We have prided ourselves on our individualism, and look what it's gotten us. A bunch of people who feel ENTITLED to receive yet feel that they have no responsibility to give. We're changing that.

If a person has a skill that is beneficial to society, they'll get food and energy. If they run the sewage plant, or the electrical plant, or provide transport, they and their families will eat.

If they are a stockbroker, a television actor, a model or a professional dog walker, they better learn how to swing a hammer or use a shovel. They'd better learn how to do something that society actually needs.

Police Chief: But, it's people, acting as individuals, that make a society strong...

Abbot: You're wrong. Just plain wrong.

Yes, "rugged individualism" is what most have been taught to believe, that fully independent action is strength. It's not. The 'Marlboro Men' out there are not faring too well right now. Learning 'interdependence' feeds people. Working together means we eat together

That false notion of individualism has put you in the position you're in right now. The question for you is: do you want to be here? That attitude had thousands of people living on your streets, begging for quarters, while tons of useless bureaucrats crowded City Hall, doing nothing but hopping from one meeting to another. Do you really want to preserve that?

Mayor: Wait a minute. What do you do with young people under 18 who don't have families? We've had a lot of young people living on the streets.

Abbot: They have a choice. They can come to us and we will put them up in dormitories, or they can continue to live on the streets. We'll take them down to the age of seven years old. We may be able to take younger later...

Police Chief: What if someone doesn't want to participate in any of your weird rituals? This is still America, and people are free...

Abbot: Our work and our ceremonies are two different things. Everyone who comes to our Center is welcome to participate in any or all of our activities, including our "Consciousness Ceremonies". However, they won't be paid for it. They are also welcome to not participate.

And, some of them may not find singing, dancing or meditating all that "weird".

Police Chief: What if someone wanted to pay for your food with sex? Or with drugs?

Abbot: They would have to demonstrate that the sexual activity or the drug use was a benefit to the entire COMMUNITY. That's never happened...

Right now, both of you are just stalling. These questions have nothing to do with whether or not we're going to make an agreement. You want to delay and delay, and hope that a miracle happens, or hope that this situation resolves itself. It won't.

I'll give you both 10 minutes to look outside your window at what's happening, then come back and make an agreement. If not, our offer is withdrawn and you will be left without our assistance.

[end of transcript]

[Afternote: The Tampa Accords, between the Awakening Center in Tampa and the Tampa city government, has become a model and template for innovative, inclusive public/private cooperation. After initial resistance, the Police Chief became one of the most ardent and active supporters of the Accords.]

News Article: "There Is NO Cannibalism in America!"

At his most recent press conference, the President categorically denied that the food crisis is so acute that people were starving, and that some people in certain areas are resorting to cannibalism.

"This is sensationalist garbage, fed by the sensationalist media, to spread fear and discontent, and to score political points in this election year!"

"My administration has been in touch with every Governor in every state. Each and every one of them assured me that they have the security situation in their state well in hand! Enough food! Enough shelter! End of story!"

The Governors were not so upbeat. Most refused to speak on the record. Three agreed to talk on condition of anonymity. A Governor of an East Coast state said, "He didn't talk to us... he threatened us! He said that if we said there were problems, he would federalize our National Guard and send them to another state! Cannibalism? That's the LEAST of our worries! There are whole sections of the state where we have no control and no contact. No food! No power! Our National Guard is spread too thin as it is.

"The President's call was clear. The Feds will be no help. All they can do is take from us. We're on our own."

On A Collection "Jumper" Team

File No:		File Name:	On a Collection "Jumper" Team
Location:	Seattle Awakening Center	Parties: Seattle Collection Team members: T1: Monk Adams, Team Leader T2: Monk Beans, Assistant Collector T3: Monk Shadow, Assistant Collector T4: Monk Beetle, Blocker T5: Apprentice Man-Onko: Assistant Blocker Plus four undercover Observers	
Monk/ Master Supervising:	Monk Adams		

Name:		Pgs:		Date:		Vol:	
Type of Transcript:	Mechanical xxx						
	Organic						

Preface by the North American Centers Archive Committee:

What's the best way to add new blood to a Center? Most found the easiest way just go out and pick it up... This was known by many names, including "Collection", "Jumping", even "Kidnapping".

Most Collections were routine. On this one, however, the Awakening Movement faced its most surprising and difficult foe.

Most of the threats facing the Centers were easy to predict and obvious to spot. Crop failures placed a food strain on some. Hostile neighbors and clueless officials had to be identified and dealt with. Weather, fire, pandemics, the military, communications...

Then there was the threat that no one predicted, no one foresaw, and no one could deal with...

This text is being provided in a rough draft format. Communication Access Realtime Translation (CART) facilitates communication accessibility and may not be a totally verbatim record of the proceedings. Let your coordinator know if you would prefer a

[start of transcript]

Monk Shadow: Heads up! Video and mics are hot!

Monk-Candidate Man-Onko: Damn! Do we really have to wear these clothes? I didn't smell this bad when I lived on the streets!

Team Leader Adams: Oh yes you did! And yes, we have to wear them. Clean skin and smelling like soap are dead giveaways that you don't belong here.

Remember that the Observers on the team have been living like this for a few months, collecting intel...

Monk-Candidate Man-Onko: Yeah, but its different when it's your own stink! I smell like... somebody else!

Team Leader Adams: Quit complaining! Focus on your job! Do you know how many monks got passed over, so you could be on this team? I get saddled with an apprentice! I still don't know how you got here...

So, what's your role, again?

Monk-Candidate Man-Onko: Come on, Adams, how many times we have to do this?

Team Leader Adams: You got somethin' better to do, APPRENTICE?

Monk-Candidate Man-Onko: Damn... Okay... I'm a "Blocker". I keep other people from interfering with the snatch.

Team Leader Adams: And?

Monk-Candidate Man-Onko: And... I keep an eye out for the "innocent bystander", make sure no one gets hurt – but me.

Team Leader Adams: Okay, watch the smart mouth. What's my job?

Monk-Candidate Man-Onko: You're the "Prime Collector". Snatch man. You're the guy who makes first contact with the collection target. These other two are secondary Collectors... they help you out if our guy gets "feisty".

Team Leader Adams: And how does this go down?

Monk-Candidate Man-Onko: Our collection truck shows up and turn on their flashers. All the folks under the bridge run... like cockroaches when the lights come on. They think it's the police. They all head our way. The undercover guys steer the collection mark toward us. We snatch 'em, bag 'em, tag 'em, gas 'em and toss his ass in the back of the truck. Just like you did me, a year ago! He wakes up in a nice clean bed back in the Center.

If it goes clean, the Observers won't be blown. If they're blown, they jump in the truck with us, and we all go back for tea and cookies. Like I said, I GOT this!

Team Leader Adams: Risk factors?

Monk-Candidate Man-Onko: Hey, we just went through all this!

Team Leader Adams: And we're going through it again! We go through it until I'm satisfied you're not going to screw us up! I already told you – I don't want you out here. You're a liability. I think you're too young and too hot-headed. I don't know HOW you got on my team.

You'll answer my questions until I'm satisfied that you won't screw up this collection. Now – risk factors!

Monk-Candidate Man-Onko: [sighs]: Okay, chill! Our mark is strong, may have martial arts training, has a history of violence, carries at least a knife in quick reach, and may have a gun. Wait... why do we even want this guy? He sounds like a walking liability inside the Center...

Team Leader Adams: Not our job. He was identified by the Observers as someone we want, someone who will benefit from being in the Center. Period. So, how do we handle this?

Monk-Candidate Man-Onko: Given his history of violence, we put him down and out FAST.

Team Leader Adams: Not "we" Apprentice... ME. Let's see you do your job. After some Jumps, if you keep your nose clean, maybe you can work as a Collector.

Monk-Candidate Man-Onko: How can I keep my nose clean when I smell like THIS?

Shadow: Look sharp! Jumper truck coming!

[flurry of activity. People on team take their assigned positions.]

Team Leader Adams: [whispers]: Here he comes! OOWF! Fuck! Bag him, quick! He kicks like a mule!

Shadow: Got him! Bag's slipping!! There, got it!

Team Leader Adams: Hey, keep him pinned, will you? And you, stop looking at us and check our perimeter... Look for the truck coming back!

Monk-Candidate Man-Onko: Perimeter is secure... Wait a minute – somethin's not right!

Team Leader Adams: What're you talking about? The mark is secure and no one is attacking... what's not right?

Monk-Candidate Man-Onko: Look, those 4 guys – they're not runnin', they're not attackin', and they're standin' way too close. Wait! I know that guy!

Team Leader Adams: What?

Monk-Candidate Man-Onko: That one! I saw him in Denver! HE DON'T SMELL RIGHT!!!

Beans: He's right! We're blown! This is a set-up! Wave off the truck!

Monk-Candidate Man-Onko: GUN! He's got a gun!

Beans: Dart 'em! Dart 'em!

[Sounds of struggles]

Shadow: Which ones?

Beans: Dart ALL of 'em!

[Gunshots and darts fly...]

Shadow: Shit! I'm hit! God... it hurts!

Team Leader Adams: Report! Hold it down! Everybody else report!

Monk-Candidate Man-Onko: All bad guys down. Shadow's hit in the leg... looks bad. Everyone else looks okay.

Team Leader Adams: Okay... Damn... we just darted over 20 people! Can you tell which ones are bad?

Monk-Candidate Man-Onko: Yeah... my guess is that everyone who's darted in the back was tryin' to run away – we bag all the ones who got darts in the front.

Team Leader Adams: Good idea...

Monk-Candidate Man-Onko: And we dart the target, too. He was BAIT.

Team Leader Adams: You think...

Monk-Candidate Man-Onko: He's not a "collection candidate". He's with THEM.

And you find the Observer who recommended him and dart him TOO!

Team Leader Adams: Our people? That can't be...

Monk-Candidate Man-Onko: Hey man, THIS WAS A SET-UP. Now, who do you think set us up?

Team Leader Adams: Jesus... I don't think I can handle this...

Monk-Candidate Man-Onko: Look, just call the truck back, and call all the Observers in. The one who doesn't show up is your man.

Beans: That's gonna blow everyone's cover...

Monk-Candidate Man-Onko: Your cover is already blown!

Team Leader Adams: Do what he says – call the truck back and call them all in.

Monk-Candidate Man-Onko: And get these marks secured before they wake up...

Team Leader Adams: What if they have back-up? What if they have a rescue mission?

Monk-Candidate Man-Onko: I think these guys WERE the rescue mission...

Beans: We can't take them in! They're probably Feds!

Monk-Candidate Man-Onko: Feds aren't this smart! We've got to find out exactly who they are and what they want. We can't leave them running around...

Beans: Someone's gonna come for them...

Monk-Candidate Man-Onko: Which means we better get moving!

Team Leader Adams: I don't know...

Monk-Candidate Man-Onko: Look... if we snatch them now, we can always put 'em back. If you DON'T take 'em – you'll regret it for a long time.

Team Leader Adams: [pauses]: Bag 'em and tag 'em.

Beans: We don't have that many bags!

Team Leader Adams: Come on... improvise! Tie their hands with their belts! Pull their shirts over their heads! Just get them on the truck!

Monk-Candidate Man-Onko: I'll tie off Shadow's leg and get him in the cab.

Team Leader Adams: No. Let Beans do that. You and Beetle check on the bystanders... make sure none of them are hurt and that they'll wake up okay.

Monk-Candidate Man-Onko: Will do. This is a mess...

Team Leader Adams: You said it.

[end of transcript]

Counseling after Collection Incident

File No:		File Name:	Counseling After Collection Incident
Location:	Seattle Awakening Center	Parties:	Monk-Candidate Man-Onko
Monk/ Master Supervising:	Sierra, Master and Abbot, assisted by Monk Adams		

Name:		Pgs:		Date:		Vol:	
Type of Transcript:	Mechanical xxx						
	Organic						

Preface by the North American Centers Archive Committee:

People make the mistake in thinking that the old Breaker Society had no values. That is not the case... the Breakers had a rich set of values. They just never knew how to apply them.

As the Awakening Centers matured, it was important to instill in everyone how important our values are...

This text is being provided in a rough draft format. Communication Access Realtime Translation (CART) facilitates communication accessibility and may not be a totally verbatim record of the proceedings. Let your coordinator know if you would prefer a more verbatim option.

[start of transcript]

Abbot Sierra: Okay, let's get started...

Monk-Candidate Man-Onko: Hey, aren't we going to wait for the other guys?

Abbot Sierra: No, we're all assembled here.

Monk-Candidate Man-Onko: Huh? I never heard of an after-mission exit interview without the whole team present.

Abbot Sierra: This isn't an exit interview... it's a counseling session.

Monk-Candidate Man-Onko: I don't think Adams did anything to deserve counseling...

Abbot Sierra: Monk-Candidate, this is YOUR counseling session.

Monk-Candidate Man-Onko: WHAT? Why me? Only thing I did was help take out a bunch of bad guys!

Abbot Sierra: Yes... that's what I want to talk about.

Monk-Candidate Man-Onko: What? What were we supposed to do... give 'em a kiss an' let 'em GO?!

Abbot Sierra: Calm down, Monk-Candidate. This is not punishment. We just want to talk about what happened...

And, if you don't mind, I'd like to start off the conversation?

Monk-Candidate Man-Onko: [pauses]: Okay with me... but if this is counseling, why's he here? [Indicating Adams]

Abbot Sierra: As Team Leader, he has ultimate responsibility for the behavior of the entire team...

Monk-Candidate Man-Onko: Did he rat on me?

Abbot Sierra: [sighs]: Why are you so defensive? No one "ratted". I called this session, after looking at the video feeds. Now, if you don't mind... may I start?

Monk-Candidate Man-Onko: [pauses]: Okay... 'long as we're all straight.

Abbot Sierra: Monk-Candidate, what do you think we found when we opened up that truck?

Monk-Candidate Man-Onko: Probably some sore ass--; some sore collectees. We didn't have time to arrange them...

Abbot Sierra: No. All five of them were dead.

Monk-Candidate Man-Onko: WHAT? I DIDN'T DO THAT!! WHAT THE FUCK...

Abbot Sierra: Man-Onko, SIT DOWN! No one SAID you did anything!

One of the problems that's been noted on your file is a tendency to blow up at your superiors! You MUST learn how to rein that in! You have to learn how to control your defensiveness!

Monk-Candidate Man-Onko: Cool! I mean... sorry! [Pauses.] I mean it. Sorry. I know I have a tendency to blow up sometimes.

[Pauses:] So, what happened? How did they die? All five of them? I know they were alive when we tossed 'em in the back...

Abbot Sierra: All five of them died from cyanide poisoning. They bit down on cyanide capsules that they had embedded in their teeth.

Monk-Candidate Man-Onko: Wow! Wait... including the target? The guy we were trying to collect?

Abbot Sierra: Yes... you called it absolutely right. He was just "bait" for us. Somebody set up our entire collection team.

Monk-Candidate Man-Onko: Wow...[pauses]   Wait... who would do that? Who COULD do that? That doesn't sound like the Feds... or anybody else I heard of.

Abbot Sierra: They said you were fast...

Yes. We are facing a brand-new enemy. As we are the Centers, we are referring to this new threat as "The Edge".

We don't know who they are, or what they want. It's clear that they weren't going after food, or the truck. They wanted the monks on the collection team. And, they weren't just trying to attack you. They wanted a kidnap – they could have shot you all where you stood, before the truck ever showed up.

Most importantly: the Edge has the power to BLOCK our telepathic powers. We didn't see this coming. We didn't believe that was even possible. We don't know how they can block us. We saw NOTHING wrong with this particular Collection.

That kidnap attempt cost them 6 agents, including our Observer, a monk named Cradle. It was obviously important to them... but why? By the way... it was Cradle, the false Observer, who insisted that YOU serve on the collection team. We think they were after YOU.

The Edge is a major threat to us. Up until now, all of our opposition has been "seen" by our psychics. We know who's coming over the fence... sometimes before they know themselves! We just simply did not see this coming. None of the forecasters could see it. A few of the forecasters were uneasy about Cradle, but put it down to his personal habits, not that he was a double agent.

Thanks to you, we're now aware of "The Edge"... rather than losing one of our best collection teams, we gained some valuable intelligence on a brand-new threat. We are spreading that news all around the globe, to all of our Centers, as fast as we can. Thanks to you.

Monk-Candidate Man-Onko: I think you better look inside the gate, too. That Observer...

Abbot Sierra: Stop, Monk-Candidate. I want to point out something else that shows up again and again in your file. You have a problem acknowledging praise. You usually change the subject or talk about something else.

That will change, right here, at this Center. Right now. Please stand...

[Man-Onko stands. Abbot Sierra and Monk Adams also stand.]

Abbot Sierra: Monk-Candidate Man-Onko, your service to the Collection Team, this Center and to our Movement has been invaluable, and we thank you for your quick insight, quick thinking and your decisive actions. [Both Sierra and Adams bow to Man-Onko.]

Monk-Candidate Man-Onko: Damn...

Abbot Sierra: Monk-Candidate, the proper response is to put your hands together like this, and to say "Thank you".

Monk-Candidate Man-Onko: [pauses]: Yeah, I know. [pauses]: Thank you.

Abbot Sierra: And, in recognition of your exemplary behavior, we have placed 50,000 credits in your account, in addition to your credits from the collection itself.

Monk-Candidate Man-Onko: What? But wait, all of us... Okay, sorry... "Thank you!"

Abbot Sierra: Better! And, incidentally, all of the team members got increases... but none as big as yours.

And... Monk Adams has recommended you for a special citation – but that has to be approved by the Culture Council itself.

Monk-Candidate Man-Onko: Wow, this is... [pauses] "Thank you!".

Abbot Sierra: Now, if it's alright with you... perhaps we can get to the reason for this session.

Monk-Candidate Man-Onko: Wow... I thought it was just to tell me how wonderful I am!

Abbot Sierra: [pretending to consult file]: Sarcasm to superiors... check!

[Seriously]: When I reviewed the video of the incident, I found that you displayed a degree of violence toward your assailants that was unjustified by the circumstances and not in keeping with our principles of nonviolence.

Monk-Candidate Man-Onko: Come on! Did you... Okay. Slower. Abbot Sierra, when you reviewed the video, did you happen to notice that the assailants were SHOOTING AT US?? That my guy had put a bullet in Monk Shadow and was trying to draw down on the rest of us?

Abbot Sierra: Yes, I saw that. And, I saw that, rather than just take the gun away from him, you broke his arm.

Monk-Candidate Man-Onko: Yeah... I made sure he wasn't gonna use that arm to hurt us... anymore.

Abbot Sierra: At that moment, you had a choice, and you used the higher degree of violence, although the circumstances did not indicate he would have posed a continuing threat. You broke his arm because you wanted to.

Monk-Candidate Man-Onko: Well... Yeah... He shot our guy, so I broke his arm. So what? He didn't die... at least, not until later... He didn't die from a broken arm!

Abbot Sierra: Yes, it's "so what" that we want to talk about. It's about preserving the life and health of ALL... including people who mean you harm.

Monk-Candidate Man-Onko: Yeah, I know we talk about that in class, but this was different. This fucker had a GUN!

Abbot Sierra: Apprentice! Language!

Monk-Candidate Man-Onko: Sorry, sir! The assailant had a gun.

Abbot Sierra: Not only did he have a gun, not only had he already used it... he was going to probably use it again.

Monk-Candidate Man-Onko: Yeah! So? He had to be stopped! Isn't this why you give us martial arts training? Isn't this why you taught me how to break someone's arm?

Abbot Sierra: No one questions you in stopping him. We are questioning HOW you stopped him.

Monk-Candidate Man-Onko: I don't get it. Looks like that guy isn't complaining – why are you?

Abbot Sierra: Man-Onko, I know you don't "get it". And, I really, really hope you do. Because, if you don't... you might as well take off your monk's robes RIGHT NOW, and leave the program.

[silence]

Abbot Sierra: As valuable as your Awakening Powers are, as much good as you've done on this Collection Team, you are a LIABILITY to us if you don't get this point.

I know you heard Gandhi's saying, "An eye for an eye makes the whole world blind". It's plastered all over our walls in the Center. But that isn't the issue here. Right here, "an eye for an eye" is making YOU blind.

Okay, let's say that, instead of going for a broken bone, you decided to use a leg trip to stop him. And let's say that the assailant lost his footing, fell off of the embankment and died. I would not lose one minute of sleep over that death.

This has NOTHING to do with him. It has EVERYTHING to do with YOU. I need to know that you will put your principles FIRST, ahead of every other consideration.

Monk-Candidate Man-Onko: You want me to care more for an "enemy" than for myself?

Abbot Sierra: Yes. Now, you are beginning to understand what "nonviolence" means.

Here's an example: that young girl that you've been sleeping with... what's her name?

Adams: Pret-la...

Monk-Candidate Man-Onko: You know about that?

Abbot Sierra: What if she ate something that made her temporarily insane? What if she got a gun and was threatening people in the Commons? Would you stop her?

Monk-Candidate Man-Onko: Sure... she would...

Abbot Sierra: Would you break her arm?

Monk-Candidate Man-Onko: No! I could take her down... [pauses]: Oh. I get it...

Abbot Sierra: Tell me the difference between Pret-la and the man who shot Shadow?

Monk-Candidate Man-Onko: I get it... I mean, I UNDERSTAND it. Now, I have to learn how to see some ugly... assailant... from Outside the same way I see her. And, I DON'T. Not yet. I'll try...

Abbot Sierra: Monk-Candidate, you have been exhibiting a special level of telepathic ability. You "read" that Collection situation very quickly and very correctly. That's really important to us. You can see the Edge and we can't. You may be able to teach it to the rest of us. We may have ways to boost your power.

But, we won't... not until you "get" what you just said. Not unless you control your tendencies toward violence.

Monk-Candidate Man-Onko: Okay, I'll try...

Abbot Sierra: Don't "try" to do it. Just do it.

Apprentice, I can guarantee this: you will <u>never</u> rise any higher here until you get this lesson.

Monk-Candidate Man-Onko: That important, huh?

Abbot Sierra: Yes, that important.

Monk-Candidate Man-Onko: I don't know... I mean, there's not a week goes by without me thinking that some asshole needs to get taken down.

Abbot Sierra: Monk-Candidate, I assure you... after 15 years, it's the same for me, too!

The essence of nonviolence is not about thinking those thoughts... The essence of nonviolence is not to <u>do anything</u> about it!

Monk-Candidate Man-Onko: Okay... getting it...

[end of transcript]

[Afternote: The aborted Seattle Collection Incident was the first identified incident involving "The Edge", a major security challenge to the existence of all of the Centers. The Edge was a highly trained, highly motivated shadow group with the apparent ability to block or hide from the telepathic and other Awakened Powers of the Centers. In fact, the Edge seemed to be able to use the Awakened Powers against the Centers. The Seattle Collection Incident revealed a huge blind spot in the Awakening

Centers' security systems – an over-use and over-confidence in the Awakening Powers, over the evidence of one's own eyes and ears.

Because of its unpredictability, the Edge became the single largest threat to the existence of the Awakening Centers.

Monk-Candidate Man-Onko received a Culture Council Commendation for his ability to spot and stop the danger to the Center – the youngest person and the only Apprentice to ever receive a Commendation.]

Year Three

We have come to be one of the worst ruled, one of the most completely controlled and dominated Governments in the world – no longer a Government of free opinion, no longer a Government by conviction and vote of the majority, but a Government by the opinion and duress of small groups of dominant men.

Woodrow Wilson

The Prison

File No:		File Name:	The Prison
Location:		Parties: Alan Voorhees, Superintendent of Prisons for the State of Michigan Alice Betlyn, Assistant Superintendent of Prisons	
Monk/ Master Supervising:		Dawn Light, Master, Abbot of Brandywine Awakening Center, assisted by Monk-Candidate Man-Onko.	

Name:		Pgs:		Date:		Vol:	
Type of Transcript:	Mechanical xxx						
	Organic						

Preface by the North American Centers Archive Committee:

The Awakening Centers were designed from the outset to replace the Breaker systems and structures. Sometimes that meant creating new kinds of processes and procedures. Other times, it meant taking over and reforming existing systems.

And always, it meant a change in thinking ...

This text is being provided in a rough draft format. Communication Access Realtime Translation (CART) facilitates communication accessibility and may not be a totally verbatim record of the proceedings. Let your coordinator know if you would prefer a more verbatim option.

[start of transcript]

Voorhees: This isn't a prison, it's more like a country club! You aren't punishing them, you're making them feel good!

Dawn Light: Well, what would a prison be like, in your estimation?

Voorhees: Well, it wouldn't look like a bunch of criminals running around, acting like they own the place! It wouldn't look like a goddamn college campus!

Dawn Light: And why not? What is a prison? What is the purpose of a prison?

Voorhees: This place is better than where most of these animals live! This place is a step UP for them!

Dawn Light: First of all, they're not animals. They're human beings, and we treat them as such. Second...

Voorhees: These are criminals who owe a debt, and I don't see how they're paying that debt here!

Dawn Light: What debt are you talking about? Do you mean the fact that they have all gone through the criminal justice process and have been convicted of a crime and are not allowed to leave these premises? If that's what you're talking about, this is indeed a prison.

But, if you are talking about a place with bars and armed guards and barbed wire, no we don't have that. We see no need for it. We know how to alter their behavior in such a way that those things are not only unnecessary but are counterproductive to their growth and development as human beings.

Voorhees: Growth and development! What are you talking about? These thugs are back in the prison system after being released so fast you think they were on roller skates.

Dawn Light: Not ours. This is the original idea of the prison. That's why they were first called "penitentiaries". That the prisoners were supposed to be "penitent" about their lives and their crimes. And in that way, they would change into productive citizens.

In Awakening Justice, the inmates are encouraged to look within and think about themselves and their society. And here they can do so, without worrying about being stabbed in the back or raped in the shower.

Voorhees: You have to put these men DOWN! Show them who's boss! That's what the bars and guns are for! You have to show them who's in CONTROL!

Dawn Light: We do. Every day, directly and indirectly, we tell them who's in control. THEY ARE. And, as long as they follow our few simple rules, they STAY in control of themselves and their lives.

In your prisons, the inmates are taught force and fear, every day. That's how they act as soon as you release them. And you lock them back up, for following the lessons you give them.

And... all that "power-over" stuff costs a lot of money. Our overhead is much lower than...

Betlyn: Perhaps if you told the Superintendent the rules here, he'll understand better what you are trying to achieve.

Dawn Light: Yes, we have...

Voorhees: [Directed to Betlyn:] I can't believe you authorized this nonsense! What were you thinking? I hope you've got your resume handy - when word of this gets out, you're going to need it! Heads are gonna roll, and it won't be MINE!

Betlyn: Well, uh, Sir, I was just...

Dawn Light: Perhaps we'll get to the point in this conversation where threats are not necessary. Now, I'd like to go over our few rules:

#1: No violence or intimidation, of any kind, direct or indirect.
#2: An inmate cannot approach the walls or borders, for any reason.
#3: No alcohol, drugs or anything else that diminishes consciousness. That means no television, also.
#4: Gender separation in sleeping arrangements.

Voorhees: Well, I heard you've got men and women sleeping together! I don't call that gender separation!

Dawn Light: I meant in the dormitories and cabins. Yes, we allow couples to sleep together, if they can convince us they are indeed a couple, and if they can buy a private room.

Voorhees: What about... well, you know... the queers and faggots?

Dawn Light: [Pause]: I'm sure you mean people with a different sexual orientation. We have a smaller dorm for those sleeping arrangements.

The most interesting thing about the couples arrangements is that the couples have to earn enough credits by working here on the prison campus to get private rooms. It's amazing how hard men and women will work for the opportunity of real intimacy.

In your sex-isolated prisons, men attack, kill and rape each other. In our co-ed prisons, all that energy gets channeled in productive, even beautiful endeavors. Lower negative energy, higher positive outcomes and lower overhead. How did you like the flowers that surround the main gate?

Voorhees: I'm not here to talk about your goddamn flowers! I'm a public servant. I answer directly to the Governor, an elected official. How are we going to explain to the voters, the taxpayers, that they are paying for conscripts to live in luxury and have sex?

Dawn Light: First of all, from where we sit, your list of "taxpayers" seems to be shrinking every year. Therefore, you've got a lot less explaining to do. Second, we get the same amount of money per head as your "punishing" prisons -- we just apply it differently. Third, we are the only one of your private prisons willing to take alternative payments for operating, instead of the cash you don't have and we don't want.

Voorhees: Look, we appreciate the fact that you take land and buildings instead of cash payments. But, this has just gone too far! You are going to have to comply with some rules, get some guards and bars in here, stop this sex comingling...

Dawn Light: No, we won't. We have an experiment going here, and we will see it to fruition. Or, you can take them all back. Now.

Voorhees: What? You can't do that!

Dawn Light: Sir, this is a contract evaluation and renewal. You are threatening our contract. Well, go ahead! If you want these men and women to be punished, take them all, today, and be done with it. You see, we don't need you. But, it seems that you need us.

Betlyn: [To Voorhees]: Sir, we do need them. Remember, you were going to ask them to take an additional 100 inmates, on top of what they've already got.

Dawn Light: We can't take 100 now. We can take 60 now, and an additional 90 in about 6 months, once the inmates finish the new dorms and expand the super-garden areas. But, we're not taking one more person, until you STOP this nonsense about altering our experiment!

Voorhees: Come on, be reasonable. I want to work with you. Can't you just, you know, get rid of the sex part?

Dawn Light: No. It's an integral part of our program of behavior modification. Take out any one element, and the entire program becomes unstable.

We've been running this prison for 3 years. In that time, our recidivism rate was ZERO. That's not percent, that's absolute. In the same 3 years, the rate for your old-style prisons was over 60%. Now, which way saves the taxpayers money?

Voorhees: Well, I heard that's because some of your inmates refuse to leave!

Dawn Light: Yes, that's almost correct. We have several inmates here who are staying longer than their term. Look, out the window -- do you see that couple? The ones holding hands -- the tall guy and the shorter woman? Well, he was released over a month ago. He's staying on to be with her... her term is finished in 3 weeks. Then, they will move over to our nearest Awakening Center.

Frankly, we wish we could move them over NOW. He has skills that the Awakening Center needs, and we need their beds! But, every inmate serves their full term -- no exceptions.

Voorhees: Okay, let's just talk and see if we can come up with some terms...

Dawn Light: Terms? These are the terms. I'll leave the two of you alone to decide whether to renew our contract as is, or not. For five years. If yes, I'll come back in and sign it. If no, you tell me when the buses arrive to take them away.

Voorhees: {pauses]: Does "as is" mean that you'll take the extra 100 inmates?

Dawn Light: [pauses]: "As is" means we will take an additional 150 inmates, spread as I mentioned before.

We really are trying to help you out. And, most importantly, we're trying to help the inmates out.

Voorhees: Listen... why are you folks messing around with prisons, anyway? Your Centers are very nice places, you've got an interesting educational program for the youngsters... Why mess around with prisoners? There are plenty of decent people who would jump at the chance to be inside a Center.

Dawn Light: [pauses]: We happen to think that prisoners are decent people, also.

We work with prisoners for three reasons:

First, the simple fact that they are not looking to be saved by your system. Prisoners know that the system has failed. That's why they're prisoners.

Second, prisoners tend to be smart and resourceful.

Third, many prisoners are incarcerated because of drugs. They have been early experimenters in alternative forms of consciousness.

Someone said that drugs were the mystical experiences of the ignorant. We help them have better mystical experiences.

Voorhees: I just don't get it!

Betlyn: [To Voorhees]: Sir, with all due respect, we don't HAVE to get it. They're taking our prisoners off our hands – what more do we want?

[end of transcript]

[Afternote: Superintendent Voorhees approved Awakening Justice for an additional five-year term, with an additional 150 inmates. Payment for this contract was the receipt of effective control over Tahquamenon Falls State Park.

Three years later, Dawn Light negotiated the transfer of three complete "old-style" prisons, launching the beginning of the Awakening Justice System (AJS). Payment included three additional state parks, along with various State office buildings. (The public was told that these transfers were "temporary", and that Michigan would "buy them back" as soon as the economic picture improved. It never did.)

Five years later, Superintendent Voorhees received a Presidential Commendation for his role in creating a successful alternative criminal justice system.

A year later, Alice Betlyn (a former novice in the Ann Arbor Awakening Center), replaced Dawn Light as the Coordinator of AJS.

Three years later, the criminal justice system in Michigan collapsed, due to the state's insolvency. 95% of inmates in the traditional system were incorporated into the Awakening Justice System. There were no payments for those inmates. The AJS was able to absorb those additions with minimal difficulty.

At the time of the collapse, the State of Michigan transferred the management and control of the Department of Natural Resources to the Michigan Awakening Centers. The Governor called this "streamlining" government. She said that the two events were in no way related.]

Water and Energy Wars - An Accommodation

File No:		File Name:	Water and Energy Wars – An Accommodation
Location:	Denton (TX) Awakening Center	Parties:	Jason Roberts, Commander of the Restore America Army
Monk/ Master Supervising:	Monk-Candidate Man-Onko, assigned to security		

Name:		Pgs:		Date:		Vol:	
Type of Transcript:	Mechanical xxx						
	Organic						

Preface by the North American Centers Archive Committee:

As stated previously, the Awakening Movement spent a great deal of time focused on security. How to defend oneself and defend the Movement... without violence? How is it possible to "defeat" your "enemy"... by making them go away?

Most threats were indirect – people trying to sneak into the Awakening Centers to steal food. Sometimes the threats were more straightforward...

[Confrontation at main gate of Center.]

[start of transcript]

Roberts: You better be packing something under that robe, to be talking shit like that.

Monk-Candidate Man-Onko: I am unarmed. I carry no weapons. None of us do.

Roberts: (to his 20 armed followers): Well, this is going to be easy!

Monk-Candidate Man-Onko: Not hardly. It will be very, very difficult. In fact, I think it will be impossible.

Roberts: And what exactly do you think is going to stop us from coming through that gate and getting the water, gas and food that we need?

Monk-Candidate Man-Onko: Well, for one, YOU will stop you. The fact that you are talking right now means that you are an intelligent man and trying to assess your situation.

Roberts: Well, thank you so much for the compliment! Now, will somebody give me a gun, so I can blow this sucker away!?

Monk-Candidate Man-Onko: You won't shoot, and not because I gave you a compliment. You won't shoot, for a different reason.

Roberts: Oh yeah? And what would that be?

Monk-Candidate Man-Onko: It's real simple. You won't shoot, because you don't know what will happen if you do.

Roberts: That's bullshit. I know exactly what will happen if I pull this trigger. You stop talking shit!

Monk-Candidate Man-Onko: Yes, that part would be true. The Center will need a new junior Security person. That's why they put their least valuable person on the gate...

But that's not what I'm talking about. You don't know what will happen to YOU if you pull that trigger.

We know you've been doing your homework. We know that you been probing our defenses for a while. And, we know you've been doing research on other Centers around the country.

I know that you know one fact: NO one has ever taken anything out of a Center by force. NO one. Not a biscuit, not a bottle of water. Not through legal means and not by guns.

And, I know one other thing: you don't know why that's true. You know we are pledged to nonviolence, and I just told you that we have no guns. From your point of view, there is nothing to stop you from riding in here, shooting up the place, loading up those trucks behind you, and riding off into the sunset.

The one thing that is stopping you right now is your knowledge that that has <u>never</u> ever happened. And it won't happen today.

Roberts: [pauses] Well, why don't I just take YOU, and beat the crap out of you until you tell me what kind of security you've got?

Monk Man-Onko: You don't do it, because it won't work. I'm a transfer and an apprentice – I have no idea what they do for security at this Center. I just know the same thing you do... it WORKS.

Roberts: Maybe we are so desperate, we don't care what works...

Monk-Candidate Man-Onko: If that was so, you wouldn't have sent three different recon teams over our fence. None of your men came back, did they? None of their tracking devices worked, did they? You lost 9 men and gained zero intel. Your security scan on us is nonexistent. Our security scan on you is... more than adequate.

Those men you sent over our wall on reconnaissance over a month ago – what happened to them? They never came back... and we didn't kill them. What do you think happened?

Roberts: Hey, we heard all about your mind control mumbo-jumbo. I don't believe in that crap!

Monk-Candidate Man-Onko: I didn't ask you what you believe in. I asked you what you think happened to 9 of your men.

Roberts: [Pauses]: Look, we're hungry and we're desperate. You can keep toying with us...

Monk-Candidate Man-Onko: You're hungry and you're desperate, but you're not FOOLS. A fool is someone who bites the hand that is willing to feed him. I don't think you're a fool.

And we ARE willing to feed you. We can give you all the food, water and energy you need...

Roberts: We don't want your fucking charity! We don't want to sell our souls to whatever the hell it is that you believe! Our job is to RESTORE AMERICA! We want to bring back the Constitution, and the other Democratic and capitalistic tools of government! We're having hard times, but this is America! We've been down before, but by God we will get back up again!

Monk-Candidate Man-Onko: Nice speech. You've given it a lot of thought. Now, how exactly do you plan to do that, with no food and with your troops sick and freezing to death? You ain't George Washington, and this ain't Valley Forge.

And you DO want our "charity". You just don't want to ASK for it. You don't want to PAY for it. You think there's something noble about being a THIEF.

Roberts: We're not THEIVES!!

Monk-Candidate Man-Onko: Who am I to argue with a man holding a gun on me?

You need our help. We can use yours. You can try to come in here as thieves and try to take what's not yours. You will fail, and your movement ends right here.

Or, we can make an accommodation, right here and right now. You can leave your weapons, come in and talk. You'll have to work with people that you don't like, and who don't like you. You'll have to do things that may go against your principles – things like practicing nonviolence and not stealing.

It's down to this: You've got choices to make. Turn around and face starvation. Try to come through this gate with guns and... disappear. Come through the gate ready to reach an accommodation and live. Your choice.

I'm going back inside and let you guys think about your next steps. Oh, by the way: we know that you're ready to blow up or smash down the gates. That's unnecessary – they're unlocked. Just come in when you're ready.

[end of transcript]

[Afternote: The Restore America Army and the Denton Awakening Center came to an agreement on the provision of external security in exchange for basic food and medicine.

Within two years, the bulk of the Restore America Army was absorbed into either the Denton Center or its urban Commons. A dozen die-hards refused to accept the Center principles and left the area in search of other groups with "American" values and principles.

They moved out of tracker range and have not been heard from again.]

The Time Bar

File No:		File Name:	The Time Bar
Location:	Seattle Awakening Center, Exploratory	Parties:	Monk Tannor Monk-Candidate Loro Monk-Candidate Man-Onko
Monk/ Master Supervising:	Monk Rasheed, Exploratory Lab Director		

Name:		Pgs:		Date:		Vol:	
Type of Transcript:	Mechanical xxx						
	Organic						

Preface by North American Archive Committee:

As the "Latent Powers" began to awaken, the Awakening Centers continued to explore the furthest reaches of their new abilities. Abilities that we now think of as routine had their beginnings. Some of those beginnings were quite surprising...

This text is being provided in a rough draft format. Communication Access Realtime Translation (CART) facilitates communication accessibility and may not be a totally verbatim record of the proceedings. Let your coordinator know if you would prefer a more verbatim option.

[start of transcript]

Loro: Yes? What do you want?

Monk-Candidate Man-Onko: I was talking at breakfast today, and the guys thought that I should come over and talk to you.

Loro: Why is that?

Monk-Candidate Man-Onko: I don't know. It's just something freaky happened to me this morning, and I can't explain it. I was just talking to them about it, and they said come here. What is this place?

Loro: This is the place where no one answers that question. So, what happened?

Monk-Candidate Man-Onko: Hey man, I don't think I like your attitude! I came over here because the guys at the canteen said this is the place to take freaky stuff. If you don't want it, I'll just leave.

Loro: I asked you what happened? If you don't want to talk about it, then go on and leave!

Tannor: Come on, give 'em a break! This is the newbie... The guy that scoped the new baddies in that busted collection!

Loro: I know who he is, but that don't mean I have to like him!

Tannor: Hey, Man-Onko, why don't you tell ME what happened today?

Monk-Candidate Man-Onko: Okay... It's just that something appeared in my room. And then disappeared.

[Silence]

Loro: You sure about this? Sure you weren't sleep?

Monk-Candidate Man-Onko: Yeah, I'm sure... Been up, washed and brushed my teeth. I was putting on my clothes and this metal bar appeared on my bed with some writing on it...

Loro and Tannor (together]: a BAR?

Monk-Candidate Man-Onko: Yeah, a bar of metal. Looked like silver or stainless steel. Pretty heavy. About that long. With some writing on it. Why are y'all getting excited?

Tannor: What did the writing say?

Monk-Candidate Man-Onko: It was just the word "BACKWARDS" and some numbers...

Loro and Tannor [together]: BACKWARDS?

Tannor [to Loro]: You better go get the director!

Monk-Candidate Man-Onko: So, what's going on?

Tannor [Pauses]: I sent him out so that we could talk for a bit. All the hush-hush crap around this place gives me the creeps!

We call this the "Exploratory", a cute name for a laboratory where we're looking into the Latent Powers and how to activate them. Things like telepathy, clairvoyance, bending time, and stuff like that.

Monk-Candidate Man-Onko: Cool. Far out. I never heard of "Exploratory".

Tannor: Hey, you're our star pupil right now! What you pulled with the Collection Team is now world famous! Our own celebrity!

That's why Loro is burned – Pret-la was with HIM before you showed up!

Monk-Candidate Man-Onko: Oops! But what's this got to do with something appearing on my bed today?

[Scuffling noises]

Rasheed: Hello, Apprentice, I am Master Rasheed. I run this facility. I know that Tannor has just been breaching security by telling you all about us!

Tannor: No I didn't! I just gave him a little background...

Rasheed: That's okay, that's okay! We were going to have to do that eventually.

[To Man-Onko:] I was hoping to get to meet you! Why don't you explain to me what you saw?

Monk-Candidate Man-Onko: Well, it was a metal bar, on my bed. And weighed a couple of pounds and looked like stainless steel, real shiny. Maybe half a foot long. Heavy. Printed on it was the word "BACKWARDS". Then some numbers...

Rasheed: Do you remember the numbers?

Monk-Candidate Man-Onko: Sure do. They were in the form of a date and time. And the date was two weeks from now.

Loro and Tannor [together]: TWO WEEKS?

Loro: We can't be ready by then! He must've read it wrong!

Rasheed: QUIET! It's really important to get this information right! We can't afford to blow another experiment!

Can you write down the numbers, exactly as you saw them?

Monk-Candidate Man-Onko: Sure . Here's the date [pauses] and then other numbers under it was the time I guess, which is pretty precise. Then, under that was the number five.

Rasheed: Did you touch the bar?

Monk-Candidate Man-Onko: Yeah, I picked it up and turned it all around. Seemed kind of heavy to me.

Rasheed: [To Tannor] If we do this experiment, make sure we test for fingerprints. And, test for fibers from his blankets.

How long do you think the bar was in your room?

Monk-Candidate Man-Onko: I don't know... Five minutes or so, I guess. I was gonna bring it to the canteen, to show somebody.

Rasheed: How about if I show you? Did the bar look like this?

[Takes object out of briefcase]

Monk-Candidate Man-Onko: Yeah, that's it! Except your bar doesn't have any writing or numbers on it.

Rasheed: [To Loro and Tannor): So, what do you to think of this?

Loro: I think it's another blown experiment. He saw something, but had to have gotten the date wrong! We might be ready a year from now, but clearly not two weeks!

And, the experiment was off spatially as well. I mean, why didn't it appear in our lab? Why did it appear only to HIM?

Rasheed: Is that a sign that the experiment failed? Or, is it a sign that it's succeeded?

Loro: For him to get it, we'd have to SEND it to him. And I don't know any reason why we would do that.

Tannor: And, we just don't have the resources, the power, to push that big an object backwards in time

Monk-Candidate Man-Onko: Hold the phone! What are you talking about, what do you mean " backwards in time"?

Loro: Listen, we don't have to tell you anything! You're just a delivery boy, remember?

Rasheed: That attitude just isn't helpful! I think we can give our young monk candidate a bit of a break here!

[To Man-Onko:] We have been experimenting with time displacement for a while. We can send our CONSCIOUSNESS backward or forward in time right now. That's relatively easy. We can view future events, as well as some in the past.

We want to go beyond that experiment – we want to send physical objects backwards and forwards. However, we can't get the amount of time and resources we need from the Abbot and the Council.

Monk-Candidate Man-Onko: Why not? This sounds pretty hot to me.

Rasheed: The Abbot's got Class II security breaches all over the place. She's allocating the Exploratory's resources to predicting them. Our security folks are spread pretty thin... Time dilation doesn't get much attention.

Tannor: You know, I don't think that the experiment was an accident at all! I think we purposely sent this to him...

Loro: Why him?

Tannor: Think about it! We were planning to send the first package to someone like the Abbot, to see if we can get her to give us more resources.

But... this guy is now more famous than the Abbot! Everybody around the world is hearing about him now! I'll bet the Culture Council doesn't remember our Abbot's name, but I'll bet they know HIS!

Yeah! And his telepathic powers had a real, definite effect on our security! And, as you know, security gets EVERYTHING they ask for! I think we sent it to him so that we could get the resources to conduct the experiment!

Loro: This is just so... wild! Pardon me while my mind gets blown! We sent that bar into the past, and it's already changing our Future!

Monk-Candidate Man-Onko: Wait a minute! What "telepathic ability"? I just saw some guy I'd seen back in Denver, that's all!

Rasheed: Actually, you didn't. None of the Edge assailants had ever been out of the Seattle area. And, we showed their photos to everyone in Denver, especially the folks who were collected the same time you were. No one recognizes them. I'll bet YOU wouldn't recognize them again.

I watched the video... You said something, that the guy didn't "smell right". I wanted to get you in here and test you for "synesthesia".

Monk-Candidate Man-Onko: What's that? And is it catching?

Rasheed: [Laughing]: Hah, good one! Not a disease! An... ability. We think you may access your telepathy through smell.

Tannor: Hey, back to the real world! What that bar is saying is that we get ALL the resources we need to conduct a "Time Backwards" experiment in two weeks! And that it will be successful!

Rasheed: [pauses]: Well, Mr. Apprentice, I think you should go to the Abbot to get our resources for us!

Monk-Candidate Man-Onko: Huh? What are you talking about? WHAT resources? I don't know how to get any resources! And I just met you folks ten minutes ago!

Rasheed: Well, for resources: at a minimum, we're going to need every monk and master in this place meditating for this... starting NOW! We'll need all of the monks over in the Transcendatory assigned to us FULL TIME! And we could use some of the other Centers...

Loro: Good luck with THAT! Those monks over in the Transcendatory are a bunch of prima donnas! Meditating all day, while everyone else has to pull their weight...

Rasheed: Enough of that! No running down other monks! The meditators are pulling their weight – just another kind.

[To Man-Onko:] I think the first step is for you to meet with the Abbot. It would take me two weeks just to get an appointment with her... But I'll bet you can walk into her office, right now!

Monk-Candidate Man-Onko: What? I don't know...

Rasheed: [Picking up phone]: Well, let's see how popular you are...

[end of transcript]

[Afternote: Master Rasheed received all the resources he requested. The time dilation experiment was a success. Two weeks after the initial conversation with Man-Onko, the Exploratory had a metal bar disappear from their laboratory, to reappear five minutes later... with Man-Onko's fingerprints and with fibers from his blanket on it.

As a result of the Seattle Center's successful time dilation experiments, their Exploratory has become one of the premier Research facilities into Time Dilation.]

Managing the Enemy

File No:		File Name: Managing the Enemy (Security Incident: Communication with Lord's Aryan Army)	
Location:	The "Blue Pussy" strip club, known to be frequented by LAA members. This encounter occurred in the parking lot of the club.	Parties: James Jacobson, the president of the "Lord's Aryan Army" (LAA)	
Monk/ Master Supervising:	Walbert, Master; Monk-Candidate Man-Onko, acting as Recorder		

Name:		Pgs:		Date:		Vol:	
Type of Transcript:	Mechanical xxx						
	Organic						

Preface by the North American Archives Committee:

From the beginning, "security" was a major issue for the Awakening Movement. The threats were many: from starving people trying to find food to eat, to ideological opponents attempting to end the experiment.

How to handle these threats, in a Movement pledged to nonviolence and inclusivity?

Some Centers realized that the best defense came in managing one's "enemy"...

This text is being provided in a rough draft format. Communication Access Realtime Translation (CART) facilitates communication accessibility and may not be a totally verbatim record of the proceedings. Let your coordinator know if you would prefer a more verbatim option.

[start of transcript]

Jacobson: Who are you? What the fuck you want here?

Master Walbert: I am unarmed, and I mean you no harm. I am Walbert, Head of Security at the Seattle Center. We have intelligence that your organization is about to come under attack, and we wanted to inform you...

Jacobson: What? What the fuck are you talking about? Do you know who I am?

Master Walbert: Yes, you are James Jacobson, the President of the LAA.

Jacobson: Yeah, and we hate your fucking guts! I don't know why I don't waste you right here and now, and call it self-defense! And who's that kid? He with you? Is he all the back-up you got? Do I waste you both?

Master Walbert: The fact that you hate me does not obviate the fact that you are about to come under attack in three days, by the Sons of Liberty. And yes, the "kid" is with me...

Jacobson: Give me a break! The Sons of Liberty are our FRIENDS! We're about to merge with them, asshole! You're just trying to stop the merger!

Master Walbert: We know about the merger talks. We also know that, at 10 PM on Thursday, while you are in the middle of your security shift, 20 armed commandos from the SL group will penetrate your southern perimeter, near the creek, assassinate you and your top leadership, and open the door for the rest of their comrades to take over your entire operation. It's designed to be a surgical strike. The merger talks are just a ruse...

Jacobson: So why you telling me? You defected from those zombies? Well, WE don't want you! You think I'm gonna pay for this load of crap that you call information? Why are you HERE?

Master Walbert: Our forecasters predict that, without forewarning, the Sons of Liberty surprise attack will be successful. That will leave SL in a prime position to attack us. That attack will fail, but will cost many lives on our part.

With this information, you may be able to repel the attack. The battle between your two organizations will weaken both of you, and will forestall an attack on us for many years. Keeping you alive and well is in our best interests.

If you are smart, you will cancel the merger talks and go to a full defensive position. This will forestall the attack. It will also leave two strong organizations for us to contend with. But, you will be focused on each other, not on us.

Jacobson: Fuck you! We are not giving up our friends just cause some zombie says so! You're gonna figure out that us true Americans have more on the ball than you think!

Master Walbert: I hope that one day, you realize that we are not your enemy. I hope you realize that we all gain from cooperating.

I'm giving you this information freely, for your benefit. I hope you realize that this is the first step in cooperation, and we have taken it. This is what we mean when we say we want a world that works for all.

Jacobson: Well, fuck you and fuck your "world for all"! That's just doubletalk for wanting One World Government! We're not buying ANY of your commie bullshit! Especially this load that you're selling right here!

I'm going over to Bobby at Sons of Liberty and TELL him about this little talk we had! That will show him how much I trust him, and how much I DON'T trust YOU!

Master Walbert: Do with the information as you wish. And, we will see in three days whether or not my information is "bullshit", won't we?

Jacobson: Yeah asshole, I do suggest you back away! Go crawl back into your little termite hole with your little punk girlfriend there! That's right! Get going, before I change my mind and change your face!

[end of transcript]

[Afternote: Jacobson did in fact call Robert Davis of the Sons of Liberty and informed him of the talk. This caused the SL to accelerate their timeline. SL attacked the next day.

Jacobson, fearing an attack by the Awakening Center, plugged the security gaps in his southern perimeter, and therefore was able to repel the SL sneak attack. The fighting at the main LAA gate was intense, and left many dead on both sides.

Both organizations have been substantially weakened, and neither is now a threat to the Center or the Culture Council. Both will continue to be monitored over time.]

Year Four

We are fast approaching the stage of the ultimate inversion: the stage where the government is free to do anything it pleases, while the citizens may act only by permission, which is the stage of the darkest periods of human history, the stage of rule by brute force.

Ayn Rand, "The Nature of Government"

The Banned Books: Yielding the Secrets

You see someone sitting in a chair, a small box on his lap. You want to know what's in the box. What do you do?

One approach is to respectfully ask him about the contents of the box. You may ask directly or you may be more circumspect about it. You may even mention it jokingly. You may offer some inducement or reward for revealing the contents of the box.

The other method would be to punch the guy in the face, and take the box. Slightly more subtle than that would be to threaten him, or imply a threat. Waving a gun around can be very effective in this regard.

In Switzerland, the physicists at CERN have constructed the world's largest supercollider, speeding supercharged subatomic particles to near light speed, then smashing them into each other, in their attempt to "understand the Universe".

This is their attempt at punching God in the face. We'll see what they learn...

There is another way.

Instead of "demanding" that the Universe yield secrets to us, we can ASK. We can ask, with dignity, reverence, for all for the processes that we are observing. We can ask with LOVE.

This is how our ancestors did it. This is how they moved the stones of Stonehenge, the Pyramids and Goebekli Tepe, this is how they traveled vast distances without airplanes, this is how they learned the medicinal properties of plants (more fully than any nerd with a gene sequencer), this is how they understood the mysteries of the Universe, more fully than modern astrophysicists ever will.

And this is how WE will learn, to start from basic principles, to release and reject the flawed worldview, based on the flawed philosophy of exclusivity and isolation.

This is how we will stop slavery, once and for all – instead of just transferring it to beings who cannot speak English. This is how we will forge new partnerships – with other human beings, with all other beings (especially our food beings, who deserve and should receive the most Love from us). This is how we will forge partnerships with the wind, rain and Sun itself – rejecting the mechanistic viewpoints of "global climate change".

Yes, the climate will stabilize – simply (and profoundly) because we ask it to. However, that asking cannot come from the mind and the heart that created the problem in the first place. That asking cannot come from a being tainted by EXCLUSIVITY.

"The Ecstatic Society"

Shariff M. Abdullah

(Banned by Act of Congress)

The Prisoners

File No:		File Name: The Prisoners: Negotiation for Prisoner Exchange after Unsuccessful Attack on Center
Location:	Cleveland Awakening Center	Parties: Abraham Bradley, Major General for the Army Rangers assisted by Colonel Rambliss
Monk/ Master Supervising:	David, Master, Head of Security, assisted by Monk-Candidate Man-Onko	

Name:		Pgs:		Date:		Vol:	
Type of Transcript:	Mechanical xxx						
	Organic						

Preface by the North American Centers Archive Committee:

From the beginning, the Awakening Centers understood that shifting consciousness was important. It was important for those who came into the Awakening Centers as guests and participants.

It was even more important to shift consciousness with those who came into the Awakening Centers as adversaries.

From the beginning, there were charges of "brainwashing" and "mind-wiping". Much of that was a result of the deliberate rumors that the Awakening Centers set, to discourage attackers and fence-climbers.

And some of it was true...

[start of transcript]

Bradley: Yes, I have your money, in gold, right here. But you're not going to get a penny of it until I see my men!

David: Of course. My question is simply that your case doesn't look large enough or heavy enough to hold that much gold. If you could just open it, so I can take a quick look, we can get this over with.

[Sounds of case being opened]

David: That looks satisfactory. We have 15 of your men. All are assembled right outside and they're ready to go. That's them, over there...

Bradley: THAT'S my men? They're playing basketball!

David: Yes, and not doing very well.

Bradley: Why are they playing with you? Why do they look so happy?

David: Why shouldn't they be happy?

Bradley: Because they are prisoners of war! They look happy to be here!

David: They ARE happy to be here. As happy as we possibly could make them.

Bradley: Why are they happy?!? Did you drug them?

David: We don't "drug" anybody. We did, however give them a combination of plant medicines that would...

Bradley: You drugged them!

David: As I just said, we don't drug anyone. We don't believe in drugs. We did, however, give them a combination of plant medicines and used other techniques that would guarantee that they would be both happy and nonviolent.

Bradley: You fucking drugged them, and have the nerve to stand here and spout that shit! I ought to...

David: Yes, and that's why you had to surrender your weapon when you came in here – no rash and impulsive actions, please.

Bradley: When do those drugs wear off?

David: If we did our jobs right...Never.

Bradley: WHAT?

David: As I said, it isn't just plant medicines. It's counseling, biofeedback, hypnotic suggestion, everything we possibly could think of. Our goal is for the effects to be permanent.

Right now, those are some of the happiest, most fulfilled, contented, and NONVIOLENT men on the planet. We gave them everything we had, and actually made up a few things for them. They're happy, good hard workers, and will never lift a finger to hurt anyone, ever again... Especially US.

Bradley: You assholes are going to pay for this! The Geneva Conventions specifically forbid...

David: Forbid WHAT? They forbid "cruel and unusual punishment". These guys haven't been punished at all! We have LAVISHED attention on them! Next to how we treated them, your barracks constitute cruel and unusual punishment!

Bradley: You have rendered them incapable of doing their job!

David: Nonsense! All of them are fit as a fiddle and ready for a long career in your typing pool, or as auto mechanics. They can do ANYTHING on your base – except fight.

Bradley: You fruitcake! I'm going to have your head for this...

David: More nonsense. Try to get one of them to testify against us, or to say that they had a bad time in any way while they were in our care! We have several budding love relationships between your men and our women. Do you know how many times the single men have had SEX?!? Tell me THAT's against the Geneva Convention!

Consciousness adjustment is just a small demonstration of our power. Your power lies in a bygone era. The power to punish, the power to maim and the power to kill. The power of violence. We have consciously and affirmatively rejected that.

Our power lies... somewhere else. We are becoming very good at changing consciousness. You can see it right outside this window. You see men happy, and you think something is wrong. You see your men healthy and productive, but I think you would be happier if we were handing them to you in coffins!

Bradley: The next time, there's going to be plenty of full coffins, and they won't be on our side!

David: Watch your step, General! The next time any of you try to come onto our property uninvited, we may not be so generous in how we treat our captives. We have learned techniques that are not nearly as positive and uplifting as what you see out here.

We could've returned these men to you with their minds wiped clean. That would be easy for us – actually, easier than "happy and nonviolent". They would be able to tell you their names and perhaps count to 100 – but little else. You would have to teach them how to tie their shoelaces. You would have to CARRY them into those vehicles. Now, would you prefer THAT?

Bradley: This is insufferable! You can't talk to me like that!

David: But I am! And, I'm giving you a choice! Happy pacifists or mind wipes! Next time you give the order to send spies or soldiers over my fence, you better think about it!

Bradley: You better...

David: Look, General... You <u>knew</u> how many of those men were so violent, they were regularly beating their wives and children! You <u>knew</u> some of your men were rapists! You <u>knew</u> that some of them were alcoholic, drinking to blackout!

You knew it and did <u>nothing</u> about it!

Now, <u>none</u> of them are wife beaters. <u>None</u> of them are drunkards. <u>None</u> of them are rapists – ever again! We fix three of your biggest problems, and for some reason, you think something's wrong with that!

Bradley: Look, I go where my orders take me. I don't make the rules...

David: Yeah I know... You just follow them. I can tell you this: If you ever order men across our fence ever again, if you ever FOLLOW such an order, we are going to mind wipe YOU! If you think you don't have a choice... We'll make sure you don't have one – ever again!

Ask yourself if you want to have your wife tie your shoes and button your shirt and feed you oatmeal for the rest of your life! Ask yourself if she would! And do that now... because after we get finished with you, you won't be able to!

Now...do you want these men, or not? Just say the word, and they'll keep playing basketball.

[Silence]

David: I'll take that as a "yes".

One more thing: our commitment is to deliver these 15 men outside our gate, in exchange for that bag of money. It's YOUR job keeping them outside our gate. Several have voiced the desire to stay in the Center. Others plan to collect their wives and children and come back.

They will be welcomed back if they do. See that one over there – Corporal Peters? Holding hands with that little monk? He's found true love. He's coming back for her... and I'll be interested in seeing how you try to stop him.

Bradley: We'll lock 'em up in an asylum, until we can figure out how to undo the damage you've done!

David: You'll lock up Peters, until he stops being in love? Wait until word of THAT starts spreading! Go out on a raid against a Center, and you'll get locked up if you're happy!

Colonel Rambliss: [to Bradley]: Sir, I think we should check in with Headquarters about this, before we say any more.

David: I agree with your man. Get word from your superiors. Take your time. It's close to lunchtime, please be my guest for a delicious...

Bradley: I'm not eating or drinking ANYTHING in this hellhole! I don't even want to breathe the air in this place!

David: That's okay... your men will make up for it. They love the food here!

[end of transcript]

[Afternote: After conferring with their commanding officers, Bradley paid the ransom and received the 15 former combatants. All were placed in mental institutions for "observation".

With the support of the Center, the families of the 15 filed a successful lawsuit for their freedom. 8 of the 15 returned to the Center, including Peters. Five brought families with them.]

The Banned Books: The Key to the Latent Powers

The Key to understanding the Latent Powers: these abilities do not reside in ANY INDIVIDUAL. These abilities are non-localized and non-individuated. They can only be discovered while in a group, a collective, relying on Emergence and Holonomy. Just as GRAVITY is not attributable to an object, the Latent Powers are not attributable to an individual.

The Latent Powers are latent within each of us, but can only be activated in the collective. One transistor has ability, but you need a lot more than one to do anything. A grain of sand has "gravity", but you need a LOT of them to generate a discernible gravity field.

All that the Breakers know about the Latent Powers is based on studies and experiments based on INDIVIDUALS. You cannot understand herd behavior by studying one cow.

So, the search for the Five Latent Powers is really the search for the COLLECTIVE CONSCIOUSNESS that will allow the Five Latent Powers to emerge.

And... You don't have to "search" for the collective consciousness. You just have to create/ encourage the conditions wherein it HAPPENS.

And, as it turns out, we've already been doing that. For a very long time.

"The Ecstatic Society"

Shariff M. Abdullah

(Banned by Act of Congress)

Counseling after Telepathy Class

File No:		File Name:	Counseling After Telepathy Class
Location:	Seattle Awakening Center	Parties:	Monk-Candidate Man-Onko
Monk/ Master Supervising:	Blessing, Master		

Name:		Pgs:		Date:		Vol:	
Type of Transcript:	Mechanical xxx						
	Organic						

Preface by North American Archive Committee:

The Awakening Centers strived hard for a balance between the needs of an individual, the needs of a group, and the needs of the Awakening Movement as a whole.

How is individual achievement recognized... without falling into the trap of egotism or even elitism? How do you make sure that the abilities of one are shared by all?

How do you make sure that abilities are NOT shared... until the time is right?

[start of transcript]

Master Blessing: Come in! Sit down! Will you have some tea?

Monk-Candidate Man-Onko: Thank you! Of course! The last meal of the condemned!

Master Blessing: [laughing]: Why do you think you're the condemned?

Monk-Candidate Man-Onko: Seems like the only time I get tea with a Master is when I've screwed something up. You're gonna tell me to get my shit together... without ever using the word "shit", of course.

Master Blessing: [more laughter]: That's pretty good! And pretty accurate! So, want to cut to the chase?

Monk-Candidate Man-Onko: Hey, I want my tea!

Master Blessing: [more laughter]: You really are a delight to work with! Let's see how fast you get these two points and get out of here.

[pauses for tea]

Monk-Candidate Man-Onko: Okay, shoot.

Master Blessing: First of all, you've gone to sleep in two sessions in a row during your telepathy class.

Monk-Candidate Man-Onko: Oops. Well... guilty as charged. I'll try to do better...

Master Blessing: "Trying" isn't a part of this. Your T-P work is as essential to the existence of this Awakening

Center as our food production or our gate security. You have to take this SERIOUSLY.

Monk-Candidate Man-Onko: Well, if I may speak frankly?

Master Blessing: Go ahead.

Monk-Candidate Man-Onko: Well, why do I have to attend the class? I'm not bragging or anything, but everyone's telling me that my T-P scores are off the charts. I've been training the other monks and masters in the "olfactory technique". So why do I have to sit like a novice, trying to visualize a circle or a square?

Master Blessing: Pretty boring, huh?

Monk-Candidate Man-Onko: Absolutely!

Master Blessing: So, you'd rather spend your nights screwing every female monk-candidate you can get your hands on, then sleeping it off in class – is that right?

Monk-Candidate Man-Onko: WHAT? How the hell do you...?

Master Blessing: Take it easy! We'll get to that part later. Right now, let's stay focused on the T-P class.

You are incredibly gifted. But you are undisciplined.

I've watched you playing basketball with the others during free time. You've got a mean jump shot, a fair hook, and a very effective lay-up. You're too short to dunk the ball...

Monk-Candidate Man-Onko: Hey, watch your mouth! I'm just SAVING it! One day, when they least expect it... Out of the sky! The MIGHTY MO!

Master Blessing: [laughing]: Yes, "The Mighty Mo". That's what you ask your girlfriends to call you, isn't it?

Monk-Candidate Man-Onko: Jesus... One day, you folks are gonna tell me where the cameras are hidden. Or, who's runnin' their mouths. It was Pret-La, wasn't it?

Master Blessing: You keep asking how we know everything. Well, today is the day we tell you.

But first, back to basketball: What if you only had one shot, your jumper? And what if you could only take it from one place on the floor? How good a player would you be?

Monk-Candidate Man-Onko: Not much. They other guys would just stand in my spot, or block me every time.

Master Blessing: In fact, your lay-up shot is effective, BECAUSE you have a jumper. And your jump-shot is effective, BECAUSE you have a strong lay-up.

Monk-Candidate Man-Onko: Yeah, I guess so. I never thought of it that way...

Master Blessing: Your "smell-sense" is like having a powerful jumper that you won't be able to use, because you have nothing else.

Monk-Candidate Man-Onko: [long pause]: Okay... Got that. But, why not give me private classes, special training? I spend a lot of solo time in the Exploratory now, couldn't I just spend some days there learning the other T-P techniques?

Master Blessing: Yes, you could. It would be very efficient and effective for us to do that.

Monk-Candidate Man-Onko: So? Why not do that?

Master Blessing: Because it's not about you.

Monk-Candidate Man-Onko: Uh-oh. You're gonna go all Zen on me now, right? You been talking to Master Nampa?

Master Blessing: No, I don't need to confer with your meditation teacher. And this isn't as much about Zen as it is about... well, what we're all doing here in this Center.

Monk-Candidate Man-Onko: Okay, shoot.

Master Blessing: Your ability to read intentions is truly amazing. Your "smell-o-vision" works accurately for over a kilometer.

Monk-Candidate Man-Onko: Okay... you just finished saying that this was not about "me".

Master Blessing: Your ability is truly great. And, thanks to your help, it now can be blocked.

Monk-Candidate Man-Onko: What?

Master Blessing: Yes, all that time in the Exploratory was for us to understand your ability well enough to develop effective resistance to it. Otherwise, you'd be running the show here.

Monk-Candidate Man-Onko: What's wrong with that? Hey, just kidding. How do you know you can block it?

Master Blessing: Last week, we had a monk take a knife and intend to stick it in your ribs. He walked all the way up behind you, to striking distance. You didn't detect him.

Monk-Candidate Man-Onko: [long pause]: It was last Wednesday, wasn't it? During dinner in the cafeteria? I remember feeling strange, but I couldn't figure out why...

Master Blessing: Excellent! That "strange feeling" comes from some of the other T-P powers, the ones you don't have... yet.

Man-Onko, as long as you remain a "one-trick pony", you are a short-term asset and a long-term liability.

Monk-Candidate Man-Onko: Okay, agreed. Just give me the lessons, straight.

Master Blessing: There are two other considerations...

One: This is where Master Nampa comes in. You are getting used to special treatment. Having your chores reassigned so you can spend time in the Exploratory, having the others looking up to you because of what you did for the Collection Team.

Getting calls and requests from other Centers. You get regular phone calls from the Culture Council! I've never had one, in my entire life. In fact, you're the only person I know who gets them, besides the Abbot!

Monk-Candidate Man-Onko: Hey, I'll give you my autograph! Hey, kidding!

I never asked for any of this. I was happy just being another grunt. I didn't ask for the Exploratory time, or the phone calls.

Master Blessing: Yes, we know. But, look how quickly you suggested private lessons for yourself.

Monk-Candidate Man-Onko: I was just trying to be my best – for the group.

Master Blessing: Yes... but down that path is the road to individuality and exclusivity. Down there, you start to blur the line between "what's good for the group" and "what's good for ME". Soon, you'll want your own table in the canteen, your own separate sleeping quarters...

Monk-Candidate Man-Onko: Hey, I could use that NOW!

Master Blessing: We'll get to your nocturnal activities in a minute. So, do you see why, unless it's really important that we do so, you need to do the same activities as everyone else – including trying to "see" circles and squares in T-P class.

Monk-Candidate Man-Onko: Okay... I'll try to stay awake – not making any promises, though.

Master Blessing: Well, let me see if I can give you some incentive...

How do you think the Masters "know everything" around here?

Monk-Candidate Man-Onko: WHAT? You're using T-P on us? You told us you weren't doing that!

Master Blessing: And we're not. At least, not in the sense of trying to "read" your thoughts to determine your activities and intentions. Doing that kind of "reading" is like going through someone else's journal – the only time we would do that would be under the most serious and special circumstances... which your sex life is NOT.

Monk-Candidate Man-Onko: Oh yeah? Then obviously, you don't know how great a lover I am, because...

Master Blessing: STOP! Right there! Do not use that word!

Monk-Candidate Man-Onko: What? What I do?

Master Blessing: You used the word "lover". That you are NOT.

Monk-Candidate Man-Onko: But...

Master Blessing: SILENCE!

Monk-Candidate Man-Onko: [silent]

Master Blessing: Good. For the past 9 months, you've been screwing around like a wild rabbit, visiting every vagina that would hold still long enough.

That is going to stop. Not right now, but within the next 3 months.

In the Centers, we tolerate this promiscuity for a couple of years. In some cases, we encourage it. We want you to get "sex" out of the way, so that you can start to focus on LOVE. And no, my monk-candidate, they are not the same.

From what we know, you seem to be fairly proficient at having sex. You haven't the slightest idea of what "love" is, or how to practice it. Three months from now, you will start to learn.

Monk-Candidate Man-Onko: May I speak?

Master Blessing: Yes...

Monk-Candidate Man-Onko: So, how long's it gonna take to learn this "love" you're talking about?

Master Blessing: The rest of your life.

Monk-Candidate Man-Onko: Umm...Should have seen that coming. This isn't about "celibacy", is it? Cause if that's what you're talking about, just send me out the gate right now...

Master Blessing: [laughing]: No! Some of the monks and masters practice celibacy, but only for a limited time and for a specific reason. In general, we view the desire for celibacy as a pathology.

Monk-Candidate Man-Onko: Whew! Okay, so what happens in 3 months?

Master Blessing: In 3 months, you will be forbidden to have a sexual relationship with anyone, except under two conditions:

1. You must declare the relationship in advance.
2. Someone must witness it.

Monk-Candidate Man-Onko: Hey, that's not so hard.

Master Blessing: Let's see how you do in a few months.

How many times have you had sex with Monk-Candidate Pret-la, because you couldn't find anyone else to sleep with? Or because she was bored, or didn't like her room-mate?

When you declare your relationship in advance, you have to declare the KIND of relationship you want. There's a list of potential relationships. And "Fuck-Buddy" isn't on the list.

Monk-Candidate Man-Onko: Wow. No more "one night stands"...

Master Blessing: I didn't say that. If you want a one-night stand, you can have it... if both of you AGREE, and your witness agrees that it is for the good of both of you and good for our community.

Now... how many times have you had sex by IMPLYING that you were going to be with your sex partner forever? Don't bother trying to answer... we already know.

Now... instead of whispering into a girl's ear, you will have to agree before-hand, write it down and post it over on the "Relationships" board, and have it witnessed. How many girls are going to sign up for one-night stands with you?

Monk-Candidate Man-Onko: So... no more "one night stands"...

But... what if I know someone, I really like her, but it's too soon for sex? What do I do – nothing until both of us are ready? How do we get ready?

Master Blessing: You would declare a "getting to know you" relationship, declare it for 2 or 3 weeks, have it witnessed, and then take your time getting to know each other. Sex is possible, but optional.

However, Man-Onko, I must warn you: relationships between monk-candidates and their supervisors are definitely frowned-upon. In order to pursue a relationship with Monk Pico-Laton, she would have to...

Monk-Candidate Man-Onko: [Rising]: WHAT? Tell me that you're not reading my mind now!

Master Blessing: Sit down! So, I guess we're switching back to the T-P discussion.

I did not read your mind. I don't have to. We're using another of the Activated Powers, something we call "Collective Knowing". It's an ability to "see" past the surface layer of a person, to see a bit into their motivations, intentions and actions.

It's not reading your mind. It's like you've got on a second set of clothes. Just like I can see that you're wearing your trademark red shirt, I can also see this big sign hanging around your neck, saying, "I had sex with Pret-La last night." And she's got one saying the same thing.

Monk-Candidate Man-Onko: But... but... I never did anything with Pico-Laton!

Master Blessing: I'm not looking at what you did. I'm looking at your ENERGY. And every time you get around Pico-Laton, you light up like a Christmas tree.

Monk-Candidate Man-Onko: Wait! Does she know that?

Master Blessing: Of course she knows...

Monk-Candidate Man-Onko: Oh fuck! I am so screwed! SHIT!

Master Blessing: Language, please! Although in this case, it is understandable.

Would it help at all if I told you that the energy was reciprocated?

Monk-Candidate Man-Onko: You mean... she likes me?

Master Blessing: No, she doesn't "like" you. She LOVES you. You'd know that, if you weren't asleep in the T-P class.

Monk-Candidate Man-Onko: I can't take this...

Master Blessing: Yes you can. Get your head out of your hands. Stop slumping over - sit up straight. Look me in the eye. The only thing that's changed is you just found out what everyone else has known for months.

Monk-Candidate Man-Onko: Does she know about me and Pret-La?

Master Blessing: She knows about you and everyone else. That's her job to know. And she knows that you've gone to extraordinary lengths to keep those pairings private from her. And she knows why. That's the early budding of something we would call "love".

Monk-Candidate Man-Onko: Oh, man... I feel like I've been kicked in the gut...

Master Blessing: Excellent! So you do have the capacity to love!

Monk-Candidate Man-Onko: How can I ever face her again?

Master Blessing: Don't bog down into questions like that. Instead, explore the ENERGY that lies behind those feelings. That energy is the first step in understanding your feelings of LOVE.

Monk-Candidate Man-Onko: Are we done here? I want to go dig a hole and crawl in it...

Master Blessing: Almost done... One other point regarding the classes. We want you to attend and participate, in part because of your effect on the other students. When you are present, their T-P scores go UP. By a measurable amount.

Monk-Candidate Man-Onko: Really?

Master Blessing: Yes, and it's fairly across the board. They get better, even in the areas where you yourself are not improving.

Monk-Candidate Man-Onko: Hey! Isn't this like... STUD SERVICE? Shouldn't you be payin' me a fee for making all the others smarter?

Hey! Maybe I could wear a ROBE? And you could make me a MASTER! "Master Super-Stud, at your service"!

Master Blessing: Hmmm... I wonder what Pico-Laton would think about all that?

Monk-Candidate Man-Onko: Wow. I'm gonna call you "Master Buzzkill".

Master Blessing: All buzzing aside: where do we stand on the T-P classes?

Monk-Candidate Man-Onko: I'm cool. No more skipping or sleeping. Check. I will get what everybody else has already got. Check.

Master Blessing: And your sex life?

Monk-Candidate Man-Onko: Cut down on sex, start focusing on love. Check.

Master Blessing: You don't have to cut down on it, for the next 3 months.

Monk-Candidate Man-Onko: To tell you the truth, it was starting to get a little "old" after awhile...

Master Blessing: Yes, we know...

Monk-Candidate Man-Onko: Don't remind me... you know everything...

[end of transcript]

Year Five

You cannot escape the responsibility of tomorrow by evading it today.

Abraham Lincoln

The Commons

File No:		File Name:	The Commons
Location:		Parties:	The McMinnis and Alexrod families.
Monk/ Master Supervising:	Security Outreach Man-Onko, accompanied by Forest Pod, supervised by Adam, Master of Security		

Name:		Pgs:		Date:		Vol:	
Type of Transcript:	Mechanical xxx						
	Organic						

Preface by the North American Centers Archive Committee:

Not everyone could "fit" into a Center. Not everyone had to. Not everyone had to embrace the Center's culture and behaviors. But, everyone had to let go of the dysfunctional values and behaviors that led to the Upheavals...

This text is being provided in a rough draft format. Communication Access Realtime Translation (CART) facilitates communication accessibility and may not be a totally verbatim record of the proceedings. Let your coordinator know if you would prefer a more verbatim option.

Mike McGinnis: Stop! Stop right there! Who are you? Go away! We're armed!

Man-Onko: Take it easy. We mean you no harm. We are unarmed.

Mike McGinnis: Just go away! We don't have enough for our people. We can't help you. Just keep moving...

Alice McGinnis: Mike, it just isn't... RIGHT to send people away like that! We can offer them something, even a cup of water. We shouldn't be just turning people away. We've got to be CIVILIZED.

Mike McGinnis: I don't know if we can afford to be civilized, not after what happened that time...

Man-Onko: Please! We want nothing from you. And we have food and water we'd like to share with you.

Mike McGinnis: And why are we the recipients of your generosity?

Alice McGinnis: Mike! Your manners!

Man-Onko: I'd like to share a meal with you, me and my assistants. After the meal, I'd like to talk to you for an hour, no more. Then we'll be on our way.

Mike McGinnis: What's in the food? Is it drugged?

Alice McGinnis: MIKE!

Man-Onko: Actually, it is doctored a little! We add vitamins, minerals, and some medicine to combat the giardia that you all probably have, from drinking water from these streams around here. My assistants and I will be eating the same food -- no tricks.

It looks like about 25 of you, including the kids. There are 6 of us. With your permission, we'll lay out the food, eat, and then get down to business.

[After the meal]:

Mike McGinnis: Well, you're a man of your word! That was the best meal we've had since... well, for a long time! And the ice cream! ICE CREAM! Some of the younger kids have never tasted ice cream before!

Man-Onko: I can see... some of them are wearing more than they ate!

Alice McGinnis: Nancy, take those little ones down to the stream and rinse them off!

Mike McGinnis: Well, Friend, lets get down to business. How do we pay for this generous meal?

Man-Onko: No payment - the meal is our gift.

What we want to talk about is simple. You can't stay here. But we have some alternatives...

Mike McGinnis: What the hell you talkin' about? This is the best place we can find! It's away from the madness in the cities, there's good water and enough deer for us to eat. Why can't we stay? You want it for yourself?

Alice McGinnis: Now, Mike, give him a chance to explain himself! But, Mr. Man, I think you better explain quick -- we worked hard to put up these shelters and dig the fire pit. The men all say this place is secure.

Man-Onko: It's Man-Onko. You can't stay here. And, we've got somewhere better for you to go to. Just hear me out on both of those matters.

Mike McGinnis: Why don't you start with the "somewhere better" part.

Man-Onko: No, unfortunately, I need to explain the "You can't stay" part first.

You can't stay because this land is now under the supervision of the Ann Arbor Awakening Center.

Mike McGinnis: What? We know that this is part of a State forest! And you're not the State!

Man-Onko: Actually, we are. The State of Michigan has turned over management of this State forest to us.

Alice McGinnis: You're trying to kick all the people out of the State forests?

Man-Onko: No, not all the people. Just the ones that don't know what they're doing.

That gets me to the second part of why you must leave. You don't know what you're doing. You don't have adequate resources to stay out here. You're all going to die and you're going to destroy a good part of the forest before you go.

We're here to give you an alternative.

Alice McGinnis: [crying]

Mike McGinnis: Listen, pal, we're doing the best we can out...

Alice McGinnis: HE'S RIGHT! You know he's right, Mike! We talk about this all the time! We can't live out here anymore! The kids are getting sick! We can't live in those cars, and we can't live in the woods!

You don't know how to hunt! You see a deer, blow its head off with that damn Uzi of yours, then drag it back here! I don't know how to cook it! It's either bloody or burned! I'M SICK OF IT!

Shannon Alexrod: I need a shower! A FUCKING SHOWER! When's the last time any of us had a decent bath? You guys keep telling us how good we've got it compared to the others, but I DON'T CARE!

[To Man-Onko]: Mister, I don't care what your deal is! If it includes a shower and not sleeping on the ground, count me in!

[To Mike McGinnis:] Do you SEE these guys?? They're CLEAN! They smell like SOAP! Look at their clothes!

Mike McGinnis: Okay, everybody, calm down, calm down!

[To Man-Onko]: Okay, looks like you got our attention. What's your proposal?

Man-Onko: Okay, short and sweet. We are with the Awakening Center, and...

Peter Alexrod: The Awakening Center? Are you one of the monks? You folks rejected our application over 3 years ago! Said there were too many of us.

Man-Onko: I'm an Apprentice, kind of a Monk-Trainee. My companions are novices.

And your group is still too big for the Awakening Center. But, we've got an alternative that may work for you.

We've recently taken over several buildings and lots of land in the city. We are creating an urban analog to our Awakening Center. We are inviting you to live there.

Shannon Alexrod: Back in the city!

Peter Alexrod: Not so fast! Last time we checked, the city was a pretty dangerous place to hang out.

Man-Onko: I won't lie to you... It's still pretty dangerous in some places. In lots of places. But, that's one reason why you would go back -- to change the perception and the reality.

Peter Alexrod: What do you call this place?

Man-Onko: We call it "The Commons".

Peter Alexrod: Okay, say we take you up on your offer. We give up here, and go back into the city. What do we get?

Man-Onko: On one level: You get to stop butchering innocent animals. You get to stop eating burned or bloody meat. You get to take a SHOWER!

Shannon Alexrod: I'm in! I'm in! Sign me up!

[laughter]

Man-Onko: On another level: You get to work with other families like yours, decent people trying to survive in these times. People who wanted to get into a Center. You get to work for the common good. You get to think about the future of your children... like, who are they going to MATE with in the next few years?

And then there's the spiritual level, the transcendent level. Don't raise your hands, but think about this: how many in your group have considered suicide?

[pause]

Mike McGinnis: Mister, I don't think anyone here would consider taking their own life...

Alice McGinnis: Mike, you are such a FOOL! [crying]

Shannon Alexrod: Mike, do you really think that Jake blew off his own head in a "hunting accident" two years ago?

Man-Onko: The human race is SHRINKING. Whether by suicide or homicide, by famine or flood, there are fewer and fewer of us left on the planet. We estimate that the city has shrunk to less than 25% of its former size.

And, your little group here will get even smaller. For the same reasons. Unless you band together with others, and uplift your outlook.

So, here's the deal: If you say "yes", we will arrange safe transport from here to the Commons. We've already moved in about 20 families like yours into the area. They are keeping each other safe.

Each family will get a large communal area, that they can divide any way they see fit. They'll be given bedding, cooking supplies... everything you need for a new start. Families are also given plots of land, and we encourage you to work it with the other families.

The area is secure, but you'll have to work with others to keep it that way. Patrols around your neighborhoods, some non-lethal defense techniques. No uzis.

You and the other families will control your area, make decisions, practice democracy... subject to the governance of the Awakening Center. And, most of the time, we won't be exercising that governance...

Mike McGinnis: We would need more assurance than that. It sounds like we would be like... like a colony.

Man-Onko: Very perceptive. That's exactly what you'd be. You will have near-complete freedom, unless you start doing things that will harm yourself or harm the Center. You can't discriminate against others in the Commons. You can't use violence. Or recreational drugs. Or steal. We call those the Prime Rules. In addition, you've got to take all the people we send you.

Mike McGinnis: Well, we don't want to do those things anyway.

Man-Onko: So, you probably won't feel or even notice the Center's control.

Everyone in your family will work -- no exceptions. Communal cooking, cleaning, building, school, security... everyone will be assigned work.

If you break the Prime Rules on violence, stealing, drugs, you will be brought right back here. Other than that, you make the rules there.

Mike McGinnis: What happens if we say "no"?

Shannon Alexrod: To hell with that! Hey, Mister, I'm going with you NOW!

Alice McGinnis: Me too!

Mike McGinnis: Alice! You can't leave me!

Alice McGinnis: I'm not leaving YOU, I'm leaving THIS! You can come if you want...

Man-Onko: Hold on! Let me explain a few things!

[to Shannon Alexrod:] This offer is made to this GROUP, not to the individuals. If you want to go on your own, you can apply for entry to the Commons.

Shannon Alexrod: Just point me in the right direction!

Man-Onko: Mike, if your group refuses the offer, nothing happens... EXCEPT, you will not be allowed to kill any animal with a gun, anymore. You can snare rabbits, fish, eat berries... but no hunting.

Mike McGinnis: You can't do that!

Man-Onko: I can and I did.

Mike McGinnis: How are you gonna stop me?

Man-Onko: By taking your gun away from you.

Mike McGinnis: Is that your army you're gonna use to take it away from me?

Man-Onko: [smiling]: I won't need an army. We'll take it peacefully and nonviolently.

Alice McGinnis: Oh, Mike, just can it! You know you're low on bullets anyway! We're probably 2-3 months away from either starving or getting eaten.

Man-Onko: Speaking of which: We are tracking both grizzly bears and wolves that are moving into this forest. They're about 2 months out at their present rate of movement.

Mike McGinnis: Wolves? Grizzlies? They have never been in this part of the forest!

Man-Onko: You are correct. Times have changed.

Mike McGinnis: I don't believe you! You're just trying to scare us!

Alice McGinnis: He's not trying!

Man-Onko: What we will do: My assistants and I will bed down over there for the night. In the morning, we'll serve you breakfast -- which will include fresh eggs.

[Everyone]: EGGS!

Man-Onko: Yes! My novices are getting quite good at making omelets!

Alice McGinnis: [crying]

Man-Onko: Then, we will hear your decision about whether you will move to the Commons or stay here.

And: One way or another, your gun will come with us. If you decide to stay, we will leave you with fishing gear, a book on how to make snares for rabbits and chipmunks, a few knives. But, no more butchering deer with that gun.

Mike McGinnis: Okay, Mister, you've been pretty straight with us. We'll talk it over. I think I can see which way this is going to go...

Shannon Alexrod: Damn straight!

Mike McGinnis: ... so we'll give you your answer in the morning.

[end of transcript]

[Afternote: The McMinnis and Alexrod families elected to move into the Commons. They were very hardworking and helped to establish the Detroit Commons as a model for urban transformation.]

News Article: Seizure of Center Assets

Government Orders Seizure of Center Assets; Military "Practically Refuses"

Today, Congress issued an order that all assets of Commonway Institute's "Awakening Centers" be seized. However, in a stunning statement, General Adam Popkin, the top Crisis Commander during the current Domestic Affairs Executive Order, has said that his troops will "probably" not comply with the asset seizure.

"We have inadequate resources as it is. Those folks from the Awakening Centers have been giving us very valuable assistance in nonviolent crowd control, effective and positive resource distribution, even providing their own food and organizing governing circles. In those cities where the government has completely collapsed, some of the Centers have been the difference between getting along and total anarchy. Now, why would we want to put them out of business?"

Gen. Popkin hastened to add, "Don't get me wrong. I fully intend to comply with that Congressional seizure order. I've got some of my top people working on an implementation plan, that will allow us to execute the seizure, without also creating mass disruptions on the street. They are studying the problem."

A senior staffer on General Popkins staff, speaking on condition of anonymity, was more blunt. "It will happen when Hell freezes over. There's no way to shut down the Centers without also shutting down large sectors of the country. Implementing that seizure order would be like committing national suicide. We would be cutting our own throats. I really wish Congress would get its head out of its ass and come up for air once in a while."

Nathan Wilkins, the "Abbot" for the Seattle Center was equally blunt. The former stock broker, now known by his Center name of Sierra, said, "We're helping people. Congress thinks its role is to get in the way of that. They do what they have to do, and we do our job. One day, the people in this country will realize that they simply don't need Congress anymore."

The Banned Book - The Five Latent Powers

Why five? Why not 25? Why not follow (for example) Rupert Sheldrake's research, and look for the mechanism that allows dogs to know when their masters are coming home? Why not research and develop the ability of drivers to "manifest" convenient parking places?

My work has a point. You may disagree with the point... in which case, reading the rest of the book is moot. (Well, you're into it now, so you might as well finish!)

My point is this: WHAT DO WE NEED TO KNOW/DO/BE IN ORDER TO CREATE A WORLD THAT WORKS FOR ALL? This is the test/critical focus from which I measure things – my work and the work of others.

From the "World for All" measuring stick, learning about dog telepathy or parking space manifestation is not important – gaining the power to change violent behavior among humans, or to reverse the effects of global climate damage, or to alleviate poverty and greed... these are essential for our survival and thrival on this planet.

So, looking from our "different lens", I have identified Five Latent Powers that can help us in our quest for a "World for All":

#1: Universal/ Common Knowing
This is the first and greatest of the Powers. With this, our ancestors accessed the "knowing" of the Universe.

This is not like looking at an encyclopedia. This is not the empty accumulation of not-necessarily-relevant "facts" and information. With this power, one would "know" what one NEEDED to know, when one needed to know it.

Unlike the picture painted by Breaker anthropologists, ancient holons did not live in fear or scarcity. They KNEW where their food was, when the rains would come, when to shelter from the hurricanes... They knew how to "talk" to the LIFE Energy Field (and all of the manifestations of it). They knew that they were an integral part of a well ordered whole.

They didn't <u>believe</u> in the Universal Knowing Power. Beliefs have nothing to do with it. They experienced Universal Knowing like you experience Gravity.

This form of knowing includes:

- *Group telepathy*
- *Group knowing*
- *Consciousness mental influencing*
- *Consciousness shifting (moving one's consciousness to spatial points outside one's body)*
- *Consciousness transfer (shape shifting)*
- *Communication via transcendence*

#2: Spatial Powers
Holons can affect/catalyze actions at a distance. In most cases, these actions are seen as "impossible" under current ways of perceiving "reality".

Holons could cause rain to fall where they willed. They could locate (and bring closer) food sources. They could cut, move and assemble huge stones. Other spatial powers include:

- *Transportation (moving from one location to another, at great speed, or without any time interval)*
- *Navigation (crossing vast distances while "knowing" one's destination)*
- *Trans-location (having one's consciousness in a different location/position than one's body)*
- *Bi-location (being in two or more distinct locations at once)*
- *Object moving and manipulation (for example, cutting and moving megalithic stones)*
- *Object sensing (seeing/knowing objects from a distance.)*

#3: Temporal Powers

We have an awareness of two types of "time". One is "objective" time – measured by clocks and watches. The other is "subjective" time, the sense that events are moving faster or slower than normal, the sense that time can "stand still" at profound moments.

We've been taught that "objective" time is "real" and "subjective" time is a fantasy.

The exact opposite is true.

Our latent temporal powers include:

- *Timeshifting:*
  - *Speeding up time*
  - *Slowing down time*
  - *Stopping time altogether*

- *Shifting to alternate narratives/realities*
- *Temporal forecasting/fortune-telling/seeing the future*

#4: Communication Powers

Scientists regularly report that up to 70% of our human communications are "non-verbal". They talk about the non-verbal part being made up of subtle body signs, eye cues, even pheromones.

All of this is true. And, there is a part of communication that cannot be measured and quantified. Communication is a Field, a Power. And it exists between humans. And, it exists with the more-than-human world. And it can be regularly accessed by holons.

Inclusive consciousness is not the sole domain of human beings, but is cross-, inter-, and trans-species. Therefore, Global Communications can take place with all beings who have inclusive consciousness. Inclusive consciousness crosses species, the way it crosses individuals within species. At one time, Breakers did not believe that all "human" beings were capable of consciousness. (In their world-view, my African ancestors were not capable of consciousness... and they locked the doors to their educational institutions and put my ancestors in chains to insure the survival of that "belief".) The descendants of those Breakers will scoff at my notion that yaks and I share the same consciousness.

Examples of Communication Powers include:
- *Nonverbal communication with other human beings (telepathy)*
- *Communication with transcendent beings (Gods, goddesses, avatars)*
- *Communication with other Earth beings (other species)*
- *Communication with ancestors (beings that used to have bodies)*
- *Communication with future beings*

#5: Bodily Powers
This is the most-studied, yet least important of the Five Latent Powers. Possibly because Breaker scientists can at least set up the experiments, even if they do not understand the results.

Examples of Bodily Latent Powers include:
- *Changing heart rate, respiration, etc.*
- *Entering into transcendent meditative states.*
- *Going without food and water for extended times.*
- *Returning to life/ postponing death*

"The Ecstatic Society"
Shariff M. Abdullah

(Banned by Act of Congress)

News Article: The New Police: Omaha Hires Awakening Center to Provide Security in the City.

In the most recent Omaha City Council meeting, the Council voted unanimously to disband its current Police Department, and replace security in the city with the "Agents" of the Omaha Awakening Center.

"It's simple. We can't afford to continue to spend more and more money on policing, while getting fewer and fewer returns." Mayor Gibson said after the vote. "I don't think it takes a genius to see that our police department gets smaller every year, crime goes up every year, and the whole operation gets more expensive every year."

This sentiment was echoed by Councilor Bates, who was the strongest advocate for the plan. "Fewer and fewer of our officers were willing to take city scrip instead of US dollars. The Police Union was unwilling to consider alternatives to traditional policing operations. The citizens were increasingly hostile to police attempts to manage the ongoing Upheavals. Something had to give – and it was the police force."

Under the new security plan, the Awakening Centers will supply an unspecified number of experienced security "agents" to take the place of uniformed officers. Said Abbot Fawn, "We aren't saying how many agents we are providing, when they will be on the streets, whether or not we'll be in uniform... nothing. The good folks don't need to know, and the bad folks will figure it out the hard way."

"Our security goals are simple. The people will be more secure. Not only will crime go down, people will FEEL safer. And that's because the people will be involved in providing their own security."

The new security arrangements have encountered vocal criticism. "This is outrageous! You bet we're going to court!" said Sgt. Anderson, the president of the local Police Union. "If you think crime's been bad up to now, watch what happens when you turn crime-fighting over to the CRIMINALS! We know that these "Awakening" people are taking and using drugs! They are TRAFFICKING in drugs! How can you expect them to turn around and start POLICING the drug trade! It's going to be chaos on the streets once they take over!"

When asked about the Police Union President's drug allegations, Abbot Fawn was dismissive in her reply. "How can you have MORE drug trafficking? The streets are already awash in destructive drugs. The current police don't answer emergency calls now... how can we answer FEWER calls than none? There are whole sections of the city that the current police don't patrol... how can we be MORE invisible than zero? Believe me, the only thing that will suffer from this transfer of policing authority are the city's donut shops."

"Yes, the Awakening Centers use many plants and herbs for healing. Some of them have psychoactive properties. NONE are used for "entertainment". All are used under the supervision of our healing staff. The fact that Sgt. Anderson doesn't know the difference between heroin and medical marijuana is a major part of the policing problem."

Another vocal critic of the plan is Rev. David Lawson of the People's Political Church of Jesus. "We need less talk and more action! These godless freaks over in that cult aren't even going to carry GUNS! We need MORE guns on our streets, not less! What are they going to do when an out of control gang of migrants starts raping our women?

"The only problem we've got is that we've been tying the hands of our cops, rather than letting them get tough with crime!   If we shoot some of these migrant rapists BEFORE they have a chance to harm our women, the rest of them will get the message and leave our city!"

In a strange twist of circumstances, it was the agreement of Police Chief Lewis that convinced some of the more reluctant Councilors to join the band wagon. "We just can't work in an atmosphere of crumbling budgets, fraying social structures and bureaucracies unwilling to change. Authorizing more violence will not make the violence on our streets go away. We're at a crisis point – we've got to explore another way."

The Abbot was equally adamant (and equally evasive) about the question of violence. "Violence in the city will go down, starting the first day of our work. We won't be shooting anyone – we won't carry guns. We won't need them. And, we won't need any courts, either. We're going to give all of those practicing violence a really good talking-to."

The Police Union President was dismissive of the Abbot's claims. "Anybody who walks these streets without a gun is just plain crazy.   Giving our city over to these Awakening Center lunatics is insane. Mark my words: inside of one week, they're going to be begging us to come back to work!"

News Article: "Awakening Agents" Sting Operation Results in Arrest of Rev. Lawson, 19 Others

In a stunning operation, Rev. David Lawson of the People's Political Church of Jesus, along with 18 of his followers have been arrested on a variety of charges, including manslaughter, rape, money-laundering and weapons charges.

The arrests, coming only 3 days after the Omaha Awakening Center took over the policing functions in the city, came as a complete surprise. Said Abbot Fawn, "In any city, everybody knows the perpetrators of violence and anti-social behavior. They know, and they are afraid to say. We simply took away the fear."

"David Lawson operated a "Vigilante Squad" out of his 'church'. The Squad would go out and commit beatings, killings and rapes against innocent victims, blame them on Latinos and other minorities, then go out and punish the innocent for the crimes they themselves had committed. All the time hiding behind a twisted misinterpretation of the Bible."

Anthony Lester, attorney for Rev. Lawson, said, "My client's rights have been thrown right out the window! He has a right to be held in the city jail – instead, they have all of them imprisoned down there at that "Awakening Center"! I will have a writ of habeas corpus before the courts in the morning!"

Said Abbot Fawn, "We don't use the City Jail... we see it as part of the old system. Plus, the food's better over here! The entire atmosphere is just more... friendly. More conducive to conversation.

"No, Lawson does not have the 'right' to a jail filled with his supporters and cronies. If the courts order him released, we'll release him. Until then, WE will provide them with secure detention until trial."

"Half of the men arrested have confessed. We expect the other half to do so shortly. All have implicated David Lawson. He will have a lot to answer to."

When questioned about how the Awakening Center "Agents" were able to achieve such a high number of arrests without resort to violence and guns, Abbot Fawn was evasive. "We just used the same tools of every non-violent, non-militarized, non-uniformed police department. In our arrests, no one was shot, no one was threatened, nothing was broken. No guns waved around. Not even any unpleasant language was used. All very civil and polite."

In her press conference, Abbot Fawn issued a warning to others involved in the "Vigilante Squad": "In their confessions, the former 'Vigilante Squad' members have implicated certain members of the former police staff. The allegations are serious.

"In light of your years of service to this community, I am giving you 24 hours to either turn yourselves in or get out of town. If you are still here tomorrow at this time, I am coming for you."

Neither Police Union President Anderson nor his four principal department aides have been found for comment, despite numerous attempts to do so.

The Review

File No:		File Name:	The Review
Location:	Denver Awakening Center	Parties:	Monk-Candidate Man-Onko
Monk/ Master Supervising:	Monk Ariel		Annual progress interview

Name:		Pgs:		Date:		Vol:	
Type of Transcript:	Mechanical xxx						
	Organic						

Preface by North American Archive Committee:

Over time, some things change. And some things change radically...

[start of transcript]

Ariel: It's great to see you again! Wow, you've really grown up!

Man-Onko: Yeah, it's strange... I kind of FEEL grown up.

Ariel: Weren't you the one who walked in here, saying that you were a "man" already?

Man-Onko: And thanks a lot for reminding me of that! I think the only thing grown up about me was my mouth!

Ariel: Well said. Now, let's get down to your interview. This won't take long, but it has to be done. It's why we shipped you back here, after all your fun and games in Seattle.

Man-Onko: I really like the Seattle Center. Nice and green. But, I think I'm going to wind up back here after all my assignments are over...

Ariel: We'll talk about your forward assignments last. First, we have to review your physical exam... This says you've grown a full foot since coming to the Center!

Man-Onko: You mean 30 centimeters...

Ariel: Don't even pretend to try to correct me! I know the deal is metric, but I learned in feet, and I'm not giving it up!

Man-Onko: You know I'll have to report you for expulsion from the Center.

Ariel: Your smart talk hasn't changed. Nor has your failure to notice who has your evaluation form in his grasp.

Man-Onko: Oops! I meant I'll have to report you for COMMENDATION in the Center! Let's talk about that extra foot!

Ariel: Thought so! As a result of your physical, the health staff wants to upgrade their assessment of your age. They think you're a LOT older than the initial assessment.

Man-Onko: [Pause]: Could be.

Ariel: In fact, they think you know you are older, and used your malnourished size as a survival mechanism on the Outside. They want me to ask you if know your true age.

Man-Onko: [Pauses]: Do I have to answer?

Ariel: Well... no, I guess. They are going to assign you an upgraded age assessment of 14 or 15 at entry, which would make you 19 or 20 years old now.

Man-Onko: Okay, I'll take that.

Ariel: Man-Onko, are you learning anything here? There is no punishment here for telling the truth!

Man-Onko: [pauses]: Well... it's not about telling the truth. It's about... who you get to associate with, who your age-mates are.

Ariel: Is "associate with" a euphemism for "have sex with"?

Man-Onko: God! You guys never let up, do you?

Ariel: And, apparently, neither do you! We'll discuss your sex life some other time...

How about we put you down for 19 years old now. If you feel the need to "confess" later, I can change it.

Man-Onko: Cool.

Ariel: Now, on to emotional stability... Your file says you've been making your emotional transitions very well. We were afraid that your unique psychic talent would separate you from your peers, but that hasn't happened.

Man-Onko: Yeah, "Smell-O-Vision". I think everybody else makes a bigger deal out of it than I do. I'd trade it in for the ability to do a power-dunk in basketball.

Ariel: The ability to power-dunk a basketball has never saved anyone's life, or brought a community together.

Man-Onko: No... but it... it might come in handy sometimes...

Ariel: You mean, like in getting laid?

Man-Onko: Oh, God, please! Tell me my sex life's not in my report!

Ariel: In excruciating detail! It's quite entertaining!

Come on, Apprentice, get your head out of your hands! You've got nothing to be ashamed of! The report said you made your transition from our chemically-enforced celibacy to a "full sexual experience", and then another smooth transition to emotionally-based relationships. Looks like you've no hang-ups on your horizon.

Man-Onko: [Softly]: Only one.

Ariel: By the way, you may want to know that your former pod-mates, Victory and Krista-Lin, are engaged!

Man-Onko: [Pause]: Engaged to do what?

Ariel: They are in a relationship!

Man-Onko: [Pause]: With who?

Ariel: With each other!

Man-Onko: You know, I'm hearing the words you're saying, but I'm having a lot of trouble trying to understand what you mean.

Ariel: You think you're having trouble! The counsellors freaked out when they saw that they posted that they were "dating".

Man-Onko: WAIT A MINUTE!! Are you saying that Victory and Krista-Lin are DATING!?!? EACH OTHER!?!?

Ariel: They're beyond dating! They've announced that they intend to marry!

Man-Onko: [Long pause]: You know, if you told me that Krista-Lin had sprouted wings and was flying around the Canteen, I could believe that, more than you telling me that those two would have ANYTHING to do with each other! How did that happen? Who was their witness?

Ariel: Given their history, we suspended our own rules and required that they have THREE witnesses. One of their choice, one of our choice, and their counsellor. And, we require them to undergo weekly counseling sessions – both together and separate. And, by the way, they chose Dorado as their witness.

Man-Onko: So, Gopher Pod lives on, without me!

Ariel: They said they would have chosen you, if you were still in Denver.

Man-Onko: Wow. But, what about... well you know, Krista-Lin's... history?

Ariel: She still can't talk about her experiences, still freaks out whenever anyone tries to bring it up.

Man-Onko: Yeah, I still remember that day we were in the cave, during the fire. I thought she was gonna lose it.

Ariel: So did we. All the monks were carrying dart guns that day. We were about to take her out, when Victory turned the situation. Victory! Who'd a thought he would be her rescuer?

Man-Onko: Wow... what would have happened if you knocked her out?

Ariel: We would have locked her up, isolated her. Probably forever. Gopher would have ended on a very bad note.

Man-Onko: What about Victory? Does he know about her now?

Ariel: He knows nothing. He knows something's up, he's not dumb. But he doesn't have a clue about what. He thinks all the extra counseling is about HIM.

There was a big debate among the monks and masters about whether or not to tell him. We decided that she had to be the one to tell him... and she's not talking.

And... maybe that's okay. We've had contact with one of the Hives in Asia. We hear that they've developed a technique that can make someone "forget" something that happened in their lives. We asked them to work on Krista-Lin.

Man-Onko: That would be cool! How does that work? It beats being in therapy for the rest of her life. And, I can't see her freaking out for the rest of her life, either. If the damaged part can be tossed away – that would be cool.

Ariel: Well, they offered, she agreed, and we're just working out the details right now. If it works, it would be a lot better than our work at "mind-wiping". Our folks say that her damage is so deep, they would have to wipe out most of her personality in order to get to the damage. Having her wind up a vegetable isn't in anyone's best interests.

If it works for her, we'll use it on some of the others, the ones we still have locked up. It could really change things around here.

Man-Onko: Yeah. She's cute and pretty smart, once she manages to open her mouth.

Ariel: She's been opening her mouth more and more, now that Victory is actually on her side.

By the way...None of us have forgotten that you were helpful in her healing process. And that you kept your mouth shut. You are the only person not a monk or master who knew anything at all. Most can't even guess at her damage.

Man-Onko: Well, she's cool, so glad to help.

Ariel: We think you're going to like the "new" Victory as well...

Man-Onko: Hey, don't push your luck! In the "nonviolence meditations", when we have to picture someone to be peaceful with, I still visualize him!

Ariel: Come back next week and see how you feel!

Let's move on to the rest of your evaluation...

You know, we've had you on a "fast track" for monkhood. Partly because of your talent, and partly because... well, you've "got it". You grasp the big picture really well, and you work hard to fit into the local realities. We've given you some assignments that, quite frankly, should have gone to a monk, not an apprentice. Way above your pay grade...

Man-Onko: Throw me into the deep end of the pool and see if I float or sink, right?

Ariel: [pauses]: The monk who said that to you in Seattle was out of line when he said it. As advanced as we are, we still carry some leftover baggage from Outside – like jealousy and envy.

Man-Onko: No problem... Always a few ants at the picnic, right?

Ariel: Right. But tell me... [pauses] Have you ever been on a picnic? Have you ever SEEN a picnic?

Man-Onko: [pauses] Nope. It's just a word out of a book I read. There was a nice picture of a family in a park – not a park with squatters, looters, tweakers, killboys, mad dogs, druggies... like I said, a picture.

Ariel: You've been gaining a good use of the language. You apply the things you read very well. Just make sure that you don't exchange your own reality for things you find in books. Although parts of it are painful, it's what makes you who you are.

Man-Onko: When you were talking about Krista-Lin, I was thinking that there are parts of my life I wouldn't mind forgetting.

Ariel: We've all been there... The fact that we're here, on this nice, sunny day, chatting about it means that we don't have to forget. It's only when we can't do our jobs, when we can't fit in, that we need help.

And you've got the opposite problem: when you fit in too well, when you do your job with high marks... we give you more work!

Man-Onko: Yay for me! Resting for a whole day was getting to be too much! So, where to next?

[end of transcript]

Year Six

Make no little plans; they have no magic to stir men's blood and probably themselves will not be realized. Make big plans; aim high in hope and work, remembering that a noble, logical diagram once recorded will never die... Remember that our sons and our grandsons are going to do things that would stagger us.

Daniel Burnham

Fresno Falls

File No:		File Name: Fresno Falls
Location:	Transcript of tightbeam video call	Parties: Master Morning Light, the Abbot of Fresno Center. Security Master Zorro, assisted by Monk-Candidate Man-Onko
Monk/ Master Supervising:	The Culture Council, First Councilor Tanaku presiding	

Name:		Pgs:		Date:		Vol:	
Type of Transcript:	Mechanical xxx						
	Organic						

Preface by the North American Centers Archive Committee:

This incident may represent the Awakening Movement's darkest hour.

From the beginning, the goal of the Awakening Movement was not to prevent the dissolution of society. The goal was to create NEW systems and structures, ones that respond to the needs of the butterfly.

From the beginning, it was understood that the dissolution of the Age of Waste would take tens of millions of people with it. There was nothing that the Awakening Centers could do to prevent this from happening.

This put the Awakening Centers at odds with many, who thought the Centers did too little to alleviate the suffering of humanity.

Some of the disagreement was within the Movement itself.

This text is being provided in a rough draft format. Communication Access Realtime Translation (CART) facilitates communication accessibility and may not be a totally verbatim record of the proceedings. Let your coordinator know if you would prefer a more verbatim option.

[start of transcript]

Councilor Tanaku: Yes, per your request, we have reviewed our earlier decision. The earlier decision stands. We will send you no aid.

Morning Light: What!? You're not going to help us?

Councilor Tanaku: That is correct. We are not going to set a precedent with you, of a Center disobeying our direct orders, and then having us bail them out when things turn out exactly the way we predicted they would.

Morning Light: But people are DYING here! Townspeople and our people!

Councilor Tanaku: Yes, that is exactly what we predicted would happen if you opened your doors and tried to feed everybody.

Morning Light: We've got 30 or 40 dead here! Maybe more than that... We can't count them all! Last night, the last of the clean water and the last of the food supplies were looted. We have NO FOOD! Do you understand that? No food! Where is your compassion?

Councilor Tanaku: Opening your doors is proof that you don't understand what 'compassion' means. Compassion doesn't mean doing stupid, dangerous things, in an attempt to "be nice". Compassion doesn't mean trying to feed an entire city, when you KNOW you don't have the resources to do so!

Compassion means that we sit here, on food supplies, and let this scenario play out. In our last decision, which was unanimous by the way, the entire Culture Council was in tears.

Our hearts go out to you... But our food won't.

Morning Light: But... What are we going to DO?

Councilor Tanaku: That is exactly the question you should have asked yourselves three weeks ago, when you made that decision to open your doors.

The forecasters predict that, when the townspeople discover that you no longer have any food, they will burn your Center to the ground. Our recommendation is that you LEAVE NOW. Take only what you can carry, and leave Fresno. You will not be safe anywhere in that city. Go somewhere else and try to establish a Center. Or, go to one of the nearest existing Centers and see if they will let you in. We will recommend that they do.

We've sent every available airship to your area. We are willing to assist in your evacuation as much as we can. But we feel the majority of your people will have to walk to the nearest Centers.

Morning Light: But, but... Those are hundreds of miles away! And this is our home! We've worked for years to establish this Center!

Councilor Tanaku: Yes, and those are all considerations you should've made before you made this misguided attempt at compassion.

We have sent Security Chief Zorro to you, with instructions to assist you in getting out of the Center. He is instructed to organize all available transit, including air and water transport, to save as many lives as possible. That we've put our airships above you in broad daylight shows how serious we take this matter.

But... Master Zorro will help, only AFTER you have given the order to evacuate the Center. Master Zorro?

Zorro: Yes, I'm listening...

Councilor Tanaku: You will remain in the air, remaining in contact with the Culture Council by tightbeam, until Morning Light gives the order to evacuate. If he doesn't make that decision by midnight tonight, you are instructed remove or destroy the Center's records, to remove their tightline communications equipment, and then to use your airship for your departure. You will take with you any who choose to leave the Center voluntarily. Do you understand?

Zorro: Yes... although we may have to clear out earlier than that, if the situation deteriorates.

Councilor Tanaku: Of course. You have complete authority to do what you need to do to protect yourself and to achieve your mission.

Zorro: Thank you.

Councilor Tanaku: Morning Light; we will alert the Centers at Sacramento, Santa Barbara, and San Jose to look for you. Those are small centers... They can't take all of you, so I would suggest you divide up and see who goes where. Many of you will have to walk – And I don't have to tell you how dangerous those roads are.

Morning Light: But... You helped Tucson, when they were about to be overrun by townspeople.

Councilor Tanaku: You used this argument when you first asked for aid. As we told you then, your...

Morning Light: You are signing our death sentence...

Councilor Tanaku: No, we are not! The death sentence, which you signed yourself, was when you threw away the integrity of the Center by opening the floodgates to violent, desperate and dangerous people.

And it is a death sentence. You don't want to know the probability factors the forecasters give you for getting out of there alive. That's why we suggest you give the order to leave right now.

We helped Tucson, for the same reason that we will NOT help you. Their troubles came from outside, not as a consequence of making bad internal decisions. We were PREPARED for their troubles -- we knew the old government would attack us somewhere. We had been stockpiling food and water for years, ready to help whichever Center got blockaded.

Tucson, as bloody as that conflict became, is our success story. You are not.

Morning Light: Look, just give us ten shipments of food! That will give us time to secure things around here...

Councilor Tanaku: ... Not ten shipments. Not one shipment. Anything we give you will simply make the problem WORSE. You are desperate, so you can't see the reality that you face.

Morning Light: You're all just a bunch of greedy bastards! You're sitting up in your secure buildings, not facing the realities on the streets! People are starving! We tried to feed the people!

Councilor Tanaku: No, you tried to feed the BREAKERS! The WASTERS! You tried to feed people whose consciousness created the problems in the first place! You brought that consciousness inside your Center! And you are living with the results.

You forgot the primary purpose and mission of the Centers: to feed the Global CONSCIOUSNESS! You were focused on their bellies – we are focused on their HEARTS. You were focused on individuals – we are focused on HUMANITY.

As long as our resources are limited, as long as we are forced to make choices, we will feed those bellies that are attached to good hearts, and minds not filled with delusions.

Morning Light: You don't know what it's like to see hungry people and do nothing! To stand around...

Councilor Tanaku: Of course we do! We're doing it right now! Do you think that we <u>want</u> to see you suffer? That each of us is not heart wounded by this situation, and the terrible decisions that we have to make, because of your irresponsible actions?

The Culture Council has been watching helplessly as people starve around the world. We are doing triage on a planetary level -- determining where we can intervene and where we can't. Gambling our future against our present.

This is the lesson that you fail to get – that all actions have consequences. The people of the Age of Waste failed to get that lesson, and billions are dying around the world because of it. YOU and your fellow Fresno Councilors failed to get that lesson, and you will watch your Center, and its inhabitants, die.

The Fresno situation will mark the real maturity of The Culture Council. This is the first time we've had to make these hard choices in a hard situation, choices that will lead to the deaths of our own people. We realize that we have made a terrible decision... but it's not the wrong one.

It's not about whether or not you as an individual lives or dies. It's not even about whether the Fresno Center lives or dies. It's about the MOVEMENT... That won't move very far, if we give away the seeds that we are storing for the future.

Morning Light: To hell with you. To hell with the entire Culture Council!

[end of transcript]

[Afternote: Morning Light and the Fresno Culture Council refused to give the evacuation order. Security Master Zorro removed himself and the Culture Council dirigibles from Fresno. He did so, taking 30 monks/masters and 50 of 80 novices with him.

That night, the Fresno Center was overrun, looted and burned. Of the 200 masters, monks and novices left in the Center, 90 of them arrived at the Sacramento Center three weeks later, some in critical condition. 15 died on the journey, succumbing to their wounds or to the conditions on the road. All of them were eventually redistributed to other Centers throughout the West.

According to the survivors, the 20 member Fresno Council attempted to negotiate with the townspeople. They were all killed, and their bodies mutilated.

Of the remaining 55, their whereabouts are unknown and are presumed dead.]

Year Seven:

We're about to play a strange game of musical chairs. There are 30 people circling in the room. The game starts with two chairs available. When the music stops, everyone without a chair dies.
James Harold Moore (2006)

News Alert: Global Climate Change Reverses!

It's official: This is the fifth year of dramatic declines in all of the extenuating factors of global climate change.

"It's just not possible. It's not. It's that simple. I'm looking at the data, but I just don't believe it," says Scientist Karl Johanssen of the US Climatic Data Center. "I've been doing research in this field since I was an undergraduate – these trends don't just turn around on a whim. These numbers are impossible. There must be some error in data collection."

Some attribute the spectacular change in global weather conditions to the dramatic downturn in industrial output, caused by the years of the Upheavals that have rocked governments and economies around the world. Dr. Johanssen remains skeptical.

"We're not measuring what the industrial capacity was planning to do. We're measuring what's already been done. Atmospheric carbon has been at 440 ppm and above, for decades. Then, in just 3 years, it drops to 370 ppm, and is still falling! That just doesn't happen! It CAN'T happen!"

Abbot Sierra of the Seattle Awakening Center takes a radically different position. "Of course it can happen. We've been working for this day for ten years!" Abbot Sierra says that his work takes place... in a different realm.

"Breaker technology jeopardized our ecological niche on this planet. And, the things the Breaker scientists proposed to "solve" the problem of global climate change have made everything WORSE! Don't forget that the TCP that caused 'Sick Rain' were supposed to make things better."

"We went in another direction. By apologizing to the Earth, by our constant prayers and our Ceremonies, by addressing the consciousness of the planet and all of Her systems – including us – we have been able to pull ourselves back from the brink."

"It's never been a straight-line proposition. The Breaker scientists, with their measurements and their computer modeling, have been looking too closely in only one direction. We opened up another."

Dr. Johanssen is dismissive of the Abbot's claims. "I think our good Abbot has been eating the spiked granola! He can believe that all he has to do is meditate and the CO_2 will magically fall from the sky. He can believe they can all hold hands and sing, and all the atmospheric carbon will turn to Happy Dust.

He can stay on top of his hill and keep chasing moonbeams. Those of us who live in the real world will continue to rely on computer modeling and the other tools of science.

"We just need to figure out why the data has gone so screwy."

The Power
MEMORANDUM

FR: THE NORTH AMERICAN CULTURE COUNCIL
TO: ALL AWAKENING CENTERS AND URBAN COMMONS
RE: THE NORTH AMERICAN ELECTRICAL GRID

The moment has arrived.

Our forecasters have long predicted that the North American electrical grid would collapse, and that the failure would be catastrophic. The catastrophe has arrived, and all Awakening Centers are requested to put their emergency operations plans into effect, immediately.

BACKGROUND:

In forecasting societal transformation, many primary markers were identified, including:

- Collapse of money system
- Unreliability of fossil fuels supplies, coupled with "peak oil" shortages
- Destabilized food production and distribution, including failure of petro-fertilizers and industrial bee-death
- Political instability
- Local/ regional power outages

With each of these systems, the Breaker authorities believed it was possible to "snap back" to a dysfunctional "normal". Indeed, with many of the crises in the early years of the Upheavals, the Breaker authorities were able to ignore or repair the damage. Even the collapse of the money system led to the "federal coupon" system that many still cling to, in the vain hope that dollars will once again be worth something.

However, according to our forecasters, the "point of no return" is the failure of the electrical grid. So much of the system has been automated and computerized, there were few humans who knew where the raw materials came from and where the electricity produced was going.

That system ran with inhuman efficiency. Those controlling computers ran on electricity. With no electricity, the grid failed. The failure was not so much a failure of capacity as a failure of SYSTEM.

Extent of Power Systems Collapse
Outside of isolated pockets of electrical capacity (generally centered around hydro or solar plants or nuclear power plants) the North American electrical generating capacity is permanently down. Coal shipments to the East Coast's coal-generating plants have ceased. Generation from hydro plants has largely failed, in part due to dried-up rivers and streams, and in part due to cyber-attacks on generation systems. (It is unclear if the cyber-attacks triggered the overall collapse of the grid, or whether they were a by-product of a generalized collapse. From our point of view, it does not matter.)

All Awakening Centers must generate their own power. Period. Those Awakening Centers that have continued to use supplemental power from the electrical grid should be advised that these failures are PERMANENT. They should immediately go to their own power austerity programs to reduce their electrical needs, coupled with emergency electrical generation.

ISOLATION OF GENERATING CAPACITY:
The failure of the grid, the cyber-attacks and the resulting load imbalances crashed most nuclear power generation stations. According to our information, virtually all of the

nuclear plants closed in a "safe" manner – there is little chance of nuclear contamination from these plants in the short term.

However, three plants are in imminent danger of a catastrophic collapse. The plant operators lack the resources, technical know-how (or the will) to close these plants in a safe manner. Awakening Centers and Urban Commons within a 100-mile radius of these three plants must be ready to VACATE their locations on 24-hour notice:

1. Duane Arnold Reactor – Palo, IA
2. Shearon Harris Reactor – New Hill, NC
3. Indian Point Reactor – Buchanan, NY

The Culture Council will continue to closely monitor the efforts to safely close these reactors and will advise affected Awakening Centers and Urban Commons as more information develops.

However, there are still several nuclear plants producing electricity on a local and regional level. THESE PLANTS MUST BE SHUT DOWN – OR CONTROLLED -- AS SOON AS POSSIBLE. As long as these reactors are in operation, people will continue to place false hope on the resurrection of the failed system. The Awakening Centers in the following areas must take action to remove from production (or place under their control) the following nuclear power plants:

1. Turkey Point Reactor – Homestead, FL
2. Edwin L. Hatch Reactor – Baxley, GA
3. H. B. Robinson Reactor – Hartsville, SC
4. Davis Bessel Reactor – Oak Harbor, OH
5. Cooper Reactor – Brownville, NE
6. Three Mile Island Reactor – Middletown, PA
7. Pilgrim Reactor – Plymouth, MA

We recognize that this is a tall order. The Culture Council will provide as much assistance to the local Centers as possible in achieving this goal. However, as long as these nuclear plants exist and produce power, people will attempt to cling to the failed system, instead of searching for practical, human-scale solutions.

Even worse, our forecasters predict that possession of the operational nuclear plants will become a primary source of conflict in the near future. Attacks and counter-attacks to control these facilities will increase the danger of damage to the fissionable material, dramatically increasing the threat of regional and even continental damage to the land and all beings.

This threat MUST be eliminated. Taking the operational reactors off-line will eliminate the threat. The Culture Council will work with the affected Awakening Centers to develop and execute de-activation plans.

PREDICTED, INEVITABLE... BUT NOT NECESSARY

As we reach this moment that so many have foreseen, we wish to reiterate that while this catastrophic grid failure was predicted by our forecasters, while it may seem inevitable to those who are living it, it is NOT necessary for those living now to go through the present and future turmoil that the failure of the grid will impose.

At many intervals, the Upheavals could have been ameliorated by bold, swift action. In each instance, the Breaker power structure has opted to maintain the dysfunctional status quo. It will continue to do so into the future.

Part Three: The Monk

Section 01: Under Attack

The point is, there is no feasible excuse for what we are, for what we have made of ourselves. We have chosen to put profits before people, money before morality, dividends before decency, fanaticism before fairness, and our own trivial comforts before the unspeakable agonies of others.

— Iain Banks

The Solon Fever

File No:		File Name:	The Solon Fever
Location:	Tucson Awakening Center	Parties:	
Monk/ Master Supervising:	Singing Winds, Abbot		

Name:		Pgs:		Date:		Vol:	
Type of Transcript:	Mechanical xxx						
	Organic						

Preface by the North American Centers Archive Committee:

Since the "Seattle Collection Incident", the Awakening Movement was on high alert for another attack by "The Edge".

And, when it came, we STILL did not see it.

This text is being provided in a rough draft format. Communication Access Realtime Translation (CART) facilitates communication accessibility and may not be a totally verbatim record of the proceedings. Let your coordinator know if you would prefer a more verbatim option.

MEMO

TO: ALL AWAKENING CENTERS & CULTURE COUNCIL
FR: TUCSON AWAKENING CENTER, Abbot Singing Winds
DT: XXXXX
RE: A STRANGE ILLNESS

We want to alert our brothers and sisters in other Awakening Centers about a strange illness that is sweeping our Center, and to enlist your support in effectively dealing with it.

The Disorder:
This malady started about two weeks ago. The illness starts as a severe and sharp headache, located in the forehead region. The headache subsides, but is replaced with extreme vertigo, that lasts from a few hours to several days.

The headache and vertigo eventually subside. However, the ill person is left with feelings of emptiness and lethargy, along with an inability to connect with the Holonic Mind of the Center. This effect is ongoing. Because of this, we are referring to the disorder as the "Solon Fever".

The Spread:
So far, Solon Fever has effected between 7-10% of our Center. Because some feel it may be contagious, we have isolated those who have been experiencing the symptoms. This has caused a significant disruption of our normal routine, and a very significant diminishment of our Center's holonic abilities.

It is the latter effect that causes us to bring this matter to the other Centers. As we all know, almost all Centers have had their share of illnesses among their members – everything from measles to superbugs. Some of these Center-wide illnesses have been quite horrific... the resurgence of Yellow Fever in the Savannah Awakening Center and the spread of ebola that nearly eradicated three Northeastern Centers.

These illnesses were difficult, sometimes deadly, but always UNDERSTANDABLE. We simply do not understand Solon Fever. We have applied all of our healing arts to this task, to no effect. It does not have any typical morphology of any known disease. It is not viral, bacterial or microbial. We can identify neither a source nor a path – it does not appear to be contagious, but more and more of us are becoming symptomatic. None of the stricken have developed any antibodies or resistance to Solon Fever. In two weeks, we have developed no course of treatment more significant than aspirin and bed rest.

EVERYTHING has been tested and changed at the Center. Water, food, bedding, even the incense we burn in the sanctuary.

WARNING: Although still a minority, a significant number of us believe that Solon Fever is an attack by the Edge. Given that the net effect of Solon Fever is a diminishment of our entire Center as an effective part of the Holonic Mind, this could be a very powerful way of ending the Awakening Movement.

PRECAUTIONS: Until further notice, the Tucson Center is declaring itself "off limits" to the rest of the Movement. Please do not send any crewed flights to us. If you send any shipments via drone, please make sure they are one-way flights.

UPDATES: We will do our best to respond to your inquiries about Solon Fever. Your suggestions and your prayers will be most welcome.

[Afternote: Solon Fever caught the Culture Council completely off-guard. In its attempt to cope with the challenge, they turned to a source that they had never imagined using: the enigmatic "hives" of Europe, known collectively as Unity.]

The Despair

File No:		File Name:	The Despair
Location:	Culture Council Headquarters	Parties:	The Paris Unity (Hive) The Culture Council
Monk/ Master Supervising:			

Name:		Pgs:		Date:		Vol:	
Type of Transcript:	Mechanical xxx Organic						

Preface by the North American Centers Archive Committee:

Extraordinary times led to extraordinary measures...

The North American Culture Council asked Unity, the "hives" of Europe, for help. History shows that they got more than they bargained for...

This text is being provided in a rough draft format. Communication Access Realtime Translation (CART) facilitates communication accessibility and may not be a totally verbatim record of the proceedings. Let your coordinator know if you would prefer a more verbatim option.

From: The Paris Unity (Hive)
To: The Culture Council
Re: YOU ARE UNDER ATTACK

Greetings to Our Beloved Cousins:

You have recently contacted Unity regarding the conditions you face at your Awakening Center in Tucson, the conditions you refer to as "Solon Fever". You have requested Unity's assistance.

YOU ARE UNDER ATTACK. The Tucson Center's "Solon Fever" is only a part of that attack. The Edge is responsible. You will not be able to resist this attack without the help of Unity. Unity is willing to help.

Tucson: What you refer to as "Solon Fever" is a beamed ultrasonic wave pattern interference generator, which is designed to permanently interfere with the subject's holonic functions. It is beamed at a distance via drones, triangulating on a target identified by an internal agent (someone who has had extensive time outside of the Center).

Given the nature of this weapon, it is believed that it can be used *en mass*.
There is a defense: wearing a "Faraday Helmet" that blocks specific ultrasonic frequencies. However, distribution of such a helmet in Tucson may trigger the Edge to step up their attacks. They could take over your Tucson Center before everyone is fitted with the Faraday Helmets.

You will need the assistance of Unity to end this attack. Unity may also be able to restore those who have been subject to the "Solon Fever".

Despite its seriousness and severity, Tucson is not your main challenge.

Milwaukee: "The Edge" has your Milwaukee Center under a direct and widespread attack. It is an ingenious attack. You have not been able to detect it. You will need the assistance of Unity, if you intend to repel the attack and regain your Center.

For the past two weeks, virtually all of the Milwaukee Center residents have experienced feelings of lethargy, hopelessness and failure. They feel that something is WRONG -- although no one can name it.

Novices (and some monks) have had fits of despair and crying. Many are abandoning their work. Some have attempted to leave the Center.

There have been arguments and fights – mostly between the novices but some involving monks, also.

There have been suicidal thoughts among some masters... including Abbot Tensai.

The insidious nature of this attack is that everyone in your Milwaukee Center is treating these incidents as personal failures, or the fault of a particular person or persons at the Center. They are not looking at the Edge as the assailant.

1. The most significant aspect about both of these Edge Attacks is that YOU DO NOT SEE IT. The Edge has developed the ability to massively block your holonic abilities. None of your Future Seers in your North American Centers have detected the attack. (A few have had upsights that "something is wrong", but cannot locate or identify the troubles.) Other than this message to you, you would not know of Milwaukee's troubles. This

indicates the nature of future attacks against you -- they will aim at this very obvious "blind spot".

2. The nature of these attacks is to draw you out. They do not intend to keep either the Tucson or Milwaukee Centers. Once the attacks became clear to you, you would be forced to either abandon these Centers, or pledge all of your resources to thwart the attacks. In doing so, they would get to see within your "arsenal". That is the purpose of this style of attack. (If they wanted to take over or wipe out either Tucson or Milwaukee Centers, they could have done so two weeks ago.)

3. You do not have much in your arsenal to stop them. The Edge has developed immunity to almost all of your chemical defenses -- your darts and gas grenades no longer work on them. And, even if you manage to subdue them, they will commit suicide before allowing themselves to be taken for questioning.

4. None of these aspects are challenges for Unity. Unity can repel the attacks; you cannot. Unity can capture the agents alive; you cannot.

5. Unity will perform this service for you, because you are kin to Unity. However, it must be done on Unity's terms:

1) Unity will repel the attack, without involvement from the Culture Council or the Centers. (The Unity "arsenal" will not be revealed, to anyone.)

2) Unity will not inform you of the methodology used (at least, until the Edge has been fully removed as a threat to the Movement for Humanity).

3) Unity will keep the Edge agents. (Unity is willing to share relevant information with you, but not share access to the agents themselves.)

4) Outside of the Culture Council and the Abbots in Tucson and Milwaukee, no one else must know of the direct involvement of Unity in this matter.

As you know, Unity rarely shares its abilities. This is for the protection of all parties. However, in order to repel Edge attacks in the future, Unity will give you certain aspects of Unity's technology -- including a form of "Direct Consciousness Intervention" that you have been experimenting with. Your methods are blunt and unfocused – the term "mind-wiping" is quite accurate. Unity is precise and effective.

To accept Unity's help, under the expressed terms, please send Unity a tight-line video communication from the Culture Council.

And, as always, Unity will welcome any and all of you into full Unity, if that is your destiny.

THE PARIS UNITY

[Afternote: The Culture Council immediately sought Unity's aid. Two days after sending the message, the Culture Council received the following message:

"The threats to the Tucson and Milwaukee Awakening Centers have been neutralized. The Edge agents have been apprehended and are being interviewed.

"Unity is providing an antidote to restore those who have been afflicted with "Solon Fever" and "The Despair". This will negate the damage done by the Edge. However, full re-integration into the life of the Centers of those afflicted may take weeks.

"Unity welcomed this opportunity to work with Unity's cousins, and look forward to the ongoing relationship with you."

London Unity

Based on this message, the Culture Council extended the invitation for Unity representatives to come to North America for a formal meeting.]

Year Eight

The future is not some place we are going to, but one we are creating. The paths are not to be found, but made, and the activity of making them changes both the maker and the destination.

John Schaar

The Ambassadors of Unity

File No:	File Name: The Ambassadors of Unity	
Location:	Denver Awakening Center	Parties: North American Culture Council (Seven of the 15 Councilors are present, each with an attendant. The other Councilors attend via video.) The Ambassadors of Unity in Europe (including delegates from Paris, London, Prague, Rome and Istanbul Unity (Hives)).
Monk/ Master Supervising:	Councilor El-Din, as "First Councilor" is the first to speak.	

Name:		Pgs:		Date:		Vol:	
Type of Transcript:	Mechanical XXX						
	Organic						

Preface by the North American Centers Archive Committee:

The Awakening Movement on other continents went down paths that North America did not. While "Centers" similar in scope and reach developed, there was a sub-set of that movement that went in... other directions.

At first, the other movement was referred to as "Hives". This notion was resisted – the Unity adherents were adamant that the analogy to bees and ants was grossly misleading. They were not "mindless". By releasing their individualized consciousness, they believe they have achieved "Ultimate Mindfulness".

The relationship between the Centers and the Hives (now known collectively as Unity) has always been uneasy. That is nowhere more evident than in the transcript of the first formal meeting between the Culture Council and the Ambassadors of Unity.

[start of transcript]

Unity representatives flew into the meeting in their airship. Only the five Unity Ambassadors leave the pneumatically sealed airship. As they enter the room, they carry oxygen cylinders and breathing tubes.

FC El-Din: Greetings to our esteemed guests. Perhaps the first thing we should do is exchange names? My name is Councilor El-Din, and...

Five Unity Ambassadors, in unison: WE HAVE NO NAMES.

FC El-Din: Well... how do we refer to you when we're speaking to you?

In Unison: WE ARE UNITY.

Paris Unity: Unity understands that this can be difficult for those not in Unity. For your convenience, each body of Unity may be referred to via that particular geographic Unity. For your convenience, the geographic name of each specific Unity has been sewn onto our tunics. For example, this one may be referred to as Paris Unity.

FC El-Din: Yes, I see. Well, thank you.

As I said, my name is El-Din, and this is...

Paris Unity: Unity knows who you are. There are full dossiers on each of you. And, you have placed those pieces of stiff paper with your names on them in front of each of you. It is printed on each side, in case you forget your names during the proceedings, yes?

FC El-Din: Well, okay. Let's dispense with the introductions...

Paris Unity: That was funny? That was an attempt at being humorous. Did you find it humorous? Unity does not use language much, so the nuances of verbal humor are difficult. There is no intention to offend.

FC El-Din: Well... Uh...

C. Khalifa: What First Councilor El-Din means to say is that your "joke" was humorous but unexpected. And, that given the gravity and importance of this meeting, perhaps we should leave humor until we get to know each other better.

Paris Unity: Why did not El-Din say this? If he meant to say that, why are you saying the words for him? Is this your practice called "telepathy"?

C. Khalifa: (pausing): This is a way of speaking, among those of us who use language as a means to convey information.

[All 5 Unity Ambassadors freeze in place, for a full five seconds.]

In Unison: UNDERSTOOD AND ACKNOWLEDGED.

London Unity: Continue with your talking.

C. Khalifa: Well, perhaps we should dispense with the Introductions and get down to business.

Ambassadors, we would like to thank you all, and especially Paris Unity, for warning us about the Edge attack and helping...

Istanbul Unity: You have already thanked Unity for repelling the attack. Why do you do this again? What need do you have to repeat this?

C. Soora: Jesus, this could take forever...

FC. El-Din: Okay, what do YOU want to talk about?

London Unity: The Unity agenda is relatively short:

- Unity will transfer the DCI technologies to you. You will be able to see, capture and modify Edge agents in the future. Details to be negotiated.

- Unity will transfer information gained from the Edge agents currently in possession. This information will help you in seeing and resisting further attacks.

- Seeing that you still use mechanical means for data storage and collection, Unity will give you technologies that will allow organic data storage. This will be more efficient and less expensive than your current reliance on technology for data storage.

- Unity wants access to Man-Onko and/or anyone he has trained in his olfactory viewing technique. Unity also wants access to the blocking techniques you have developed for his ability.

- Unity wants sex with your young men. Or, acceptable amounts of frozen sperm.

- Unity wants access to...

C. Soora: What? Did I hear you correctly? You came all the way over here to bang our monks?

Istanbul Unity: They do not have to be monks. Masters or even novices will do as well...

[Unintelligible voices and shouting]

FC El-Din: Wait!! We'll be here all night! I suggest we take these matters in the order that Ambassador London has suggested. Now that means...

Paris Unity: Please! Do not use that term!

FC. El-Din: What term?

In Unison: WHEN YOU REFER TO "AMBASSADOR LONDON", YOU THINK THAT THE BODY WEARING THE TUNIC WITH THE LABEL "LONDON" IS DIFFERENT FROM THE WHOLE, DIFFERENT FROM UNITY. IT IS NOT.

WE ARE UNITY.

REFERRING TO A PARTICULAR BODY WOULD BE LIKE SAYING UNITY IS SPEAKING TO EL-DIN'S EAR, OR LISTENING TO EL-DIN'S MOUTH. IT IS NOT ONLY INCORRECT, IT IS OFFENSIVE. PLEASE STOP.

[pause]

FC El-Din: We sincerely mean no offense. This is difficult for us to comprehend, and even more difficult to communicate through. I only meant that London Unity gave us a list of agenda items.

In Unison: NO. UNITY GAVE YOU THAT LIST. COUNCILOR EL-DIN MADE AN APOLOGY. THAT IT WAS COUNCILOR EL-DIN'S MOUTH THAT WAS MOVING IS OF NO CONSEQUENCE.

FC El-Din: [pauses]: Okay, let's start with...

Paris Unity: Would...

Rome Unity: It be...

London Unity: Better...

Prague Unity: If...

Istanbul Unity: Unity...

Paris Unity: Spoke...

Rome Unity: To...

London Unity: You...

Prague Unity: Like...

Istanbul Unity: This?

[pause, then]

C Khalifa: No, that is not better, not at all. Goodness...

Prague Unity: Another suggestion, then. One body will respond to you, but a different body for each question.

FC El-Din: [pauses]: Sure, okay, let's try that...

Now, where were we? I think we were about to negotiate the terms of how you... how Unity... will transfer the consciousness intervention technology to the Awakening Centers.

Istanbul Unity: There is no negotiation. These are the terms. You will send your masters to Unity. Any number between 3 and 24. They will stay a minimum of two weeks. They will return and teach the DCI technique to each Awakening Center. That is all.

FC El-Din: Ummm... can we ask questions?

Prague Unity: Certainly.

FC El-Din: Well... how effective is it? We've only had marginal success in our efforts. Kind of like super-hypnosis, with all the problems of hypnosis and post-hypnotic suggestion.

Rome Unity: Your process works on the basis of hypnosis. You can achieve such states quickly, but the deeper you go into the subject's past, the more his or her personality gets obliterated. So, your process can render a person unable to function, what you refer to as an "imbecile. Unity agrees that a nonviolent imbecile is much better than a violent antagonist. However, a fully functioning adult who no longer believes he was ever an antagonist is infinitely better than an imbecile.

Istanbul Unity: The Unity process works via the process of memory. Basically: if you can remember something, our DCI can make you forget it. Do you remember what you had for lunch yesterday?

FC El-Din: Well, yes.

London Unity: DCI can make you forget it.

FC El-Din: How far back can you... can Unity... go with that?

Prague Unity: If you can remember being breast-fed as a child, DCI can make you forget it.

C Khalifa: How selective is it? Do you erase a particular point forward? Or, can you erase, like, selective slices...

Paris Unity: DCI can make you forget your intimate partner's middle name, or forget the birth of your second child... not the child, just the birth.

C Soora: Goodness gracious. Do we really want this?

Rome Unity: Our method of DCI is not without its drawbacks. Selective consciousness intervention has the potential of creating relativistic paradoxes.

C Khalifa: What is a "relativistic paradox"?

Paris Unity: An example: What if Unity caused you to forget that your spouse had a middle name, then you saw some document that had her middle name on it? You may not be able to "see" the name. Or, perhaps you could see it, but not understand it. Or, perhaps you would treat it like a fraud, or like a supernatural phenomenon. Or, perhaps believe that you had gone insane.

London Unity: Therefore, you must be very selective in how DCI is approached. Unity will teach you both the technique and the proper ways to use it.

FC El-Din: Can you make the Edge agents forget they were Edge agents?

London Unity: Yes.

C Khalifa: You could return them to us, thinking that they were Center residents the whole time!

Istanbul Unity: Unity will not return the Edge agents. This was a part of Unity's agreement to rescue your Center. That is all.

FC El-Din: No, no, of course not. We're just asking about their abilities. And, we have a question, if you... Unity... does not mind?

In unison: ASK.

FC El-Din: Why were you insistent that you get the agents? By "you", I mean Unity, of course. What are you going to do with them?

[All Ambassadors freeze for 10 seconds. Then...]

Rome Unity: Unity does not think it is the proper time...

FC El-Din: Wait a minute... You all... the five "bodies" present... just went catatonic for a few seconds. What gives?

Paris Unity: These bodies were in communion with the aspects of Unity that are behind the glass.

FC El-Din: When do we meet the people behind the glass?

In Unison: WE ARE UNITY.

FC El-Din: Right, right. When do we get to see the aspects of Unity that are behind the one-way mirrors?

London Unity: It has been determined that viewing Level 5 aspects of Unity is too disconcerting for unprepared minds. Actual communication between yourselves and Level Five is impossible.

FC El-Din: What level are you? The five aspects of you, I should say.

In Unison: LEVEL TWO.

Prague Unity: You asked about the Edge agents. When you have developed a sufficient level of trust, Unity will share with you current operational details. Until then: the Edge agents will be used to lead Unity back to their main nest. Unity's intention is that Edge will no longer exist as an organization. When that happens, you will be informed.

FC El-Din: Why do you want Man-Onko? Please know that there are many on the Council who are not in favor of sharing this young man with you. He's only now being promoted to monk. He's still very impressionable, and, frankly, we really need him for our security training at present. Can you examine him here?

London Unity: Young Man-Onko may possess a natural and rudimentary form of the abilities that Unity uses for primary communication. As such, it would serve an historical function for Unity to witness the ability in its "pure" form.

Paris Unity: The examination must take place in one of Unity's areas. You lack the resources, and it is simply more efficient to move one body than several truckloads of bodies and equipment.

Istanbul Unity: Regarding his age and your security needs. Your concerns are noted. If you wish to wait a period of time before transferring him for examination, please do so. Would 10 years be sufficient?

C Soora: God... Yes, yes, let's revisit this in 10 years...

Prague Unity: You misunderstand. There is no discussion of "IF" Man-Onko will be examined by Unity. The only question is "WHEN". 10 years seems reasonable to Unity, but if you have some other date in mind, please propose it.

C Khalifa: How long will you want him?

Paris Unity: A minimum of 30 days. He will be welcome to stay as long as he wishes.

FC El-Din: Within 10 years, the Culture Council will transfer Man-Onko to... Paris Unity? For a period of at least 30 days?

In Unison: AGREED.

Rome Unity: We detect that more than one of you will wish the masters learning DCI or Man-Onko to be "spies" for the Culture Council, returning information on our practices and behaviors.

Please do not wait so long! Unity will welcome Culture Council Ambassadors to all geographic locations, for any length of time.

FC El-Din: At any level? Even Level Five?

Unity Ambassadors freeze, for 4 seconds. Then:

London Unity: Culture Council Ambassadors will be welcome at any length of time, and at all levels. However, please be advised that no person going to Levels Four or Five has ever returned.

C Soora: You keep them?

Paris Unity: No. They keep themselves. They would not be able to leave with their minds intact. At that level the experience of Unity is too intense to be survived as an individual.

Istanbul Unity: Consider this: What if you had all of your communication senses removed from you? You could not see, hear, smell, touch, feel, taste... you could communicate with no one, but you know that communication is possible! It is believed that you would go mad.

Leaving Level Four would be like that.

FC El-Din: What would leaving Level Five be like?

Istanbul Unity: There are no words/ concepts that would convey the experience. Ancients have used terms like "Enlightenment", "Samadhi", or "Bliss" to describe the experience of Level Five. One thing that happens is the complete loss of "language" as a mechanism of communication.

C Soora: So how do folks at Level Five communicate with each other?

In unison: WE ARE UNITY.

C Soora: I walked right into that one...

London Unity: Your Ambassadors can come to any Unity they wish, and stay for any length of time you wish. However, if they are to act as spies for you, Unity will not allow them to proceed deeper than Level Three. This will facilitate their re-introduction into your Center society.

FC El-Din: I think "spies" is too strong a word.

Prague Unity: Forgive the use of terms. Is "Information Gathering Agent" less offensive?

FC El-Din: "Spies" infers a lack of trust. It's not that we don't trust you, it's that we don't really KNOW you.

Paris Unity: You do not trust Unity. That is why half of your Culture Council is not physically present, but is watching via video feed. You believe that will protect the Culture Council from Unity. Despite your work toward the Holonic Mind, you still do not trust what you cannot control. Unity is not offended.

C Soora: I've got a question: could we visit Level Five if we wore, like an oxygen tank?

Istanbul Unity: You would need a space suit. Our pheromone-based language includes the tactile – you would experience it on contact. Perhaps even a space suit would not be enough.

London Unity: Even then, you simply would not understand what you saw. Just as Solons cannot understand the Holonic Mind, you cannot comprehend Unity. It would be like you seeing a close-up video of someone's mouth moving, without hearing any sound. The movements would seem chaotic and random, meaningless.

FC El-Din: Does Unity ever have... disagreements?

Paris Unity: Do you ever face internal contradictions?

FC El-Din: I'll take that as a "yes". How do you resolve them?

Istanbul Unity: How do you resolve your own inner conflicts?

FC El-Din: Yes, but how...

C Soora: Look, we're not getting anywhere! I want to move on, to this "sex and sperm" issue. Issue! That's funny!

In Unison: WE AGREE!

C Soora: Why are you so interested in sperm from us? Something wrong with your European boys?

London Unity: Not at all. The problem is Unity's ACCESS to them.

Istanbul Unity: Unity has an accelerated birthrate. Because of our breeding programs, Unity has many, many more babies than you would expect. In a short period of time, without the introduction of outside genetic material, Unity would face birth defects and other challenges to continued existence.

Rome Unity: At first, Unity would simply obtain any available healthy single male, have him engage for a few days or weeks, then return him to his home. However, after some time, this practice started to generate negative attention from the remnants of the governmental system. Unity now looks for other ways to gather undomesticated sperm.

Paris Unity: One way is to ask for it.

FC El-Din: I think about the number of men on this continent who would gladly give you all the sperm they've got, in exchange for food and a roof!

Istanbul Unity: Unity has considered this. In fact, that step may be taken in the future. However, like you, Unity would prefer to work with people who are already predisposed to the Holonic Mind, rather than struggle with dedicated Solons.

Rome Unity: Unity is asking only for volunteers who are not in committed relationships. Given the present rate of sexual promiscuity among your senior novices, Unity would not impose a burden on them. Six months in Europe may be a highlight of their lives. Some may not want to come back.

Istanbul Unity: The experience of Unity is intense. Just like your Solons having their first holonic experience, Holons have the same kind of intense experience when entering Unity. And, like your own Solons in this country, many do not want to return.

Paris Unity: However, if they have agreed to be spies for you, Unity will guarantee that they will return. They can come back later if they choose to. Unity will always welcome them back.

C Soora: How can you do that? How can you take more and more into your... your Unities? The economics of food, shelter and space are the same in Europe as in North America...

Rome Unity: The error that the Masters of the Age of Waste made was in thinking that their belief in individuality was a fundamental construct. They created political economies based on individuality. That made it right for some people to be billionaires and others to starve.

London Unity: You have a belief in "community". This is a fundamental construct for you. You create political economies based on "community". This is infinitely better than the solon-based political economies. But, they are not nearly as efficient as Unity.

Istanbul Unity: Do you understand this? Just as Solons see the Awakening Centers as "impossible", you see Unity as impossible. You don't understand how we can have ten times the population, living on just 10% of the land you occupy.

Rome Unity: No, Councilor, the economics of food, shelter and space are NOT the same for us. They are not the same, because our basic stories diverge.

C Soora: Can you... can you teach us about your political economy?

Paris Unity: We can try, but your abilities to grasp our Reality is relatively limited. This is why we welcome your spying on us.

London Unity: Right now, we perceive that you have approximately 8,000 people living at this Center in Denver. We know that you intend to double the size of your Center in the next five years.

Paris Unity: Right now, there are close to one-half million bodies living in Paris Unity, living on about the same size land mass. We expand by over 10,000 in just one week.

C Khalifa: Goodness! How is that even possible?

In Unison: THAT IS WHAT WE INVITE YOU TO FIND OUT.

London Unity: However, before these proceedings go any further, these air cylinders are getting low. It is also detected that a few of you would like to relieve your bladders. Perhaps a break is in order.

FC El-Din: Agreed. But, a question before you go... what's in the air tanks? And, do they pose any danger to us?

Istanbul Unity: The air tanks contain a mixture of the air that we breathe at Level Two. It helps the Ambassadors to stay in contact with each other and with the aspects of Unity that exist beyond the windows.

Rome Unity: Unity's function is not impaired by not having the air. If it is disconcerting to you, the practice can stop. However, over several days, breathing untreated air would experience gradually increasing levels of unease and disorientation. In 3 or 4 days, Unity would be functioning as... you.

London Unity: If you used Unity's air tanks, you would feel... alert. More connected.

FC El-Din: Umm, we'll pass on that for now. Okay, let's take our break and reconvene...

[end of transcript]

Lessons in Time Dilation

File No:		File Name: Lessons in Time Dilation
Location:	Denver Awakening Center	Parties: North American Culture Council (Seven of the 15 Councilors are present, each with an attendant. The other Councilors attend via video.) The Ambassadors of Unity in Europe (including delegates from Paris, London, Prague, Rome and Istanbul Unity (Hives)).
Monk/ Master Supervising:	Councilor El-Din, as "First Councilor" is the first to speak.	

Name:		Pgs:		Date:		Vol:	
Type of Transcript:	Mechanical						
	XXX						
	Organic						

Preface by the North American Centers Archive Committee:

It was in this second part of the first formal meeting between the Culture Council and Unity of Europe, that the Culture Council realized the profound disconnect they experienced at the hands of their "Hive" cousins...

This text is being provided in a rough draft format. Communication Access Realtime Translation (CART) facilitates communication accessibility and may not be a totally verbatim record of the proceedings. Let your coordinator know if you would prefer a more verbatim option.

[start of transcript]

FC El-Din: Now that our representatives... excuse me, "representative"... of Unity has returned, hopefully with suitably full air tanks, we can continue our discussions.

Paris Unity: Thank you for correcting yourself. Unity sincerely hopes that you return to our meeting with suitably empty bladders.

[Laughter]

London Unity: That was funny? It was intended to be humorous. Unity believes that gatherings such as this may go better if there is good will between the parties.

FC El-Din: Yes, we got that one.

Now, we see that our prior hour was dominated by only a few voices. During our break, several Councilors expressed some issues we would like to address. We will approach them in our usual manner – seniority, with our most junior going first. Councilor Andres?

C. Andres: Thank you, El-Din. Greetings to Unity.

In Unison: GREETINGS, ANDRES.

C. Andres: Wow. Someday I'll probably get used to that. Okay...

I know that you are reluctant to share the details on how you ended the Edge attack on our Centers. But, is it possible for you to give us any information, just a general idea how you did it? I am curious how you effected such a profound change, so quickly.

Istanbul Unity: Unity is not reluctant to share the details. Unity will not share the details. That is all.

Rome Unity: Unity will give you general information only. The attack on your Centers was ended through a combination of time dilation and consciousness intervention. Unity went into your past, identified the Edge agents, and neutralized them.

C. Andres: Wow again. You used consciousness intervention to identify the agents?

[All aspects of Unity freeze for 3 seconds]

Paris Unity: No. We used... other means to identify and secure the agents. The consciousness intervention was necessary to prevent time paradoxes.

FC El-Din: We're still not too sure what you mean by "time paradox"...

[FROM THE VIDEO RECORD: Suddenly, five men wearing white tunics appear behind the Culture Council members. They are exact copies of the five sitting Ambassadors of Unity, wearing black. They each have a red rose pinned above the name on their tunic.

For two seconds, they move so quickly their actions are a blur. When they slow down to normal speed, Paris in white takes the pen from Councilor Khalifa's pocket, walks across the room and puts it in the pocket of Paris in black. London in white speaks to Councilor El-Din, who then writes something on a piece of paper, then puts the paper in his own jacket pocket. Istanbul in white speaks to Councilor's Soora's aide, who does something with his tablet. When they are finished, they vanish.]

FC El-Din: Could you give us an example of what you mean by a time paradox?

Rome Unity: Would you like a demonstration of a time paradox?

FC El-Din: Yes, an example or a demonstration would help our understanding...

London Unity: Please be specific. Are you asking for a demonstration?

FC El-Din: Yes. I am asking for a demonstration of a time paradox.

Paris Unity: Very well. Please ask yourself how and when Councilor Khalifa's favorite gold pen arrived in my pocket.

[General uproar and commotion]

FC El-Din: Okay, SILENCE! [Long pause, while Council composes itself.]

C. Andres: We would really, really, really like to know how you did that.

Istanbul Unity: How this was achieved is completely obvious to the half of the Culture Council watching on video. They are probably screaming for attention right now – but their mics have been cut.

C. Soora: How did you cut their mics!?!

London Unity: Unity did not... you did.

Paris Unity: Before you open their mics and bring in the other Councilors, we'd like to point out a third anomaly. We would like Councilor El-Din to reach into his jacket pocket and read the slip of paper there.

FC El-Din: [pauses]: It's my personal password to the Council's main computer... They've got our passwords!

Rome Unity: Actually, no. If you notice, that paper is in your handwriting.

Istanbul Unity: Now, we suggest that we pause these proceedings for ten minutes, to give you time to confer with your other colleagues, examine your video recording, and regain your composure.

[TEN MINUTE BREAK]

FC El-Din: That was a quite unnerving demonstration. I saw it, but I STILL don't understand what happened...

London Unity: And that is what we mean by a time paradox.

C. Soora: I've got a basic question: from the video, it is clear that you performed the time dilation BEFORE you got our permission. How do you reconcile...

In Unison: UNITY DID NOT.

Paris Unity: Please understand. Unity has a strict code of ethics when it comes to working in Time. Unity would not, under any circumstances, interfere with the timeline of any time-aware being, without that being's permission. We would no more do time-interference than you would shoot and kill another human being.

C. Andres: Okay... I think I'm getting this... You got our permission, THEN sent your doubles back in time, so it looks like it was in our past.

Rome Unity: Almost correct. Those were not "doubles" of us. Nor were they future versions of the beings you see here.

C. Andres: Okay, I'll bite: Who were they?

Prague Unity: They were from a different Narrative, a different... Universe.

Istanbul Unity: This is beyond you. Unity will come back to Narratives. Let's concentrate on what you can see on the video.

Paris Unity: Also, Councilor Andres, your analysis was almost correct... Unity just obtained your permission, but will not design the demonstration for another two or three weeks, not until the Unity Ambassadors are back in Europe.

C. Andres: But... how do you... [pauses] Okay, I think I get it. Until the demonstration took place, you didn't know there would be a demo, did you?

Rome Unity: It is difficult to answer the question as you have asked it. However, at the level upon which your question is based, the answer is "yes". While Unity knew something would happen, Unity did not know any of the details of the demonstration.

Paris Unity: Unity will design the demonstration in a few weeks.

C. Andres: Why did the "other" Unity come BEFORE you obtained our permission... well, our permission in this Narrative, this Reality?

London Unity: Your question is well phrased, as well as you can perceive from your limited perspective.

Paris Unity: Please examine your question. You are asking why Unity "did" something that it has not yet "done".

Istanbul Unity: Therefore, Unity's "guess" as to Unity's motives for doing something it has not yet done are as valid as your own guesses. Perhaps less so.

Prague Unity: Therefore, Councilor Andres, please tell us: Why did/will Unity conduct its demonstration out of sequence in this Narrative?

C. Andres: Goodness gracious...

C. Soora: Probably just to confuse the hell out of us...

[In unison:] UNITY ACCEPTS YOUR EXPLANATION! BASED ON YOUR RECOMMENDATION, UNITY WILL CREATE A DEMONSTRATION WITH A SEQUENCING PARADOX.

C. Soora: [pauses] If this gets any weirder, my head is going to explode.

Paris Unity: If there were any danger of cerebral explosion, Unity would not conduct the experiment.

C. Andres: Let me get this straight: You... all of you... Unity... will create a sequencing paradox because we just ASKED for it?

[In unison:] YES.

C. Andres: [pauses] Can we change this subject, before we ask for something truly stupid, like meeting our own doubles?

Istanbul Unity: Is this something you are asking for? Would you like to meet your Self from another Narrative?

C. Andres: NO! No, I'm NOT!

Rome Unity: Are you so afraid of yourself?

C. Andres: It's not that I'm afraid...

C. Soora: Wait! How would you select our double?

London Unity: How many doubles would you like to meet? 20? 2,000?

Paris Unity: How alike or different would you want them to be? Identical down to your fingerprints?

Prague Unity: Or, covered with fur? With prehensile tails and movable ears?

Rome Unity: Or, a female version? Or one that's 9 feet tall and has horns?

Istanbul Unity: Or, a version that lays eggs? Or how about...

FC El-Din: Stop! Enough! I don't mean to be rude to our guests, but I've heard about all that I can take.

London Unity: Unity meant no harm. Unity's purpose was to let you know the multiplicity of narratives that exist. Some are so foreign to you that you would be toxic to each other. Others are so similar, you would have to talk with them for 20 years before you discovered a difference in your experiences.

Prague Unity: An example: You each made a decision about which Awakening Center to live in. Each of you had choices... some of you had more choices than others.

Paris Unity: At each of your choice points, several different Narratives spun out before you. For every choice you made, a different El-Din, a different Soora, a different Andres made a different choice. Each of those choices catalyzed a different Narrative.

C. Soora: But... but.... Each of us is making choices all the time! That would mean millions, BILLIONS of narratives spinning out, each second!

Istanbul Unity: True... which is why you should always choose wisely.

C. Soora: So, I could meet a Soora who is identical to me in all ways, except he chose to not get married.

Rome Unity: Would you like to meet him?

FC El-Din: No! No more demonstrations, at least for this visit! No demonstrations for ANY of us!

[In unison:] AS YOU WISH.

C. Andres: Wait, one more question, before we change subjects. Have any of you ever met your own doubles?

[In unison:] WE ARE UNITY.

C. Soora: Good grief...

Prague Unity: As there is the experience of "Unity-in-Place", there is also experience of "Unity-in-Time". As consciousness flows from London to Paris to Istanbul, consciousness can also flow from Narrative 001 to Narrative 002 to Narrative 003.

C. Andres: Okay, just one more question: can a Narrative become so... different?... from your experience that consciousness cannot flow?

[All Ambassadors freeze, for 5 seconds. Then:]

Paris Unity: Councilor Andres asks very interesting and relevant questions. Unity would like to respond fully; however, Unity detects that other Councilors would like to ask different questions. Perhaps Councilor Andres would like to engage with Unity outside the meeting?

C. Andres: Yes, if we can work out logistics...

Prague Unity: To partially answer your question: Just as one can be so distant from the Sun that its light would be negligible, Unity in a different Narrative could be so conceptually distant as to be invisible to this Unity.

C. Andres: Is there a Narrative where we fight? Where Unity is in conflict with the Culture Council?

[All Ambassadors freeze, for 5 seconds. Then:]

Istanbul Unity: There are Narratives where the Culture Council and Unity never contact each other. There are Narratives where the Edge defeats the Culture Council, and Unity defeats the Edge. There are Narratives where the Culture Council partners with the Edge to attempt to defeat Unity. There are Narratives where the Culture Council votes to fully embrace Unity.

Paris Unity: This current Unity prefers the current Narrative, where Unity and the Culture Council work together, get to know each other, and cooperate for the benefit of all.

C. Andres: Is there a Narrative where a Culture Council defeats Unity?

[In unison:] NO.

London Unity: If it is any comfort to you, please know that almost all of the Narratives where the two perspectives have contact are Narratives where there is cooperation.

FC El-Din: While this is fascinating... and more than a little disturbing... we have other Councilors we haven't heard from yet. Councilor Jenau?

C. Jenau: [via video]: Thank you. Greetings, Ambassadors. We saw you... them... enter, then speed up, then slow down to do their... your... actions. What was going on in the speed-up time?

London Unity: That was our DCI technique. They were entering the consciousness of the councilors in the room.

C. Jenau: Why was it sped up?

Paris Unity: Technically, they were slowing time down. From this time vantage point, they appeared sped up.

Rome Unity: It was done so that you could not see the DCI process.

C. Jenau: Why can't we see it? I thought you were giving it to us?

Prague Unity: Unity will give it to your selected masters... along with specific instructions on its proper use.

Istanbul Unity: Let us move on to the next time paradox: the pen.

London Unity: Councilor Khalifa did not notice his own pen sitting in the Paris pocket until after it was specifically referred to. Is that correct?

C. Khalifa: Correct. I don't know how...

Paris Unity: Is it not also correct that the pen suddenly appeared or "popped" into existence for you in this pocket?

C. Khalifa: Correct.

Prague Unity: Did you carefully examine your own pocket, after seeing the pen in the Paris pocket?

C. Khalifa: Correct.

Rome Unity: Finally: Even after seeing your pen in the Paris pocket, and after carefully examining your own pocket, did you still not believe your own senses?

C. Khalifa: I STILL DON'T!

Istanbul Unity: How does that make you feel?

C. Khalifa: God... I saw the video. Several times. On the video, I can SEE you... I mean, some other "you"... take it out of my pocket and waltz across the floor to that other "you" and stick it in his pocket. My eyes are open! I can see it! But, I have NO MEMORY of it happening!

London Unity: And that is another type of time paradox.

FC El-Din: I'd like to address what is for me the most troubling aspect of this matter. None of us are comfortable with Unity having our passwords...

In Unison: UNITY DOES NOT HAVE YOUR PASSWORDS.

FC El-Din: But, we just saw you...

Paris Unity: You saw beings from another Universe, another Narrative, take your passwords. The likelihood that those passwords will work... or even EXIST... in their Universe is unlikely.

FC El-Din: But, you are all Unity!   As soon as they popped into being, aren't you all on the same connection? Weren't you talking to them?

[Ambassadors freeze for five full seconds. Then:]

Rome Unity: There is much Unity cannot tell you, but please know this.   To reduce the number of time paradoxes, Unity almost always switches agents with other Narratives. That way, what is seen in Narrative A is not useful to the agent from Narrative B.

Prague Unity: This is done because Unity does not WANT to know your passwords.   If we wanted your passwords, we would simply ask you for them.

C. Soora: Would we be compelled to give them to you?

Rome Unity: Yes. You have no techniques, individually or collectively, to resist Unity.

C. Soora: Jesus...

Istanbul Unity: However, only in the most dire case, with many lives on the line, would Unity compel you, in anything. Only in a situation where many lives could be lost through Unity's inaction.   Frankly, Unity cannot imagine a circumstance where Unity would compel you to do anything. You do not have anything that Unity wants.

C. Soora: Except sperm.

[laughing]

London Unity: Unity sincerely hopes you will not have to be compelled for THAT.

[More laughter]

FC El Din: Back to this "other Narrative" business... how did you communicate with your doubles?

Paris Unity: This cannot be conveyed to you in a way that you could understand. The colleagues you saw are not "doubles".   In subtle and profound ways, they are different from the Unity before you now.

Rome Unity: Also: the communications with the other Narrative has not taken place yet in this Narrative, and will not for weeks to come.

FC El Din: But... but... How do you know that...

Prague Unity: No more questions about this. We have explained as much as you can absorb. Any more will lead to further confusions.

C. Soora: Will we ever understand this stuff?

In unison: YES.

Istanbul Unity: Unity will train your young masters in our philosophy and some of our techniques. Hopefully, they will be able to impart the concepts to all of your Centers.

C. Soora: I'm sorry... First Councilor, I've got to go back to this power thing... I am really bothered by what the Ambassadors of Unity are saying to us, and the power that they demonstrated here.

FC El-Din: Go on, Councilor.

C. Soora: [to Unity]: I mean... you just told us that you can do ANYTHING to us, and we'd be helpless to resist, right?

[In Unison]: THAT IS CORRECT.

C. Soora: So, you could order us to all commit suicide, and we'd have to do it, right? And the only reason you don't is because you don't want to?

Prague Unity: Councilor Soora, using your techniques that you refer to as "mind-wiping", you can induce a suicidal state in old style humans, correct?

C. Soora: Well, yes. But it's not the same!

Istanbul Unity: The difference being?

C. Soora: Our process is vetted through dozens of people. Any one of them able to stop the process. Your process isn't ever vetted or discussed!

Rome Unity: To the contrary. From your perspective, the decisions of Unity are vetted... tens of millions of times.

C. Soora: You know, you people just aren't... human anymore.

In Unison: BE CAREFUL WHAT YOU SAY. BE CAREFUL HOW YOU SAY IT. BE CAREFUL NOT TO SOUND LIKE THOSE YOU CALL BREAKERS AND WASTERS.

C. Soora: This isn't what the Imaginal Group planned! YOU aren't what they planned!

Paris Unity: The caterpillar doesn't "plan" the butterfly. If they did, they'd simply design a different caterpillar.

C. Soora: This business with "The Edge" and "The Despair". All that could have just been fabricated and fed to us by you!

London Unity: Yes... but for what purpose?

C. Soora: To take us over!

Paris Unity: If Unity wanted to take you over, Unity would just take you over. No need to be evasive about it.

Prague Unity: The easiest thing to do would be just to replace each one of you with your double from another Narrative.

Istanbul Unity: After having you hand over your passwords, of course!

Rome Unity: Or, intervene in the consciousness of each of you, so that you take orders from Unity.

London Unity: Or, take over your communications network, so that –

C. Soora: Okay, okay, I get the picture!

Look, you've already told us you can get our passwords, our security systems, our defenses. You're not slowed down by individual thought processes. You breed faster than we ever can. You can make us do whatever it is you want us to do. You can swap us out for a different Narrative! Why do you keep us alive? Why not just wipe us out?

In Unison: BE CAREFUL WHAT YOU ASK FOR.

London Unity: Reverse the question: Why do you keep whole camps, whole cities of "old style" humans alive? Why are you feeding and providing services for groups like the Mormons, or the Amish? Why do you keep Las Vegas supplied with water? What is your rationale?

Rome Unity: Unity already knows your answer. That the world is more interesting with them in it. That the Breakers add to the diversity, the inclusivity of the world. They just shouldn't be in control.

Istanbul Unity: Unity feels the same about you. It is important that you stay here, stay alive, stay viable. You are necessary. Unity does not fully understand why or how, but you are an integral part of Unity's unfolding. Part of this unfolding Unity understands. And part is... a larger butterfly.

C. Soora: What's a "larger butterfly" mean? That people will get freakier than... you?

FC El-Din: Please watch your language, Councilor! We're all under stress here, but that is no reason for us not to be... civil.

C. Soora: My apologies to Unity.

Paris Unity: Unity is not offended. Just as your old-style humans find the Awakening Centers hard to accept, you find Unity hard to accept.

Prague Unity: Your notion of "inclusivity" has been filtered through your implicit assumption that you were in the superior position because of your Awakened Powers. Unity provides you an opportunity to adjust your assumptions.

C. Soora: I already feel like I'm back in school.

But, let's get back to this "larger butterfly" bit. What do you mean?

London Unity: There is much about the ongoing human metamorphosis that even Unity does not know or understand. And the part that Unity does know, is not being revealed to you at present.

Paris Unity: Unity will deliver on the commitments made. Unity will host your spies. After your spies have reported back to you, perhaps you will understand us well enough to trust us.

C. Soora: What do you expect of us?

Istanbul Unity: We expect you to live your lives – to do the best that you can. And, when more is revealed to you, we expect you to ... act appropriately.

FC El-Din: Will this "more" be revealed to us in our lifetimes?

Prague Unity: Yes... within the next 15 years, if our calculations are correct.

FC El-Din: What calculations? What's going to happen?

In Unison: YOU ARE ABOUT TO BE... VISITED. MORE THAN THAT, UNITY IS NOT READY TO DISCUSS.

C. Soora: Please don't tell me we're going to be visited by space aliens!!

Paris Unity: Nothing of the sort. However, you may find that what is produced from human DNA can be every bit as strange as what you refer to as a "space alien".

Prague Unity: The visitations have already commenced. Unity suggests you pay close attention to the... children being born in your Centers.

C. Soora: What about our children? What have you done
—

FC El-Din: I'm going to call a halt to today's proceedings. I think I speak for all of us in saying I've had as much as I can take. We will reconvene tomorrow.

[end of transcript]

Evaluation and Commencement

File No:		File Name:	Evaluation and Advancement of Man-Onko to "Monk" status
Location:	Denver Awakening Center	Parties:	
Monk/ Master Supervising:	Master Auroron Master Pico-Laton		

Name:		Pgs:		Date:		Vol:	
Type of Transcript:	Mechanical						
	Organic						

Preface by the North American Centers Archive Committee:

There was not a prescribed course for the entry into monk status. Movement happened when all felt that the apprentice was "ready". And, on a few occasions, external circumstances played a part.

This text is being provided in a rough draft format. Communication Access Realtime Translation (CART) facilitates communication accessibility and may not be a totally verbatim record of the proceedings. Let your coordinator know if you would prefer a more verbatim option.

[start of transcript]

Monk-Candidate Man-Onko: Thanks for dragging me back to home base! Wow! It seems like a million years! Everything seems... smaller.

Master Pico-Laton: Well, it is, compared to you! You've really grown up! Who would've guessed that you'd be closing in on 6 feet tall!

Monk-Candidate Man-Onko: Well, that's what plenty of fresh air, sunshine, and gun-toting Outsiders do for you! I had plenty of motivation to grow up.

Master Pico-Laton: Indeed you did. I read about –

Master Auroron: You two will have plenty of time for catching up. I suggest that we get down to the business at hand.

Monk-Candidate Man-Onko: And it's great to see you too, Master Auroron! Thanks so much for inquiring about my health and well-being!

Master Auroron: I can see that your sarcasm has survived intact all of these years. I was afraid –

Monk-Candidate Man-Onko: Excuse me, Master, but before you go rattling on, I was wondering if we could pause for a few minutes of meditation?

Master Pico-Laton: [Laughing]

Master Auroron: [pauses] By all means. Before I forget why we're having this meeting!

[pause for meditation]

Master Auroron: Now, before we go off on another tangent, I'd like to convene this meeting and get on with your next assignments.

This is a "graduation" of sorts. Because each of the novices and apprentices are on individual trajectories, without correlation, there can't be a formal graduation ceremony, the way things were done in the old school system.

Monk-Candidate Man-Onko: Graduation? From what to what?

Master Auroron: You are now a monk.

Monk-Candidate Man-Onko: Wow. [Pauses.] Who determines this? You? Both of you? No other input?

Master Auroron: I will answer your questions. But, I first would like to point out that virtually every other apprentice has said, "Thank you!" at this point.

Monk-Candidate Man-Onko: It's not that I'm not grateful. I am. Really. But, after all this time, I really haven't been thinking at all about moving on to being a monk. I guess I'm having a ball where I am.

Master Auroron: Yes... What other apprentice has the numbers of the Culture Council on his speed dialer?

Monk-Candidate Man-Onko: What's a speed dialer?

Master Auroron: Never mind. Let's just say you're chummy with people I've only heard about. It would alter one's point of view.

Monk-Candidate Man-Onko: Thanks. Now, do you have any idea how I can make them go away?

Master Auroron: It is truly delightful to get to know your mind. You've got an amazingly healthy ego.

Now, to your questions about how you were evaluated for monkhood: We've been "tracking" you for some time. All of us here in Denver. Every monk and master you encountered on your journeys through the other Centers. Even some of the novices and apprentices were interviewed.

Monk-Candidate Man-Onko: I can imagine Abbot Sierra had some choice words about me after I screwed up and broke that guy's arm on that busted collection incident.

Master Pico-Laton: Yes, very choice words. He gave you the highest praise possible in his report on the incident.

Monk-Candidate Man-Onko: You're kidding! The way he sounded, he was about to buy me a one-way ticket to Old Town!

Master Pico-Laton: His job was to impress upon you the gravity of the situation... which it seems he did. His report says that you "got" the situation almost immediately, and have applied the lesson of practical non-violence in all of your subsequent actions.

Monk-Candidate Man-Onko: Wow. So, I've been avoiding him all these years for nothing!

Master Pico-Laton: [Laughing] So it seems!

Master Auroron: You could have applied for monk status years ago. You showed so much promise, we would have probably admitted you early. Instead, you showed no interest in moving ahead, leaving it to us to "draft" you.

Monk-Candidate Man-Onko: Okay, so... thank you! Although, I need to know what happens next... except that I get a sash and a cute little hat! Is this all about my wardrobe? Why now?

Master Auroron: Leaving alone your sarcasm about the monk's wardrobe, there are a few external circumstances that moved our hand in making this decision at this time.

Master Pico-Laton: In fact, it was the Culture Council that suggested we look into your status and elevate you – if appropriate.

Monk-Candidate Man-Onko: God! The "CC" again! I wonder what my life would look like if they weren't in it?

Master Auroron: Probably a lot less exciting. Now, let's go through the three external circumstances that pushed forward your monk evaluation. I'm presenting them in the direct order of importance to you, and reverse order of importance to the Culture Council.

First of all, we've located your sister, Paulette. She's in –

Monk-Candidate Man-Onko: WHAT? You've got my sister? Where...?

Master Auroron: PLEASE! Let me finish, and I think I'll answer all of your questions.

We've located her. She's in the Chicago area. She's in a very dangerous situation. To extract her will take almost a third of the credits you have in –

Monk-Candidate Man-Onko: Do it. No problem.

Master Auroron: I have to tell you this: It does not appear that she's being held against her will. Under these circumstances, we can only hold her in a Center for one week. You could wind up spending those credits for nothing. You may want –

Monk-Candidate Man-Onko: I don't care how much it costs, and I don't care if I lose the credits. If she goes back, that's her choice. But, I want her to have the same opportunity I had – an opportunity to change her life around.

When will she be picked up? Which Center will do the collecting? And, how soon can I get to Chicago?

Master Auroron: I'll give the order once we leave here. She'll be in our custody by tomorrow this time. And, we'll have an airship waiting to take you to Chicago. A bit of bending of the rules, but I rarely get an opportunity to throw my weight around in this place, so it isn't a problem.

Monk-Candidate Man-Onko: That is REALLY cool! Thank you!

Master Auroron: Now, shall we go on to the second item?

Monk-Candidate Man-Onko: Check! Shoot!

Master Pico-Laton: This is a bit unprecedented. We frankly don't know what's happening and don't know how to handle it... You remember that Victory and Krista-Lin have been romantically involved?

Monk-Candidate Man-Onko: Yes. Even when I see them together, my mind still refuses to believe it.

Master Pico-Laton: Well, here's the next mind-blowing element: Krista-Lin is pregnant.

Monk-Candidate Man-Onko: [pauses]: Isn't that, like... IMPOSSIBLE?

Master Pico-Laton: So we thought. As you know, all of the women here are given natural contraceptives, AND engaged in "women-only" ceremonies during their fertile cycles. Double insurance... which didn't work with Krista-Lin.

Monk-Candidate Man-Onko: [pauses]: I'm waiting to hear how any of this has anything to do with ME.

Master Pico-Laton: Everything about this pregnancy indicates that this child will be "special". Looks like a very short gestation period... Seven months. Pregnancy tests are coming back... screwy. Ultrasound readings aren't working at all. Which is impossible.

Monk-Candidate Man-Onko: [pauses]: Still waiting...

Master Pico-Laton: [pauses:] Okay, here it is: Krista-Lin, backed up by every monk and master in the Forecasting Unit, says that you have to be present, to attend to this child.

Monk-Candidate Man-Onko: ME? You're kidding! I don't know anything about babies! What am I supposed to do – change its diapers? Okay, okay... I'll agree to visit Victory and Krista-Lin and the little sucker, okay? But I'm not promising I'll pick it up or anything...

Master Pico-Laton: Krista-Lin and everyone else – including me – says that you have to be present at this child's birth.

Monk-Candidate Man-Onko: AT BIRTH? Are you CRAZY? You mean, when it comes OUT? YUCK!! When it's all covered with... gunk? NASTY!

Master Pico-Laton: Oh, come on! Weren't you the one telling us how you had "seen shit" when you first came in here?

Monk-Candidate Man-Onko: Yeah, but not THAT shit! Not Krista-Lin's shit!

Master Pico-Laton: Get a grip! It will be fine!

Monk-Candidate Man-Onko: I think I'm gonna be out of town that month!

Master Pico-Laton: Krista-Lin is adamant: she'll fly out to wherever you are, if necessary. Anyway, you should be thinking about this as a "blessed event"!

Monk-Candidate Man-Onko: So someone else should get the blessing! Can I appeal to the Culture Council?

Master Pico-Laton: Good luck with that. Every monk in the Forecasting Unit will be against you. And the only thing going for you will be your squeamish stomach.

Monk-Candidate Man-Onko: Good grief... Okay, I'll be in the room, but I'm NOT gonna watch it coming out!

Master Pico-Laton: That may be the best we can hope for.

None of us know why this baby is being born, or what's so special about it. But, whatever it is, you and that baby are a key to our future.

Master Auroron: This is interesting. Your sister and Krista-Lin's baby. Your past and our future. All of it coming up for resolution, right now.

Monk-Candidate Man-Onko: Okay, what's the third thing? I've got to babysit the brat?

Master Auroron: Something more to your liking: travel, intrigue and danger. And, your friends on the Culture Council are behind it.

You've heard that we have been hosting our counterparts from Europe, known as the "Ambassadors of Unity"?

Monk-Candidate Man-Onko: Yeah. Rumor has it that they've got the CC freaked out pretty bad – and it takes a lot for them to get freaked out. I've heard that they can do everything we can do, only faster. Is it true that they aren't individuals, that they don't have any names, that they all talk at the same time?

Master Auroron: What they are... is beyond my ability to convey with words. Anything you've heard is a lot less than what they are and what they can do.

Monk-Candidate Man-Onko: And, I'll dare ask the question: what has this got to do with me?

Master Auroron: The Ambassadors of Unity have requested your presence in their Paris Hive.

Monk-Candidate Man-Onko: [pauses] You know, next to the Krista-Lin situation, this doesn't even seem surprising. Hey, if I go to Paris NOW, can I get out of watching K-L squirt out her brat?

Master Pico-Laton: NO! If you go to Paris now, we'll send Krista-Lin in the airship with you! Imagine her having her baby at 20,000 feet...

Monk-Candidate Man-Onko: Okay! Okay! Back to Unity! Why do they want me?

Master Auroron: They claim that they want to study your "olfactory sense". However, some on the Culture Council are concerned that they may have more ulterior purposes in mind. You are the ONLY person they've asked for by name.

At first, the Council did not want you to go – some thought that you were too inexperienced. Others did not trust that Unity would let you come back.

In the end, it was thought that we need to establish some good will, a show of our sincerity, to help get things on a better footing with the Ambassadors of Unity.

Monk-Candidate Man-Onko: [pauses]: Or... the Culture Council realizes it's got no cards in its hands, so they decided to play me.

Master Auroron: [pauses]: As I've always said, your insight in situations like this is truly amazing.

Monk-Candidate Man-Onko: What's the danger assessment?

Master Auroron: [pauses]: There is no danger assessment. We can't "read" Unity – not beyond anything they want us to know. They're not hiding from us... we just don't have the right "equipment" to pick up any signals from them. We're blind. You'll be going in blind.

Master Pico-Laton: We do have their... its... assurances that you will be free to observe their Paris Hive and that they will return you whenever you wish to return, and in any event no longer than six months.

Monk-Candidate Man-Onko: Am I going by myself?

Master Auroron: Yes and no. There will be three monks going to Paris to pick up their mind-wiping techniques. They will return in 3 months. Also, you will have your own security detail and your own tightline communications setup.

Monk-Candidate Man-Onko: I thought the folks in the Hives over there already had tightlines.

Master Auroron: They do. They've been using the tightline to monitor what's been happening with us in North America. We thought we were monitoring them, but as it turns out, we saw only the tip of their very large iceberg.

This tightline setup is exclusively for your use. It's going to be super-encrypted, and coded only to your DNA. You will be the first person in history to have a personal tightline communicator.

Monk-Candidate Man-Onko: Cool! I assume you guys are gonna pick up my long-distance charges?

Master Pico-Laton: You can assume we'll be listening in on all of your conversations. You may want to be mindful about what you say to all those girlfriends of yours!

Monk-Candidate Man-Onko: [silence]

Master Pico-Laton: What, no witty, sarcastic remarks? Cat got your crotch?

Master Auroron: Enough of that, my young Master. Let's see if we can elevate this conversation.

Master Pico-Laton: Sorry. Too tempting a target.

Master Auroron: We will have everything set up in a month. It will take you that long to learn a new mnemonic code that will verify that your messages are in fact coming from you, not Unity.

Monk-Candidate Man-Onko: What's a "mnemonic code"?

Master Auroron: Actually... none of us knows, except the handful of folks who've come up with it.   And, theoretically, YOU won't even know it, or know that you're using it.   It's something that will alert us if your mind has been tampered with.

So... are you willing to go into the spying business?

Monk-Candidate Man-Onko: Okay, let's see if I get this: You made me a monk, you found my sister, I've got to watch Krista-Lin have a baby – and I don't even LIKE babies – and I get to go to Europe and spy on people who might roast me and eat me. And I'll have security and communications equipment that even the Culture Council doesn't have. Did I leave anything out?

Master Auroron: No, that sums it up pretty well...

Monk-Candidate Man-Onko: Sure. Bring on the sashes and the funny hats! Just don't give me a suicide pill... I might take it to get out of watching Krista-Lin have her baby!

[laughing]

Master Auroron: Just one more matter. As a monk, you have the right to choose your own name. Most monks just continue with the name they received as novices. A few choose to revert to their original names. And some...

Monk-Candidate Man-Onko: Original name? You mean, the name my parents gave me? Wow! I can barely remember it! It's like a name that belongs to somebody else!

Master Auroron: In a way, it does. In your time here, you've changed almost all of the neural pathways in your brain and heart. You are a fundamentally different person now.

Monk-Candidate Man-Onko: So, if I go back to that name, does that mean I revert to the stupid little shit who thought he knew everything?

[laughing]

Master Auroron: I think there's little danger of that! And, don't be too hard on your former self. He knew how to survive when the odds were against him, and showed enough humanity to attract our attention.

But, there's a third option for naming: you can keep your existing name, revert to your original name, or discover a completely new name for yourself. You may know that your old pod-mate, Dorado, is now Monk Fierce Light.

Monk-Candidate Man-Onko: Well, that's cool for him, but... what's wrong with the name I've got?

[end of transcript]

[Afternote: As Monk Man-Onko, he chose to return to the Denver Awakening Center as his Home Base. His chosen specialty is "Future Forecasting/ Big Picture Division" following in the footsteps of his Sponsor, Monk (now Master) Pico-Laton.]

Next in the Series:

Book Two: The Chronicles of the Awakening (2055-2085)

Book Three: The Chronicles of the Metamorphosis (2085-2120)

Other Books by Shariff M. Abdullah:

The Power of One: Authentic Leadership in Turbulent Times
[New Society Publishers, (1990); New Catalyst Books (2007)].

Creating a World That Works for All
[Berrett-Koehler Publishers, 1999].

Seven Seeds for a New Society
[Commonway Press, 2009].

Practicing Inclusivity
(with Leslie Hamilton) [CreateSpace Publishing, 2015].

Appendix A: The Sponsors of the Series:

The Early Supporters

Reviewers, Editors and Commenters:
Many people think that writing is a solitary process, where the writer retreats into a dark attic, quill pen in hand, and pumps out pages of deathless prose (by candlelight, of course).

Lots of the writing process IS solitary. However, a lot of it is communicating with others... the writing, review and editing process involves a community of people. From catching plot failures to catching typos, it took a lot of people to get "Chronicles" beyond the barely legible entries in my travel journal to the finished book in your hands.

While many people helped with the writing process, one name stands out for me. Next to myself, **Susan Belchamber** has read more copies of the manuscripts and made more editorial comments and suggestions than anyone else, period. Her unselfish generosity of time and energy was a true gift. Our ongoing dialog about the book, over the course of several months, helped make the book what it is today.

Another key contributor was **Regina LaRocca**, whose detailed comments helped shape parts of my thinking around what being a "holon" really means. Many of her comments are already shaping Book Two (along with my Sri Lankan friend **Kashyapa Yapa**, who helped me realize that the focus of the next two books has to be more "globally" focused).

Many thanks to **Maria Carlo** for critical assistance in the last stages of getting the finished manuscript accepted by the paper and digital online book printers.

Other early readers, editors, reviewers and commenters include:

John Brown
Susan Buckley

Greg Burrill
Jaelle Dragomir
Lois Isbell
Ted Polozov
Liana Rein
Janet Sussman

My thanks to them all.

FINANCIAL CONTRIBUTORS:
Several people questioned why I chose to release "Chronicles" through the medium of a crowdfunding campaign. Simple answers:
1. I needed resources for the graphics, printing and marketing expenses that will accrue in any book marketing campaign.
2. In order to "globalize" Books Two and Three, I need the funds to spend significant research time in Europe, Asia and Africa.
3. I want the book to reach the widest possible audience. One of the key components of "crowdfunding" is the CROWD. The idea was to attempt to reach beyond Commonway's database, to access potentially millions of people via Kickstarter.

According to Kickstarter's statistics, 98% of the funds collected came from people in the Commonway database (or their contacts). Once again, the Commonway "crowd" comes through!

Significant Crowdfunding Support:
Many thanks to **Eric Foster** for his valuable volunteer efforts and suggestions in managing the crowdfunding campaign. His assistance and suggestions were a LOT more valuable than the "paid" help that I received. I look forward to working with him again in the future.

Significant Financial Backers:

Pat Adams, Raffi Aftandelian, Elaine S. Alexander, Pamela Allee, Catherine Norwood Anderson, Tom Atlee, Sherry Banaka, Donna Beegle, Susan Belchamber, David Berry, Karen Bettin, Tahdi Blackstone, Kathleen Boyer, Teresa Bright, Carol Brouillet, Helene Brown, John D. Brown, Rev. Marj Bryant, Barbara Buckingham-Hayes, Greg Burrill, Sandra Campbell, Maria Carlo, Joan E. Caruthers, Heather Carver, Dinah Chapman, Lynda Coates, Catherine Condon, Gary Corbin, Dana Cummings, Mary Cummings, Lakshmi Dady, Marcia Danab, Maja Daniels, Bob Davis, Sara DeHoff, Rev. Douglas Duerr, Jay Earley, Jane Engel, Gaya Erlandson, Bill Evans, Suzanne Fischer Reynolds, Jeffrey Fowler, Erica L. Frank, Jim & Rebecca Gaudino, Robert Gilman, Amari Gold, Veta Goler, Ernestine Griffin, Leslie Hamilton, Paula Hannan, Carol Hansen Grey, Christine Harbaugh, Carol Hart, Holly Hatch, Jacquelyn Hawkins, Fred Heutte, Peggy Holman, Debbie Hornibrook, Jeffrey Hutner, Anita Hyatt, Rick Ingrasci, Miki Kashtan, Hank Keeton, Dottie Koontz, David Kyle, Robert Kyser, Eon LaJoie, Ed Lantz, Regina LaRocca, Dominic Le Fave, Stewart Levine, David Levinger, Rev. Judith Marshall, Andolie Marten, Austin Marx, Konda Mason, Rev. Joslyn Mason, Krishna K. Mayo-Smith, Leta Mullen, Patricia S. Murrell, Abdisalan Muse, Linda Norlin, Jeanne E. Nyquist, Joyce O'Halloran, Veena Fox Parekh, Eileen Patra, Ted Polozov, Lane Poncy, Edward Preston, David Rankin, Liza Rankow, Arthur Rashap, Liana Rein, Jzonay Reitz, Ben Roberts, Adin Rogovin, Robert J. Romanski, Erin Ross, Tim Rouse, Laura Schlafly, Rev. Ted Schneider, Brian Setzler, Anna Shook, Tesa Silvestre, Sally Slick, Gregory Smith, Tara Steele, Susie Steffes, Muriel Strand, Paul Sunderland, Debbie Susnjara, Janet Sussman, Jill Sutton, Catherine Thomas, Shirlene Warnock, Zoe Weil, W. Thunder Williams, Chuck Willis, Barbara Wuest

Additional Crowdfunding Support:

Corliss Acosta, Michael Baroff, Deborah Bellony, Don Berg, Shyama Blaise, Liviu Caliman, Suzanne Caubet, Joel E. Conarton, Jo Ann DeFrancesco, Jaelle Dragomir, Erica L. Frank, Eric Gamonal , Anthony Mtuaswa Johnson, P+T Johnson-Lenz, Koty Juliano, Jennifer Kahnweiler, Gerald Landrum, Richard Lerman, Rev. Jim Marshall, Casey Mullen, Leonie Ramondt, Joanne Rowden, Richard Seidman, Kashyapa Yapa, Cathy Zheutlin,

Appendix B: Acknowledgement of Influences

My friends know that I am a voracious reader of "science fiction" (I prefer the term "speculative fiction", since a lot of it has nothing to do with "science".) Starting with "Dune" as a teenager and moving on to whatever is rattling around in my book bag right now, I've been regularly ingesting other people's views on what our future will look like.

My reason for reading it is simple: outside of science fiction writers, few people in this society spend much time thinking about our future. (While many people think about an aspect of the future, like the environment or social justice or energy, few pay attention to the whole thing.)

When it came time for me to make my own contribution to future thinking, how do I give proper credit to all who went before me, all who possibly influenced my writing? The answer: I can't. So, I hereby issue this

GENERAL DISCLAIMER:
Many of the concepts in the "Chronicles" series came from somewhere else. (ALL of the concepts, when you include Divine Inspiration.) Perhaps they came from your book. If so, thanks! (And sorry for not mentioning you by name.)

Primary Influences:

ANATHEM (Neal Stephenson): Monks and masters. A monastery that is not an artifact of religion. Young people "collected" into a community and eventually coming to understand their role. An alternative to mainstream society...

EMERGENT (Stephen Baxter): This is THE book on what eusociality, "human hives" could be like. Baxter based his speculations on some pretty solid science. I borrowed lots of ideas, including the shortened fertility cycles, pheromonal communications, underground living...

DUNE (Frank Herbert): The top of my list for the greatest science fiction book/series of all time. When I read Dune as a teenager, I identified with the young Paul Atreides, forced to grow into challenging circumstances. Like young Man-Onko, finding both shelter and opportunity in a very different community.

CHILDHOOD'S END (Arthur C. Clarke): Weird children, and what to do with them... "Evolution" is not a straight mechanical line... ask any butterfly. Other books with strange kids include "Beggars in Spain" by Nancy Kress and "Darwin's Children" by Greg Bear.

THE FOUNDATION SERIES (Isaac Asimov): Hari Seldon, the man with the plan... This series posits the notion that it is possible to take a LONG look at the forces changing society. Through Seldon's "psychohistory", we see what happens when you know that the existing society, seemingly eternal and invulnerable, finally collapses. A very big concept: isolation will allow the alternative society to grow and mature to the point that it can compete for resources and consciousness with the declining society.

THE PARABLE OF THE SOWER (Octavia Butler): Written by the Grand Dame of Science Fiction, the late Octavia Butler got the gritty stuff of near-in dystopia depressingly accurate. Also: brain-dead politicians trying to land humans on Mars, while people starve in the streets and cannibals roam the hills...

THE MARS TRILOGY (Kim Stanley Robinson): This amazing series has an amazing premise: what would happen if you took 100 "normal" people and transport them to Mars... with limited resources and limitless possibilities? Why, they'd start FIGHTING, of course...

Were there other influences on "Chronicles"? Yes. And thanks to them all.

Appendix C: The Origin of the Series

There's one easy answer to where this book came from. It was a "download" (what more mystical people would call a "revelation") while fasting in a cave at the 15,000 foot level in Ladakh, deep in the Himalayas. (I had a good friend ask the rhetorical question, "How many black guys from Camden, NJ can begin a sentence, 'While I was fasting in a cave in the Himalayas...?' " Probably not many...)

If you've ever had a "Divine Inspiration", you know what it felt like. If you haven't... I don't know how to describe it to you. One minute it wasn't there, and the next minute it was. The whole thing. Complete. The book feels like "mine" and also "not-mine".

Getting the revelation took less than a minute. Writing it down took... just about 3 years.

The first year was spent ignoring it. As it turned out, I received TWO books, right at the same time! And the second book (my working title is "The Ecstatic Society") felt more immediate to me. More in alignment with my usual writing style and content. It felt "familiar". So, I dived into writing that book, and "dabbled" in the fiction at odd times and places.

Then, two years ago, "The Ecstatic Society" dried up, completely. No more juice. Like the Universe was saying that the fiction had to come FIRST, for some reason. (And who am I to question the Universe?)

Once I started writing "Chronicles" in earnest, a second challenge presented itself: where do I stop? The revelation came through as a glimpse of a complete world -- the more I wrote, the more there was to write! When it started taking on the dimensions of "War and Peace" , I realized that "Chronicles" wasn't just one book, but a series. (That's given me a lot of relief! Instead of trying to get the whole thing "right", I've just focused on getting the first one completed...)

Then, the next hurdle: what came through in the cave was a complete story, but it wasn't particularly ENGAGING. I was interested, because it was my revelation. Why would anyone else read it? Some of the timelines were absent or didn't make sense. There were lots of characters who were less than appealing. Settings were nonexistent. What to do?

So... while remaining true to the download, I've written a lot to improve the readability, continuity, engagement and flow of the book.

Many of the chapters were written in response to people wondering how various issues would be handled inside of a transforming society. For example: when the "Occupy" phenomenon was occurring some years ago, a lot of questions quickly arose regarding security and discipline. How do you deal with negative and antisocial behavior, when violent control is not an option? How do you deal with issues of "money" and value... without falling into familiar patterns of greed and poverty? How about simple issues, like transportation... when energy is not available or reliable?

Once I got the format and a good idea of the timeline, the rest was filling in the blank spaces and lots (and lots...) of rewriting.

I've had some serious critical comments about some of the tone and tenor of the book, including:

Profanity: One commenter stated that, for some, profanity is as offensive as racist and sexist language. I tend to agree. And, I placed it in the story for the same reasons I would (and perhaps will) use racist and sexist language: to make the point. A street kid like Man-Onko, coming into the Awakening Center, is not going to be using language like "gosh" and "darn". The fact that the monks keep after him about his use of language, and his growing ability to be mindful in his language choices, makes the point without damaging the authenticity of the story.

Security: I've had many comments on the issue of how security plays out in the Awakening Centers. I've had strong pushback on how many chapters are devoted to "security" issues (as opposed to environmental, social, economic...). Even stronger were disagreements about the notion of dropping off adversaries in locations where there was a likelihood that they would be killed (the 'Return to Kind' policy articulated in the chapter "A Lesson in Center Justice"). Finally: NO ONE agreed to the idea/concept of "mind-wiping" that pops up throughout the book.

First: each of these security concepts came from the initial "download" from the cave in Ladakh. Taking them out would mean not being true to the original impetus for the book. Second: when you struggle with the challenges posed by the Upheavals, you will quickly see that everything does revolve around security -- get that wrong, and you won't be around to do anything else right.

I took my lesson for security issues in part from my friends at the Oregon Country Fair, an annual event that attracts 40,000+ people from around the world, all in various stages festivity, nudity and inebriation. Their security is excellent... and nonviolent. (Some may argue that holding the arms and legs of someone having a psychotic episode is "violent". I do not. Helping them not hurt themselves or others is the highest form of compassion.)

The Lessons: For me, every chapter is a potential lesson. If you disagree with how I presented it... great! Come up with your own solution to the challenge presented. Better yet: get together with your friends and associates (and maybe even a few "adversaries") to discuss solutions. In other words: feel free to join me in INVENTING THE FUTURE!

Peace,

Shariff M. Abdullah
July, 2016

About the Author

DR. SHARIFF M. ABDULLAH is an award-winning author and advocate for inclusivity and societal transformation. Shariff's meta-vision and mission are simple: we can create a world that works for all beings.

Consultant and Trainer: As a consultant and trainer, Shariff has trained thousands of executives, managers and workers in the skills and techniques of authentic, effective leadership.

Wisdom Teacher: Shariff has been a sought-after speaker and teacher for Consciousness and Human Potential organizations, as well as several international forums.

Award-Winning Author: As an author, Shariff has written several paradigm-shifting books, including:

The Power of One: Authentic Leadership in Turbulent Times [New Society Publishers, (1990); New Catalyst Books (2007)]. This book makes the case for a new type of leadership and a new understanding of why we need it. This slim book has been referred to as "a revolution in consciousness", and has been in continuous print for over 25 years.

Creating a World That Works for All [Berrett-Koehler Publishers, 1999]. Winner of the "Book of the Year" award from the Independent Book Publishers Association, this comprehensive book makes the case for a global society based on the value of inclusivity: "We are One".

Seven Seeds for a New Society [Commonway Press, 2009]. Articulates the philosophy, theory and practice of a radically new way to envision society.

Practicing Inclusivity (with Leslie Hamilton) [CreateSpace Publishing, 2015]. A self-guided training workbook for inclusivity, Practicing Inclusivity is used by individuals, small groups and large organizations to develop greater degrees of inclusivity and connectedness.